A MAGIC+CITY WONDERS NOVEL

TAYLOR THOMAS SMYTHE

LAMPLIGHT
UNIVERSE

WEST PALM BEACH, FLORIDA

Cover design and interior layout by Taylor Thomas Smythe

Published by Lamplight Universe
ISBN: 978-1-959345-15-2

Lamplight Universe
West Palm Beach, FL

www.lamplightuniverse.com

To Mom & Dad—
thank you for loving me,
supporting me, and
teaching me about the firm foundation
on which to stand when things
don't go the way I plan.

MAGIC✦CITY WONDERS

TIMELINE

1980

Goldie

1981

1990

NIGHTMARE ARRAY

COMING SOON!

ALSO BY TAYLOR THOMAS SMYTHE

KINGDOM OF FLORIDA SERIES:

I. The Golden Alligator

II. The Lamplight Society

III. The Place Beyond the Sea

IV. The Fountain of Youth

V. The Curse of Coronado

VI. Coral and the Treasure Hunters

VII. Guardians of the Willow

MAGIC CITY WONDERS SERIES:

Goldie

The Dream Team

Nightmare Array

Song of the Starling (Coming Soon!)

More stories coming soon!

Visit lamplightuniverse.com *for more.*

Table of Contents

(continued)

(continued)

A

MAGIC✦CITY WONDERS

NOVEL

CHAPTER 1

Late Summer 1981.
Freeport, Grand Bahama, The Bahamas.

The moon shone bright and full—a distant beacon overlooking the night market at the edge of Grand Bahama's southern end. Lanterns and string lights relegated lingering shadows to the spaces between narrow stalls of eclectic merchandise. A trio of crackling boomboxes competed to define the ambience of one particular avenue, though the resulting cacophony wasn't quite what any of their owners had hoped for.

A woman rounded the corner onto this section of the crowded market, walking with her head bent low. She wore a lightweight, neutral scarf to hide her blonde hair and the bottom portion of her face. The woman paused near a graffitied phone booth and shoved a hand inside one of her deep trenchcoat pockets. She withdrew her hand discreetly, clutching a small, folded note between gloved fingers.

A breeze carrying salt and cinnamon fluttered the slip of

paper as the woman unfolded it. She read it again for what must have been the twentieth time:

Row 7. Stall 34. Ask for the Duke.

The handwriting was barely legible—*a dead giveaway that a doctor wrote it*, the woman thought with a quick grin. She scanned the painted numbering at the edges of the nearest seller's tables.

2, 3, 4—long way to go.

The woman tucked the scrap back into her pocket and started moving again.

"Donna!" A harsh whisper crackled through her obscured earpiece, followed by a burst of irritating feedback.

The woman pressed a finger to her ear and ducked back into a shadow. "What is it, Rico? I'm getting close."

"We're in range. Just keep moving, okay? We don't have much time."

"Guys!" Came a third voice—a woman's. "Codenames, please!"

Rico crackled back: "Sorry, Tracy—I mean *Katanga.*" He could almost hear her rolling her eyes on the end of the line.

"Brody—" Donna whispered into the hidden microphone, then lowered her head again as a couple of shoppers passed by. She started over: "Brody, do you still have eyes on the buyer?"

"Roger that, Ravenwood," Rico answered. "I'm right behind them—we're pulling up to the market. Over."

Donna tucked a few loose strands of her blonde hair back behind her ear and moved through the crowded marketplace. The stalls were covered in rainbows of spices and dyed fabrics, and nearly every object one could imagine fashioned from brittle straw. As she walked, the woman feigned interest in various items so as not to appear suspicious. If she weren't under such pressure, Donna would have enjoyed browsing the local wares.

As she ran her gloved fingers along a large woven basket, Donna glanced ahead. Her heart nearly stopped and she felt her jaw slacken. There was a man a couple stalls ahead, his back turned to her.

It can't be...

Donna started toward him in what felt like a trance. She noted his broad shoulders, the way his black hair was trimmed, faded, immaculate.

Marcus—?

Donna's pulse quickened. The man turned. The blonde woman exhaled slowly as she realized he was just another face in the crowd.

We're so close, she reminded herself and kept strolling with purpose. *I'm going to find you.*

"The buyer's parking," came Rico's voice again. "You gotta hurry. I'll follow from a distance on foot."

"Try not to let your gun go off this time, *Brody,*" Tracy insisted. "We're out of our jurisdiction here and I'd rather not have to convince Metro-Dade to bail you out of a Bahamian prison."

"Got it, Katanga."

"Ravenwood, don't worry," said Tracy. "I've got your back. I'll just be one row over in case they get too close."

"Roger that." Donna took a deep breath.

The two voices vanished once more from Donna's ear. She scanned the stalls that lay before her. *32, 33*... Her eyes alighted on a table full of enormous pink and white shells. *34!*

"Eyes on the prize," Donna spoke quietly into the earpiece, then started walking.

"Good!" Rico snapped. "Buyer is moving *fast* and she's almost there."

Donna's pulse quickened. "Can't you distract her?"

"Working on it."

Donna gulped and made a beeline to the display, keeping her head low once more. A diminutive man with leathery skin and short white hair appeared from behind a curtain. "Hello, miss!"

"Uh, hello," Donna forced a nervous grin.

"What can I interest you in tonight—for the pretty American lady? We have queen conch, king conch—" He began to point at the different varieties strewn across the table.

Donna pretended to be interested, then remembered the slip of paper. *This better work.* "Actually," she said. "I'm looking for the *Duke?*"

The old merchant paused, his expression growing stoic. Then he cracked a smile, his wrinkles squishing his weathered eyes into mere slits. He nodded and quickly disappeared through the curtain at the back of the stall.

Donna tapped her foot and glanced back over her shoulder. *No sign of Rico or the buyer yet. Good.*

After a few more long moments, the fabric parted and the merchant returned holding an enormous conch shell with both hands. A swath of vibrant pink spilled across one side, while a set of dull, stubby knobs spiked around the spiraled top.

A flurry of motion out of the corner of her eye made Donna turn back toward the thoroughfare's entry point: *the buyer!* A woman in a long, dark trenchcoat and a black scarf traced the same steps Donna had taken minutes earlier. She was moving fast.

"Forty dollars." The merchant's voice snapped Donna's attention back to the large shell.

Donna's jaw dropped. "Forty?"

"Yes. Forty dollars." The old man tucked the shell under one arm and held out his other hand to receive his requested payment.

"It's worth thirty *max*," Donna retorted and crossed her arms. She watched the buyer from the corner of her eye, nearly halfway down the row already. *Where are Rico and Tracy? Why aren't they intercepting her?*

"Forty dollars." The merchant insisted.

Donna looked back down the row again then felt a sharp elbow in the side from a passerby. "Hey!"

"Hurry it up, Ravenwood," whispered a familiar voice. The speaker turned to face Donna, flashed a grin, then quickly continued moving toward the approaching buyer.

Tracy! Seeing the dark-eyed officer granted her a momentary relief, but Donna wasn't about to let a local vendor scam her like all of the other tourists.

Donna doubled down. "I could get *two* of those for that price at the seller just down the way!"

"Other sellers don't have one of these." The man shook his head.

Donna caught the sound of Tracy's voice in the distance: "Oh, miss, I love your scarf."

The buyer snapped. "Thank you, but I'm kind of busy—"

"Where did you get it, may I ask?"

"Uh," the buyer was distracted, clearly focused on getting to the shell vendor as fast as possible. "I don't remember. Now will you please—"

"Don't remember?" Tracy now widened her stance to block the woman from moving forward.

Their voices faded as Donna returned her full attention to the shell seller. "Would you take thirty-five?" She fished through a loose bag and pulled out a wad of cash. "Thirty-five *American* dollars?"

The ensuing seconds were agonizing as Donna's eyes fluttered from the man to the shell to the buyer then back to the seller. Finally, he smiled.

"I will sell it to you for forty dollars."

Donna rolled her eyes and exhaled dramatically, then produced another five-dollar bill. She thrust the money across the table and into the man's eager hand. Satisfied, the seller passed the large shell into Donna's gloved hands.

She nearly dropped it, not realizing how heavy the object

would be, but quickly tucked it halfway under her overcoat. "Thanks." She smiled, nodded, then rushed off down the avenue.

"I've secured the Duke," Donna whispered into the earpiece. "Repeat: I have secured the Duke." The blonde woman scanned all directions before tucking herself into another corner away from the foot traffic. She inspected the large shell's top side, then turned it over. As she looked closer, Donna noticed an object lodged inside the gap along the inside of the shell. She reached her fingers into the space and managed to grab the corner of it, then carefully removed it—a piece of paper.

"There's something in here," Donna narrated through the earpiece. "It's some kind of ad ripped out of the newspaper."

Rico's voice returned, "What's it say? Does it have what we're looking for?"

Donna unfolded the wrinkly black-and-white advertisement and read aloud: "It says, 'Enjoy the wonders of the Banyan Beach Club & Casino.' Then underneath that it mentions a 'masquerade party' happening tonight at nine." She held the torn fragment so that a bit more light spread across it. "Oh, wait, there's something else—letters circled in black ink in the news story beneath it."

"Do they spell out anything—a code word, perhaps?" Tracy suggested.

"Maybe," Donna muttered as her eyes began to flick from character to character. *J. E. R.* Her eyes moved to the next paragraph. *I. C. H.* Donna almost missed the last letter. The drawn circle was small as it followed the character's form tightly: O. "It spells *Jericho*. Mean anything to you guys?"

Rico's voice crackled through the earpiece. "I think Katanga's right: it's a codeword. Or a clue to how we access the underground market from the Beach Club."

"Well, good news is that the Banyan Club is just up the street." Tracy replied. "Ravenwood and I can get there on foot. Brody, get the truck as close as you can without drawing attention. Our window might be tight to get the package loaded up."

"Roger that. Heading back now."

"The package has a *name*." Donna chimed, insistent but not quite irritated.

"Sorry, Ravenwood," Tracy answered. "But we don't know if any others are listening in. I know how much he... *the package*... means to you."

Donna closed her eyes and nodded. For a moment, in the darkness, she pushed away the lively hubbub of the market and conjured up an image of the man—tall, trim, and handsome in his Metro-Dade uniform. *That dimpled smirk*. So many details. And yet: he appeared blurry. Out of reach.

Marcus—I'm almost there.

"Ravenwood," Tracy's voice interrupted her reverie. "I'll meet you at the flagpole in four. Gotta do some quick haggling."

Donna inhaled the savory aroma of a barbecued meat stall nearby, tucked the conch shell into her bag, then took off through the market, once again lowering her head as she weaved in and out of the throng.

A few minutes passed as Donna navigated the marketplace. Ahead, the market spread out into a large town square. String lights criss-crossed high above the space, mimicking the starry, twinkling night sky beyond. In the center of the courtyard rose a sturdy pole upon which fluttered the national flag: a black triangle, a pair of blue bars, and a thick stripe of yellow between them. Spotlights illuminated the flag and attracted swarms of curious moths.

When she reached the flagpole, Donna scanned the area.

Tracy, where are you?

She checked her watch.

Four minutes. On the dot.

"Katanga?" She spoke into the earpiece.

No response.

A few men brushed past, and Donna instinctively clutched her bag tighter. Suddenly, the woman became acutely aware that any one of the dozens of strangers around her could have been listening in—could be looking for her. Her pulse began to increase rapidly. *We told them exactly where and when we were meeting! What if—?*

Donna felt a firm hand grab her arm. She gasped and whipped around, eyes wide. Her entire body loosened when she saw the stranger's face: Tracy.

"What took you so long?" Donna's voice rose, shrill.

"Shh!" Tracy pushed in, raising a finger to silence Donna as she glanced over her shoulder. "I had to pick up something. I'll show you later." The woman maintained her grip on Donna's arm and nudged her along as she started off into the crowd again. "C'mon!"

The two women hurried down an alleyway in silence. The moon's glow offered ample light to guide them, while still allowing the pair to remain mostly unseen by any curious or wandering eyes.

Within minutes, Tracy and Donna had left the market far behind and now found themselves weaving through a maze of brief streets lined with colorfully-painted houses, though their luster was muted by the dusk that hung over the whole port town.

Finally, they came to the end of a row of homes. Tracy urged Donna to press her back to the wall as the confident leader peered around the corner.

Tracy's shadowed face caught the vibrant, pulsing glow from an illuminated sign across the street—*Banyan Beach Club & Casino*, written in flashing, colorful lights.

"Any sign of him?" Donna whispered, glimpsing the sign for a brief second before ducking back.

Tracy shook her head.

"He'll be here," Donna muttered, mostly to assure herself. "Just give him some time."

Tracy joined Donna against the wall and leaned her head back. A pair of cars rumbled past, giving way to a soft chorus of crickets that filled the silence.

Donna tapped softly, instinctively on the stucco wall at her back.

"You alright?" Tracy Jones, a Metro-Dade police officer,

wasn't one to miss a tell.

The blonde woman exhaled and nodded unconvincingly.

Officer Jones raised an eyebrow. "Donna...?"

"I just—" Donna started, then closed her eyes. "I don't know. If he's really in there, I—it's been so long since I've seen him—spoken to him. What if after all we've been through to find him—what if things are *different* now—between us, I mean?"

Jones took a deep breath, waiting to make sure Donna was finished before she answered, "Donna, everyone has their rough patches. Hardships." She swallowed, then added quietly, "*Disappointments.*" Tracy lowered her head in thought, then looked back at Donna. "But the bad parts don't nullify the good moments—what you *had.*"

Donna drifted off in thought but made no reply.

"You care about Marcus, right?"

"Of course."

"Then," the officer paused. She seemed to weigh whether she believed the words she was about to speak. "Then no matter what happens, your time together was worth it. And what you had—what you *have*—is real."

Donna nodded slowly.

"But I wouldn't worry about it so much," Tracy added. "From everything Rico tells me, you and Marcus had something truly special. A little time apart isn't going to change that."

With a nod of agreement, Donna allowed Tracy's words to sink in. Then she turned to the officer with a growing smirk:

"Speaking of *you* and *Rico*—"

The sudden sputter of an old engine startled the women before Donna could finish, and they both peered around the corner. A beat-up delivery truck rounded the bend and came to a stop in the quiet side street. The driver killed the engine. He jumped down to the cobblestone road and approached them.

It was Rico, a smug smile stretched across his face: "Made it in record time."

Tracy rolled her eyes, her arms crossed. "We came on foot and we got here *minutes* ago."

"Crazy traffic," he offered. "And I'll never quite get used to driving on the wrong side of the road."

"It's the *right* side here," Donna smiled and went in for a hug. "Just glad you made it."

As Donna stepped back, Rico became more somber and maintained eye contact. "I'm sure he's in there, Donna. We're not leaving without him."

The woman nodded.

"I identified a loading dock around the back," he continued. "No doubt that connects to the market, but I won't be sure til we're inside. And it's too conspicuous a spot for us to park the truck. Once we secure M—*the package*—Jones will bring 'er around and we can make the getaway." Rico tossed the keys to Tracy.

She caught them, then stepped forward and rifled through a satchel. "I grabbed these at the market." Tracy withdrew a set of simple masks with elastic straps and handed them to

Donna and Rico. "Figured these are kind of important if you two are showing up to a masquerade party."

Rico struggled with the elastic band on his, but managed to slip the mask over his head. "A little tight," he quipped as he straightened it. The stiff black material covered the top half of his face, with holes for his eyes.

Donna adjusted her own. "I kinda like it—the anonymity. I feel like some sort of comic book super hero."

"You sort of *are* like one, too," Tracy noted. "When the gloves come off, I mean." She gestured to the leathery pair that covered Donna's hands. "Alright, time to get in there and find this mysterious *Jericho*."

Donna and Rico nodded.

They started to walk away, but Rico turned back. "B-be careful," he stammered.

Tracy smirked. "You, too, *partner*."

"Don't worry," the man lifted one side of his coat, revealing a metallic glint near his belt. "If things get rough, I've got a few tricks up my sleeve."

Tracy took a deep breath and gave a stern look of concern, then shook her head. "Let's pray they don't." She turned and climbed into the truck.

Rico returned to Donna's side and the two masked figures quickly and silently slinked across the street.

Donna and Rico neared the entrance to the Banyan Beach Club & Casino, each obscured by both a mask and a loose-fitting trenchcoat. As they approached, they were bathed in fluttering lights and the rising pulse of synthesized drum beats issuing from the door.

The pair stepped into a short queue of other partygoers dressed in masks—most of which were more ornate than Donna or Rico's and covered in feathers or rhinestones. A hulking bouncer waved each person through after inspecting their masks. Then it was Donna's turn. The man's droopy eyes sized her up and lingered on the simple black mask.

Donna stammered: "It was the best I could do on short notice—"

The man interrupted her with a disinterested wave of his hand, ushering her into the dark doorway. He nodded for Rico to follow her.

"Someone woke up on the wrong side of the bed," Rico mumbled under his breath.

Donna led the way into the main room of the casino, which spread out in carpeted avenues lined with card games, pinball sets, and slot machines along the outer areas closest to the wall. The entire space was crowded and thick with smoking revelers and loud talkers.

"Keep your eyes peeled," Rico uttered into Donna's ear, speaking loud enough to be heard over the music. "We find Jericho, we find Marcus."

As she inhaled a whiff of cigar smoke, Donna surveyed the space again. "Split up?"

"Yeah." Rico nodded. "You know how to reach me if you find anything." He tapped his earpiece.

Donna adjusted her mask and started off through the dim

space. She passed under a decorative arch into a smaller side wing of the room, where a number of tables brimmed with boozy, boisterous bachelors looking to score big on blackjack.

Tourists, by the looks of them. Then again, most people in this quarter of the island were—the sort that only came for a quick weekend getaway. The proximity to Miami and its port accounted for hundreds of millions of dollars pumped into the local economy back home. Flights and cruises to the islands comprised a major portion of that, and they made it easy for the rich and famous (and those with sufficient credit) to live a lavish tropical fantasy for a couple of nights—or simply escape from a city that was becoming increasingly famous for all the worst reasons.

And with direct flights clocking in at just one hour, who *wouldn't* take advantage of such an opportunity?

A group of rambunctious frat boys cheered and shouted, drawing Donna back to the moment at hand. She squeezed between a group of couples chatting in the middle of the carpeted walkway, keeping her gloved hands close to her sides as she brushed past.

No sign of Jericho yet.

And no idea what—or who—it might mean. Donna took a deep breath. She only hoped she'd know it when she saw it.

As she scanned the room, Donna froze. A masked figure, dressed in red and wearing a black coat, stood on the far side of the space and appeared to be staring right at her. When the figure realized Donna had noticed, they vanished into the crowd.

Donna pushed past the throng with haste, making her way to the spot where the stranger was last seen. She came to a series of slot machines and arcade-style games that followed the contours of the wall, and Donna spun to try and discern where the enigma had gone.

They were watching me. I'm sure of it. Her breathing was quicker now. *A spy for the black market dealers, no doubt.* Or worse: *a spy for Angela.*

If she wasn't indoors, Donna would've spit at the mere thought. Donna Locke wasn't one to hold to grudges, but there were two people with whom she made easy exceptions: Angela Hyde and Rolf Ducane. The two people responsible for ruining her life.

This thought gave Donna a new vigor as she walked swiftly past the blinking slots. The masked figure was nowhere to be found. Finally, Donna came to a stop at the far end of the room, just ahead of a small alcove that housed a couple more of the colorful machines. The woman leaned against a half-wall and took another look around the large room. She pressed her finger to her ear discreetly.

"Anything yet, Brody?"

"Negative," came Rico's voice. "You?"

"I thought I saw something—someone. In a mask. *Watching* me." She realized how paranoid it sounded. "But I might've just imagined it," she added to allay any suspicion that she was losing her ability to think rationally.

Rico exhaled sharply. "Everyone's in masks, Ravenwood."

"I know," Donna said dismissively as she took another

look at the machines nearby.

"Keep looking. We're bound to find something soon enough, right?"

Donna didn't respond. She squinted and cocked her head to peer into the darkened alcove. *It's just more slots,* she told herself. But the large, colorful lettering across the top of one of the machines made her move closer.

"Ravenwood, you still there?" Rico's voice crackled.

Donna slowly approached the slot machine and an involuntary smile flashed across her face when she could finally read the name emblazoned on the console. "Brody. Get over here. Far side, past the blackjack tables."

"You alright?"

"Yeah," Donna nodded. "I found it. I found *Jericho.*"

CHAPTER 2

When Rico arrived half-a-minute later, Donna was running her hands along the back edge of the large slot machine. The stylized lettering across the bottom panel of the unit glowed brightly in yellow and red: *Jericho.*

"It's attached to the wall," she noted of the machine as he approached.

Rico studied it before turning to the lit-up digital display in the center: the pixelated images spun, simulating the movement of reels on the more classic, analog kind of gambling machines. A flurry of icons rotated in and out of view: cherries, lemons, melons, oranges, numbers. Rico scratched his chin then pulled the lever on the side of the machine.

Nothing happened.

"You got a nickel?" Donna suggested, reading the large-printed instructions across the top of the machine:

5 cents per spin.

Immediately, Rico thrust a hand into his pocket and fished his fingers around. He withdrew a handful of coins: some pennies, a quarter, and a pair of nickels. The officer plucked one of the nickels from his hand and passed it to Donna. "Care to do the honors?"

Donna carefully slid the nickel into the narrow slot. The small coin clinked as it made its way down a series of unseen slides and chutes behind the machine's facade until, finally, the screen flashed: *Ready!*

She turned to Rico. He nodded. Donna inhaled deeply, then pulled the lever.

Click. Click. Click.

As the lever rose back to its upright position, the digital reels began to spin rapidly. The left-most reel slowed first, coming to a stop: cherries.

C'mon, c'mon!

Donna had no idea how or why she suddenly felt so invested in the game, but then again, something inside told her that this was important.

The middle reel came next, also landing on cherries.

"Yes!" Donna didn't mean to say it out loud—it just slipped out.

The final reel's spin was agonizing. Rico and Donna leaned in instinctively. Donna memorized the sequence: the gold bars, lemon, orange, then came the cherries. They disappeared as quickly as they came, then rotated around once more.

Slower.

Lemon?

Slower.

Orange?

Stop.

"Cherries!"

The trio of simple graphics flashed red, and a celebratory song began to play in all its 8-bit, chiptune glory. Donna and Rico were so busy celebrating the win that they almost failed to notice a deep *click* behind the device. One of the back corners of the machine pushed away from the wall slightly, forming a small gap.

"Look," Donna pointed. "Help me push." She planted her feet beside the glowing apparatus as the song continued. With Rico's help, the duo managed to slide the machine in a perfect arc along a rusted, dirty track on the floor that had been obscured by the base of the device. A cool draft issued from behind it, and the pair could now see a small opening—a hallway barely large enough for an average adult to pass through. It was too dark to see much farther into the passage.

Rico sang under his breath: "And the walls came tumblin' down."

Donna's pulse quickened. "Do you think—?"

"Yeah," the man nodded. "Definitely." Rico touched his earpiece. "Katanga, I think we're in. Looks like the south side of the building."

"Roger that." Tracy's voice answered back. "I'll be ready.

You two be careful in there."

Neither Rico nor Donna replied. Donna glanced back over her shoulder at the crowded casino floor then took a step into the narrow unlit corridor. The two moved cautiously, feeling along the rough concrete wall to maintain their balance and bearings as the music and chatter faded away behind them.

Donna's shoes navigated the space ahead of her, discovering that she was now confronted with a series of steps heading downward. She relayed this to Rico and the two continued in silence. Soon, the pair saw a dim light ahead, where the passage veered to the right. The ground leveled out and Donna and Rico found themselves looking into the entryway to another massive room like the one they had just left behind.

This room was dark, though, save for overhead blacklights and glitchy greenish neon shapes attached to the otherwise barren walls. The entire space was packed with people in ornate masks and glitzy attire, who all seemed to be looking ahead to a sort of stage area, where a lone spotlight cast a thick beam on an auctioneer calling out bids.

"We'll start the bids on Lot 16 at five-thousand dollars," he said through a skinny microphone. The man was an island local—and he made for a natural auction caller.

Donna leaned to Rico as more of the room came into view. "What's all this?"

"How do you mean?" He replied, keeping his eyes ahead.

"When Roger told us about a black market, this is not exactly what I had in mind." She gestured at a woman with an inordinately-large diamond ring. "The clientele—they're not the seedy underbelly I envisioned."

"Whoever runs this place knows the wealthy are willing to pay for this stuff, even if the legality is questionable," Rico explained as he guided Donna toward the side of the room. "I'll bet they love the intrigue—the danger of it all. Come on," he muttered. "Let's get a number."

"They've already started." Donna noted.

"Don't worry," her friend assured her. "They save the best for last. No way they let some crumbly old mask steal the limelight when... *the package* is in the mix."

The item beside the auctioneer on the stage looked old—ancient, even. It was a painted wooden mask with deteriorating stag horns protruding from the top of it. A custom-designed stand allowed it to be displayed without the need for anyone to touch it.

"—Eight. Make it nine. Do I hear ten-thousand dollars?"

Donna and Rico made a beeline for a registration table.

"Hi," Donna smiled winsomely at the surly woman behind it. "I'm here to pick up a number—"

"You're late."

Donna caught herself before she said something snide, and took a calming breath instead. "You're right. Traffic's brutal." She searched for a way forward, then recalled the buyer from the market. "But I was told there would be a number reserved for me."

The attendant raised a doubtful, lazy eyebrow. "Name?"

"Um, LaRoque—" She stammered. "Cheyenne LaRoque."

"And who's he?" The grumpy woman nodded at Rico.

"That's, um, my uh—bodyguard." Donna bit her lip as she said it.

While the surly woman ran her finger down a clipboard, Donna glanced back to Rico, mouthed, "*Sorry!*" then caught the tail end of the continued haggling over the old artifact on stage.

"Twelve-thousand—the woman in red."

"Fourteen!" A deep voice shouted.

The auctioneer pointed to the shouter. "Fourteen-thousand. Do I hear fifteen—"

"Hello?" The grumpy woman nearly yelled.

Donna looked down to see the paddle in the lady's hand—bearing the number *031*—and quickly grabbed it. "Thanks," she said, disappearing into the crowd with Rico.

The two shuffled their way across the room to get a better view of the stage and the area as a whole. Rico noted that the only visible exit was the hallway through which they had just entered. He leaned to Donna. "That corridor's too narrow and too conspicuous to haul their contraband merchandise in and out. That means there's some sort of loading area behind the stage."

"Right where Tra—I mean Katanga will be waiting?"

"You got it." Rico smiled.

Donna wriggled her fingers nervously, clenching and unclenching them around the numbered paddle.

"Twenty thousand," the auctioneer pointed at someone holding a numbered paddle, then another, spewing words in rapid time. "Twenty-five, thirty, do I hear thirty-five? Thirty-five? Thirty-five?"

Someone in the crowd shouted and held up their number.

"Thirty-five! Going once—"

The man scanned the half-covered faces.

"Going twice."

The tension rose.

"Sold! Lot 16 goes to bidder number 108." The auctioneer pointed to the winners—a couple draped in light-colored furs—as a pair of attendants carefully carted the ancient artifact offstage. "Please bring out Lot 17."

The room began to fill with light chatter as another object was wheeled out on to the stage. It was large, draped in a thin white sheet, and roughly resembled a human form.

Donna took quick breaths. Her heart started to race. Instinctively, she clutched Rico's arm. "It's him," she whispered, her eyes glued to the stage.

In what felt to her like slow motion, Donna watched as the auctioneer tugged on the sheet. The cloth billowed and danced, casting shadows with its cloud-like form as it finally floated to the ground. Donna let out a silent gasp and covered her mouth.

The audience had a similar reaction. An almost deafening murmur came over the crowd as all eyes became locked on Lot 17. It was the figure of a man who seemed to be frozen in time, his hands spread in front of his face and chest in a gesture of defense—or to stop a fall. Every detail, contour, line, and hair was present, perfect and lifelike. The thing that caused such an uproar, however, was that the man was fashioned not of flesh, but of pure, glimmering, solid gold.

Marcus.

Memories flooded back to Donna, gaining clarity as she took in the shape of his face. His tight, faded haircut. Those deep brown eyes now lifeless and metallic. Her reverie was interrupted by the auctioneer.

"While the artist of Lot 17 is unknown, its *purity* has been independently verified—three times over. The object you see before you is indisputably constructed of *solid*, twenty-four karat gold—a true feat." As he spoke the words, the energy in the room began to rise even more. Gasps could be heard throughout the throng. "We'll start the bidding at forty-thousand."

Immediately, nearly every numbered paddle shot up. The flurry of the ensuing moments was disorienting. Donna couldn't take her eyes off Marcus—that helpless expression plastered on his face for an entire year.

Ow! Donna felt an elbow nudge her in the side. It was Rico.

"You gonna bid or not?"

Donna remembered the paddle in her hand, nodded, then threw it up high above her head.

"Sixty-thousand—bidder 31." The auctioneer continued, "Seventy, seventy-five, eighty!"

"We're going to have to do better than that," Rico inhaled quickly. "Let's get up closer to the front—I have a feeling this is gonna get ugly."

The two meandered their way through the dense collection of perfumed partygoers, Rico clearing the way for Donna to follow.

"Eighty-five, do I hear ninety?"

The number of bidders had dwindled considerably by this point, but the room remained full—no one wanted to miss the thrill of a high-dollar bidding war. Donna noted that a short old man and a rotund woman with reddish hair seemed to be her only remaining competitors. She flung up her sign again.

"Ninety-thousand," the auctioneer pointed at Donna. "Do I hear ninety-one?"

The red-haired woman flashed her sign with a sneer.

"Ninety-one, ninety-two?"

The old man snorted in the woman's direction and raised his paddle.

"Ninety-two, do I hear ninety-three?"

Donna was sweating. She raised the paddle again.

"Bidder 31 at ninety-three. Going once."

Again the old man bid, shouting, "Ninety-four!"

"Ninety-four, do I hear ninety-five? Ninety-five thousand dollars?"

Any hope of exiting the room as a mere anonymous number in the crowd had faded long ago. Donna had no choice. She was leaving with Marcus. She'd find the money—*or make it*. Her paddle flew up once more.

"Ninety-five *thousand* dollars," the auctioneer said, shock his voice. "Going once."

Donna looked around.

"Going twice."

She glanced at Rico, took a deep breath. *Finally,* she thought. *We're bringing Marcus home—*

A voice from a far, shadowed corner of the room shouted over the room: "Imposter!"

Donna whipped toward the voice. It was a woman's voice. A voice she recognized. A voice she hadn't heard in a very long time. Donna muttered under her breath, "*Angela!*"

"She's an imposter!" The woman exclaimed again, pointing a slender finger in Donna's direction. "She's not supposed to be here!"

The room was electric. Donna felt every eye in the room suddenly focus on her. She glanced to her side and watched as Rico reached inside his trenchcoat.

"Get ready—this is gonna be a little loud," he whispered in her ear, then raised his arm above his head, revealing a shiny silver handgun.

Donna cupped her hands over her ears as a pair of shots rang out.

The crowd was in an uproar. Everyone scrambled to the floor and frantically began to climb and claw over one another to move toward the exit. Rico looked across the room at the one person who stood unfazed: Angela Hyde. Though the upper half of her face was adorned in a mask, Rico instantly recognized her cold, beautiful lips and thick blackish hair. She was dressed in a flashy scarlet dress and now reached for a handbag. *A weapon?*

Rico swung back to face the stage, where the auctioneer

and his attendants began wheeling Marcus away. Rico's gaze locked in on Donna's as he gripped her forearm: "The package. Don't let him out of your sight!" He waved his gun in the direction of the stage, which Donna took as a cue to hurry after the quickly-vanishing golden man.

As Donna made her way to the stage, Rico thought fast: he toppled a high-top table and crouched behind it just as a series of shots rang out from the opposite corner of the room. He peered around the circular edge of the table to witness Angela aiming a small pistol right at him. Rico put his finger to his ear: "Katanga, you in position?"

There was no reply.

Drat!

Rico sucked in a quick breath and sidestepped the table to aim at Angela. The bullet missed, shattering a glass pitcher full of ice-water which quickly slickened the concrete floor nearby. The woman ducked behind a thick support column.

Donna sprinted across the stage. "Stop right there!" She shouted at the trio of men carting away the golden man. "Don't move him another inch."

The auctioneer turned to her and raised an eyebrow, then subtly cocked his head to the side—a signal to the two attendants. Immediately, they removed their hands from the golden sculpture and slipped them to their sides, from which they each drew a handgun.

"He's mine," said Donna confidently.

The armed attendants took short steps toward her, but

she held her ground.

"Impersonation is a crime, miss," the auctioneer muttered, his voice having traded its bright showman's tone for a slimier color. "I'm afraid that tiny detail nullifies your bid."

Thinking quickly, Donna reached into the bag slung at her side and produced the heavy conch shell. With a grunt, she hurled it toward one of the gun-wielding men. He sidestepped it, and the shell crashed somewhere behind him. Donna gulped and quickly looked around.

The thin white sheet that had covered Marcus now lay in a heap at Donna's feet. She glanced down at it, then back up to the two guns aimed right at her. Both men cocked them and readied to fire.

The auctioneer approached the golden man and looked back at Donna. "Why don't you run along now before someone gets hurt?"

With her hands behind her back, Donna carefully removed one of her leathery gloves and tucked it into a coat pocket. She took a deep breath then thrust the one still-gloved hand downward. Donna crouched, grabbed hold of the white sheet, and yanked it up in the air. The draft caught it and the whole cloth billowed just as it had earlier. Donna extended her ungloved hand toward an edge of the fabric.

The instant her skin touched the hem of the cloth, the sheet's form began to change before their eyes. Donna heard a series of gunshots in succession, ducked, and squeezed her eyes shut. When she realized she had felt no bullet pangs, Donna slowly opened her eyes as the shots continued.

It worked.

The white sheet no longer consisted of a colorless piece of fabric. Instead, before her stood a solid gold object, shaped with the exact contours of the billowing sheet as if it had frozen in time and space. The long edge of it that pooled at the ground kept it standing upright like a thin golden wall.

Then she heard the sounds she was waiting for:

Click. Click. Click.

Both guns out of ammo. Donna rose and pushed the golden wall with all her might. The wide, heavy object toppled over, trapping the two men underneath it. Donna caught her breath then looked ahead.

The auctioneer—and Marcus—had disappeared.

Not on my watch.

Donna breathed in deep and hurried ahead into the darkness backstage. She nearly tripped on a curtain pulley system, but kept moving.

The darkness finally gave way to the dim, violet glow of night seeping in through some unseen opening around the corner. Donna cleared the bend and found herself on a loading dock. A large bay door had been opened and Donna's eyes locked on to the glint of her gilded boyfriend. The auctioneer gave the final push to roll the prized item into the back of a truck.

Donna shouted: "Hey, stop!"

When he saw her, the man turned to Donna and flashed a half-faced grin. He fished inside his coat and withdrew a surprisingly long, serrated bowie knife, which shone in the moonlight.

"I don't know what witchcraft you conjured in there," the armed auctioneer waved the blade in her direction. "But the statue is mine now."

With a glance down at her hands—one gloved, the other bare—Donna paused for a breath. She knew her powers would be useless if the man's blade kept her from getting close enough to touch him—and even still, turning another human to gold was a last resort. *No one deserves that fate. Time to improvise.* Her eyes scanned the dock.

The auctioneer made a slimy lick of his lips and took a step toward her. "What a waste of such a beautiful creature."

Under other circumstances, Donna would have retched in her mouth a little and made a snarky comeback. But she had no time for quips and witty banter.

Think!

Her eyes moved along the wall: from a rope to a grimy bucket to a wooden broom.

Yes—that'll do.

He was getting closer. Donna made a run for it. The man gave chase, quickly gaining on her. She reached out her hand, felt the flimsy wooden pole of the broom become dense, heavy, metallic. *Pure gold.* Donna gripped it tightly and swung the solid golden broom behind her.

The auctioneer ducked to evade the swipe then lunged at Donna with the bowie knife. He'd seen it coming. Donna's gaze narrowed as she brought the broom around, gripped between two hands in front of her to meet the man's blow.

She smelled spices and fish on his breath.

"Going to make me work for it, eh?" He taunted, sizing her up.

Donna pushed, sending the man a few steps backward. She raised the broom behind her like a baseball bat and hurried at the auctioneer. She swung.

The man bent to his side, allowed the golden pole to pass, then reached out a quick hand. His fingers gripped it, holding the broom tightly. Donna's eyebrows shot up as she watched the auctioneer raise the blade with his other hand and slowly point it toward her chest.

"Now," he said, his mouth full of spittle as he pressed her back to the wall. "What do you say you take off that coat?"

Donna's ungloved wrist was pressed against the cinder-block wall, trapped and immovable.

The man licked his lips again. Donna clenched her teeth and tried to resist, but the man was too strong. She couldn't budge the broom that kept her locked in place.

"Poor, pretty lady." The auctioneer touched the tip of the knife to Donna's exposed neck. She held her breath.

An ear-splitting crack rang out—a pistol shot. Donna gasped, then looked into the face of the auctioneer. His eyes betrayed the look of sudden pain as he drooped into a heap at Donna's feet. She looked up to the end of the dock.

There stood Tracy, her feet planted firmly in a wide stance and both hands on a smoking gun. Behind her, the door to the idling truck hung open.

"Tracy!" Donna gasped with momentary relief. She

pushed the limp man away and tossed aside the broom with a clatter.

Tracy Jones holstered the weapon and approached Donna. "Where's Rico?"

Donna slipped her other glove back over her bare hand and nodded in the direction she'd come. "I dunno," she explained. "But we saw Angela—"

A voice echoed down the hall, unseen, hurried, and crackled through their earpieces: "Ravenwood! Ravenwood!"

Donna winced at the static feedback then looked ahead. Rico rounded the corner, frantic.

"Did you get him?" He shouted as he approached.

Tracy raised a concerned eyebrow: "Yeah, he's in the back—"

"Good—we gotta go!" Rico reached the two women and began to nudge them down the ramp. "It's Angela—she just called in backup."

The trio climbed into the vehicle, with Marcus secure in the back, and slammed the doors shut.

Tracy thrust the vehicle into drive and wheeled out of the cargo bay. "What kind of backup?" As the truck rounded the corner into the alley, Tracy's eyes flicked to the side mirror. Her heart sank. "You gotta be kidding me."

Donna, squished between the two officers on the long front bench, leaned over Rico to look out the opposite mirror. A series of boxy cars appeared at the end of the alley, tailing them, with sirens on their roofs flashing blinding reds and blues against the building walls on either side. "Wait—the *cops* are after us?"

"Angela's got 'em wrapped around her finger, no doubt," Rico mused, still catching his breath.

Tracy yanked the steering wheel in a sharp turn down another sidestreet. Quickly, though, the police cars were back on their tail.

"How far to the airstrip?" Donna asked.

"A few minutes." Tracy muttered, dodging a car in front of her. "Hang on!"

The officer floored the gas pedal as the truck reached the highway. They were picking up speed slowly; that's where the compact cop cars had the advantage. The hulking tank of a truck couldn't maintain its lead much longer.

At this hour of the night, traffic was sparse enough that Tracy began to weave between cars, searching for the next gap to keep their forward momentum. Miraculously, this allowed them to gain a considerable lead on the squad of police cars that followed.

Soon, the truck reached the airport. Instead of slowing at a security checkpoint, Tracy accelerated, busting through the lowered boom bar at full-speed. She made a fleeting glance in the mirror to ensure no one was harmed, then turned her eyes back to the darkened space ahead of her.

They had rehearsed the route many times before this moment. Tracy knew exactly where the plane would be docked—but they hadn't planned on cops giving chase. She eyed Rico, then a walkie talkie attached to the dashboard.

Rico grabbed it and pressed the button: "Mayday!

Mayday! This is Brody. We're coming in hot, Jock. Gonna need to board on the runway."

A man's voice shot back, "You got lucky—I'm pulling away now and all systems are go. Gonna be a tight window—meet you on strip four."

"Roger that, Jock," Rico released the talk button and nodded to Tracy. "You heard the man."

She nodded and accelerated, following the lighted beacons that lined the airstrips.

Donna pointed out the guides for strip four. As Tracy navigated the vehicle in a wide turn, they cleared the airport's main building and could now see straight ahead down the runway: a beat-up cargo plane had started down the strip and was just now straightening itself out to prepare for its rapid acceleration and takeoff. The back ramp was lowered so that it nearly scraped the rough concrete below, revealing an open space just large enough for the truck to fit inside—if it could make it in time.

Donna glanced at the side mirror again and saw that there were now at least a half-dozen squad cars on their tail—and they were gaining on the truck fast. "I have a bad feeling about this," she muttered over the rising sound of sirens.

The pilot's voice crackled through the walkie: "Beginning takeoff in five. Four—"

The truck was at least a hundred yards behind the plane. "There's no way we're going to reach him in time," Rico snapped.

"—Three. Two. One."

Donna, Rico, and Tracy watched as the large turbines rotated into blurs, and the deafening roar pierced and pervaded all ears in proximity to the runway. Tracy kept her focus on the plane's back ramp, which was drawing closer and closer. The large plane lurched and started to move forward.

"They're gaining on us!" Donna instinctively clutched Rico's arm. Red and blue lights dappled the airstrip asphalt.

"Hang on," Tracy gripped the wheel tighter and sunk her foot as far as the gas pedal would go. The gap between them and the cargo ramp was closing, but now the plane was beginning to pick up speed.

A series of gunshots rang out. Rico and Donna huddled low in the front bench.

Officer Jones bit her lip. "Almost there."

The front wheels of the truck neared the thick metal ramp, which bounced and sparked against the concrete ground. Finally, the tires touched the ramp and Tracy guided the vehicle up into the cargo bay.

"We're in, Jock! Close 'er up!" Rico shouted through the walkie.

Immediately, the ramp began to rise. As they watched through the mirrors once more, the reds and blues faded as the truck was quickly engulfed in darkness. The hatch door clicked and locked, and the trio within the truck let out a collective sigh of relief. A moment later, a series of thick metal blocks rose from the floor to lock the truck's wheels in position right as the plane lifted off from the ground and pitched at a sharp incline, roaring away from the island.

We did it, Donna thought and closed her eyes. *Marcus. Finally.*

CHAPTER 3

Donna Locke shivered. The plane droned on through the night at just above thirty-thousand feet in the air. It was a short flight, but Donna couldn't sit still.

Rico and Tracy had disappeared to check in with the pilot (an old friend of Rico's from his grade-school days), leaving Donna in the glow of the cargo bay's dim red lights. She squeezed along the space between the truck and the plane's curved walls. A small battery-powered lantern caught her eye. She unstrapped it and carried it with her while she approached the back of the truck.

Donna clenched her gloved fingers—a habit—then yanked on the big truck's back hatch. After some effort, the rusty door creaked and swung open. At that moment, the cargo plane made the slightest turn, causing Donna to stagger before quickly reaching out for the door to keep her balance. The lantern dangled from her other hand. As the plane leveled again, the blonde woman placed the powered-off light in the back of the truck, heaved herself up, and crawled across the floor.

When she could sense Marcus Myles' silhouetted form, Donna paused, bracing herself against the truck wall in the dark. Her breathing was quick and deep. She flicked the lamp on, casting a vibrant yellowish glow over the man before her.

In the flurry of their rescue mission, Donna hadn't been able to stop and observe him this closely. But now she felt her chest rise and fall in a calm, assured cadence. She reached out a hand and placed it gently on the golden man's shimmering, statuesque face.

"I'm so sorry," she whispered, barely audible.

For a few moments, Donna stood in silence, allowing her eyes to linger and study every line, contour, and feature on the man's face—features she once knew by heart and now wished to bring again to mind.

"We're almost home," Donna continued softly, though she knew he couldn't hear. "As soon as we land, Roger's going to fix you—turn you back. Doc says he's finally recreated the compound—the formula that will reverse all of *this*." She slid her hand down to his chest, where her fingers settled into the faintest indentation of a handprint—*her* handprint—on his now-solid shirt.

Then she had an idea. Donna set the lantern on the ground and began to shuffle through her messenger bag. She withdrew a clunky walkman with bulky headphones and a pair of cassette tapes, and sat down on a wooden crate.

"I know I've got it in here somewhere," Donna mumbled, half to herself and half directed at Marcus, as she fished around for something else. "A-ha!" She announced, pulling a third tape from the bag. The woman carefully placed it in the deck of the walkman and closed the tray with a satisfying click. She placed the big, muff-like earphones on her head.

Donna turned to Marcus and spoke wistfully. "Remember when you took that class at MDCC? You had to do that project where you interviewed someone about their goals or something," she sort of chuckled. "We barely knew each other, but you chose me."

The woman smiled, pressed the clunky *play* button, and looked up at Marcus' inanimate face. The player began to spin its tiny twin spools, visible through a plastic window in the walkman's front plate.

Marcus' rich voice broke through the grainy crackle of the tape, and Donna imagined the golden man speaking before her: "So, uh—" It was a nervous start. "I guess I'll just start. This is Marcus Myles and I'm recording this for Vocational Exploration 101—" A pause as he took a heavy breath. "And so I guess you go now—I mean, can you state your name for the recording?"

The tape now played Donna's reply: "My name is Donna Locke—"

Donna's fingers flicked from *play* to *stop*. She inhaled deeply. "And I've missed you so much," she added in a breathy sigh. Donna started the tape again.

"So I guess, uh," the voice of Marcus continued, "now

I can ask you the first real question. When you were a kid, what did you want to be when you grew up?"

Donna spoke in unison with her younger voice. "When I was a kid, I always wanted to be a famous singer." Donna had lost track of how many times she had listened to the tape. She knew every word, every breath, every grainy static blip.

"A singer, huh?"

"Yeah." Donna's unrecorded voice spoke a split second after her taped one.

"What happened?"

Donna's weary, recorded sigh played through the headphones. Though it was only a few years ago, the woman wondered at how long ago the moment felt—how much *older* she felt now. "I dunno," her two voices spoke, aligned once more. "Real life, I guess. It's hard enough to make ends meet, let alone follow my dreams."

"But it would be worth it, wouldn't it?" Donna imagined the statuesque man's gilded lips moving as his voice resounded in her ears. "To chase after what you want even though it's hard? After all, doesn't all the blood, sweat, and tears it took to get there make the dream that much sweeter?"

Before either Donna or her recorded voice could respond, the woman was startled by a motion in the corner of her eye. She turned. It was Rico.

"Oh, hey," she said. Donna clicked *stop* and yanked off the headphones as the tape spools jolted to a standstill. "Sorry I couldn't hear you over the tape."

"All good, Donna," Rico grinned. "Captain says we're

coming in for a landing. You should strap in."

The woman nodded.

Rico's eyes flicked to Marcus. "I still can't believe it," he muttered. "That's he's just been hidden away, encased in solid gold for the past year."

"*Changed*," Donna corrected as she stuffed the walkman and headset back into her bag. "Not encased. And we're going to change him back." She moved to the edge of the truck bed. Rico extended his hand to help her down.

"You ready?" He asked.

Donna placed her own warm, gloved hand in his. "Yeah," she nodded and took a nervous breath. "Never been more ready."

The cargo plane landed on an airstrip at Miami International Airport in the dead of night, and the craft taxied to a private hangar on the property's outskirts. Donna placed a quick call from a nearby payphone while Tracy and Rico oversaw the transfer of Marcus to another large truck that would better obscure his gold from curious eyes. As an extra measure, they wrapped the inanimate man in protective blankets tied with twine.

When she got off the phone, Donna hopped into the vehicle. "Roger says everything's ready," she said, a slight tinge of disbelief in her voice. "You remember the way?"

Tracy nodded from the driver's seat as she peeled out of the parking lot.

The three drove in relative silence as they entered the

city's downtown area. Towering buildings glittered and flashed as light caught rows of glass windows and reflected off parked cars. In spite of all of that, though, the city seemed empty and devoid of activity—particularly in the industrial area in which the truck pulled to stop.

The trio piled out of the vehicle beside a nondescript warehouse. While Rico and Tracy carefully rolled Marcus down a ramp from the truckbed, Donna approached the warehouse and knocked on a large garage door. A few moments later, she heard an unpleasant metallic grating sound, then the door began to slowly retract. She peered into the open space, well-lit by a series of old fluorescent overhead lights; Donna was momentarily blinded until a man's approaching silhouette shaded her from the brightness.

"So it worked?" The man said, adjusting a set of oily spectacles. "You found him?"

Donna smiled nervously and nodded toward the truck's ramp.

"Hey, Doc," Rico waved with one hand while he kept the other gripped firmly to the shrouded golden man.

The doctor, Roger Lansing, adjusted his glasses again as he tried to discern the form of the inanimate man underneath the thick protective blankets. "Donna Locke," he muttered. "You truly never cease to amaze me."

Donna smirked. "Thanks, Doc. We did our part. Now it's time for you to do yours."

Tracy and Rico wheeled Marcus over the threshold and into the large space.

"You *are* ready for this, aren't you?" Donna pressed.

"Yes, yes, of course." The man snapped out of his reverie, pressed a button to close the garage door, then scurried back into the well-lit warehouse. He approached a tangle of large machinery and equipment in the center of the room as the bay door sealed them inside with a resounding metallic thud.

When they reached the testing area, Tracy and Rico began to untie the cords that bound the blankets and quilting around Marcus. In the buzzing yellow-green light, the man's current form now cast scintillating dapples across the space as he stood motionless and uncovered.

Roger's jaw sank slightly and his eyes glistened. "Well done," he said. The others who overheard weren't sure if it was a nod to their work in rescuing Marcus, or a self-congratulatory comment intended to be left unspoken. Either way, the doctor stood mesmerized for several seconds before moving toward a blinking console.

"We'll need to nudge him into the isolation chamber," Roger instructed with a wag of a finger, "in order for the vaporized formula to provide even coverage since he can't ingest it. Don't want to take any chances."

Rico followed Roger's instructive gesture to a large capsule made of a transparent glass-like material. One half of it acted as a door, which hung slightly ajar. The man now opened it all the way as he and Tracy pushed Marcus—still attached to the wheeled base—into the oversized tube. When they had secured and locked the casters in place, the two backed away and Rico closed and pressed the door until it made a satisfying click to indicate that it was properly sealed.

"Is he gonna be able to breathe in there?" Tracy wondered aloud.

Roger nodded and answered without looking toward her as his fingers fluttered out a sequence of keystrokes. "There's plenty of oxygen being pumped in there, and we'll regulate it and adjust as the formula takes effect so it's less of a shock to his system." The doctor flicked a few more buttons and switches then moved near to the group, who stood just a few feet from the glass tank which now encased Marcus.

Donna's eyes pored over every shimmering detail of the man behind the glass. *It's time.*

"Y-you know, Miss Locke," Roger stammered, interrupting her thoughts. "We've never tested the formula on an object that's been, er, *gilded* for as long as your dear Marcus has."

A look of concern washed over Donna. "And?"

"I just—" He began, then started again: "I'm not entirely sure what the side effects might be when he rematerializes—nausea, generalized hibernation sickness, disorientation, mutation, memory lo—"

Donna gripped Roger's shoulder, squeaking her leathery gloves. "Is it going to work or isn't it?"

The doctor took a deep breath, then another, before bobbing his head up and down. "It's going to work." He forced an unconvincing grin.

"Alright, then." She turned back to Marcus. "Let's do this."

Rico could sense Donna's anticipation, the nerves causing

her to clench and unclench her gloved fist out of habit. He took a step closer to her and allowed his hand to meet hers. "You gonna be okay, Don?"

She closed her eyes and inhaled slowly, then nodded. "It doesn't feel real. After all we've been through, we're finally here."

The man didn't reply, but felt the same. Rico moved his arm to hug her from the side, his comforting brotherly presence easing Donna's internal tension ever-so-slightly.

Roger looked down to a small remote control in his hand. "Let the countdown commence," he said, eyeing a big red button in the remote's center. "Ten. Nine. Eight—"

Donna controlled her respiration as much as possible, attempting to slow her racing heart by way of a series of deep breaths.

"Seven. Six—"

It's time we had the life we always wanted, Donna bit her lip.

"Five. Four—"

You and me—together again.

"Three. Two—"

A second chance.

"One." Roger placed a firm finger on the red button and pressed down.

See you on the other side, Marcus.

Donna held her breath. A cloud of thick gaseous material shot into the tube, quickly obscuring Marcus from view. The glass canister filled fast, and the colorless matter danced around the space in curious clumps and wisps. The pneumatics slowed their pumping to a stop, allowing the trapped vapors to drift.

Instinctively, Donna stepped forward. Then another few slow steps. She placed her hand on the cloudy glass and peered in, hoping to catch a glimpse of Marcus' transformation. Donna waited, her warm breath fogging the outside of the convex glass.

Then something remarkable happened. From the mist emerged an arm—a hand which pressed itself gently to the transparent casing of the tube, mirroring Donna's own. As the gaseous formula began to subside, Donna could now see the familiar, human face—with all of its beautiful features. Donna gasped as her eyes began to glisten. No one spoke a word; they dared not interrupt this long-awaited moment.

Marcus gazed from behind the glass, his soft brown eyes piercing gently into Donna's own—into her soul, she felt—a look she'd seen many times before. He did not speak, but stood mesmerized, conscious for the first time in over a year.

It's really happened, was all Donna could think. *Finally.* She smiled. "Marcus, I—"

Thwack!

The loud and sudden appearance of Marcus' other hand from the sinking mist—a fist, to be precise—startled Donna, sending her stumbling backwards reflexively. She tripped and fell to the ground, then looked up in wonderment.

"Marcus—?"

Thwackkk! It resounded again, his heavy, dark fist hammering against the interior of the glass.

"What's happening, Doc?" Rico asked as he assumed a combative stance and reached toward a weapon at his side. Tracy did the same.

"I-I don't know—"

Thwack-crrrack!

This time, the fist left a large fissure in the glass, snaking quickly into tiny, tendril-like splinters across the tube. Both hands pressed against the glass, and Marcus' eyes conveyed a look of fear and confusion. Or was it anger?

Before Donna or the others could think, Marcus punched his fist against the glass door again. This time it shattered and his hand broke through the fragile tube.

"Marcus, what are you doing?" Donna shouted. "Marcus?"

As fragments of the broken glass scattered across the floor, Marcus turned his head to lock eyes with Donna. "Who are you?"

His words sent a chill down her spine. She started to open her lips to reply, but quickly threw her arms to cover her face as Marcus shattered more of the glass with his bare hands. Donna lowered her arms slightly to take another look at the man.

Zzzzsssap!

The lights cut out—all of them at once. The overheads, the indicators on the console and remote, the exit sign. The room was suddenly pitch black. Cold.

What the—? Donna gasped and shouted. "Marcus, please—"

She heard the sound of shoes crunching on broken

glass, then running across the cavernous warehouse. Donna scrambled to stand up, extending her hands to guide her in the dark.

"Donna?" Rico's voice startled her, closer than she anticipated.

"I'm here," she shouted. "But Marcus—"

The footsteps hurried away, unseen, toward a far corner of the darkened space, echoing softly. As Donna squinted to try and make her eyes adjust, she heard a door click and a sudden bluish beam of moonlight flood in. For a moment, this glow illuminated the silhouette of Marcus, but he quickly passed across the threshold and the door swung closed behind him.

Frantic, Donna sprinted toward the exit, with the others close behind. She burst through the door and her heels clacked across the parking lot, craning her head rapidly in every direction.

"Marcus?" She shouted, cupping her hands around her mouth. "*Marcus!*"

The only sounds that called back were the distant rumblings of midnight traffic and police sirens. Marcus was gone.

Rico and Tracy reached Donna's side.

"Donna," Tracy placed a hand on her shoulder. "What just happened in there?"

Donna trembled. She shook her head. "I don't know. One minute it was him—the way he looked at me—just like I remember. Then—" Here she choked up and tried to hold her tears at bay. After a moment, though, she burst into uncontrollable sobs.

Rico patted her back gently, moved closer. "Did he say something to you?"

The blonde woman nodded and wiped her dripping nose with the back of her glove. She took a deep breath. "He said," Donna could hardly move herself to repeat the words. "He said, 'Who are you?'"

Neither of the officers knew how to respond, but gave each other a worried glance.

Just then, Roger's voice shouted from the small warehouse door. "The lights are back on!"

Tracy turned to him and hollered across the parking lot. "Some kinda power outage?"

The doctor shook his head. "I don't think so. The remote's indicator lights went out and came back. But the thing is—the remote is *battery* powered." His jaw hung agape as he had this realization.

Donna sniveled again, then walked quickly toward the doctor, a fury in her eyes. "Roger, what did you do to him?"

"D-do to him?" Roger stuttered and backed himself through the door and into the warehouse once more. "What do you mean?"

"Something was *wrong* with Marcus!" Donna followed him inside, clenching her gloved fists. "He didn't remember who I am. Something's *very* wrong. What did you do differently to the formula?"

The doctor waved his hands defensively. "I assure you, Miss Locke: the formula was recreated as closely to the original as possible. It *did* work correctly. The effects of your, er, powers on him were reversed, just as intended."

Donna pressed in, her pulse quickening. "But *why* didn't he remember me? Why did he freak out like that? None of that happened when we turned Starla back."

Rico interjected himself between the two. "Hey, hey, guys—Donna—if he says he didn't do anything wrong, then he didn't. Doc knows his stuff." The young officer waited as Donna took deep breaths. "Whatever *that* was," he pointed toward the fractured glass tube, "was something beyond Roger's doing. Fact is, he did exactly what he was supposed to do. He *fixed* Marcus."

Donna shook her head and turned to look out the open door. "Something was *not* right with him, though—I could see it in his eyes. And now he's gone. Again."

"We'll find him, Donna," Tracy assured her. "We did it once; we'll do it again."

"And then what?" Donna spoke in a near-whisper. Her eyes began to glisten again. "What if this time he doesn't want to be found? What if he's not... the *same* Marcus he used to be?"

"I suggest we cross that bridge when we come to it," Roger offered calmly.

Donna hesitated, then nodded.

"C'mon, Don," Rico said, leading her back out the door. "Let's get you home to the girls."

The woman complied, trailing Rico as they moved toward the truck parked on the warehouse's side. Before she entered,

Donna glanced back over her shoulder. The dark streets seemed colder, emptier, more unknown now, and a plastic bag crinkled past like a tumbleweed in the seabreeze.

Marcus. Donna strained her eyes to see in the moonlight. *Where are you?*

CHAPTER 4

October 1981. A Few Months Later.
Citrus Springs: A Western Suburb of Miami.

It was a muggy evening in the middle of October. A cool breeze fluttered the Spanish moss that clung lazily to a series of drooping oak trees on the canal behind the Barley family's gated housing development. Biff, the youngest of the Barley children, was halfway through his first semester of middle school and hadn't exactly thrived in the experience so far. He was terrible at sports, and he was a portly boy—everyone expected him to sprout and spread his girth more evenly about his awkward body, but that hadn't happened yet.

Add to that a name like Biff Barley and it wasn't hard to see why the boy might've been an easy target for bullies. His solution? Not rage. Not physical force. Not curling up into a ball and never speaking to a soul. No. It was his *words* that carried the power, and he would lob a choice few when he felt so inclined—or threatened.

After dinner, Biff snuck out through the back gate and

down to the canal, wearing Reebok sneakers and a red baseball cap. Mr. and Mrs. Barley always warned him to watch for alligators, but in all their years of living there, there was yet to be a single credible sighting. The boy remained cautious and planned to stay on dry land just to be safe. He sat down in the soft grass and took a deep breath. The sounds of cicadas and croaking frogs floated from somewhere up the canal, and Biff imagined where the stream might take him if he happened upon a canoe or a raft one day.

A few bubbles fluttered up to the surface, catching Biff's eye. He leaned forward, wondering what sort of fish or turtle or other nocturnal creature might be coming up for a breath.

The sound of snickering at his side startled Biff and he whipped toward it. His wide, freckled cheeks became flushed and he took a nervous gulp. He couldn't see their faces, but from the sound of the approaching voices, Biff knew who was behind them: Tommy and Travis. Tommy lived in the house next-door and Travis lived a neighborhood over, but they were nearly inseparable.

Biff clenched his sweaty hands. He could run, but they'd catch up to him, maybe beat the pulp out of him just for the fun of it—just to prove to each other that they *could*.

"Well, well, well," Travis jeered as he stepped into the waning half-beam of a far-off streetlight. "If it isn't the biggest dweeb of the century."

Sure, Biff was into standard "nerd" hobbies like reading comic books and playing *Donkey Kong*, but even if he was a *dweeb*, it clearly wasn't a compliment coming from Travis's slobbery lips. *Mouthbreather.*

"Go away, Travis," Biff mumbled, turning to look back at the still water of the canal.

"You first," interjected Tommy. "You're on my land."

Biff craned his neck back to look at the houses that sat up the embankment. The fences of the two houses looked identical, merging into one long wooden wall across the backyards. Tommy might have been correct that Biff was *technically* in the neighbor's lot, but what did it matter? "Funny, I didn't know they let eleven-year-olds own land," Biff said, mustering a smirk.

Tommy scowled and his whole body clenched. "What'd you say?"

A gentle breeze disturbed the surface of the canal ever-so-slightly, and another flurry of small bubbles appeared, this time closer to the water's edge.

Biff took a deep breath. "I said it's not *your* land, Tommy, and I'm pretty sure your mom and dad don't care—"

"And he said *scram*, dweeb!" Travis balled a hand into a fist and slapped it against his open other hand. "Before we beat the crap outta you til your stupid freckles fall off."

Biff felt his armpits sweating, soaking his t-shirt. As if the duo needed any more ammunition against him. *Thank God it's too dark to see.*

"Did you hear what we said, dweeb?"

The rotund child gulped and shook his head. "No."

"No?"

"I don't have to leave. The canal's no-man's-land."

Travis sneered and moved toward Biff. He gave him an aggressive shove. "Beat it, butthole!"

Biff braced himself from falling, then tried to ignore the angry bullies standing over him. His pulse was racing.

"What a sissy!" Tommy spouted and came in with punch.

The fist felt like a heavy tap—nothing too painful. Biff recoiled and caught himself again. Tommy swung again. A few more punches and Biff put his hands up to try and shield himself. Travis joined in with a second forceful shove, this time toppling Biff.

Biff started to roll down the embankment, and the two boys continued to throw more punches—even some kicks—their clean white sneakers triggering short, labored breaths out of Biff. Soon, the boy was forced down to the edge of the water.

"Let's dunk him," Tommy suggested in a mock whisper, grinning.

Travis nodded.

Biff glanced back at the water, thought he saw the strange air bubbles again, then turned to the pair of red-faced boys. "C'mon, this isn't funny! You know I can't swim—"

"Should float, though," Travis chuckled. Tommy followed suit.

"That's not funny," Biff insisted.

"I dunno," Tommy said. "Seems like it'd be pretty funny to me."

The two boys moved closer. Biff had nowhere to go,

nowhere to run. One foot shifted backward, landing with a splash in the murky canal water and soaking his shoe. Biff winced, a tad embarrassed.

"Ready, Tommy? We dunk the wuss on the count of three."

Biff watched the boys' fists clench again.

"One."

The boys were all too distracted to catch the latest set of air bubbles rising to the surface of the water.

"Two."

Biff gulped.

"Three—!"

Instead of lunging at Biff, the two boys screamed and leaped backwards, their eyes enlarging as they tumbled onto the matted grass. In a flurry of motion, something large and scaled emerged from the water, latched onto Biff, and yanked him backwards with a splash. Biff started to scream, but all sound was garbled as his mouth—his entire body—was submerged in the canal. Neither Tommy nor Travis spoke as they watched a momentary struggle in the water. In a matter of seconds, the waters returned to a calm ripple, with a series of small bubbles rising to the air with a few wet *plops*. There was no sign of Biff Barley.

After lingering for just a moment longer, Tommy and Travis took off, sprinted up the embankment toward the house, and pushed through the fence gate. In the dark behind them, the breeze brushed through the sagging trees and danced across the waters of the canal.

All was quiet.

Too quiet.

Officer Rico Castillo turned off the engine and opened the driver's side door to step out.

"Rico, c'mon—" Tracy spoke in a serious tone from the passenger seat, trying hard to hide a growing smile. "Where are you taking me?" She wore a bandana over her eyes, tied tightly at the back of her head.

"You'll see," Rico said cryptically as he closed his door and circled around to the other side of the car.

Tracy heard the door click open and listened for more clues as she felt Rico's hand touch her own in that gentle but firm way that he always did—the way he showed he cared and that he had no intentions of letting go.

"Careful." Castillo guided the woman out of her seat and onto the pavement.

Immediately, Officer Tracy Jones's ears were met with the distant, calming roar of the ocean, muffled by a salinated, humid breeze that she'd grown somewhat accustomed to since relocating to Miami from the cold northeast.

Both wore well-fitting blue jeans, with Tracy sporting a matching light denim jacket over a t-shirt. Rico's signature short-sleeve button-down fluttered a little in the wind, its floral print design still clearly visible in the moonlight. He was often playfully accused by his colleagues of ripping off Magnum, though Castillo swore he'd sported the signature tropical shirt look long before Tom Selleck ever splashed into primetime.

Rico closed the passenger door, fiddled with the key to open the trunk, and removed a battery-powered boombox. When he'd shut the trunk, he took Tracy's hand again. "This way—watch your step."

Jones complied, her face betraying a mix of intrigue and frustration. She took her first few steps cautiously, her feet sinking into the top layer of soft sand. "Sand's loose—not packed down like the popular spots. You taking me to one of your secret beaches?"

"Trace," Rico exhaled sharply. "Can you maybe try *not* to be a detective for like five minutes?"

His partner didn't reply.

Rico puffed: "I know they're covered, but I can still tell when you're rolling your eyes."

Tracy masked a creeping smile.

"Just trust me, okay?"

The woman breathed in deeply, then sighed. "Fine."

The two trudged up and over the soft dune, at which point the sound of the rumbling sea became more pronounced. Rico spotted a landmark in the distance and continued on with Tracy still grasping his hand.

After a few quiet moments, the pair reached their destination and came to a stop.

"Can I take this ridiculous thing off now?" Tracy reached for the bandana without awaiting the answer.

"Yeah, we're here."

As she removed the blindfold, Jones braced herself for a

surprise. Directly ahead of her was the ocean, vast and foamy and roiling. Exactly what she expected. She breathed in, taking a quick hit of the salty air. "Impressive," Tracy said with a hint of sarcasm to Rico, who stood closely at her side. "You, uh, know I love the ocean..." If she was being honest, Tracy felt a little underwhelmed—what with the lengths to which Rico had gone to keep the night a secret and all.

Rico smiled. "Turn around," he whispered.

With a hint of cautious hopefulness, Jones leaned her neck and turned her whole body to face back toward the dunes. She was almost startled by the appearance of a large wooden structure just feet in front of her. Even in the darkness, the lifeguard tower's vibrant lime-green and baby blue paint job were hard to miss.

"Go on," Rico nodded toward the wooden staircase on the front of the tower.

"You mean go *inside*?" Tracy raised a skeptical brow then quickly glanced up and down the beach. "That's not exactly legal—"

"Tracy, who's going to arrest us? The *cops*?" The breeze swept back his thick black hair and he snickered like a schoolboy who had just succeeded in playing a prank that only he found funny.

Jones puffed, rolled her eyes, then started up the rickety steps with Rico close behind. When she reached the top of the stairs, she paused and made an audible gasp. Rico wrapped an arm around her as he came to her level.

A checkered tablecloth had been laid out across the floor

slats. A trio of candles flickered in the center of the space, casting a yellowish glow on a pair of plates with their accompanying silverware and place settings.

"Rico, you did all this? I don't know what to say." Tracy was admittedly hard to surprise and not exactly what one would call a *romantic*, but if there was anyone who knew how to get her in the mood, it was Rico.

"My sister helped a little," he muttered, guiding Tracy to take a seat. Rico came to a squat in the place opposite her and set the boombox beside him. He fished inside a large picnic basket in the corner of the compact, square room and produced a brown paper bag. When he opened it, the room immediately filled with the savory scent of garlic, chili, and something fried.

"Chinese?" Tracy guessed.

"Bingo." Rico reached a hand into the bag and pulled out a couple small white cardboard takeout boxes—the kind with the swirling designs and characters in thinly-printed red ink. "General Tso's for you. Orange chicken for me."

Tracy reached for the box as he moved toward her, but Rico motioned for her to sit back as he dumped the warm, gooey chicken onto her plate. Flecks of chili floated in the sauce that covered the fried meat and broccoli.

"I know it isn't the same as whatever they got in New York," Rico said as he scraped from the other box onto his own plate. "But this is supposed to be the best Chinese food in town." He finished divvying scoops from a styrofoam container of white rice, tossed a pair of chopsticks to Tracy, and then leaned back.

Tracy looked Rico in the eyes. "I'm sure it's perfect."

Rico raised a finger. "Wait." The young officer clicked a cassette into the boombox and pressed a chunky button on top. Immediately, the lifeguard tower filled with the sound of a sultry saxophone solo. "*Now* it's perfect," he smiled. "Bon appetit."

With the music playing over the calming ocean rumble, the two dug into the steaming meals with haste. Rico popped a cork from a bottle of wine and poured a small portion into two stemmed glasses. He handed one to Tracy. "So?"

Mid-bite, Tracy nodded, chewed, then swallowed. "Not bad," she grinned, then took a sip of the wine. "Can't beat Chinatown, of course, but it's really not too bad at all."

Satisfied with himself, Castillo reclined a little and took a large swig from his glass.

He looked like he wanted to say something—Tracy read it in his posture and face. "What's up?"

"Listen, Trace," he started in a somewhat serious tone. "I know it's only been a few months—"

"Four," Tracy spoke through a mouthful, "but who's counting?"

Rico exhaled, set his glass down, smiled. "Yeah, four. Right. So I know it's only been *four* months, but I've been thinking a lot about," he gulped, "the future."

His tone caused Tracy to tense instinctively, matching his furtive breathing.

"We've been through a lot together," he continued.

Tracy nodded. She thought of the rescue mission in the Bahamas just a few months prior, a drug ring they had disrupted earlier in the summer, and their first assignment—the one where they met while investigating an inexplicable murder. *We've been through a lot together.* "Sure have," she muttered. *Where's he going with this?*

Castillo's candlelit expression looked pasty. "And I guess with all of that, I've been thinking about what could be next for us—"

A sudden piercing beep shot through the guard tower. Tracy nearly spilled her glass of wine but gripped it tightly as Rico reached for something on his belt while the high-pitched beeping continued.

He glanced at the small device and pressed a button. The beeping ceased. "Sorry, just my pager—"

"You needa get that?"

"It can wait," Rico dismissed it as the saxophone music continued softly. He turned to again meet Tracy's gaze. "What I'm trying to say is that if there's anyone I want to spend my life with—"

Instantly, Tracy knew what was coming. And she dreaded it.

"—anyone I would want to raise a family with—"

"A *family*?" Tracy's fists clenched. "You mean like *kids?*"

Rico thought for a moment, then nodded slowly. "Yeah, that's what people mean when they say they want to raise a family, right?"

"Sure."

Rico raised an eyebrow. "Sure, like, that's what people

say? Or *sure*, like that's what you want, too—?"

The pager blurted out another sequence of deafening bleeps. Tracy scrunched her face as Rico scrambled for the button to mute it.

"You should really probably check that, huh? Is that the station?"

"It can wait," he exhaled, almost frustrated. "If they need to reach me that bad, they'll try again." Rico clicked *stop* on the boombox and turned back to Tracy with a soft expression in his eyes. "Listen, Tracy, I've never felt the way I feel around you with anyone else. I know we've been through a lot—and things are moving fast—but I finally realized I want you by my side through it all. Whatever comes next."

Jones swirled her chopsticks in circles around a pool of gooey chili sauce and tried not to look Rico in the eye. "I *will* be by your side," she muttered, then looked up to add, "*partner*."

"No, I don't mean our jobs," Rico puffed. "I mean like you and me and—"

Breep! Breep!

This time the sonic beeps came from Tracy's pager. The sound startled her, but she felt a momentary wave of relief. Jones looked at the small display. "It's the chief. We gotta go." She was already rising, scraping her plate into one of the open take-out boxes.

Castillo exhaled slowly.

Tracy was glad to be off the hook from a conversation she wasn't ready to have, but she saw the disappointment welling in Rico's body language as he refilled the picnic basket. "Hey, Rico," she said, putting her hand on his. He turned so that their eyes met. "I meant it when I said it," Tracy's dark eyes were big and kind. "Tonight was perfect."

The man smiled, a tinge bashful, romantic. Then a dose of Rico's usual sarcasm: "I guess it can only get worse from here, then," he mumbled as he threw the last few items into the basket and grabbed the boombox with his other hand. "Gotta be bad if they called us both at this hour. Wonder what's up this time."

"Guess we're about to find out," Tracy said, leading the way back down the wooden steps of the lifeguard tower. The two started across the long beach toward the dunes as the wind whipped salt and sand at their ankles.

Officers Jones and Castillo rolled up to the police station and hurried inside, brushing off chunks of sand that still clung to their shoes. They were immediately greeted by several sounds issuing down the hall—clicking keys, shoes treading furious paths across laminate floors, and voices answering phones with an air of haste. The two officers were surprised at how busy the station was, given the hour. It worried Rico.

They rounded a corner into the central space—where all the action happened—just as their chief emerged from his own private office. "Oh, thank God," he spoke above the flurry of ringing phones and activity. "Castillo. Jones. Get in here." The chief's forehead glistened and he dabbed a damp handkerchief across it. With his other hand, he took a draw from a withering cigarette.

The pair complied and walked quickly into the chief's office, shutting the door behind them. The chief made his way to his desk and leaned on a corner of it. He took another puff of his cigarette.

Rico started to apologize for failing to heed the pager's initial signal: "Chief, sorry we didn't get here sooner—"

The chief held up a hand. "Save it. We got a missing child."

"When?" Jones asked, her brow furrowing.

"'Bout an hour ago. Citrus Springs, just west of 33rd."

"When you say *child,* what are we talking?"

The chief puffed. "Sixth-grader. His name's Biff Barley."

"And what do we know about what happened to him?" Tracy crossed her arms.

There was a moment of quiet as the chief considered his words carefully. "Gator attack," he said finally. "Kid was playing near the canal out back of their house when it got him. Two of his buddies saw the whole thing."

Rico thought for a moment. "I hate to ask it," he gulped. "But do you think he's still—"

"Alive? Not a chance."

"Then why—" Tracy started.

The chief shook his head quickly, then leaned in close, a plume of smoke billowing in front of his face. "You wanna tell that to his crying mother out there? Be my guest." Neither of the two officers spoke as they glanced at the frosted glass door. "Just humor me and carry out the investigation. It'll be quick and easy—search the area, maybe find a piece of clothing or a scrap of a comic book upstream in a few days—*then* you call it. But we gotta give the family *some*thing to hope for."

Tracy raised an eyebrow. "Something like a chewed-up piece of his clothing?"

"Something like *hope* that we can actually help," the chief clarified. "You can start with the two witnesses—they're in the interrogation room. Haven't said much since they got here. Just do me a favor and try not to get them *too* riled up, or we'll be dealing with *their* angry parents, too."

"We can handle a couple kids," Rico said confidently. "Right, Officer Jones?"

Jones exhaled slowly, then nodded. "Right, *partner*," she said with a forced half-grin.

"Alright now get outta here," the chief nodded toward the door, then orbited his desk and sunk into its leathery chair.

Rico and Tracy closed the door behind them as they walked back through the busy central office area and down a hallway. The woman caught a glimpse of a small group of men and women in the waiting area, their eyes puffy and red. *The parents,* Tracy noted. *The pain they're feeling right now—*

She pushed the thought away.

The officers passed through a door into a dark room, where a large window let in a fluorescent glow that outlined a woman's face on the far side of the space. She wore large glasses, had big, curly hair, and she sat at a desk with a sketchpad and a bunch of charcoal pencils. The woman looked up when the officers entered.

"Hey, Barb," Rico said as they approached the woman and the window. On the other side of the glass, two teenage boys sat sniveling at a simple table.

"It's *Barbara*. And hey *yourself*," Barbara answered with more than a hint of irritation. She was the station's resident forensic artist. "What took ya so long?" The woman squinted and cocked her head, noticing their still-sandy ankles.

The newly-arrived officers made split-second eye contact before turning back to the artist. "We got here as fast as we could," Tracy answered tactfully. Barbara didn't seem satisfied with this answer, but the officer continued to quickly change the subject. "So no one's spoken to them yet?"

"Just the intake," Barbara replied. She turned to get another look at the boys. "Poor kids. Gotta be traumatizing—"

"What, being a teenage boy?" Rico muttered under his breath.

Barbara rolled her eyes under her chunky frames. "Seeing... *that* happen, I mean. The whole alligator thing."

"And so they brought you in to draw a sketch of it—the *alligator*?" Tracy raised both eyebrows this time.

The artist tightened her grip on one of the pencils instinctively. "Whatever gets us closer to finding that missing kid. I'm just doing my job; maybe you should do yours."

Tracy backed down. As the officers took another glance at the boys behind the two-way mirror, Rico spoke softly. "You wanna do this together?"

Officer Jones kept her eyes fixed straight ahead. "Might

be better if you take this one. Wouldn't want to overwhelm them." Two officers looming over them, sitting in a cold interrogation room late at night after witnessing a horrible tragedy. It would be a lot for anyone. "They're just kids," she added.

"Alright." Officer Castillo nodded, took a deep breath and rounded the corner to the entrance to the contained inner room. He swiped a tiny notepad and pen from the corner of the table. "Wish me luck."

A brief buzzing sound filled the space, indicating that the door was unlocked. Rico swung it open and entered the smaller room. The latch clicked behind him; the buzz dissipated. Tracy watched the two boys—nervous, afraid. She took a deep breath as Rico approached them.

CHAPTER 5

The small island upon which Donna Locke had purchased her home was situated in an enviable location. The house itself was a massive, multi-storied structure with its own private dock access to Biscayne Bay. Sandwiched between the mainland and the large offshore strip known as Miami Beach, Star Island was home to some of the wealthiest residents in the nation—politicians, investors, and even television and movie stars.

But Donna could have cared less about the social clout her zip code afforded her. For her, this was an escape, a second chance, the earnings of years of hard work—*and* the fruit of a freakish science experiment that left her with the ability to turn any object to gold at the touch of her hand. Many in the philanthropic community wondered where she had gained the sudden wealth that she distributed so graciously to needy non-profits in the area. Thankfully for her, even rich people had taboos when it came to discussing money, so Donna Locke kept mum about her powers. And that was just how she liked it.

It wasn't all allure and flashy cars, though. Just like her legendary progenitor King Midas, Donna had learned the hard way that her abilities came at a cost. First there was the accident that left her niece Starla paralyzed as a solid golden statue. Thankfully, with the guidance of Dr. Roger Lansing who had helped invent the power-imbuing experiment, Donna secured the antidote and turned the girl back into her lively, flesh-and-blood self. And later he invented a special set of gloves for the woman that allowed her to live a somewhat normal existence without turning everything she touched to shimmering gold.

But not before another tragedy struck: Marcus. Donna clenched her fists, stretching the leathery outer material of the gloves as she thought of him. Marcus Myles hadn't been as lucky as Starla. It was an accident, too. But there was only one vial of the formula...

All that glitters isn't gold. Indeed.

Then *she* took him.

Angela Hyde—another one of the scientists who was part of the original experiment with Roger. No one saw Angela or Marcus for months after the incident happened. It took a dangerous, convoluted series of missions to finally track them down. During that time, Dr. Lansing was able to conduct further research and procure the elements needed to recreate a new, single vial of antidote to eventually reverse the golden touch's effects on Marcus.

Under the moonlight, Donna stood at the edge of the seawall, staring out across the bay as her mind swirled and tossed like the dark waters in the evening breeze. Twinkling city lights dazzled from downtown Miami to her left and the ritzier island to her right as she recalled the scenes in her mind.

The lights.

It was all she thought about lately. Ever since she watched that golden statue melt away into skin and flesh, felt the pulse, heard Marcus' rich voice like it was the first time:

Who are you?

He disappeared again, but his words still haunted her.

I'll find you again, Marcus. I'm trying. I just don't know if you want *to be found...*

"There you are!" A woman's voice yanked Donna out of her reverie.

Donna turned, her big blonde hair bouncing in the breeze. The approaching woman had black hair fastened in a large ponytail: Susanna Castillo—Sue for short.

"You're missing all the fun, Don!" Sue said with a genuine smile, reaching for Donna's gloved hand. She started to pull her back toward the house, then paused when she saw the somber look in the other woman's expression. "You okay?"

There was no immediate answer from Donna, who let out a quiet sigh and wiped an unseen tear from the side of her face.

"You're thinking about *him*," Sue presumed correctly and

stepped closer. "He's out there somewhere, Donna. We'll find him again."

"I *know* he's out there." Donna spoke softly, barely audible over the choppy waves. "I just don't know if he even *wants* to be found or if he even remembers who I am—remembers what we had. After all we went through to find him the first time, what if it's just a waste?"

Sue hung an arm over Donna's shoulder. "You love him right?"

Donna breathed in deep, then exhaled slowly before nodding. "Course I do."

"Then it isn't a waste." Sue chose her words carefully. "Just because it takes work—takes risks—doesn't mean it isn't real or good or worth it. Good things take *risks*, Donna. You can't give up on him. Whatever's gotten into him, your Marcus is still in there... somewhere."

The two shared a moment of silence. Donna leaned her head on Sue's shoulder.

"C'mon," Sue said, craning her neck to look back to the house. "Lisa's bringing out the presents—and there's *cake*."

"Thanks, Sue." Donna smiled softly.

"Don't mention it, Don."

The women turned and walked back toward the rear of the house, where an outdoor area was bedecked in warm string lights and paper lanterns. A cluster of children crowded around a wooden picnic table, upon which a red-haired woman—Lisa—placed a large, frosted cake with nine thin candles glowing, flickering.

Donna wrapped her arms around the young girl who sat at the head of the table, half of her face obscured by a large cup of red liquid.

The girl put the cup down, licked her stained lips and smiled, scrunching her freckled face upwards. "Aunt Donna! Just in time!"

"Wouldn't miss it, little Starling." Donna brushed a few strands of the girl's ruddy hair behind her ear. Starla reached across the table for a translucent pitcher of more of the red drink. "Don't you think you've had enough Kool-Aid for one night?"

The girl didn't respond, but continued to refill her plastic cup.

Lisa gave Donna a smirk.

"What?" The girl's aunt cocked her head defensively. "Do you *know* how much sugar's in there?"

"Relax, Don. It's her birthday. Let her enjoy it!"

Donna exhaled—a motherly sigh—then stooped to Starla's seated level, gathering the eye-contact of as many of the children as she could. "Ready?" A few nods.

In near-unison, the group erupted in song while Starla watched the candles dance in the wind: "Happy birthday to you! Happy birthday to you—"

Finally they reached the end: "—Happy birthday, dear Starla. Happy birthday to *you*!"

Starla took a deep breath then blew out the candles. Her one, big breath managed to extinguish all but one, so she breathed in again. It took a couple more tries but finally the last little flame was gone, leaving a charred, smokey wick in its place. The girl smiled to Donna. "That was a tricky one." Her friends giggled and began their loud conversations once more as Lisa began to cut the cake into thick slices.

As the pieces were distributed to the many little guests and the birthday girl, Donna's eyes drifted to a stack of wrapped gifts on an end table nearby. "Time for presents, I think?"

With frosting smeared across her cheek, Starla grinned and nodded, shoving her plate away.

Sue helped Donna transport the boxes and bags to the picnic table, all within Starla's reach, while Lisa collected the quickly-emptied cake plates.

"This one's from Tiffany," Starla said, reading the tag on the box. She made eye-contact with Tiffany across the table, who shuffled her knees on the bench anxiously.

"It's a My Pretty Pony," Tiffany blurted.

Lisa leaned over and whispered to the little girl, "C'mon, Tiffany, don't ruin it. You know it's better when it's a surprise."

Starla seemed to ignore this exchange as she ripped the wrapping paper from the box. Her face lit up when she saw the pink plastic horse inside. "A My Pretty Pony! I've always wanted one of these," she beamed. "Thanks, Tiffany!"

Lisa mumbled to herself and took a step back. "Guess it *didn't* ruin it."

The girl opened a few more gifts until only one remained on the table—a small box, only a few inches long. "Who's this one from?"

Donna crouched beside her chair. "That's from me, kiddo. You gonna open it?"

Curious, Starla carefully removed the ribbon, then the wrapping, then a small lid. Inside was an object that sparkled in the dim light. The girl removed it and held it up to get a better look. It appeared to be some sort of jewelry fashioned in the shape of a colorful bird. "Is this—?"

"A starling," Donna smiled as Starla turned the brooch over and over in her hands. "That one's a special type called Hildebrandt's starling—see all the colors: purple, blue, green, and rusty orange. That's what the birds look like when they've grown up—" Here Donna felt an unexpected flash of wonder at how fast the girl had matured in the short time she'd been under her care. "You'll always be my little Starling; and someday you'll show us all your colors." Donna planted a soft kiss on the top of Starla's hair.

"Thanks, Aunt Donna," answered the girl, enamored with the object. "Can you pin it on me?"

"Of course." Donna unfastened the tiny clasp and carefully attached it to the girl's shirt.

Starla smiled, wide and toothy. "I love it." Out of what must have certainly been part of some unspoken child-code, the rest of the kids cheered and clapped.

Lisa waved her hands to gather the attention of the children. "There's *one* more special gift—" She motioned toward Sue, who had run into the house and now returned with a huge square box. Sue walked carefully. "This one's from both of us."

A muffled thumping sound came from the box—the sound of some sort of living creature inside. Donna raised her eyebrow and cocked her head toward her friends—*really, girls?*

Sue set the box in front of Starla, who's eyes conveyed her wonder. She quickly tore off a bow and removed the lid. Her face lit up with a huge smile as a high-pitched *bark!* resounded from inside the package.

"It's a puppy!"

Starla's friends clamored and climbed across the picnic table to see as the girl carefully removed a fluffy, black-eyed golden retriever puppy.

Donna locked eyes with Sue then Lisa and shook her head, amused. Starla giggled as the puppy lapped its light-pink tongue toward her, slobbering over her chin.

In a season of such darkness, such uncertainty, Donna clung to every smile and moment of joy afforded to her. There were still so many unanswered questions she had about Marcus, about her family, about her sister who even now missed her own daughter's ninth birthday party as she rested in a coma upstairs. Just months ago, Donna had learned that so much of her life was a lie. The man responsible for the company that developed the formula that had given her the golden touch—Rolf Ducane—was more acquainted with her family than she thought; he seemed to know more about them than Donna did. He claimed that Donna, her sister, and her niece all had something in common—their special blood—and that there was more to the story...

Of course there was no way to verify it all. He only said those things so he could get away. Besides, in her mind, Ducane was a villain. He couldn't be trusted.

Still, every time she looked into that sweet, innocent, freckled, nine-year-old face, the questions gnawed at Donna from the inside.

A motion out of the corner of her eye pulled Donna back to the present moment. She looked up toward the house to see a man standing inside the sliding glass door, waving to her.

Donna verified that Sue and Lisa had a handle on the kids, then moved swiftly toward the house. The chatter, giggles, and barks faded as she reached the door and slid it open.

"Sorry," the man said, running a hand through his chestnut hair. "I didn't realize I'd be crashing a party."

Donna offered a soft smile and the two shared a quick embrace through the open door. "You're welcome here anytime, Declan. There's some extra cake if you want?" She pointed a thumb toward the patio behind her.

"Thanks, but I'm trying to go easy on the sweets." Declan smirked, then his handsome expression became more somber.

Donna sensed this gravitas and leaned in, whispering: "You found something?" She wanted to say "you found *him*," but she could barely stand to have her hopes dashed one more time. And, more importantly, she hadn't yet looped in Declan on that tiny, important detail of Marcus' second disappearance—nor that they'd found him in the first place.

Declan nodded, then made a glance at the partygoers outside. "Is there somewhere more quiet we can talk?"

"Oh, yeah, of course," Donna said, sliding the glass door closed and pointing through the kitchen. "Roger will want to hear anything you've found, too. He's been a huge help." The woman started walking through the house with Declan trailing closely behind.

As they wound through the maze of halls, Declan noted the tall ceilings, lavish finishes, and interestingly-shaped, trendy furniture.

"Is everything okay, Donna?" Declan asked as they walked.

"Yeah," she answered dismissively.

He puffed. "You sure? You didn't return any of my calls after the incident with my father—" Declan followed Donna around a corner, trying to keep up. "Then you call me out of the blue a couple months ago—"

Donna paused and turned to face him. Her expression was almost stern—the man sensed that this was just the facade she put up to avoid showing the true emotion underneath. "I'm sorry, Declan. We've all been through a lot. I really do appreciate you doing me this favor."

Without another word, Donna Locke pivoted and the pair ascended a small staircase on the side of the house that led up to a garage apartment. Donna rapped on the door with the back of a gloved hand. There was no immediate answer, but she could hear the light thumping of music coming from within. She knocked harder and shouted: "Doc! You home?" *Knock-knock-knock.* "Roger? Doc?"

Finally, the door swung open and a disheveled, bespectacled man stood in the threshold.

"Doc, what took—"

"One moment," the man held up a finger. "This is the best part." An elaborate, crashing drum solo blasted through a boombox speaker behind him and the doctor closed his eyes, bobbed his head, lost in the beat.

"Phil Collins?" Declan asked, almost shouting.

Roger nodded and smiled, his eyes still shut. After a few more seconds, he opened his eyes and moved over to the boombox then clicked the chunky *power* button. Donna and Declan immediately felt their bodies release some tension.

"Sorry," Roger said. "Had to catch it while the station had it playing. It comes on each night at precisely 8:15."

"Why don't you just get it on tape?" Declan raised an eyebrow as he followed Donna into the room.

The doctor shook his head. "There's just something about hearing it on the broadcast in real-time—a sense that you know there's hundreds or thousands of others experiencing the exact same feeling." Roger smiled. "Well, *that*, and I don't exactly make it to the record store very often."

Donna shut the door behind her and the doctor gestured to a small loveseat covered in loose articles of clothing. Hesitantly, Donna and Declan sat down. They sunk into the couch, prompting the pair to involuntarily lean toward each other. With a quick motion, the two reshuffled and scooted further toward the edges of the sofa.

"Now," said Roger. "What brings you two for a visit?"

"Declan has something to share—an update."

The man nodded. "Yes, you asked me to keep an eye out for any sort of strange outages or blackouts." Though Declan had received a large inheritance from his father, Rolf Ducane, the son made his own fortune by cornering the market on an essential utility—electricity. Miami Power and Light quickly beat out all competition, and earned the younger man his first of many millions.

"And?" Donna's tone came off as a little impatient. She caught herself and almost apologized, but decided to let it slide. She *was* impatient. *I'm ready for this to be over—to find him and fix whatever's wrong.*

"There's always a handful of small blackouts, especially when it storms," explained Declan. "But ever since you reached out, I've noticed a surge in outages at times when the weather's perfectly clear." Here he reached into a jacket pocket and pulled out a piece of folded paper. He opened it, crinkled and creased, and Donna leaned over his shoulder. "These are the addresses and intersections where the reports came in—"

"Thanks, Dec," Donna snatched the paper, stood up, and moved to a far wall that was covered in a wrinkly sheet hung with pushpins at its upper corners. She swept the sheet to the side and fastened it on a hook, revealing a large map on the wall underneath.

Declan rose slowly, craning his head slightly. "So what is this exactly? Why are you so interested in these shadow spots all of a sudden?"

Donna read the first address from the paper then reached into a container of red pushpins. Without looking back at the man, she answered: "We're mapping them."

The visitor exhaled sharply through his nostrils, took a step forward. "Mapping them for *what* reason?"

As she stabbed a second red pin into the map, Donna let her gloved hand linger in place and she thought for a moment. "To find Marcus," she said finally. "He's on the run, out there somewhere, and these are going to help us find him again."

"*Again?*" Declan's voice brightened. "You mean you *found* him—the files from my father's vault—they weren't a waste after all?"

Donna cast a knowing glance at Roger and took a deep breath. "We found him," she said softly.

"But you said he's on the run?" Declan clarified, shifting his gaze to the doctor. "Which means you found a way to turn him back from gold to his normal human state?"

"The, er, overall effects of his gilded state were reversed," Doctor Lansing nodded, idly twirling a golden ballpoint pen he'd snatched from his cluttered desk.

"But?" Declan's eyes flicked from Roger to Donna then back again.

"*But* there was something... *wrong* with him," Donna lowered and shook her head, reliving the scene from the warehouse just a few months prior.

For a moment, no one spoke. Declan was growing impatient with Donna, but sensed that the memory was painful. He moved closer. "What was wrong with him, Donna?"

"He didn't know who I was," she said, choking up. "He didn't remember *us*."

Declan placed a gentle, comforting hand near the woman's shoulder and allowed her to linger in the quiet moment. His eyes drifted to the crinkled paper in her hand. "Pardon me for my ignorance," the man said, "but I'm not seeing the connection between the shadow spots and Marcus."

"When the formula ran its course," Roger began timidly, "it seemed to work correctly—in much the same way it did with Starla. But when Officer Myles regained consciousness, he seemed to be disoriented—afraid." The doctor paused. "Then all of a sudden, all the light in the room was gone."

"Like the power went out?" Declan suggested. "One of your machines blew a fuse?"

Doctor Lansing shook his head. "No. All the light was literally *gone*. From the room—even indicator lights that weren't connected to the building's power supply. It was like it just got sucked away."

Declan raised an eyebrow. "And you think it was Marcus that did it?"

"I *know* it was Marcus." Donna punched another pin into the drawing of the city streets.

Roger gestured to the map. "And that's why we need the information from the shadow spots—"

"To track him down again," Declan finished the thought. He stroked his chin as he inspected the pins. "I hate to say this, but... what if Marcus doesn't *want* to be found."

His words lingered in the stuffy apartment-laboratory,

echoing the thoughts that Donna continued to fight in her own mind. She busied herself with adding another pushpin to the wall.

"Maybe he *doesn't* wanna be found," Donna admitted. "But if there's even a chance that we could still be together, I'm going to take it."

For the next few moments, the men watched in relative silence as Donna made her way down the list of coordinates to flesh out the wall map.

As she did this, Declan questioned the doctor: "So what do you think happened to him, Doc?"

"Well," began Roger, moving to a large chalkboard. He picked up a small dusty piece with which to write and quickly sketched a crude outline of a man. "My working hypothesis is that Officer Myles was altered on a molecular level when he underwent the transformation from man to gold then back again." The doctor drew a small circle on the figure's chest. "I believe it bestowed on him some strange abilities to manipulate—or possibly absorb—light." Here he marked dashed lines moving toward the chalk man, like beams or rays. "I'm not certain whether he has any control over it, or if it happens involuntarily."

Declan stared at the chalk drawing, his arms crossed. "What about Starla?"

Donna jabbed a pin into the map then turned. "What about her?"

"If Doc used the same basic formula to revert Marcus back from his golden state as he did for Starla, how come none of this is happening to her?"

Donna had asked herself the same question months ago, but she didn't have a good answer then and she didn't have one now. Rolf Ducane implied that all of her living family members had at least some measure of the same, special blood—the blood that was a vital part of allowing Donna's own powers to flourish. But if that was true of Starla, time had yet to reveal that the birthday girl had any powers of her own.

Roger interjected his own explanation. "Perhaps it's a similar phenomenon to radioactive decay." The two blank stares directed at him indicated that he needed to explain. "What I mean is that maybe the longer one's body is in such a rigid state, the more drastically the molecular structure is altered."

It made sense. Starla was only golden for a day; Marcus spent a whole year that way. Donna nodded and flexed a hand. "That could certainly be *one* logical explanation." If Starla had abilities, surely they would've made themselves apparent by now. *She would've told me. Right?*

Donna placed a red pin on the final location from Declan's slip of paper and stood back. The red dots formed a sort of scatter plot across the city map, increasing in density as they neared the downtown area.

The woman gestured toward the cluster. "It's happening more often," Donna noted. "At least we've narrowed it down." She turned to the doctor and Declan. "We're getting close. I can feel it."

"Now that we know the area to keep an eye on," Roger said, "we just have to wait for another report and we'll be right on his tail."

"So that's the plan?" Declan raised an eyebrow. "Wait for a new report and then—what?—snatch him up and force him to give up his powers?"

Donna tensed. "You have a better idea?"

The visitor was silent. He sighed then shook his head slowly. "But," he said. "I'll call you the *minute* we hear of another outage."

The two exchanged knowing, warm smiles and Declan moved toward the door.

Donna took a few steps after him. "Declan."

"Yeah?"

"I should've told you sooner. I'm sorry for keeping you in the dark."

For a split-second, he considered pressing more, then nodded. "Don't worry about it, Donna. I know things haven't been easy."

"Thanks," she exhaled. "Thanks for everything."

With a quick nod of acknowledgment, Declan turned and left the apartment lab quietly.

When he had gone, Donna returned her attention to the map, poring over each and every pin. *We're close, Marcus. I'm coming. Hold on.*

CHAPTER 6

Click. Officer Tracy Jones switched on the intercom. The faint buzz of a cold, dying fluorescent light crackled through the speaker in the outer observation room, underscoring the unease of the interrogation room's three occupants. Inside, Rico sauntered over to the seat opposite the two trembling middle-school boys, hunched in the stiff metal chairs like they were awaiting a parental reprimand. The officer glanced over his shoulder, sensing his partner's gaze beyond the shiny glass at his back—a bit of one-way eye-contact, Tracy mused—before turning to address the two kids.

"Good evening, boys," he started. "I'm Officer Enrico Castillo, and I'm sorry we kept you waiting so long. Can you state your names for the record?" The man hovered a pen over a small notepad like he was about to write.

The boy on the left gulped. "Are w-we under arrest?"

Rico bit his lip to mask a smile. "No. I just need to ask you some questions."

Poor things. Jones felt relieved that she didn't have to hide her own grin. *And this is why he's the one dealing with the kids, not me.*

Barbara, the artist who sat at the table beside Tracy, let out a sigh—a sigh that was clearly intended to make her impatience known. "Those kids are definitely hiding something."

Tracy kept her eyes fixed ahead, rolled them a little. "Officer Castillo will get it out of 'em," she said, pursing her lips.

"You can go first," Rico instructed to the boy on the left.

"T-Tommy Lambert," he stuttered.

"And I'm Travis," the other replied. "Travis Hodgkins."

"Thank you. You know why we're here?" Castillo continued.

Both gave hesitant nods.

"Chief says you two were—I mean *are*—friends of Biff Barley."

The boy on the right furrowed his brow. "Is that a question?"

Rico grinned. "Sorry. Is it true that you're friends with Biff Barley?"

"H-his house is right next to mine," answered Tommy, the boy on the left.

A non-answer, Tracy noted. *People can be so clever. Even at their age.*

"We've known him for a long time," Travis sniveled.

Rico shifted, craning head to the opposite side. "So you

aren't friends with him?"

Both boys gulped, then made shifty eye-contact. Tommy shook his head slowly. Rico pretended to write something, which made the boys squirm a little more.

"We, uh," Travis started. "We might've been..." He took a long pause to garner the courage to speak the words. "We might've been *teasing* him... when it happened."

Tracy had a clear view of the scene, and watched Tommy land a soft but determined kick to Travis' ankle under the table. The boy winced, scrunched his nose. *Maybe* he *should've been the one that got*—she caught herself before she could finish the thought, macabre as it was.

"Thanks for your transparency," Rico nodded. "Like I said, you're not under arrest—we just want to find out what happened to Mr. Barley tonight. Every moment counts, though, so don't hold back, okay?"

Both boys nodded—Tommy with a bit of reluctance. Officer Jones smiled softly, involuntarily.

"He's a natural," Barbara said, interrupting a thought.

Sure is, Tracy thought, not wanting to gratify the annoyed artist with a verbal response. *Better him than me.*

The questions continued.

"So can you tell me anything about what happened before—" Rico chose his words carefully, "before Biff, uh, went missing, and the events leading up to that moment?"

It took a moment for the sixth-graders to gather their thoughts, but finally Tommy spoke. "We went out back after dinner... we were supposed to be doing homework. Then we saw him."

"Biff Barley?" The officer listened intently.

Tommy and Travis nodded in unison.

"We thought it would be funny to mess with the dweeb—I mean Biff." Tommy stuttered, before a crushing wave of guilt spawned fresh glossy tears at the edges of his eyes. "But I promise we never meant for anyone to get *really* hurt—"

Rico raised a gentle, knowing hand for the boy to calm down. "Right now, we just need to know what happened. No one's in trouble." He exhaled, then added: "Not yet, anyway."

"We sort of cornered him," Travis spoke now, his head lowered. "You know, pushed him back toward the water. None of us saw it until it was too late..."

"Saw what?"

Both boys became quiet, remembering a yet unspoken horror.

"I-I don't know how t-to—" Tommy stammered.

Officer Castillo extended a hand across the table and placed it gently in front of the boy. "It's alright, kid. Breathe." The boy nodded and followed the officer's instruction. "There ya go. Let's try again. Now, can you describe what you saw?"

Tommy breathed in deep again. "It was dark—"

"It had scales all over," Travis interjected.

"A gator?"

"Not sure."

Tommy added: "It just sort of walked out of the water, then grabbed the dweeb and pulled him under."

"Walked?" Castillo cocked his head. "You mean *crawled?*"

Tommy shook his head slowly. "No. I mean *walked.* Just like any of us in here do."

On the other side of the glass, Tracy leaned forward, intrigue getting the best of her.

"What are you saying, exactly?" Rico had set the pen down by this time. "This *thing* walked out of the water on—what, you mean like... two legs?"

The pair of boys nodded again.

"And it had scales all over?"

"Well, it was wearing some kinda pants," Travis elaborated. "But its head was like a—" Here he placed his hands in front of his face and tried to suggest a shape protruding about a foot out from his nose.

"A snout?"

"Yeah."

"Scaly gator snout?"

"Yes."

"Walking on two legs... with... *pants* on?" Rico felt ridiculous even saying the words. "If you kids are yanking my chain—"

"It's all true!" Travis insisted. "I promise!"

Tommy agreed. "I'd never seen anything like it—ever. When it grabbed Biff, it chomped down on him, yanked him under, then..." The boy trailed off in a whimper.

"I think I get the picture," Rico said. "Can you just repeat your address for the record so we can investigate the scene?" The boys complied and the officer scribbled on the notepad.

Tracy could tell the boys were deeply affected by what they had seen. *Sometimes trauma messes with your perceptions of reality*, she recalled learning during her training. *And sometimes kids just don't know the difference between their imagination and what's real. But this is kind of ridiculous...*

"Thank you both for your time," Rico said, standing. "You've been a great help." He shook the timid duo's sweaty, limp hands then motioned for the door. Tracy held the lock switch and the door buzzed while they left the inner room. Rico guided the boys into the hall, where another officer chaperoned them back to their mothers. When the door had closed once again on the dim room, Castillo turned to Tracy.

"You did good," Tracy muttered, restraining herself from placing a hand on his arm when she remembered the artist who scribbled furiously behind her in the shadows.

"Yeah," Barbara spoke up, dropped her pencil. "Great job. I never knew all those years sketching comic book characters would come in so handy."

Rico lifted a curious eyebrow and looked toward Barbara. The woman held up the large pad, upon which was drawn a charcoal sketch of a vaguely humanoid creature. It looked exactly as the boys had described: something like a half-man, half-alligator hybrid, with its large reptilian snout extending from a hunched, scaly torso. He wore a pair of pants, tattered—the artist's own embellishment. Barbara was right; the creature looked like something straight out of a comic book. *Or a horror flick*, Rico gulped.

"What the..." Tracy trailed off as she looked at it. "You

think they're *actually* telling the truth? You know how kids can be—"

"I've seen a lot of crazy things in this city, Trace," Rico said, completely serious. "Those kids were convinced of what they saw. I mean, in all likelihood it was just some guy in a costume—Halloween's right around the corner."

Officer Jones sensed there was more he was leaving unsaid. "*But...?*"

"*But* we can't rule out anything until we've had a chance to take a look at the scene," Officer Castillo said. He moved closer to Barbara and ripped the piece of paper from the pad.

"Hey, careful with that!" she exclaimed. "It's some of my best work!"

"I'll be careful," the man said, already heading toward the exit. "Jones, you wanna check in with chief before we go? I'll fax this over to the folks at the next precinct, just so they can be on the lookout."

The partners started into the hall when Rico stuck his head back through the door. "Thanks, Barb."

The artist gritted her teeth. "It's *Barbara*," she grunted.

The door slammed.

Officer Castillo hurried to the copier alcove, drawing in hand, while Tracy vanished around a corner toward the chief's office. Rico examined the chunky devices and located the fax machine on a sliver of laminate counter, a newer addition to the office lineup. He'd seen bulkier ones before. Rico stood before it, wondering which buttons to press. A glance over his shoulder verified that there were no office assistants in-house at that hour of the night.

Drat.

The man noted what looked like a feeder tray near the back of the machine and slid the drawing into it with care. Then there was the keypad. Rico bit his lip and looked up to find a set of phone numbers pinned to a corkboard above the fax machine. *Guess I just dial it in?*

The chunky buttons clicked and clattered as Castillo typed out the number for the precinct. His finger hovered over a large button on the console before finally pressing down. The machine rattled, buzzing loudly as rotors inside the device began to turn, catching the page in the feeder. Rico watched the half-alligator, half-man sink beneath the surface, dragged under and into the machine by the slow motion of some unseen force.

Castillo tapped his foot as he waited for the document to scan. He perked up when he heard the dial tone, then the ringing. He waited again. Then: the most frightening alert sound followed by a flashing red indicator light.

Rico cursed under his breath.

The machine spat out the paper.

"You've gotta be kidding me," he shook his head. "Stupid machine."

He was about to give it another try when he heard Tracy's voice.

"Officer Castillo," she said.

That's an odd way to greet your boyfriend—

Rico turned to find Tracy beside a young man who stood a

half step behind her. "I want you to meet Matt Calvin—" she motioned toward him. "He's a new recruit."

"How ya doin?" Castillo offered a quick, disingenuous smile to the lanky post-pubescent recruit before turning back to the fax machine.

"It's a pleasure to meet you, Officer Castillo," the young man spoke quickly, an eager, boyish grin wiping across his bespectacled face. His short black hair was neatly-trimmed and saturated with hairspray and a smattering of unknown products, judging by the strong scent that followed him. "I've heard a lot about you, so when Chief called me in I—"

"Nice to meet you, too." Rico grunted and tapped a few buttons on the device. "Sorry, I gotta send this so we can get on the road."

The pair hovered behind him, which the officer found odd. He glanced out of the corner of his eye. "There something else you wanted to say?"

Calvin stepped toward the fax machine. "I can help you with that if you want—"

Rico grunted again, then stepped aside while the recruit fiddled with the device.

"Calvin is, uh," Tracy started, searching for the most tactful choice of words to balance the volatile state Rico appeared to be in as a result of his feud with the machine. *And there's something deeper there.* She pushed that part out of her mind. "Chief wants Calvin here to join us."

"Great," Rico muttered. "We'll fit you in on a ridealong sometime this week."

Tracy winced. "Uh, Chief was thinking... *tonight*."

The officer whipped around. "Tonight?"

The woman nodded. Calvin pressed a button and the machine began to hum.

"Trac—uh, *Officer Jones*," Castillo clenched his teeth. "The last thing we need is some cadet bungling around behind us on the scene of a dangerous crime," Rico said. "No offense," he added with a snide nod to Calvin.

"N-none taken." Calvin pointed to the fax. "It should be sending properly now."

Rico exhaled slowly. "Thanks."

Tracy motioned for Rico to come closer, then spoke in a whisper: "Chief didn't give us a *choice* in the matter. The recruit is coming with us."

The man gritted his teeth, puffed warm air out his nose again. "Fine," Rico mumbled. "But he better stay out of the way."

The two officers inspected the recruit once more. Calvin flashed a toothy smile and slid his massive glasses toward his brow with a tremulous finger motion.

Officer Castillo wasted no time in moving down the hall to the garage. "Alright, let's go."

The car ride to the Barleys' neighborhood in Citrus Springs was swift. At that late hour of the night, traffic was almost nonexistent. The Octobertime air flowed in through the open windows, lending a refreshing second wind to the officers while also—Rico hoped—muffling any attempts at conversation from the recruit in the backseat. Rico glanced in the rearview mirror. Calvin leaned forward with eager anticipation for what seemed to be his first time out on the field.

Officer Castillo's attention shifted to Tracy, who sat quietly in the passenger seat with her eyes fixed on the road ahead. Rico moved a hand to one of his pockets, felt a small object, while he kept the other hand on the wheel. A phlegmy lump began to form in his throat. *Now's your chance...* The officer opened his mouth to speak—

"How much farther?" A passing fluorescent sign reflected off Calvin's large glasses as his head appeared between the front headrests, only a few inches from Rico's face.

Rico exhaled and glanced at a passing street sign. "It's just up here on the next block."

"I really appreciate this chance to join you on an important mission," the recruit said. "It's been my dream since I was just a little kid."

"And I would really appreciate it if you could keep *quiet* from the moment we step out of this car," Rico grunted as he wheeled the vehicle around a corner then brought it to a slow stop in a driveway. He shifted into park and turned to look Calvin in the eyes. "Got it?"

Calvin was about to speak, but instead clamped his lips and nodded.

"Good."

The officers exited the vehicle with Calvin close behind. Officer Jones stepped beside Rico as they rounded the house toward the fence to the backyard.

"You okay?" She asked. "You could at least try to be a little easier on him."

"Course I'm okay," he snapped back. *Does that count as a lie?*

Tracy considered pressing again, but they had now made their way through the fence and toward the canal beyond it. Calvin tripped as he reached the sloped earth that led down the embankment to the water, dislodging a patch of loose grass and dirt.

"Careful," Rico said, reaching out a quick arm to stop the recruit's descent.

Calvin steadied himself. "Thanks, Officer Castillo."

"Don't mention it."

The two officers began to scan the ground, clicking on a pair of flashlights. The beams glinted off muddy prints near the water's edge, and Tracy approached them with caution.

Jones quickly identified three different sets of prints. "Boys' sneakers." She continued along the bank. "Looks like a bit of a struggle," she noted.

"The neighbor kids pushed the victim," Rico remembered them saying, "toward the water." He remained a step behind Tracy as she tried to formulate the picture in her mind.

"Keep your eyes peeled," Tracy said over her shoulder, nodding to Calvin.

"W-what are we looking for exactly?" He fumbled with a third flashlight, finally turning it on as he reached the canal's murky, muddy edge.

"Footprints from whatever creep snatched Biff Barley," Rico mumbled.

The two officers moved along the water while the recruit stepped carefully in the opposite direction. Rico exhaled, a hint of irritation. Tracy cocked her head toward him.

"What are we doing out here?"

"What do you mean?"

"Those kids are young," said Tracy. "I mean, whatever they think they saw, it's just gotta be some kind of prank. Right?"

Rico didn't answer right away, but allowed his eyes to linger on Tracy's for a moment. "We've seen a lot of crazy things in the last year." He flicked the light back toward the wet ground. "I'm not ruling out anything yet."

Cicadas and other insects chirped night songs up and down the canal, and the wind blew moss in lazy, greenish-gray tufts in the trees nearby. The surface of the water became eerily still.

Then Calvin's voice echoed from down the embankment. "Uh, guys?"

"What is it?" Rico and Tracy hurried toward him, sensing fear in his tone.

The two officers crowded over Calvin's shoulders. His flashlight cast a shaky, oblong circle on a patch of mud and scum, wherein sat the indentations of sneakers. And another nearly indistinguishable set of indentations that were definitely *not* sneakers. "I, um—I'm not sure, but those look like—"

"Prints," Tracy finished, casting a concerned look to Rico.

"The shoe prints match Biff's from up the bank. But those two—"

"Two..." Rico echoed in a whisper. "Holy crap—the kids were telling the truth..."

He bent lower, waving his own light toward the large, indentations. The two prints were longer than a human foot, and the ends bent out in five web-like branches.

"Those aren't footprints from a *person*." Castillo breathed quickly. "Those belong to a reptile—an alligator."

"Uh, not to be *that* guy," Calvin interjected, "but gators move on all fours... d-don't they?"

The officers shared another flash of concerned eye-contact.

Officer Castillo placed a hand inside a pocket and withdrew a folded piece of paper. He opened it slowly, then turned it toward Tracy and Calvin with a nervous gulp. It was Barbara's drawing from the interrogation—a bipedal creature with the posture of a hunched human and the features of an enormous reptile.

"That's no gator." Rico felt his hands shaking. "This is something else entirely."

All three were silent, in shock.

Calvin finally garnered the gall to speak up again. "So, do we think there's any chance this kid's still, uh... out there?"

Tracy looked out and pointed a finger at something across the water. "I don't think so."

The men followed her gaze to a soggy red baseball cap floating halfway above the surface of the canal waters.

"I think Biff Barley's gone," Officer Jones said quietly,

reverently.

Officer Castillo looked back to the two huge gator prints beside the lapping waters. He shivered in the cool air.

"Uh, guys?" Calvin interrupted Rico's thoughts.

Rico puffed. "Yes?"

"Is it a fair assumption to believe that… *thing* is still out there?"

Neither officer replied. It didn't need to be spoken; they all knew the answer.

That thing is most definitely still out there, Rico shuddered.

But what on earth is it?

CHAPTER 7

A small flock of seabirds alighted on the unplugged string lights on Donna Locke's back porch while their songs drifted away on the breeze. One bird swooped to gather loose birthday cake crumbs from the party the night before. The sunlight slanted in over the neighbor's hedge, making droplets of steam appear thick and misty over the mug of coffee in Donna's hand. She exhaled and looked out across the choppy bay.

Donna felt a wave of gratitude—she'd come from nothing and yet here she was in a mansion—a mansion that she *owned*. On a near-private island. With a back patio and a bay view, no less. *A back patio!* She smiled, almost laughed to herself. *If you'd told that waitress at the Seaside Diner that barely a year after she stopped serving tables she'd be here...*

Intermingled with these thoughts were images of the people and faces she loved. Sue and Lisa. Rico and Tracy.

Sondra. Marcus. *Starla...*

The question Declan had voiced in the lab the prior night arose again:

What about Starla?

Donna had always sensed there was something special about the girl. But having supernatural abilities? *I would've known. Wouldn't I?*

The woman took a sip of her coffee as the breeze fluttered her loose blonde hair. A loud *bark-bark!* startled her and she whipped around toward the sliding glass door. Starla hurried out of the house, running after the golden-furred puppy that she'd received as a birthday gift.

"Wait for me, Max!"

The dog sprinted across the lawn toward the seawall.

Starla tackled the puppy and the two fell into a rolling heap on the grass. Max licked Starla's face and the girl laughed then stood and carried the sweet creature back toward Donna.

"So he has a name now?" Donna smiled and reached a gloved hand to scratch the puppy's fuzzy wrinkles and folds.

"Yep! Aunt Donna, meet Max."

The puppy's irresistible black marble eyes stared up at the girl and woman, his light pink tongue flopping out.

"Nice to meet you, Max," Donna melted into the kind of blubbery voice people usually took when speaking to an adorable little animal. "You must've been reading your favorite book again last night."

Starla nodded and scrunched her freckled nose, then spoke to the pup: "I'll eat you up, I love you so!"

Donna leaned back against the cushion of the outdoor sofa and watched Starla give the puppy a good back scratch. A colorful piece of jewelry on Starla's shirt caught Donna's eye—the starling brooch she had gifted to the girl.

"Hey, little Starling," Donna started. "You remember a few months ago—before you were, um... taken—" She hated to remind the girl of such a traumatic moment, but she'd put off asking about it for far too long. "You remember when you said your mom, er, *told* you things?"

Starla nodded. "Mhm."

"Do you think...?" The woman paused.

"Do I think *what?*"

Donna shook her head. "It's nothing..."

She was young, but Starla could still tell when adults were keeping secrets. "Do I think *what*, Aunt Donna?"

The blonde woman inhaled then exhaled slowly, taking a brief glance out at the breezy bay. "That bad man that took you—he said that me, your mom, and *you* all have blood that's *special*. He said it's the reason that those experiments I took part in gave me my powers. And I just wondered if..." Here she trailed off.

The girl's mouth hung agape as she processed her aunt's words. "If... I have powers, too?"

Donna nodded.

This revelation seemed new to Starla, and Donna could tell that her mind was racing as she continued to pet Max.

"It's okay if you don't know."

"I mean, when mom spoke to me without speaking—"

Starla recalled the scene and closed her eyes. "It sort of just happened. I don't know how to explain it—" She looked at Donna in earnest.

"That's alright," Donna assured her. "I just had to ask." She was about to leave the conversation alone when she added: "But if anything like... *that*... happens again, you can talk to me about it, okay?"

The girl smiled, her freckles dappled in the morning light. Max yapped, startling both Donna and her niece.

"I think he's hungry," said Starla.

"Lisa said they left a bag of food for him on the counter," Donna replied as she rose from her seat. The two left the serene backyard, leading the puppy back into the air-conditioned house. "Let's get him fed or we're going to have a wild thing on our hands."

Dusk fell quickly that day as the off-duty police car swung around a curvy street toward Donna Locke's waterfront mansion. Rico lowered his window and a man in a compact guard tower waved him through a mechanically-operated gate that slowly inched open. Tracy gripped the edge of her seat as the vehicle lurched up the driveway and looped around so that the car parked neatly right at the front stoop.

Castillo shifted into park and let the car idle for a moment, then turned it off and removed the key. The pair exited the vehicle—Tracy carrying a bottle of wine and a large gift bag.

As he slipped the keys into his pocket, Rico fingered another small object—cold, metallic, light. *Expensive.* He inhaled sharply and turned his eyes to Officer Jones. *Just ask her.*

"You okay?" Tracy raised an eyebrow.

Rico wasn't the best at masking his emotions, but he tried. "Yeah, all good," he scrambled. "Just, uh, a little shaken up about the case and the kid and everything."

Tracy nodded and placed a gentle hand on his arm as they ascended the steps toward the front door. "That's normal. It means your *alive*," she said. "Just don't let it stay bottled up too long."

They reached the door and Rico pressed the doorbell. He heard it ring, muffled, through the house. A few moments later, the door swung open to reveal Donna, wearing a huge smile and an apron spattered in red. "Hey! Come on in," she motioned.

Rico raised an eyebrow and pointed toward the reddish liquid that had nearly dried on the apron. "Is that...?" He didn't finish the thought.

"Oh, gosh!" Donna said, reaching her gloved hands to untie the apron. "It was the tomatoes—" She slipped it over her head and rolled it up, casting it onto a side table as they moved toward the kitchen area. "Everything's almost ready."

As they walked down the hall, the television blared from the living room—a commercial for toothpaste.

"Can you turn that off, Star?" Donna shouted down the hallway as they passed.

Starla hollered back: "But *The Incredible Hulk* is just about to start!"

"We'll have to catch the re-run. We have company!" Donna craned her head toward the guests, made eye-contact with Starla, and pointed at the TV. "*Off*, please."

Starla shrugged, rolled her eyes, and punched the power button on the remote before tossing it aside on the couch. Max sniffed then swabbed his slobbery tongue all over it, while the girl slumped over to greet the guests.

Castillo half-crouched to her level and spread his arms for a hug. "Starlita!"

"Rico!" The girl's attitude changed as she leaped into his arms for a squeeze. When she let go, Starla moved toward Tracy—who stood with an awkward, uncomfortable expression—and wrapped her arms around the woman's waist.

"Oh! Uh, hey there... kid," Tracy said, trying to mask her discomfort as she readjusted her grip on the large bag she had brought inside. It wasn't the hugging that made her uncomfortable, per se; it was more the fact that she might be thrust into an interaction with a child for which she felt fully unprepared. *Just move along—it'll be okay.* Of course, there was more to it than that, but Officer Jones quickly pushed those thoughts aside as the girl hurried ahead of them into the dining area. Tracy breathed a sigh of relief.

Max clumsily flopped over to greet both of the guests with slobbery dog kisses.

"Who's this?" Tracy asked, crouching to scratch the dog's neck.

"That's Max," the girl answered. "He was my birthday present from Sue and Lisa."

"My sister gave you *that?*" Rico gulped, then muttered: "Tough act to follow." The man nodded to Tracy, who handed the large gift bag to Starla.

Immediately, the girl took it and began to tear away the crepe paper until she could see the gift beneath it. "No way!" Starla smiled. She pulled a tall box out of the bag, revealing a large doll. "It's a My Living Baby doll—I've been wanting this! It's the kind that talks when you press it—"

Rico chuckled and looked over to Tracy. She seemed absent, her eyes glazed over, her mind elsewhere as she watched Starla gush over the doll.

"You okay, Trace?"

"Yeah," she replied quickly, forcing a smile. "Think I'm just hungry."

Rico wasn't convinced, but decided not to pry any further.

"What can I get you to drink?" Donna interjected, moving toward a set of empty stemware on the counter.

"Oh, almost forgot," Tracy held out the wine bottle as they followed her through the kitchen.

"Interesting gift for a nine-year-old's birthday celebration," Donna grinned. "Let's crack it open."

Rico joined Starla at the table. "So sorry we couldn't make it last night, Starlita. We were planning to swing over after dinner, but got called into a case."

Plop! Donna removed the cork from the wine bottle and poured a generous portion into each of the three glasses. "Nothing too bad, I hope?"

"Oh, it was pretty bad," Tracy started as Donna handed

her a drink. "There were these, uh, kids who came in reporting that their neighbor had been—"

Officer Jones' eyes caught Rico making a strange, exaggerated expression with his face. He nodded discreetly toward Starla and shook his head quickly—a wordless gesture intended to mean something like, *"not in front of the kid!"*

"Right," Jones took a swig of wine, gulped it hastily. "I mean it was just your typical missing persons case. That's pretty much it..." She eyed Rico to verify that this rephrasing was to his satisfaction. He gave a thumbs-up with one hand beside the table, out of Starla's view.

Donna handed Rico a glass as she and Tracy sat down. "That's terrible," said the hostess. "I hope everything sorts itself out soon."

Rico took a deep breath, exhaled through his nose. "Me, too," he said in a soft, reflective manner.

Tracy placed a gentle hand over Rico's and the two made eye-contact for a brief moment before Donna offered a quick prayer.

"Well," Donna said when she'd finished, reaching toward the salad in the middle of the table. "Dig in."

The group began to dish portions of food from the serving platters that crowded the tablescape, engaging in lively chatter that was far less somber than talk of missing children.

"So, Starla," Tracy began as she swallowed a bite of meat, "have you figured out your costume for tomorrow night?"

The girl spoke through a mouthful of bread: "I've got an idea, but I'll put the finishing touches on it tomorrow before we go trick-or-treating."

"So mysterious," Rico grinned and sliced something with a knife on his plate. "What are the odds Doctor Lansing comes out of his cave for trick-or-treating?"

"Oh, gosh! Roger!" Donna dropped her silverware and slid back her chair. "Totally forgot to call him down."

Tracy raised an eyebrow. "Call him?"

Donna moved toward a small speaker on the wall. "I had this intercom system installed recently—I'm always forgetting about it. The house is too big, honestly. Been thinking about downsizing." She pressed a button on the interface. "Roger? Dinner's ready if you're hungry. Rico and Tracy are here." Donna nodded at the pair as she held the button down.

"Hi, Roger!" Both shouted across the table.

After a couple moments of silence, the speaker crackled and the doctor's voice came through. "Thank you, Miss Locke. And, uh, hello, officers. I'm in the middle of something at present, but save me a bite and I'll get to it later."

"Roger, Roger," Donna spoke into the microphone, then took her seat once more.

The four enjoyed their meal and were nearly finished when Rico asked, "Any word on Marcus?"

Donna washed a bite down with a swig of wine. "Declan's supposed to call me the *minute* he hears of another blackout. With some information he brought over last night, we're getting closer. The outages are more concentrated lately—near downtown."

A sudden loud *beep* emanated from near Rico. He shot a

glance down at his pager, pressed a button to silence it, and ignored the message. "Sorry about that."

"It's okay—"

Tracy's pager chimed in turn. She bit her lip as she tried not to get distracted by its message, then silenced her device and tried to bring them back to the subject at hand: "So you think Declan's close to finding him, then?"

"I can only hope." Donna could tell the two officers were distracted now. "If you two need to go, it's perfectly fine—"

Brrrrrrinnngg!

The phone startled the entire group at the table. Donna lost her grip on her glass, splashing what wine was left across the tablecloth. "Crap," she muttered as she grabbed a napkin to try and absorb some of the liquid.

Brrrrrrinnngg!

"I'll just get that," Donna said as she pushed her chair back and hurried toward the phone that hung on a kitchen wall. She picked up the receiver. "Hello?"

"Hello, is this the Locke residence?" A woman's voice asked on the other end of the line.

"Yes, it is. May I ask who's calling?"

"Hi, yes, my name is Judy and I'm calling from Texas Implements. Is Mr. Locke available to speak for a few moments about some of our new product offerings that can make life easier?"

Donna rolled her eyes. "There's no such beast."

"I'm sorry—?"

"Have a nice evening, *Judy*." Donna slammed the receiver

back and puffed.

Rico raised an eyebrow as Donna moved back toward the dining table. "Who was that?"

"Sales call."

"What were they trying to sell you?"

"Sexism, I think." Donna rolled her eyes and took her seat once more. "Now, where were we?"

Starla's fork and knife grated on the plate—an unpleasant sound.

"You sure you guys don't need to go?" Donna asked, gesturing toward their beepers.

"Yeah, we'll check in with the station after dinner," Tracy assured her.

Max let out a yappy bark in the living room. The television turned on at full volume as the group heard the remote control clatter onto the tile floor.

"Starla, can you get that?" Donna nearly shouted over a blaring newscast.

The girl scooted her chair out from the table and pattered with soft, sock-covered feet toward the living room.

On the TV, the news anchor's voice was somber. "... marks the third report of this kind in the Miami metro area..." The screen flashed a gruesome image of what looked like a cat that had been severely underfed for months.

Brrrrrrinnngg!

Donna started toward the phone again. She answered it eagerly, hoping the voice on the other end bore some news that would bring her one step closer to Marcus. "Hello, this is Donna."

"Uh, hi," came a garbled, measly voice. "This is, uh, Matt Calvin—I'm trying to reach Officers Castillo and Jones."

Donna shot a glance at the two still-seated officers and covered the microphone with one hand. "It's someone named Calvin?"

Rico's eyes shot wide as he turned to Tracy. "You gave *Calvin* Donna's number?"

Before Tracy could answer, Donna whispered harshly: "Who's Calvin?"

"Just a new recruit that Chief wants us to babysit—"

The television continued to drown out all other sounds: "... in all three instances, it appears that the blood had been drained from the animals before they passed..."

Max whimpered and scurried behind a piece of furniture.

"Starla!" Donna shouted from the kitchen. "Turn it down or turn it off!"

"I'm trying!" Starla crouched on hands and knees, searching under the couch for a stray battery that had escaped from the remote control when it took its tumble onto the tile.

"... no information yet on who—or *what*—caused this strange phenomenon..."

"Uh, hello?" Calvin's timid voice came through the receiver again.

Donna was irritated: "One of you gonna take this?"

Rico exhaled slowly and rose from his seat. "Fine."

"... authorities want to remind you to keep your pets safely inside at night until more is known about this bizarre case that has everyone in Miami on edge..."

"This is Rico." He pressed the receiver to his ear.

"O-officer Castillo!" Calvin sputtered. "I've been trying to page you and Officer Jones—"

"Yeah, yeah, what is it, kid?"

"Um, it's going to sound kind of crazy—"

"Let me guess," Rico turned so that he could see the TV. "Little pets with the blood drained out of 'em?"

"Gross," said Calvin. "No. We've already got people on that one—"

"Okay, then spill it, kid!"

"Right. Um, uh—so basically there are several people missing."

"*Basically*?" Rico leaned in. "You mean the kid from last night?"

"N-no. I mean several... *bodies*... that should be buried in the ground... went *missing*."

Though she couldn't hear the conversation on the other end of the line, Tracy caught the look of concern that washed over Rico's face. *Like he's seen a ghost, as they say.*

Rico nodded as Calvin finished relaying the relevant details of the case. "Okay," said Officer Castillo. "We'll get over there as soon as we can."

"Got it!" Starla clicked the battery panel into place and pointed the remote at the television set.

"... for Channel 4 Action News, I'm Inez Quirantes. More on this at eleven—"

Zzzapp!

The screen went black, once more bringing quiet to the house.

Rico hung up the phone and Donna let out a breath, releasing a wave of tension.

"Sorry, Don," said Rico. "But it looks like we've gotta dine and dash."

"What did Calvin say?" Tracy inquired as she stood up from her seat.

Rico glanced toward Starla, wrestling with Max on the living room floor. "Not in front of the kid," he muttered. "I'll tell you on the way."

The adults exchanged hugs and the officers thanked Donna for dinner.

"Adiós, Starlita," Rico waved.

Starla smiled and waved back. "Thanks for the present!"

Donna showed the officers out the front door, gave her last goodbyes, then returned into the now-quiet house. She stood behind the door for a moment, taking deep breaths.

She was interrupted once more when the phone began to ring yet again. Donna moved toward the kitchen swiftly and picked up the receiver on the third chime. "Hello? This is Donna Locke."

"Donna," came a familiar male voice. "It's Declan. MPL just reported another blackout downtown—the museum quarter."

Donna's breaths were short. "And?"

"I think it's him," answered Declan. "I think it's Marcus."

CHAPTER 8

An eerie mist hung over the lawn through the gate up ahead as Officers Castillo and Jones pulled up beside a second car. They rolled down the windows as the driver of the other car did the same, revealing a tense Calvin.

"What took you two so long?" Calvin asked, almost trembling.

"We had to drive halfway across town," Tracy explained as Rico turned off the car and got out.

"C'mon," Rico said. "Let's make this quick, okay? I've had enough of these late night calls." Castillo walked in front of the car, his body breaking the thick beams of the still-glowing headlights. He clicked on a flashlight and waved it at the wrought-iron arch up ahead.

Trinity Brethren Cemetery.

Tracy and Calvin joined Rico, moving as quietly as they could along the gravel path. Calvin's own flashlight was shaking.

"You okay?" Tracy muttered.

"Uh, not exactly," said the recruit. "We're investigating bodies... missing from a graveyard... in the dark... the night before Halloween. Am I the only one who sees where this is going?"

"Relax, kid. Don't be so superstitious." If Rico was being honest, he felt a little nervous himself. He'd seen some wild things, but still had reservations about putting too much stock in ghost stories.

"Being superstitious in this situation would mean my fear is *irrational* and based on weird coincidences," Calvin mumbled. "But I think I'm being *completely* rational when I say that our current scenario is just a little bit creepy."

Neither of the officers replied.

Rico pushed one door of the unlocked gate, eliciting a rusty creak. The officer led the way down an earthen path lined with dewy grass. Headstones dotted the landscape almost as far as the eye could see in the dark, though the lights from downtown skyscrapers pierced through the thick fog beyond the cemetery walls.

Officer Jones scanned the expansive, misty horizon. "Did our contact give any indication as to *which* bodies are supposed to be missing?" She didn't see any immediate signs of a disturbance of earth or dirt. *So help me, if this is some kind of prank—*

"I've got the names right here." Calvin fished inside a pocket for a crumpled piece of note paper and held it out under his flashlight.

Jason Sunder. Marjory Beauregard.

The names didn't trigger any memories or associations for either of the cops, except that Rico thought the woman's name sounded old and rich.

"Our source said both of their plots were along the south edge of the cemetery," Calvin added. "Which should be—" He closed his eyes mentally orienting himself, then opened them and pointed. "*That* way."

Calvin's feet scrunched off across the damp grass, his flashlight beam jostling and creating jittery shadows beyond the rows of mossy stone tablets that lined the nearly non-existent path. Jones and Castillo followed close behind.

The cemetery was a surprisingly-large plot of land, situated just outside the densest part of Miami's proper downtown core. Land was worth a lot here, once owned by a church that had now gone dark but thankfully had the foresight to secure such an extensive plat for what would become a growing city. The church was long gone—its building abandoned and crumbling just beyond the graveyard walls—but a retired old sexton still made his rounds from time to time to check on those that rested in the earth. After all, the dead deserved some care. Some respect.

The sexton was the one who had reported the bodies missing, Calvin explained, mostly to fill the eerie quiet as they continued their slow plod.

"Did he say if he had any idea how long the bodies have been missing?" Rico inquired.

"No."

Rico pressed him. "He didn't *say*, or he didn't *know?*"

"He said it could have been days," Calvin explained, keeping his eyes on the distance for any signs of disturbed earth. "Or weeks."

Tracy puffed. "Pretty broad timeframe we're working with."

"Yeah, well, that's just what the guy told me—sorry," Calvin said, apologetic. As they kept walking, the recruit noted how close the officers stood to each other. "So, uh, how long have you two been together?"

"None of your business," Rico grunted.

"I mean it seems pretty serious."

The pair of officers shot a glance at each other, their eyes meeting in the dark. There was so much to be said, but the field was not the place for such personal conversations. Nor was Rico interested in having Calvin serve as a third party witness.

Castillo shifted the attention back to the younger man. "Didn't know they were letting recruits conduct interrogations," he mumbled under his breath, still loud enough for Calvin to hear.

"It wasn't an *interrogation*, it was an intake." Calvin exhaled sharply, completely missing the sarcasm in Rico's voice. "And besides, I was the only one at the station. I tried to page you—"

"There." Tracy had stopped walking and now aimed her flashlight at the farthest corner of the cemetery. Not far off, she could make out the shape of a small mound of ruddy, brown dirt, loose and piled. "Think that's them."

In an almost reverential quiet, the three moved toward the mound. When they were upon it, it became clear to the officers how the missing bodies had gone unnoticed for so long. The mound had been built up in a sort of barrier of displaced dirt, formed in such a way that it covered two gaping cavities in the ground beyond it—two rectangular, four-to-six-foot-deep, human-sized holes. Any visitor would have had to walk right up to the barrier to be able to see the twin recesses.

Rico raised a foot onto the mound and shone his flashlight into the holes. Each contained the imprint of a coffin, but the caskets had been removed. "Well, would ya look at that?" Castillo muttered with a hint of a smile. "Somebody stole some bodies."

Tracy peered into the dark chasms. "Somebody *strong*." She noted straight-edged scrape marks on either side of the dirt walls—signs that the large caskets had been dragged out.

"No way one guy did that," Calvin said. "You ever been a pallbearer? I have," he continued without waiting for a response. "Took at least four of us for my uncle Curtis and even then it was still heavy as a—"

Castillo craned his head, looking away from the holes, distracted. "Quiet, kid."

"—no, I'm telling you it was pretty darn *heavy*—"

"Shh!"

"Did you just *shh* me?"

"No, I mean *shut up*, kid—listen!"

The recruit finally became silent.

"I don't hear anything."

"That's why I'm telling you to *be quiet*," Rico whispered. "Just wait."

At first, the three could only hear the hums of car engines drifting from the city in the distance, though the vehicle sounds had nearly faded to the periphery of their awareness.

But then: a stirring.

"We're not alone," Tracy barely breathed.

A *crunch* of a blade-like metal jabbed into soft, resistant earth. A shovel.

The officers crouched out of instinct behind the mound of dirt and waved for Calvin to do the same: "Get down!"

In the silence, Castillo located the source of the sound as the unseen shovel lodged itself in the dirt once more: it came from just a few plots away. *A miracle we weren't spotted,* he thought, only slightly relieved.

Dense fog lingered over the whole property, but the three hidden Metro-Dade team members saw the unmistakable silhouette of a man with a long shovel, his back toward them.

"Think we found our grave robber." Tracy hunched close to Rico. "What's our move?"

Her partner's eyes narrowed as he tried to get a better look at the shadow-man. "I'm thinking," Rico said.

"Shouldn't we start by nicely asking him what he's doing?" Calvin interjected in a whisper that was just a little too loud for Rico's comfort.

Immediately, the digger stopped digging. Rico yanked his

companions further out of sight, his eyes wide and breathing short. Calvin looked like he was about to speak again, but Castillo placed a firm, meaty finger over his mouth to signal for the recruit to stay quiet. With his other hand, Rico threw a hand over his stomach, which now made a low gurgling sound.

Dangit, Donna. Whatever she'd cooked for dinner that night, it didn't agree with Rico's digestive system. Slowly, though, the bubbling faded and Rico relaxed slightly.

The following seconds passed slowly, silently. No one spoke. The three huddled behind the dirt mound, nearly on top of one another.

Then: digging again.

The officers and the recruit exhaled discreetly. Rico hazarded a glance over the top of the earth pile to ensure the shadowy digger was still in the same spot. "Alright," he began to the others. "We approach him slowly so he doesn't get spooked. Then, let me do the talking." He directed this last part at Calvin, who gulped and nodded.

With one hand at his side, ready to draw his handgun in a moment's notice, Rico rose and started across the soft grass toward the digger. The officer held his breath and trod lightly, calculating each step with slow, careful motion. Sure, he just wanted to have a conversation with the man, but Castillo needed to get close enough that he could apprehend the suspect if he started to run.

Alright, Rico, you can do this, he thought. *Speak firmly on the count of three. One. Two. Three—*

Rico's stomach let out another growl before he could speak, louder than before. His eyes locked onto the shadow digger, who lifted his shovel from the ground and pivoted swiftly toward the officer.

What the—

As the digger rotated to face Castillo, the officer gasped: the digger had no *face*! All of the standard facial features were missing, except for a pair of tiny slits that passed as nostrils. The rest of the front of the digger's head was covered in a frightening assortment of what looked like scars or burns or patchy skin grafts—Rico wasn't quite sure which.

As the officer stood, mouth agape, the faceless digger raised the long shovel and swung. Rico reached for his gun, but the metal blade-edge of the spade nicked it and sent the weapon sailing into the moist grass several feet away. The officer took an instinctive step back and the digger swung again. This time, the shovel blade met flesh, slicing the skin of Rico's forearm.

He winced and tumbled to the ground to get away. The digger moved close, until he stood over the fallen officer, ready to bring the shovel down on him even harder.

"Hey!" Tracy shouted. "Back off, creep!"

The officer fired a warning shot that set off a minor explosion of dirt near the digger's feet. The man with no face recoiled, sniffed the air like a hound catching a scent, then hurled the heavy shovel in Tracy's general direction.

The woman leaped out of its path and rolled across the grass and dirt. When she gathered her composure, Officer

Jones turned back toward the digger, drawing her weapon, but discovered that he was gone. A quick glance toward a blur of motion in her periphery revealed that the faceless man was getting away. Tracy considered running after him, but realized he was already too far off. The officer rose and dusted off her clothes then took one more look toward the runaway digger. The strange man jumped up toward the cemetery wall and easily cleared it with only a light kick off its top edge.

"Uh, guys?" Calvin trembled, rising from behind the dirt mound when he determined the danger was no longer imminent. "What was that?"

Neither officer answered. After a moment of silence, Castillo and Jones approached each other, the woman placing a concerned hand toward the bleeding wound on Rico's forearm. "Does it hurt?"

"Gah!" The man winced.

"Sorry," Tracy said, pulling away. "Guess that's a *yes*." The gash from the shovel blade was nearly six inches long, running parallel to his arteries, which the wound had narrowly missed. "We've got some bandages in the car."

The recruit interrupted Tracy's inspection of the wound: "Um, hello? Did anybody hear me?"

"We heard you, kid," Rico snapped.

"And?"

"We don't know any more than you," Tracy answered.

"Was it just me, or did that *thing* have—"

"No face." Rico finished, almost shuddering at the

thought. "Looked like just... patches of skin or something."

Calvin retched. "Gag! That's totally disgusting."

Officer Castillo nodded in agreement then gazed off across the darkened, misty lawn. He had never seen anything quite like that strange creature. *But it must have been a mask, right? A costume? There's no way someone without eyes could move like that, run at that speed, dig such a precise hole—*

"The grave," Rico recalled. "We interrupted him before he could finish digging them up."

"Digging *who* up?" Calvin asked.

The older of the two men nodded toward the half-dug-up plot just ahead. "Let's find out."

With caution, the three traversed the lawn toward the place where they had first seen the faceless digger. The man had not made much progress on the dig before the cops blew their cover, but there was still a large amount of dirt displaced, sitting at the foot of a weathered headstone.

"Hazel Vance," Calvin read aloud, hoping it would trigger some memory or recognition. "Never heard of 'er." He produced a pen, clicked it, and scribbled the name on the wrinkly piece of paper along with the names of the two missing bodies.

"Me neither." Rico shook his head and glanced at Tracy. She shrugged.

For a moment, the three stood in silence, hovering over the grave.

"Says she died just a few years ago," the recruit said, bending closer. "There should still be paperwork somewhere on her and the missing bodies."

"Paperwork." Rico snickered. "My favorite."

"Kid's right, though," Tracy said quietly, more serious. "We don't have much else to go on at this point—not unless you want to put out a notice for a man with no face to go along with our half-man, half-alligator suspect?"

Officer Castillo exhaled sharply. "Alright. Let's get to it then."

Rico gently kicked a clump of the loose dirt back into the shallow hole in front of Hazel Vance's tombstone before turning to follow the others back to the cemetery gates. The three walked in silence across the foggy lawn as the moon shone bright and full above the city skyline. The clouds above darkened, gathered, ready to release the rain at any moment.

CHAPTER 9

The museum quarter was pitch black as Donna pulled up to the rendezvous point in her yellow convertible with the top up. She parallel parked behind another car just as a man exited the vehicle. In the quick flash of the headlights, she could make out Declan's silhouette. Donna turned off the car and walked briskly to meet him, clenching her gloved hands nervously, instinctively.

"This was him, alright," Donna said, noting that even the streetlamps, with their emergency backup power grid, had gone dark. A radius of a couple blocks in every direction was shrouded in shadow and darkness, assisted by the fact that the moon was hiding behind thick nimbostratus clouds. The alley smelled of impending rain.

"We're right near the epicenter," Declan explained. "Based on our data, it seems Marcus is headed for The MORA." He nodded over his shoulder and moved ahead, leading Donna to the corner of the alleyway where they could more easily see across the darkened street.

The Museum of Rare Antiquities—or The MORA—was a large building, taking up almost an entire block. A set of extra-wide steps led up toward its main pedestrian entrance, where a sort of plateau allowed for weary climbers to have respite before entering the air-conditioned lobby.

Donna's eyes followed the steps up to the glass doors. "He's in there now?"

Typically the facade was aglow in colorful lights, accentuating monolithic mid-century architecture and the narrow exhibit banners that hung above the entryway—*Age of the Conquistadors* was printed in large lettering down each of them. But now the entire building was cloaked in darkness, just like the rest of the block.

"Yeah, he's in there." Declan scanned the street. "Unless he moves at the speed of light, too." The man turned back to Donna, his expression softened. "You sure you wanna do this?"

She hesitated. "Am I sure I want to break into a ritzy museum in the middle of the night? Not really."

"No," Declan replied, still somber. "I mean, are you sure you want to find Marcus? You said yourself there's something wrong with him. He's clearly not the man he used to be."

Donna took deep breaths. "You're right," she whispered. "He didn't recognize me. But maybe he was just in a daze or something—you know, from coming out of hibernation. I can't let that stop me. This has gone on too long. I need to end it—need to find him. And I need to know for *sure*."

The man inhaled quickly. "Alright, then. Let's find out."

"The front entrance looks undisturbed," Donna noted. "He wouldn't have chanced that kind of visibility, even in the dark."

"Should be a loading area around back for when they change exhibits." Declan had already started out from their hiding place in the alley, and Donna followed him across the quiet street. A rumble of thunder echoed off the blackened skyscrapers that surrounded the museum's block.

Donna barely had time to gather her thoughts on the drive over from her house, so her mind raced as the pair slinked through shadows. *What on earth could Marcus possibly want with a bunch of ancient relics? Why couldn't he remember me?* It still didn't make sense.

As they rounded the corner to the back side of the building, Declan held out an arm to signal for Donna to stop. They pushed their backs against the wall and Declan peered around the corner. No signs of movement.

"All clear." The man started to move, but Donna grabbed his arm.

"Wait," she said. "Did you take your dose?"

Declan shook his head. "Not tonight. Might need my powers if things go south."

The woman raised her eyebrows. "What about *me*? Last time you lost control." Donna thought back to an incident months ago, where she'd first learned the man had unnatural abilities like hers. Only Declan's powers were a little more unpredictable and wild, shifting his shape into a large, hairy brown beast of a creature—*with very bad manners,* Donna shuddered. *It was frightening, to say the least.*

"I've been practicing," he assured her. "And plus, I've been going to therapy. That's helped immensely. If I have a handle on my emotions, I can reign in the beast instead of letting *it* control *me*."

Donna cracked a soft smile. "Good," she nodded. "Then let's keep moving."

They snuck around toward the back door of the museum, splashing through a murky puddle on the sidewalk. As they approached, Declan pointed out a set of cameras.

"Too dark for them to capture anything useful," he noted. "Your Marcus seems like a natural at this."

Donna was about to make a snide remark, but something else diverted her attention. Muddy footprints, barely visible in the double-darkness, led up a ramp toward the back door. "Look," she said quietly, crouching to inspect the prints more closely. "There's two different sizes of shoeprints here." One set was smaller than the other. Donna looked up at Declan as he spoke her thought out loud:

"He's not alone."

Another rumble of thunder rang out—louder and closer than before. In the distance, Donna could make out the faint sound of approaching rain.

Cautiously, the pair crept up the rest of the ramp and followed the footprints to the entry. The prints led straight up to the door, where they terminated abruptly.

That's odd, Donna thought.

A narrow cut-out slit of reinforced glass formed a window through the door into the hallway beyond it, but neither the door nor glass showed signs of damage. Declan produced a small flashlight and clicked it on. He moved closer to the narrow window and looked inside.

"Both sets of prints continue inside," he said, almost a gasp. He placed his gloved hands on the handle of the door. It was locked. "How'd they get in?"

"Maybe they had a key?" Donna suggested.

Declan craned to view a panel on the wall just inside the door. "Alarm's been disabled, too," he said as his light shone over the display screen.

"So whoever Marcus is working with has inside access?"

"That, or else someone who's *really* good at extracting information," Declan said. "Here." He handed the flashlight to Donna.

The rain reached the museum quarter at last, sweeping over the building. From their position under the loading area, Donna and Declan were kept dry, but the rain beat loudly and echoed around them.

Declan was pretty certain the intruders wouldn't have taken the trouble to sneak in under cover of complete darkness if they had a key, but he didn't have a better hypothesis. Instead, he reached under the side of his light jacket and withdrew a handgun and a silencer tip. He screwed them together then waved for Donna to stand back. "Look away."

Donna started to protest: "Wait, someone will hear—"

Plink-crashhh!

The glass shattered, clattering to the ground. The rain did much to muddle the sound. "Don't worry, I'll cover the bill." Declan reached his hand through the jagged glass and unlocked the door from the inside, then yanked it open. "After you, Miss Locke."

It was an inelegant solution, but an effective one, she thought, rolling her eyes at the man's bravado. Donna stepped carefully over the pieces of glass, some crunching underfoot, and shone the flashlight into the darker hallway. Declan followed closely at her side, keeping his gun at the ready.

At the end of the initial corridor, they found a set of thick double doors that closed off the loading area from the rest of the museum. Donna breathed a slight sigh of relief when she realized the doors would've likely muffled the sound of shattering glass from anyone inside. Still, she and Declan moved with caution. *We have no idea what Marcus (or whoever's with him) is doing in here.*

She nearly held her breath as they pressed through the double doors and entered a more vast gallery space, where an overhead skylight window let in a faint and diffused moonglow. The rain pattered softly down the slanted panes. As the doors closed quietly behind them, Donna and Declan paused and stood still to listen. Donna clicked off the flashlight. The museum was quiet—only the faint purr of a distant air conditioning unit could be heard above the rain.

Then a metallic clattering rang out from the right. Both Donna and Declan whipped immediately toward the sound and started moving down a narrow, winding hall. Donna's heart pounded loudly, pulsing, beating, thumping over her thoughts—thoughts of the man she knew and loved. *He's still in there—inside Marcus' body... somewhere... isn't he?*

Finally, Donna and Declan rounded a corner and could see straight ahead. The clanging continued, now clearly visible as three figures—no, it was just two—struggling with a suit of old conquistador armor. A faint glint of the cloudy moon overhead shone through another skylight. One figure stood with his back to the approaching duo; Donna recognized the man in an instant. *Marcus.* Her heart rose, jolted like it did every time she saw him, every time she heard his rich voice or fell prey to his charming, dimpled grin. She moved nearer. Closer.

Neither Donna nor Declan could discern the identity of the second figure, for Marcus now placed the final pieces of the oxidized armor on to the unseen person, ending with a half-moon-crested morion helmet with a detailed mask that nearly covered the face.

Donna pressed into the shadowy wall to stay out of sight but accidentally leaned against a pedestal upon which a large, engraved silver platter rested. As if in slow motion, Donna watched the plate topple from its perch, making a beeline for the solid tile floor. Her eyes grew wide and she reached out a gloved hand to grab it.

She missed it by an inch.

The resounding clatter was inescapable. Marcus and the armored stranger whipped immediately toward the sound.

Donna wasn't sure what frightened her more: the fact that Marcus couldn't seem to remember her, or the look of sheer fury on his face in that exact moment—a look she had never seen before.

"Marcus," Donna started, taking a short step forward. "It's me—Donna—"

Marcus furrowed his eyebrows as he recognized her. "*You!*"

Declan muttered: "Your boyfriend doesn't look too happy to see us." The man fingered the gun and raised it to a ready stance.

Even in the dim light from above, Marcus saw the weapon. His brown eyes widened, and his pupils shrunk. Marcus raised a hand and held it out in front of him, the palm angled toward Declan.

Then: a sudden burst of light.

A beam, piercing and vibrant, emanated from Marcus' outstretched hand. The movement sent what looked like a thick, almost solid ray that instantly blasted the handgun from Declan's grasp. It all happened in a flash—a blink. Declan felt the warmth, the sting as the beam grazed the flesh on his hand while the gun clattered away down the hall and spun out of reach.

Declan's jaw sank. "What the—"

Donna saw it, too. Though baffled, she barely had time to respond, for now the armored stranger produced a pair of twin blades—long, curving knives—and started toward the two interlopers.

"What's with the costume?" Donna shouted, trying to buy herself a few precious moments as the stranger clinked across the polished floor. "Halloween's not til tomorrow."

Thinking quickly, Donna scanned the large room. It was peppered with artifacts—pottery, medallions, amulets, textiles, shields, weapons. *Yes.* Swords, spears, knives. She moved toward the closest item she could reach: a long spear with a wooden shaft and a rusty, ornamented tip. Donna yanked it from the clasps that mounted it to the wall, turned, and swung. The armored stranger's knives hammered against the spear, locking for only a moment. Lightning struck outside, strobing through the skylight before vanishing just as suddenly.

In the darkness, Donna peered into the shadows beneath the ancient helmet's visor. The eyes of her attacker were barely visible, but they had an almost fiery glow. The face covering creaked and slipped lower as the armored stranger leaned in, weight pressing against Donna and the spear. Now it was clear—the attacker was a woman, with eyes weathered and hollow.

A host of insecurities and questions flashed through Donna's mind, but her immediate goal prevailed: *Get her away, and get Marcus!* Donna shoved with all her might, pressing off the wall behind her to gain traction. The armored woman flew backwards, clattering to the ground.

Meanwhile, Marcus ran and hurled himself toward Declan. The two nearly collided, swinging fists and kicks, but each dodged the other's blows with skill.

As the armored woman rose from the ground, she sneered at Donna. "Careful. Someone might get hurt."

Donna took quick breaths. "I'd prefer that someone *isn't* me," she quipped, pointing the spear at the woman to ward her off.

The armored lady grinned. "Two can play this game, niña," she muttered as she scraped the knives together quickly, emitting a flurry of momentary sparks.

Donna raised an eyebrow. Right before her eyes, Donna watched as the shape of the armored woman seemed to split apart—ripped and stringy like gooey cheese pizza torn right down the middle. The two halves continued to morph and ripple, until finally they each became wholes. Now two identical figures stood before Donna. The only indication of which halves were original were the twin knives in their hands.

Donna's eyebrows ascended. *Uh... that's frightening!*

Before Donna could make a move, both figures shifted their balance in unison, each gripping her knife in the same way, albeit mirrored. The two women stepped forward, mirrored conquistadoric silhouettes ready to fight.

"How—?" was all Donna could spit out before one of the two came running at her. Donna gripped the wooden shaft of the spear and swung—*hard,* aimed for the head.

Crrra-clunk!

The blow was swift. The spearhead collided with the duplicate's helmet and sent the ancient metal head-covering—and the woman inside it—flying backward. Donna tried to mask the subtle, satisfied grin that washed over her, but to no avail. It wasn't delight at the thought of wounding an enemy. No; she'd been practicing, taking lessons in self-defense in the months since the extraction in the Bahamas. And now, to her satisfaction, the training had paid off.

And I didn't even have to turn anyone else to gold, she thought. *Not yet, anyway.*

The duplicate woman tumbled to the ground, a sea of silver-gray hair pouring out from inside the helmet as it sailed away. Her skin was visible now—porous, pock-marked, and deteriorating. Donna scrunched her face at the sight, but she only got a brief glance at the downed knight under the armor before a motion in her periphery alerted her that the woman's counterpart was running toward her.

In the dark corridor a few meters away, the two men struggled. Declan had only heard stories of Marcus before then, but something seemed off even as he looked into his face for the first time. There was a rage in his expression, the whites of his eyes dim and gray.

"We're not here to hurt you," Declan offered, struggling to keep a calculated handle on his emotions. *Don't want any... accidents.* He spotted the gun out of the corner of his eye. *I can get to it—just need a few extra seconds.*

Marcus caught this glance. "Not here to hurt? What's that for, then?" He aimed his finger at the pistol. Another blinding, focused beam shot out from the glowing phalanx, this time meeting the gun with a flash. Declan watched as the weapon glowed, red then white-hot, and warped—melted into a distorted, lumpy, useless shell.

"We just want you to come with us," Declan pleaded, eyes wide as a legitimate fear coursed through him. If Marcus could melt a solid metal gun with the point of a finger, he could surely do some damage to the man's own flesh.

"You're with her," Marcus nodded toward Donna, locked in her own skirmish with the armored women. "Which means you must be eliminated."

Eliminated? Declan wasn't about to let that happen—not with all the trouble they'd gone through to find Marcus again. He kicked Marcus in the gut, sending him recoiling a few steps back. He glanced across to the other side of the larger room: Donna managed to *thwack!* one of her attackers back and make eye-contact with Declan.

Marcus' hands began to glow, filled with some energy as if from within.

Donna shattered a glass display case, freeing a large, round shield. She quickly removed one of her leathery gloves and placed her bare hand on the old, wooden object. In an instant, a wave of shimmering gold washed over it—its very essence changed. Donna felt the weight of it increase dramatically as she wound up to toss the now-golden shield across the room.

"Dec! Catch!"

She heaved it.

Swoosh!

The object flew through the air toward Declan, hitting the floor just before it reached him. The golden shield skidded and scraped on its way toward the man's feet. Marcus seemed mesmerized, fixated on the glittering object as it skimmed across the tile.

"So it is true," Marcus muttered, looking from the gilded shield to Donna and back. He clenched his fists, and his hands started to glow once more.

Declan picked up the shield and held it out as Marcus' hands became incandescent, aimed right at the man. A new pair of light-beams emanated from his outstretched hands. Declan tilted the shield, its shiny metallic surface glinting in the light. Then: it worked. The shield's surface was reflective. The beams bounced back toward their source—Marcus.

"Gah!" Marcus hurled himself away, momentarily blinded and stunned by the stinging light and heat refracted back at him.

"Donna, c'mon!" Declan allowed the shield to fall to the ground with a loud clang as he nodded down a hall toward the museum lobby. Donna hurried after him.

A million questions rushed through Donna's mind as she caught up to him, winding through a maze of short hallways until they were spat out into a large, glass-lined foyer. The rain coursed down the panes and another rumble of thunder vibrated the room. Declan tried the door—it was locked. He fumbled with a latch, but it wouldn't budge.

Donna glanced over her shoulder. "Hurry it up, Dec!"

"It won't unlock!"

The armored twins appeared from within the darkness—one still missing her helmet—with Marcus close behind. An eerie glow emanated from his body, but everything around him still seemed somehow masked in darkness, a black haze. The trio had Donna and Declan cornered.

When he realized they were empty-handed with nowhere to run, Marcus slowed his steps, lingering in the shadow. "It's your fault!" Marcus shouted, his voice echoing across the expansive lobby space.

Donna felt his words sting—more than any beam of heat or light ever could.

"You're the reason I'm like this—it's your fault this happened." He continued.

Donna couldn't speak. Truth be told, he was right. It was *her* hands that turned him to gold that night. *Her* cursed, wretched, clammy hands. She clenched her lone, sweaty gloved hand, glanced at the two armored women who stood at either side of Marcus, and started to speak: "Marcus, I'm sorry. I never meant for any of this—"

"You're *sorry*?" He chuckled, exposing one of those irresistible dimples that seemed so much less attractive to Donna in the present moment. "So it's true."

"Yes," she fumbled. "I mean, no—"

"You'd only be *sorry* if you'd done something wrong." Marcus sighed, tightened his fists. "I was afraid of this." He nodded to the armored woman who still wore a helmet.

She and her mirror counterpart turned toward Donna and Declan, held out their knives, and lunged in unison toward the would-be escapees.

"Declan?" Donna's eyes grew wide as she braced for a fight. "Wouldn't *now* be a good time to take *control*?"

"Workin' on it!" He closed his eyes and took deep breaths. His teeth ground together. Then, his mouth began to foam, his arms bulged and he seemed to grow larger.

Donna only caught the motion out of the corner of her eye, for she was too focused on the two knife-wielding women charging at her from across the room. Donna, defenseless, braced herself in a fighting stance, her ungloved hand outstretched—a threat. Try to hurt her, and she'd turn them to solid gold—no more life, breath, blood, warmth. Life would be over—except on the occasion of a rare, expensive scientific intervention. Not likely. *I swore I'd never do it again.*

To Donna's relief, she didn't have to. A loud growling roar beside Donna startled her. She turned in time to see an immense, brown hairy beast standing in Declan's place. With his giant furry arms, the beast swiped one of the two women aside. Her armor caused her to skid across the lobby floor like a gangly hockey puck, sailing toward the restrooms.

Donna barely had a moment to take it in when the beast swung his massive claws at the second woman. This time, he grabbed her by the arms—he'd grown to more than twice her size—and swung her as hard as he could toward the large panes of glass that shielded the foyer from the outdoors.

Smash!

The conquistador sailed through the shattered glass and clunked across the wet, grand masonry steps outside, tumbling down toward the street. The beast turned to Donna and grabbed her by the arm. Out of instinct, she resisted at first, but relaxed slightly when she saw where he was leading her: through the now-gaping hole in the front door. Rain flooded in and coursed across the tile.

Donna took a fleeting glance across the room, making bleary eye contact with Marcus. He stood still in the shadows, glaring at her. Donna's lips quivered. *What was he thinking? What's gotten into him? How has he settled on painting me as the villain in his story?*

Marcus shouted across the vacant space. "You can't stop what's coming, Donna!"

The words hit deep. Donna gulped. A threat made more ominous by how indefinite it sounded; vagueness had a way of doing that.

"Hurry," the beast growled at Donna as he ducked through the hole in the glass, leading her with his paw.

Donna nodded, breathed in deep, and turned away, leaving Marcus behind in the wreckage of the museum—the place and the moment where all she'd known and hoped for had been shattered in one night. She wiped a stream of tears and raindrops with the back of her hand as Declan—the beast—threw her across his shoulders and leaped in huge strides down the stone steps.

As the breeze and wet fur whipped across her face, Donna turned to look back one more time. There, in the shattered, fragmented doorway, she thought she saw the silhouette of Marcus. The faintest flickering glow of light from his hands. It was all too much. Donna turned away and buried her face in the soft fur, her body rising and falling through tears and the steady cadence of the beast as it tramped through the storm.

But those words echoed back:
You can't stop what's coming.

CHAPTER 10

Rico trudged into the police station conference room with little haste, flicking the light on while he pressed a loose bandage against his forearm. He didn't bother looking at the time—he didn't even want to know how long it had been since he first left dinner at Donna's place. Thunder rumbled, and the wounded officer's stomach growled at the same time, as if on cue.

"Anyone else craving Chinese food?"

Tracy and Calvin were only a few steps behind and filed into the stuffy room.

"I don't think anything's open at this hour," Calvin chimed, his eyes drooping slightly but his voice still full of his typical cheekiness. He separated a pair of blinds and looked out through the window at the light rain that began to sweep down the block.

Officer Jones switched on a box fan in the corner. "Calvin's right," she said. "And we can't waste any time while that faceless grave-digger is on the loose."

"Don't forget about the human-alligator hybrid that's roaming the suburbs of Citrus Springs," Calvin shot back with a smirk.

Rico rolled his eyes and crossed his arms. "How about you *roam* on out into the filing room and bring us back something useful? You got the names?"

"Yeah." The recruit fished a hand in his pocket and withdrew the crinkled piece of paper with the names from the tombstones.

"Good," Castillo nodded.

"But," Calvin continued, "won't they only show up in our system if they were part of a criminal case?"

"It's kind of our only option at this hour," the older man replied. "You can use the computer to look 'em up."

He seemed like he wanted to say something smart, but Calvin kept his mouth shut and slinked out of the conference room.

Tracy raised an eyebrow and sat against the table. "You could be a little nicer, ya know?"

Her partner puffed. "I *am* nice," Rico smiled, then winced as he felt a sharp pain run down his arm.

"Lemme see it." Officer Jones moved closer and placed her hand on the side of his arm.

"Gah—it stings!"

"Just let me look at it."

Cautiously, Rico relaxed, loosened his shoulders, and

allowed the woman to inspect his poorly-bandaged wound. "You should clean that," was her diagnosis. "Or else it'll get infected."

"Been kinda busy," Rico quipped.

Tracy had a glow in her eyes, like she'd just thought of something. "C'mon. Let's go to the breakroom—lemme at least wipe up some of that blood before it dries."

Officer Castillo took a deep breath, then exhaled slowly. "Alright. Lead the way."

In the narrow galley-kitchen, the sink squealed as Tracy turned the left-side knob to usher in a stream of lukewarm water. She splashed her hand under it. "Gonna take a minute to get hot." The woman turned and began to open and shut a series of drawers under the counter's edge, searching.

Rico sat on the narrow mauve laminate countertop, his legs dangling like a kid at the doctor's office about to get a reflex test. He rested his wounded arm on his leg while he awaited his surrogate nurse's next instructions.

"That *thing* really got you good," Tracy said, once again eyeing the gash as she shut another drawer.

The other officer half-smiled, half-winced. "For someone who doesn't have eyes, he sure knew how to aim."

"Sure did." Officer Jones answered, her mind focused on the task at hand. Or, more specifically, she tried to avoid thinking about all the frightening impossibilities that could explain what the trio had witnessed at the graveyard. "Here we go," Tracy said, finally pulling a couple of clean white dishrags from an open drawer then moving back toward the sink.

Officer Jones ran the cloth under the steady stream of water—now visibly steaming—then placed it gently on Rico's forearm. He winced again.

"Sorry." She eased the pressure, but continued to wipe off the congealed blood and pus.

Rico inhaled through pursed lips. "It's okay. Just stings, is all."

Tracy smiled, recollecting a fond memory. "My, um—a friend back home used to say 'things don't get better without a little sting.' Always stuck with me."

"Sounds like a smart friend."

"He was." Tracy glanced up to make quick eye contact before diverting her attention back to the cleaning of the wound.

Officer Castillo cocked his head. "You okay, Trace?"

She nodded quickly. "Yeah, I'm fine."

One didn't need to be a detective to tell it wasn't an entirely truthful response. But fortunately Rico *was* a detective; he saw right through it and was about to press further when Calvin appeared in the doorway with a large box.

"Hey there, lovebirds," Calvin grinned. "Sorry to interrupt, but I think we might be in luck."

"What'd you find?" Tracy asked, scrubbing the last bits of blood from Rico's arm. The washcloth was now a ruddy, off-brown color.

Calvin set the edge of the heavy box on the corner of the

counter. "One of the names from the headstones—Jason Sunder—he's in the files."

"And?"

"Let's take a look," Calvin said, removing the cardboard lid and beginning to sort through the alphabetized case files. "Should be right... *here*!" The recruit lifted a thin manila folder and slid the box out of the way to make room.

Rico and Tracy leaned over Calvin's shoulders—Castillo still seated on the counter.

"Name's Jason M. Sunder," Calvin read from the file. "He was a victim in a housefire a few years back—1977."

Tracy raised an eyebrow. "Victim?"

"Arson," Calvin answered, pointing to a typewritten field on the file sheet. "Let's see, uh..." He scanned a large block of text, the narrative account of the case. "Apparently, some guy named Wayne Erkhart lit up Sunder's house—he was trying to target someone who ripped him off on a drug sale, according to his court testimony. Toxicology report later revealed that the perp was coked-up when he did it. Sunder was sound asleep in his house when it happened."

The others became somber, almost reverent as Calvin finished.

"Firefighters put out the flames before it spread to the neighbors' houses," he continued. "But Sunder didn't make it out. His body was taken to Orange Street Mortuary & Funeral Home. Erkhart was tried, convicted of second-degree manslaughter and arson, then the case was closed." Calvin flipped the page and made a squeamish gulp as he saw a pair of gruesome photos. He looked away and handed the folder to Tracy.

She took it, cautious, and scanned some text. "Notes from the autopsy say Sunder died of asphyxiation from smoke and burns all over his body," Tracy looked up, "including his face."

Rico took a deep breath and his expression betrayed serious concern. "You think that..." He trailed off.

Jones shrugged. "I don't know what to think."

"Wait a minute," Calvin said. "Are you saying this deceased burn-victim is our grave-robber?"

"We've seen *stranger* things, kid," Rico smirked. "But it's more than likely just a weird coincidence. Or someone trying to play a Halloween prank."

The three lingered in silence for a moment. None of them wanted Rico's first hypothesis to be proven right, but with all they'd seen, the idea really didn't seem too far-fetched.

"Who was Sunder's next of kin?" Tracy asked finally. "Any family or friends we can reach out to so we can piece this together?" She had finished cleaning Rico's wound by this time and now reached for a spool of gauze and bandage tape.

Calvin flipped a few pages in the folder then looked up. "None on record. Looks like he immigrated here as a kid and kept to himself most of the time."

Rico "How about the arsonist—Erkhart?"

"Deceased," Calvin read off the sheet.

"Fantastic." Rico sighed.

"Well what about the other names," Tracy asked, concentrated on wrapping a strip of bandage around Rico's forearm. "Hazel Vance and Marjory Beauregard. You find anything on them that might show us a connection?"

"Unfortunately, they're not showing up in our files," Calvin answered. "Or maybe it's *fortunately* for them, since it means they weren't involved in any crimes. I left a note on Miss Marge's desk for her to run the more detailed intelligence reports in the morning."

"Good thinking, kid," Rico nodded. The compliment caught Calvin off-guard.

Tracy ran her finger along the edge of the bandage's adhesive to press it down. "There," she said. "All clean and ready for action." She looked up into Rico's eyes, smiled softly, then turned away quickly to clean her hands under the faucet.

After another moment of thought, Rico turned to Calvin and extended his good arm toward the folder. "Hey, lemme see that."

"Sure." Calvin handed the pages to the officer, who began to scan the report.

"What about the mortuary?" Rico said, his finger landing on line halfway down. "Orange Street," he read.

Tracy nodded, flicked off the tap. "Good call. They would've been the last ones to handle the body before he, uh... you know."

The others agreed and they moved back down the hall to a conference room. In one corner of the room, there was a telephone and a thick phone book. Calvin flipped the pages furiously.

"Doubt they're open at this hour," Tracy noted.

"That faceless *thing* is out there somewhere," said Rico, "just waiting—searching for the next innocent arm they can slice with a shovel."

His counterpart rolled her eyes.

"But actually," Rico continued, "these places usually have someone on premises around the clock. You never know when death will strike."

Calvin perked up. "Found it." He picked up the phone and punched in the number. The three waited patiently as the dial tone came through the receiver.

Finally, there was a click as someone picked up the phone on the other end.

"Hello?" The voice was a woman's—tired and old. "Orange Street Mortuary & Funeral Home. How may I help you?"

"Y-yes, uh, hi," Calvin sputtered, then shoved the receiver at Rico.

The officer pressed it to his ear and continued. "Good evening, this is Officer Enrico Castillo, Metro-Dade PD. Who am I speaking with?"

The woman's tone became slightly more tense. "Oh, hello, officer. This is Dr. Blanche—I'm the director here. Is there a problem?"

He sidestepped her question. "We just need to ask you a few questions about a, uh, client of yours. Mind if we drop in?"

There was a long pause, then: "Not at all. You have the address?"

"Got it right here. Thanks, Dr. Blanche."

"Of course, officer," she said, then hung up.

Rico turned to the others. "There's something *off* about her."

"You probably just woke her up," Tracy raised an eyebrow. "And she works with dead people for a living," she smirked. "I think it's a job requirement that you're at least a *little* bit strange."

Officer Castillo nodded then moved toward the hall. "Let's go. Don't wanna keep the doctor waiting."

Orange Street Mortuary & Funeral Home was located in an odd part of town—or, more specifically, an odd part of town for a building its size. The two-story ramshackle structure was sandwiched between towering monolithic office buildings which, in comparison, could only be described as skyscrapers. The mortuary had outlived many other small, local, and immigrant-owned businesses that caved to the promise of profit afforded them by rising real estate prices. Of course, it was common knowledge that the momentary inflation was a direct result of the burgeoning drug trade, but savvy entrepreneurs knew not to ask too many questions when that much cash was at stake. That money was a lifeline to them, regardless of its source.

So Rico found it odd that this mysterious Dr. Blanche had held on to the plot of land and the deteriorating wooden structure that sat on it. *What's she holding out for?*

The question faded from his mind as Rico pulled the car through a large puddle and into a parallel parking space in front of the funeral home. It was still raining, so the trio shared a pair of umbrellas as they piled out onto the sidewalk. It was quiet on Orange Street—eerie and barren and dark on account of a burned-out streetlamp.

"We sure she's home?" Calvin asked, pointing at the darkened windows near the entrance.

"She said it was fine for us to drop in," Rico reminded him.

Tracy cocked her head and gestured toward the side of the building. "Some lights on in the back. Mortuary entrance, I'd wager."

The woman led her companions through the rain toward the side door, where she took a deep breath then knocked softly three times.

Shadows danced across the curtained windows, indicating that someone inside was moving toward the door. A moment later, the team from Metro-Dade heard the *click* of the lock and the door swung open a few inches—enough for a short old woman's head to appear in the gap. Rain trickled in clumps from the edge of the roof, which lacked a functioning gutter.

Rico was the next closest to the door, so he took the lead. "Good evening. Dr. Blanche?"

"Eudora Blanche—that's me," the lady nodded, peering at the shadowed faces outside. "And you're Officer Castillo, I presume?" She said, while her eyes flitted to Calvin and Tracy.

"Uh, y-yes," Rico sputtered, quickly flashing his badge then extending a hand. "Officer Enrico Castillo. Metro-Dade. Pleased to meet you." The woman offered a frail, bony hand to match his greeting. Rico noticed a small bandage on her pointer finger as he shook her hand. "Oh, and this is Officer Tracy Jones and, uh... Matt Calvin. Our intern," he added.

"*Recruit*," Calvin gritted his teeth and corrected under his breath.

Tracy stepped forward. "Thank you for meeting us on such short notice, Dr. Blanche."

"Of course, Officer Jones," Dr. Blanche replied, finally opening the door the rest of the way. "I understand how this sort of thing works. Death doesn't wait for office hours." Rico thought it sounded like the kind of pithy saying one might find on a line of tacky inspirational wall posters—ones designed *specifically* for the incredibly niche market of those who worked in the funerary industry.

"Please, come inside," Dr. Blanche said, extending her arm in a sweeping motion. "It's ghastly out there." The trio stepped over the threshold and entered a small hallway, shaking off their umbrellas, which they quickly set aside. When she had closed and locked the door behind them, Eudora again took the lead and started down the hall. The others followed as she ushered them through a set of swinging double doors and turned on a light.

The room was stark, with polished checker-tile floors and an almost greenish tint to the fluorescent lights overhead.

A set of bleach-white built-in cabinets adorned one of the smaller walls, while the largest wall featured a grid of small square doors with large vertical metal handles—these compact refrigerator doors were also white. There was an oversized stainless steel table filling the center of the room.

Calvin gulped when he realized where they were, and he pointed a shaky finger toward the doors. "Is that where..." He didn't finish.

Dr. Blanche smirked. "Yes. That's where the bodies are kept until they're ready to go to their new residences in the earth."

Though none of them wanted to speak up, Rico was pretty sure they were all wondering how many of the doors had actual frigid corpses behind them.

The doctor's next words brought his mind back to attention.

"So," she began, "you said you had some questions about a client of mine?"

"That's right," Castillo nodded. "Does the name *Jason M. Sunder* ring a bell for you?"

As he spoke the name, Rico thought he sensed a subtle flutter of Eudora's eyelashes, a slight clenching of her jaw. Or maybe he had compelled himself to see those things—to imagine something that wasn't *actually* there. After all of the wild experiences of the past couple days—and years, for that matter—he was ready for an easy answer, an explanation, a quick admittance of guilt. He wouldn't put it past his imagination to conjure up that sort of doubt.

But then Dr. Blanche spoke again, stroking one of her old, skeletal fingers across her chin. "Doesn't ring any bells," she said, then started off toward a filing cabinet. "When did you say he died?"

"I didn't," Rico answered, with a quick glance to Tracy.

"1977—" Calvin interjected eagerly. Officer Castillo offered a moment of uncomfortable, stern eye-contact that immediately sobered the recruit.

"Thank you, dear," Eudora nodded without looking and heaved open a heavy drawer. Her frail eyes scanned a series of nearly-identical folders with small tabs scrawled in ink from a bleeding pen. "Q... R... S—here we go—Saunders—no. Sunday... Sunder. Jason." The woman grabbed and carefully removed the folder and held it out toward the officers. "Well, look at that! Guess he did come through here after all."

Tracy received it from the lady and noticed the manila had faded to more of an orange color, with a small reddish stain along the name tab.

"What is it you're hoping to find, exactly?" The doctor moved back toward the large metal table, where a number of other folders and files were strewn about. Eudora collected them, straightened them into a neat stack, and set the pile near a corner of the surface—the farthest corner away from her guests.

"Anything, really," Rico said, sauntering toward her while Tracy flipped through the file. "Anything strange or unique about the way he died—or about what happened to him afterward."

Dr. Blanche tensed and her eyes narrowed. "Afterward—?"

Calvin interrupted, moving toward the filing cabinet. "Mind if I scan through some other files?"

"Um, uh, of course not," Eudora sputtered, a little flustered. "Go right ahead."

The storm continued outside, muffled only slightly by the few small windows. As the recruit began to flip through the folders in the open drawer, Eudora continued:

"Where was I? Ah, yes. As I noted, I don't recall the details of this specific client—Mr. Sunder—but I can assure you that I follow a very strict set of procedures to ensure that each and every body is well-cared for on its journey to wherever's next."

"You're religious?" Rico asked, beginning to pace, orbiting the table.

The old woman's face was cast in oblong shadows from a lamp on the table. She seemed to choose her words carefully before speaking: "I believe that there's more to life than what happens before we die."

Officer Castillo grinned, satisfied with the coy answer, then looked down at his bandaged arm. This sparked a thought, and he turned back to the doctor. "How'd that happen?" He gestured and shifted his gaze toward her bandaged finger.

"How did *what* happen?" It took her a moment, then Eudora raised her hand above the edge of the table. "Oh, this? Paper cut," she answered dismissively.

"That happen often?"

"Not really."

Rico didn't respond, but waited for her to say more.

She did: "Normally, I'm wearing gloves. Not sure how it slipped my mind."

By this time, Castillo reached the far corner of the table, where Dr. Blanche had hastily gathered the pile of loose folders. He used two fingers to nudge and rotate the top folder so he could read it and the folders beneath it, but found that they weren't labeled like the one with Jason Sunder's records. The tabs were blank.

Hmm. Maybe nothing.

"You're a doctor," Rico stated, trying to buy Tracy more time to find something—anything—in Sunder's file.

"Is that a question, officer?" Eudora's voice was gritty and a hint defensive.

"Just curious," he answered. "What does someone like you have to study to go into a business like this?" With his unbandaged arm, the officer made a sweeping motion toward the wall of square refrigerator doors.

"Each person's path is his or her own," she started. "For me, it began, oddly-enough, with studies in music, but my career was cut short by the war." Here, Dr. Blanche's eyes became gray and glassy, then she continued. "I served as a medic—with very little training, mind you. But I learned quickly. When my time was complete, I decided I rather enjoyed it and continued my education before going on to teach." Here her glazed-over look turned to one of apparent reverie—recollections of years of students, the lives she touched, perhaps.

Calvin slammed a drawer of the metal filing cabinet—a little harder than intended—then chimed in from across the room. "So how'd you end up *here?*"

Dr. Blanche exhaled a slow, weary breath. "I'd had enough of the politics and pandering of higher education. That wasn't for me—it was exhausting." Eudora sighed again. "I do miss the students, though," she said more softly. "So bright and full of life."

At this point, Tracy closed Sunder's file and handed it across the table to Dr. Blanche.

"Find what you were looking for?"

Tracy puffed. "Nothing of note."

"I think that's enough for tonight," said Officer Castillo. He gave a light kick to Calvin, who was hunched over the lowest drawer of the cabinet. He winced, shut the drawer, and stood up.

"Thank you, Dr. Blanche," Calvin sputtered.

"Of course," she answered, moving the group toward the exit. They started down the hall ahead of her. "I'm happy to be of assistance in whatever way I can, so please don't hesitate to call if anything else comes up."

The three left the building quietly, grabbing their umbrellas once again, with Eudora waving goodbye in the doorway.

"Thank you again," Rico shouted over the storm before entering the car. The engine roared and the headlights lit up the mortuary's wall. As they pulled away, Rico watched in the rearview mirror as Dr. Blanche closed the side door and turned out the lights.

When they had rounded the block, Castillo leaned toward Tracy. "Find anything?"

The woman lowered and shook her head. "Everything matched up with our case file at the station," Officer Jones explained. "I looked for any details that might've been off or inconsistent, but... nothing out of the ordinary."

Rico tightened his grip on the steering wheel, his knuckles bulging. Raindrops danced in tiny rivulets down the windshield.

"Aren't you going to ask *me* if I found anything?" Calvin said from the backseat.

Officer Castillo grunted, exhaled, then made eye-contact with the recruit via the rearview mirror. "Hey intern: you find anything?"

Calvin crossed his arms. "As a matter of fact, I found *nothing*."

"Great." Rico muttered, bringing the car around a sharp turn.

"No, I mean, there should have been *something*," Calvin continued, leaning forward between the front seats. "But I couldn't find it."

Tracy and Rico made eye-contact, then Officer Jones asked: "What do you mean?"

Calvin smiled, apparently satisfied at the discovery he was about to unveil. "While you were distracting Dr. Blanche with your little interrogation about her past, I discovered an index to the files in her cabinets."

"Riveting," snapped Rico. "How does that help us

exactly?"

"Well, I located the years and names of our two other persons of interest: Hazel Vance and Marjory Beauregard."

Castillo slammed the brakes. "You found their files and didn't say anything?"

"N-no," the recruit braced himself on the seatbacks. "That's just it—what I'm trying to tell you. I *didn't* find their files."

The driver leaned toward Officer Jones. "This kid making sense to you?"

"I think I'm following," Tracy nodded, then turned toward Calvin. "You mean they were in the index, but their files were missing from the drawers?"

"Exactly!" Calvin smiled, delighted.

Rico's impatience was difficult to hide. "Which means...?"

"It means Dr. Eudora Blanche is as suspicious as she seemed," Tracy clarified. "Or... it could just be a coincidence that the files are missing..."

"Or the files were misplaced." Castillo grunted.

"I assure you, Officer Castillo: I was thorough in my search."

The car became silent for a moment, save for the rain and rumbling of the engine as they sped back to the station. Castillo spoke up again:

"We still can't prove she's done anything wrong. Or that she has anything to do with that *thing* in the graveyard." He paused, lost in a thought. "Anyway, let's all get some sleep and meet back at the station in the morning. Maybe Marge'll have something for us."

Before anyone could respond, Rico reached down and clicked on the radio. A blaring electric guitar line burst through the speakers as the car screeched through the city in the rain and moonlight.

CHAPTER 11

Declan awoke to the feeling of cold, wet slobber on his face. He blinked his eyes open to find a furry puppy face staring at him with round black eyes and a lopsided pink tongue that hung out of its mouth. When it sensed him stirring, the dog yapped and scurried away. The man stretched his arms, felt a strain in his lower back, then sat upright. He had been sprawled on a trendy, white sectional sofa in a living room with high ceilings and lucite end-tables. Undulating dapples of morning sunlight danced across the wall in a sort of rhombus shape as Declan took in the bright space. Finally, he recognized the scene: Donna Locke's living room.

He was draped in a large woven blanket, which he quickly realized was the only thing covering his body besides a pair of loose-fitting boxer shorts that he did not recognize. Declan pulled the blanket closer around him as he heard footsteps coming from the kitchen.

Donna appeared around the corner. “Hey, sleepyhead,” she smirked. “Hungry?”

Declan’s face contorted, as if he didn’t quite understand the question. “How did we get here? And where are my clothes?”

“Relax,” Donna answered. “I didn’t, ya know… *see* anything. Roger made sure you were all settled in. Your clothes were all torn and wet. There’s some dry things on the end table over there.”

The man followed the direction of her gloved finger to a stack of neatly-folded clothes.

“Doc didn’t mind,” Donna continued as Declan shifted toward them, an arm still clutching the large blanket. “Don’t worry; they’re clean. You really don’t remember how we got here?”

Declan shook his head. “I remember the museum, Marcus and the knights, and that it was raining.”

“You carried me all the way here, then you passed out as soon as we hit the foyer and all your fur started, um, *ungrowing*. Doc dragged you out here and got you dried off. You know, I’m impressed, Dec—you’ve come a long way in just a short time. Controlling your abilities, I mean.”

“Sorry you had to see me like that.”

“Don’t mention it.” Donna paused. “Thanks, by the way. For saving me, I mean.”

The man nodded.

Donna cocked her head. “You still didn’t answer my question.”

"Huh?"

"You hungry?"

"Oh, yes, very much so."

She smiled and pointed around the corner. "Restroom's that way. Food'll be ready in a minute."

With that, Declan took the pile of clothes and disappeared toward the bathroom. A couple minutes later, he returned to the dining area, dressed in a loose-fitting gray sweatsuit.

"Not exactly my color," Declan smiled as he took a seat at the table. "But I suppose it'll do. Thank you, Donna."

"No. Thank *you*, Dec." She placed a plate in front of him with eggs, toast, and slices of fresh fruit. Donna turned, hung her head through the open doorway, and shouted toward the staircase: "Starla!" There was no answer. Donna shrugged, then remembered the intercom. She pressed the button. "Starla, breakfast is ready."

A moment later, the pair heard small footsteps pattering down the stairs. Starla appeared, her reddish hair in a mangled mess across her freckled face.

"Morning, Aunt Donna," she mumbled as she reached for a plastic cup on the counter. She noticed their guest, but said nothing. Instead she eyed him with curiosity as she moved toward the fridge.

"Starla, you remember our friend Declan?" Donna asked as she sat down near the man and took a bite of eggs.

The girl nodded. "I remember you. You helped save me and my mom and Aunt Donna."

He smiled, recalling the underwater rescue mission a few

months prior. "That's right. Good to see you again, Starla."

Starla closed the fridge as she produced a large pitcher of red Kool-Aid. She filled up her cup then set the container on the counter.

Donna puffed. "Starla, what have I told you about drinking Kool-Aid for breakfast?"

"You said it has a lot of sugar and that sugar makes kids hyper," Starla said, taking a generous sip of the red drink.

"And...?"

She took a breath. "And when I'm hyper I get cranky."

Donna nodded. "Right. And it'll make you crash. Don't you wanna stay awake for trick-or-treating tonight?"

Starla took another swig out of the plastic cup then nodded.

"You want some breakfast, kiddo? There's eggs. No pepper."

"I'm not hungry yet." The child shook her head. "I'll just get some Lucky Charms later. I'm busy right now."

Donna rolled her eyes as the girl ran off down the hall. Max followed, trailing at her feet to lick up little splashes of red on the tile.

"Just keep it off the carpet!" Donna shouted after her. "Please," she added with a weary sigh as she heard the girl ascend the stairs once more.

Declan grinned as he took a bite of buttery toast. "What's it like taking care of a kid?" He said through a mouthful.

"It's the hardest thing I've ever done," Donna said, her eyes lost in a sea of golden scrambled eggs on her plate. "And it's the most *important* thing I've ever done."

"She's lucky to have you," Declan offered softly.

Donna nodded and took another bite. Declan sensed her mind drifting elsewhere.

Finally, the woman spoke again, shaking her lowered head as she continued to swirl her eggs with her fork. "I just can't get it out of my head—what Marcus said last night: *You can't stop what's coming*." Here her voice quavered and her speech began to accelerate. "What does it mean? Why is he doing this? Who's he working for? I mean, did you see the way he... *looked* at me—"

"Donna," Declan interrupted, placing a gentle hand on her wrist.

She looked up at him and wiped a small tear from the corner of her eye.

"I'm sorry about Marcus," the man said. "He's clearly not in his right mind."

Donna shook her head. "I'm not so sure, Dec. He seemed perfectly *present*. It's just that he's... remembering things wrong—he thinks *I* turned him to gold."

"Well, didn't you...?"

The woman puffed. "It was an accident. I would never do that on purpose—it was this damned *curse*. I loved him. I mean, I *do* love him—or, I did—I—sorry, I don't know what I'm saying anymore." Donna stood up from the table abruptly and carried her plate over to the trashcan. She scraped off the loose crumbs then placed the dish in the sink to rinse it. Donna flipped on the faucet.

"I hate to say it," Declan said when she'd finished running the water. "But I don't think Marcus is the same man you knew before, Donna. I mean, did you see what he did with his hands—and the *light*? I've never seen anything like it." He stood and brought his plate over to the sink, where Donna took it in her gloved hands without making eye contact. Declan thought he saw a tear forming at the edge of her eye. "*You can't stop what's coming*," he repeated the words. "It sounds like a threat."

Donna finally looked up into Declan's eyes. "I'm not scared of him," she said. "I'm just afraid he'll never be the man he *was* again."

"He's grown very powerful, Donna," the man pointed out. "And whoever—*what*ever that armored *thing* was is just as dangerous."

"We held our own."

"Barely."

Donna began scrubbing the second plate with a sponge.

"Donna, if they're out to get you, that's not something to shrug off. Think of Starla—and your sister—"

"We're fine."

The man sighed. "You know, me and my team can offer you protection."

"I don't need protecting," Donna snapped. "I just want Marcus back. And I want everything to go back to the way it was before any of this ever happened." Here the woman dropped the plate and sponge in the sink and took a few steps away. Donna lowered her head, her back to Declan, and began to cry. The man moved toward her slowly and placed a gentle hand on her shoulder.

"Do you think he can be turned?" Declan asked softly, almost a whisper.

The woman's breathing was heavy. Finally, Donna gave a breathy answer: "I don't know."

"Well," said Declan, stepping away, "if you need anything, you call me right away, okay?"

She turned to him and nodded. "Thanks, Dec."

The two shared an embrace then Donna moved to the phone. "I'll call you a cab," she said as she started dialing. "You're welcome to join us for trick-or-treating tonight—if you don't have plans?" Donna put the receiver to her ear as she waited for someone to pick up.

"I appreciate the invitation," the man answered. "I may lie low tonight. I've had enough action for a while." Declan offered a grateful smile as Donna finished arrangements with the taxi service.

Upstairs, Starla tiptoed across the carpeted second-floor landing, moving toward a closed door at the end of the hall. She did her best to keep her big cup of red Kool-Aid balanced while Max slobbered along after her. The dog let out a yap.

"Quiet, Max!" She whispered, placing a finger over her mouth. Starla crouched to rub the young golden retriever's furry neck. This seemed to calm him down.

She rose again and, with her free hand, the nine-year-old girl reached out for the handle and clicked open the door.

It swung slowly with a faint creak, the gap widening so that Starla could see inside. Max nestled his way between her legs and pounced toward the rug that rested under the bed in the middle of the room.

When she was inside, Starla quietly closed the door behind her. The light hissing of an oxygen tube and faint hum of various electronics filled the space. The girl rounded the corner to get a better view of the bed.

"Good morning, mom," the girl said softly.

Sondra Gordon—the woman on the bed—did not answer. Her eyes were closed and one might easily assume she were not alive, save for the slightest motion—the rise and fall of her chest—as she took unconscious breaths.

Starla moved toward the side of the bed. She set her red drink on the end table and scooted a chair closer to Sondra's bedside. When it was near enough, Starla sat down and leaned toward her mother.

"It's me," the girl said. "Your daughter Starla. Can you hear me?"

Again, Sondra made no reply. Starla glanced at a screen that displayed a squiggly line indicating her mother's heart rate. *Not even a little flutter of her eyelids or a change in her pulse.*

Max whimpered at Starla's feet, offering his big, glassy black eyes as a plea to be held.

"What's that, Max? You want to try and talk to mom, too?"

The girl caved and picked him up. She set Max on her lap, where he curled close.

"Aunt Donna says she thinks I might have powers," she spoke to the puppy. "And I think she's right."

The pup squirmed and yipped again, as if trying to carry on the conversation.

"What powers? Well, I think I may have used them once before—I think I can talk to people through their minds." Here Starla looked to her mother again. "I think I once read mother's mind. And I'm going to give it another try."

Apparently satisfied, the puppy relaxed. Starla took her mother's hand.

"Mother, it's me. Are you listening?"

No answer.

Starla inhaled deeply, then closed her eyes.

Think. Listen for mom's mind, her voice. You can do this.

The girl felt the rise and fall of Max's breaths, and the slow, steady pulse of her mother's veins. *I'm listening, mom. Talk to me.*

Slowly, gradually, the noises of the room faded away. With her eyes shut tight, Starla began to imagine the room without walls or its other trappings and decorations. Just her mother, the bed, the chair. She imagined her mother's eyes opening, turning toward her. Those kind eyes—she hadn't seen them in nearly two years and could barely remember their true color.

"Mother, I'm listening," Starla whispered. "D-did you know—?" Did she dare ask the questions that kept her up at night? Her breaths were short and quick. "Did you know that I would have... powers? And did you know that Aunt Donna did, too—?"

A light knock at the door snapped Starla out of her thoughts.

"Starla?"

Her eyes shot open as the door swung in. A face appeared in the gap: Donna.

"Hey, kiddo," she said. "Everything okay?"

The girl nodded quickly. Max jumped down from her lap.

"What were you doing in here?" Donna opened the door wider and moved toward her niece. She crouched next to her as she waited for the girl to answer.

"I just wanted to know—to see if..." Starla trailed off.

"You wanted to see if you have powers after all," she finished the girl's thought.

Starla nodded.

"Any luck?"

The girl shook her head.

"That's okay," Donna wrapped her arms around the girl. "You'll always be my little Starling—whether you have special powers or not." She looked the girl in the eyes. "You know, you don't need super powers to change the world anyway, kiddo. You changed mine just by showing up in it."

Here Starla's somber expression softened to a contented smile and she gave her aunt another squeeze.

"How's your costume coming along?" Donna asked. "Gonna be ready for tonight?"

"Almost ready," the girl answered. "I can't wait. I heard the neighbors are giving out whole candy bars this year!"

"No pressure for the rest of us," Donna quipped under her breath. "How about you hop to it and we'll let your mom get her beauty rest?"

The girl complied and scampered out of the room with Max at her heels. Donna took another look at her sister, peaceful and silent. She crouched and leaned in close. "Did you know about all of this?" She asked, knowing Sondra wouldn't hear. *Why did you never tell me? Why did you push me away?* Donna didn't bother asking the rest of her questions out loud—there were too many to count. If she'd learned anything over the past few years, it was that questions weren't meant to be answered. *They're just meant to gnaw at you until you decide you've had enough and finally cast them aside. Right?*

Of course, she didn't really believe that. Donna knew there were answers out there—somewhere. Answers about Marcus, about her family. She was determined to find them—to know the truth. The *whole* truth.

Donna clenched her gloved hands.

So help me, God.

CHAPTER 12

After the long, eventful night, including the near-midnight visit to the Orange Street Mortuary, Rico overslept and arrived to the police station much later than he'd hoped. When he walked in late that morning, the station was crowded and full of chatter as phones rang almost non-stop. Officer Castillo tried to pick up on conversations as he squeezed past a group of teary-eyed civilians in the waiting area.

"—we demand some answers!" One woman shouted through the glass divider that separated her from a dispatch officer.

"I already told you," the officer answered as calmly as possible, "I can take your written report and we'll follow up as soon as we're able—"

"But I want to *speak* to someone now! I need to know if my children are going to be *safe*—"

Ah, Rico thought as he pushed through a door and left the waiting area behind. *So it appears the news has gotten out. Blood-sucking phantom, alligator-human hybrid that eats children, faceless grave-digger... Terrific.*

As he moved into the galley kitchen to grab a cup of coffee, Tracy appeared in the doorway.

"Where have you been?" She asked, moving to inspect his bandaged arm.

"Ouch!" Rico winced at her touch as he reached for a styrofoam cup with his other hand. "Just lost track of time, is all. Forgot set an alarm." He handled the coffee pot and poured its final, viscous dregs into his cup, filling it to only about a quarter of its capacity. "Great."

"C'mon," Tracy nodded. "Chief's waiting for us."

Without another word, Rico followed, taking a quick sip of the lukewarm coffee. He scrunched his face as he tasted the gritty texture of stray coffee grounds between his teeth.

"Marge find anything?"

"Not yet," Tracy answered without looking back.

The duo rounded the corner and entered the crowded meeting room. Castillo scanned the room, noting the familiar faces of many of his colleagues—and scrawny Calvin, sandwiched between two burly officers on the far side of the space.

"Well there he is," the chief said when he saw Rico. "Nice of you to show up, officer."

"Sorry, I forgot to—"

"Save it, Castillo." The chief turned to address the room.

"Alright, team. We've really got our hands full. With everything that's going on, I thought it best that we take some time to get on the same page, to make sure everyone's clear on our response."

Here he gestured to a corkboard, upon which were pinned various photographs, newspaper clippings, and illustrations.

"As you all know," he continued, "a kid went missing near his home in Citrus Springs two nights ago. Name's Biff Barley. Castillo and Jones interrogated two eyewitnesses—the kid's neighbors—which led us to learn that there's someone wearing some kind of alligator costume that's behind this."

A woman across the room—Officer Ruby Sanchez—raised her hand.

Chief pointed at her and nodded for her to speak.

"Was it some kind of prank?"

"Don't know," the chief answered.

"It's a sick one, if so," someone chimed in.

Rico took a deep breath, made a glance at Tracy, then spoke up: "Respectfully, I don't think it was a prank. Or a costume."

"Go on," said the chief, gritting his teeth.

"We found prints—from a gator—in the mud."

"Gators live in canals," the chief nodded. "Tell me something I don't know."

Castillo hesitated, then said: "Gators walk on all fours, right? There were only *two* prints."

The room suddenly filled with chatter, mumblings and whispers between colleagues. Rico could feel the judgmental stares. *They think I'm crazy—or worse: that I'm making all of this up.*

"Alright, alright, calm down." The chief made wide motions with his hands to regain the attention and focus of the team. "Whatever the hell it is, it ate some kid and I get to be the one to tell his parents he's gone. Lucky me. What's more, we're investigating a series of grave robberies—a couple bodies missing with no apparent connections to each other. More on that as we learn it." Here he eyed Castillo, then took a deep breath and continued. "In other news, I'd like Officer Sanchez to give her report on last night's... pet incident."

Ruby nodded and picked up a large manila envelope from a side table. "Thanks, chief," she said, turning to address the group. "We received several reports throughout the past couple days about pets going missing, but they seemed unrelated. Yesterday, two of the pets were found in different parts of the city." Here she removed two large photos from the envelope and pinned them to the bulletin board. "Two dogs: when we found them, they were drained of all of their blood."

Even though he'd seen the news report on Donna's TV, Rico still had to hold back the urge to regurgitate. The images were terrifying: the dogs looked like mummified corpses—emaciated, starved, and colorless.

"Do we know how it happened?" Tracy asked. "Or who did this?"

Sanchez shook her head. "Nope. There's no clear motive or connection between the pets' owners." She produced two more photos from the envelope. "However, upon closer inspection we found marks near the neck of each subject."

Rico leaned in and craned his neck to view the images. "Are those... *bite* marks?"

Ruby nodded slowly. "Appears so. There's identical markings on both pets."

"So the good news is that they don't look like alligator teeth marks," someone snickered.

"Yeah," Rico added. "More like a vampire. Great news."

Tracy elbowed Rico in the side then glared at him.

"I'm afraid we're not quite to the good news yet," the chief said with a weary sigh. "Around the time that the news was busy covering the pet incidents, there was a break-in at The MORA. I just got off the phone with the museum's executive director and they've had to close down the whole place until repairs can be completed."

Someone asked: "Was anything taken?"

"The director's team is still conducting a full inventory, but so far they've identified that they're missing a suit of armor."

"Armor?" An officer asked. "What kind of armor?"

"Very *valuable* and very old," the chief answered. "Part of that conquistador exhibit." The man felt his shirt pocket and removed a polaroid photo: "Oh, and they found this." He pinned it to the board.

Rico and Tracy moved closer to inspect the item. The photograph depicted a circular shield, fashioned of what looked like solid gold.

"What is it?" Rico asked. "Is that shield part of the exhibit?"

The chief exhaled slowly, coughed, then raised his eyebrows. "You guys aren't going to believe this—it doesn't really make any sense yet—but the director says they had a shield with a description matching this one *exactly*—same shape, markings, patterns. Except," here he paused and shook his head before taking another breath, "it was made of *wood*, not gold."

Tracy touched Rico's hand and the two made eye-contact. Both had the same thought:

Donna.

It didn't quite make sense. But then again, nothing else they'd just covered in the briefing made much sense either.

"The museum director indicated that there were signs of struggle," the chief continued. "Broken displays, something like burn marks on the walls, and an entire section of the building's glass facade was shattered."

Could Donna have been involved? Officer Castillo felt uneasy and anxious. *There's only one reason Donna would go to those lengths: Marcus.* He sensed that Tracy had a similar revelation.

An officer interrupted his thoughts. "Burn marks?"

"He described them as circular," said the police chief. "Smallest one about the circumference of a grapefruit." He held his big hands in the shape to emphasize the point.

"Any idea who was behind it?" Rico asked, hoping the answer was negative. "Did their cameras catch anything?"

The chief sort of chuckled. "Funny you should ask. The

cameras were rolling the whole night, but it was too dark—they showed me the tapes. There's nothing usable."

Everyone in the room seemed to have the same question, but one officer asked it: "Too dark? Aren't the cameras configured for capturing footage at night?"

"Sorry, I should've clarified. The lights went dark. The cameras usually rely on streetlamps and emergency lights to capture usable footage."

Calvin asked: "How come the cameras kept rolling if the power went out?"

"I didn't say the power went out." The chief became somber. "I said the *lights* went *dark*."

"W-what do you mean—?"

"I mean what I said. I'm just telling you what I heard straight from the museum director."

"Maybe it was the boogeyman," someone jested, making eye contact with Rico. He rolled his eyes back at the officer.

"So what you're saying is that we don't have any leads on the break-in yet?" Officer Sanchez asked, crossing her arms.

"That's correct."

There was a moment of silence before someone suggested, "Maybe we should just cancel Halloween."

Someone else chuckled and shot back, "You can't *cancel* Halloween. It's the best night of the year."

The whole room began to mutter their own versions of the same arguments, the volume rising to a muddled roar.

"Quiet, quiet!" The chief once again raised his hands to speak. The room became silent. "There's nothing to indicate that any of these incidents are connected, or that we have any reason to worry about an imminent danger to the masses. But," he paused for effect, "it may be a good idea to consider a curfew—"

Here the room broke out once more in a flurry of conversation and objections. The chief shook his head and conceded. "Fine. No curfew. But that's going to mean overtime—we'll need patrols in as many neighborhoods as we can—especially Citrus Springs."

At this point, the crowd grouped off as higher-ranking members began to assign the units for patrol. The rest of the team members were dismissed. Rico and Tracy started for the door when the chief barked toward them.

"Castillo. My office."

Rico caught the serious look in the man's eyes and followed quietly.

The office door slammed shut behind them.

"What the hell is wrong with you, Castillo?"

That's always a great way to start a constructive conversation, Rico thought. He wondered if the chief expected an honest answer. He decided to remain silent to see if the man would elaborate as he took large paces across the room. He did:

"You okay?"

Rico started to answer. "I'm fine—"

"I'm serious," the man moved behind his desk and leaned over it. "You know, I took a big risk letting you walk back in here. Now you're talking with a straight face about alligator-men and vampires?"

I'm guessing he hasn't heard about the man with no face, Rico mused. *Probably best not to bring it up right now.* Once again, he wasn't sure how to respond. The question was more rhetorical, anyway.

"All I'm asking is: are you sure you're okay? You're one of my best officers—always have been—but the things you're saying are just... out of the realm of possibility. I'm worried about you. Are you sure you can handle all this job requires of you?"

"Yes, sir." Castillo replied. "Just got... a lot on my mind lately." He raised his chin confidently. "I'll do better. I promise, chief."

The chief raised an eyebrow, giving Rico a once-over. "You're serious, aren't you?"

"I'm sorry, chief—?"

"You think there could really be some alligator walking around on two legs, eating kids?"

Rico took short breaths, and waited some time before answering. "Sir, I've seen things that I couldn't explain if I tried, and I—"

"Just answer the question, Castillo. You think something like this is possible or not?"

The officer nodded his compliance, then spoke. "Yes. I think it's *very* possible."

For the first time all morning, it was clear that the chief took Rico's words seriously.

"I was afraid you'd say that," muttered the chief. He sank

back into his large chair and his gaze drifted off toward a corner of the ceiling. "That'll be all, Castillo." Chief gestured toward the door.

Rico nodded, hesitated—as if he wanted to say more—then moved swiftly out the door.

Tracy and Calvin intercepted Officer Castillo as he returned to his office. Officer Jones handed Rico a stack of files.

"What's this?" Rico asked, inspecting the manila folders as they continued walking.

"It's everything Miss Marge could find on our three persons of interest," Tracy replied.

"And?" The man turned back, raised his eyebrows, and flicked his eyes from Tracy to the recruit.

Officer Jones sighed. "No leads."

"Fantastic." Rico pivoted and continued into the office. The others followed.

"But," Calvin chimed in, "there was one important detail that might be of interest."

Tracy raised a curious eyebrow.

"I'm all ears, kid," said Rico.

The recruit looked eager to share his morsel of intelligence and rubbed his hands together. "Marge didn't find much connecting Jason Sunder, Hazel Vance, or Marjory Beauregard, per se—"

"But?"

"But," the young man continued. "There was one thing

they all have in common: none of the three have any living relatives." Calvin waited in anticipation for the officers to react.

Tracy crossed her arms. "How is that important, exactly?"

"Yeah," said Rico. "That just means there's no one we can interview, no way to follow-up—you know the drill by now."

"But I think we were all in agreement that there was something fishy about Dr. Blanche," Calvin spoke quickly. "I think she's hiding something, and this little detail may be important enough to—"

"It isn't." Castillo shot the young man a stern look. He inhaled deeply and started to pace. "I agree that it might not be a coincidence—all of these bizarre happenings all at once. But just because weird stuff is going on, it doesn't mean we can throw logic and process out the window."

"But—"

"You heard me, kid."

"Yes, sir." Calvin nodded quickly. "O-of course." With that, he turned and hurried out of the office, closing the door on his way out.

Tracy grinned.

Rico caught it out of the corner of his eye. "What's so funny?"

"Listen to you," she said. "Talking about *logic* and *process*... what happened to the loose cannon I met months ago?"

"I dunno," he muttered. "He just... grew up a little, I guess."

Tracy moved closer, so that the two were now standing toe-to-toe. "I'm proud of you, Rico. You've come a long way, and I know it wasn't easy." She moved closer, reaching for his hand. They touched—softly, gently.

Rico's mind shifted to the weight in his side pocket—the tiny, metallic object for which he'd saved up for months. "Trace, I know we've been pretty busy lately, but..."

Officer Jones tensed, anticipating the conversation that was coming. She wasn't ready to have *that* talk.

"You know how I feel about you..." He started.

And I feel the same about you but—

"... and I don't want to put this off any longer—"

There was a sharp rap on the office door. Both officers were startled, but let out momentary breaths of relief.

"Come in!" Rico shouted.

A woman's head appeared in the doorway—one of the secretaries. "Donna Locke is on the line for you," she pointed toward the phone at Rico's desk, where a button glowed to indicate the incoming call.

"Thanks, Sarah," Rico affirmed as she disappeared once more. He moved toward the desk quickly and was about to pick up the phone. The officer stopped himself and looked back up at Tracy, who was heading for the door. "Hey," he said. "Where you goin'?"

Jones turned her neck, keeping most of her body angled toward the door. "Gonna make sure we're ready for the patrol tonight," she said quickly. "Tell Donna I said hello?"

Rico nodded as Tracy exited in a hurry. The man let out a defeated breath then picked up the receiver. "Donna? Is everything okay?"

"Rico," Donna's voice answered back with an immediately-detectable sharpness. "It's about Marcus. We found him, but there's been some... *developments*."

Officer Castillo braced himself against the desk.

"Tell me everything."

CHAPTER 13

The sun completed its slow descent, painting the sky like the insides of a ruby red grapefruit with wisps of sugary clouds streaked across it. From Donna's long, paved driveway, the solar orb was already invisible, having ducked behind the banyans and other tropical trees that lined the shady streets of Star Island. The whole man-made landmass consisted of a single, curvilinear street that formed a loop. Donna's home at the farthest tip from the island's entry bridge was a covetable mansion, and served as staging ground for the most lucrative trick-or-treating in the whole Miami area.

Donna's heels clacked down the tile front steps. The blonde woman was clad in black dress shoes and jeans, a leopard-print blouse, and a fuzzy cat-eared headband. She wore a facemask that covered the area around her eyes, fastened with a stretchy elastic band.

As she stood in the entryway, Donna motioned after

Starla, who was dressed in black from head to toe. "Hang on, kiddo!" The girl turned, revealing bones painted in white all over the front of her outfit. Her face was covered by a surprisingly-realistic store-bought skull—so realistic, in fact, that Donna jumped when she saw it.

A little giggle snuck through the faux-rotting teeth and Starla lifted the mask. Her freckles framed a delighted smile.

"Don't scare me like that," Donna muttered, still catching her breath. "Now c'mere and let me grab a photo for the fridge." The girl complied and moved a little closer, clutching a brown paper grocery bag for her soon-to-be-acquired treats.

Donna held the clunky camera over her eye: "Say cheese!"

"Cheeees—" Starla's attention drifted down to the edge of the driveway past the open front gate. Another child about Starla's own height and build approached carrying an orange plastic pumpkin-shaped bucket. Starla did little to hide a scowl.

Click!

The girl shielded her face from the flash then took another look down the paved drive. "Can you believe it?" She muttered to her aunt. "Tiffany wore the same costume." Her little bone-gloved hand gestured toward the approaching skeleton twin.

Donna flapped the polaroid back and forth and eyed Tiffany herself. "Not *exactly* the same," she said, a little preoccupied with inspecting the emerging image. "Yours is homemade, Star. Mostly." Using a black marker pulled from her pocket, Donna wrote something on the bottom of the photo.

When she realized the girl was actually upset, Donna crouched to her level and took the girl's hand in one of her own, glove to glove. "Hey, little Starling. It's gonna be okay. You know when me and Sondra were little, people used to think we were twins?"

Starla raised an eyebrow. "Really?"

"Mhm. She was six years older than me—I mean, she *still* is—but some people still couldn't tell us apart. Mom used to dress us in matching outfits..." Donna shook her head as she recalled the clothes, shoes, ribbons—she *hated* those ribbons. "Anyway, it used to drive me crazy, because as much as I wanted to be like her, I really just wanted to be my own person—to be independent. But you know what our mother used to say?"

Starla shook her head.

"She'd say, 'Now Donna, being independent isn't all it's cracked up to be, you know. We *need* other people—to be kind, to laugh with us, and to help us out when things get scary. That's what sisters are for,' she'd always say." Here Donna seemed to be lost in a memory, a wistful thought.

"Uh, Aunt Donna? Tiffany is *not* my sister."

"Yeah, yeah. You get the idea." Donna stood upright. "You can at least be nice to her, okay? Maybe she just... needs a friend."

The girl didn't immediately reply, but eyed Tiffany once more.

"C'mon, kiddo, don't worry about it," Donna whispered

to the girl. "Have some fun, and find the biggest Hershey's bar imaginable, okay? Now run along, ya little Argonaut," she added under her breath as Starla hesitantly shuffled down the driveway, acknowledged Tiffany with a timid wave, then scurried off and away from the other girl. Donna sighed and shook her head.

As the sky faded to a dusky purple and street lamps clicked on to illuminate the island loop, Donna's gaze drifted to a pair of jack-o-lanterns perched atop columns at either side of her open front gate. The little votive candles inside flickered in the breeze off the bay, and Donna crossed her arms as she felt a slight chill in the air, a shiver.

Her thoughts were interrupted by a police siren. Rounding the bend, the top of the squad car flashed the signature blue and red. The car rolled slowly around the loop until it reached Donna's driveway, where the vehicle turned off and its doors popped open almost simultaneously. Rico and Tracy disembarked and moved to greet Donna.

The blonde woman nearly threw herself at Rico.

"Hey, Donna," the man said softly as Donna buried her face in his coat. Donna let out a burst of silent tears, during which Castillo stole a glance to Tracy, who offered an understanding nod.

After a few moments had passed, Donna regained her composure, wiping tears from her face with her gloved hands while taking care to avoid smearing her makeup any more than she already had. "Do you think—" She started, then sniffled and pointed toward the army of children in costumes orbiting along the island's inner road. "Do you think it's safe for them to be out here like this?"

"Don't worry, Donna," Tracy assured her. "We're here to make sure nothing happens." The cop tilted her head and glanced toward the gun holstered at her side, which seemed to give some comfort to Donna. "Metro-Dade's got patrols all over the city tonight, just to be on the safe side," the officer added.

Donna made a few steps down the driveway and craned her neck to spot Starla. The girl was already quite far down the island, but still within shouting distance. If the aunt wanted to call her home, she could easily do so.

Pushing her fears aside, Donna turned back to the cops. "I take it you're not allowed to drink on the job?"

Rico side-smirked. "We try not to."

"How about a couple Cokes?"

Tracy nodded. "That sounds perfect."

"Alright, you two just hang tight and keep an eye on the kids," Donna said, starting toward the house. "I'll be right back."

When the hostess was inside, Rico and Tracy turned to face the street, standing side-by-side. Officer Castillo counted at least fifty kids in costumes, with a few parents guiding along the youngest bunches.

Tracy leaned toward Rico: "You seen the recruit yet?"

Officer Castillo took another look to survey the island road, imagining the entrance beyond the thick central treeline. "He was right behind us leaving the station, so he should be posted up at the entrance to the island by now." Rico took a few steps forward and opened the car door. He withdrew a walkie talkie and clicked the *talk* button a couple times. After double-checking the channel was correct, Castillo held down the button: "Come in, recruit, this is Castillo. What's your 20? Over."

The pair stood in silence for a few seconds. Finally, a response crackled over the comm: "Roger. This is... Recruit Matt Calvin. In position at... front gate. Over."

The young man's voice was uncharacteristically soft and wavering, but the officer chocked it up to the signal quality. "10-4, recruit. Let us know if you see anything fishy. Over."

"10-4," came the quick reply.

Castillo lowered the walkie and looked to Tracy.

"What's up with the signal?" She asked.

Rico shook his head. "I dunno. Probably just a lot of interference with everyone out tonight." He set the walkie on the top of the car and leaned against the vehicle. A boy walked up the driveway dressed in cheap greenish-gray armor and a mask with a t-shaped black visor. *Boba Fett*—Rico recognized the character from his brief appearance in *The Empire Strikes Back*. In the dusk and lantern-glow, the kid nodded casually at the officers and moved toward the house. Rico watched as he arrived at the front step and looked around.

"Where's the candy?" The kid shouted back to them.

Tracy glanced at Rico, who tried to hide a smirk. Rico shook his head quickly and was about to reply when Donna opened the front door and appeared again.

“Oh, so sorry, kiddo,” she said, setting two Coke bottles and a glass on a tiny outdoor side table. Max, the golden puppy, snuck outside through the gap between the door and Donna’s legs. “Forgot the most important thing!” Donna hurried back inside and returned a few seconds later with an enormous basket full of tiny candy bars and other goodies. She held it out as the boy buried both fists in the sea of sweets and withdrew overflowing handfuls. The kid stuffed his bag full, thanked Donna, and ran off toward the next house.

Donna set the basket on the step, grabbed the drinks again, and rejoined the officers at the edge of the driveway. “Here ya go. Ice cold Coca-Cola.”

“What are you sipping?” Rico nodded with his chin as Max nestled himself at the officer’s feet. The man crouched to pet the dog’s soft coat.

Donna, mid-sip, nearly spit, then covered her mouth with her hand and smiled. Donna gulped. “I, uh, spiked some Kool-Aid,” she answered finally. “It’s actually not bad.”

The group was interrupted by the two-beat honking of a high-pitched car horn. All three turned to watch as a baby-blue compact hatchback rolled up the driveway. The windows rolled down and a woman stuck her head out.

It was Sue: “Hey, Don!” She squealed as her counterpart Lisa waved from the other side. Sue turned off the car and they stepped onto the paved drive. Max greeted them with a couple of playful *yaps*.

Donna came in for an embrace, careful not to spill her drink. “Thought you guys weren’t going to make it. It’s already getting dark." She gestured toward the sky, where stars twinkled faintly, and moved around the vehicle to hug Lisa. Her red hair was pulled up in a bun fastened by a scrunchie glued to a plastic bone, and she wore a ragged knee-length dress and a chunky white necklace.

"Wilma Flintstone?" Donna guessed correctly. "I love it."

Sue spotted her brother and Tracy.

"Hey, little sis," Rico smiled as the two went in for a hug. "Nice costume. What are you supposed to be? A janitor?"

Susana was dressed in a gray-blue jumpsuit with semi-circular patches hot-glued to each shoulder. Her black hair hung in its usual tight curls, with an extra puffiness aided by what most certainly had been a full bottle of hairspray. She showed off a pair of white, high-top Converse All-Stars with a flourish of her ankle. "I'm Ripley," she said matter-of-factly.

"Who?"

"Ellen Ripley," Sue offered again, faced with blank looks from both her brother and Tracy. "You know, from *Alien*?"

Rico nodded. "Oh, you mean the one with the—" Here he pressed one arm against his chest then shot his hand out toward his sister, fingers wiggling, in a sudden motion that imitated the chest-bursting creature from the film.

Sue and Lisa both jumped, startled, then the former slapped her brother on the shoulder. "*Not* funny!"

The man slumped his shoulders and muttered to Tracy. "It was kinda funny... right?"

His counterpart rolled her eyes, smiled then nodded toward the street. "We should get going. We're on the clock, remember?"

Officer Castillo moved toward Donna once more and spoke softly. "You gonna be okay?"

She nodded and took a gulp. "Yeah. We'll be fine. Sue and Lisa will keep me company."

He smiled. "Alright, but you just call us if you see anything suspicious, okay?" Here Rico handed her a bulky walkie-talkie. "Just press and hold that button to talk," he added, pointing.

Donna affirmed that she understood and the two officers headed back down the driveway to begin their patrol down the opposite side of the loop from which Starla had run. As they moved under the light of a lamppost, Max started barking. Donna crouched to the dog's level and ran a gloved hand over his golden fur.

"It's okay, buddy," she said. "They'll be back soon."

This seemed to calm the dog somewhat, but he continued to stare off in the direction in which the cops had walked. Donna rubbed under his neck and ears and looked out to make sure she could still see Starla. For a moment, her pulse quickened. *Where is she?* Her eyes flicked from one side of the street to the other. *Starla?* She couldn't see her. Donna stood and took a step forward.

"Donna?" Lisa asked, grabbing her arm. "Everything alright?"

Donna whipped around, exhaling heavily. She looked back toward the street, caught sight of the little skeleton girl, and let out a deep sigh of relief. "Yeah," she answered.

"Everything's fine."

Lisa raised an eyebrow and shot a knowing glance to Sue, who nodded. "You don't *look* fine, Don. If you want, I can go keep an eye on Starla?"

The blonde woman thought it over for a moment. "You sure?"

Her red-headed friend nodded.

"Thanks, Leese." Donna fished into the back pocket of her jeans. "Wait, here you go—" She handed Lisa the polaroid photo of Starla in her skeleton costume and candy bag. "There's a lotta kiddos out there that are dressed alike."

Lisa gratefully accepted the photo. The women hugged, then Lisa hurried off down the long driveway, her chunky fake-rock necklace clacking as she walked.

Sue put an arm around Donna as the two looked down the driveway. "She's okay," said Sue. "Now relax—enjoy yourself a little."

Donna allowed her breathing to slow and took a light sip of her drink. *Everything's fine,* she repeated in her head. *She's fine.*

Officers Castillo and Jones strolled down Star Island Drive, the island's interior road that was devoid of sidewalks and lined instead with palm trees on one side and massive mansions on the other. Halloween was the one night that the homeowners' hedge-bordered front gates were left wide open, allowing floods of Miami-area children to scavenge through what was generally known as the best selection of candy and treats in the entire county.

Rico waved and smiled at an old woman who stood at her curb dressed in a nun's habit. She nodded back as a flock of children in costumes hurried toward her to dig through a large bucket of candy at her feet.

Tracy noticed her partner wince as he lowered his hand again. "How's your arm?"

"Still stings a little," he admitted. "But my nurse cleaned it up pretty well." Here Rico glanced at Tracy out of the corner of his eye.

She met his gaze and cracked a smile.

"I'm serious!" He chuckled. "You did a great job with it—I'm impressed."

"Thanks," Jones answered finally, and the two continued to wade through the sea of costumed children.

As they walked under a street lamp, Rico looked up at it, then reached into his pocket. He took a deep breath, withdrew his clenched-fist from the pocket, and stopped walking.

Tracy had already taken a couple steps further when she realized he was no longer keeping apace. "Rico? You okay?"

He gulped and nodded, and offered a sweaty smile. "More than okay," he muttered.

Officer Jones raised an eyebrow and walked slowly toward him. When Tracy was close enough, Rico lowered himself so that he was crouched on one knee.

Jones started to breathe heavily. "Rico, I—"

"Tracy," he interrupted. "I can't put this off anymore." He held out his fist, still clenched. "You know I'm crazy about you, and I can't imagine going through life without you by my side, and I want to start a family together, and—"

"Rico, we don't have to do this here—"

"I can't wait any longer." The man paused, gulped, then opened his fist. In his outstretched palm sat a simple golden ring.

The woman put a hand over her mouth to hide her shock. She knew the moment was coming, but it had still caught her off guard. Tracy was silent for several moments.

"Y-you don't have to give me an answer right now," Rico offered, trying to fill the space of his own discomfort. "But I have to ask: Tracy Jones, will you—"

"Stop." A tear formed at the corner of Tracy's eye. "Rico, it's..." Tracy started, then thought about her words before continuing. "It's not that simple for me."

His brow furrowed. "What do you mean?"

She took a deep breath. "I mean... I know you want a family, but I can't be a mother."

"Then we'll adopt—"

"That's not what I'm saying."

"Then what *are* you saying, Tracy?" Rico closed his fingers and tightened his grip on the ring again as he stood up.

Tracy's gaze drifted toward the ground. "I was *engaged*, Rico," she said softly, before taking a few breaths. "He had kids—two beautiful little girls. I was... I was looking forward to it—I had dreamed of being a mother my whole life. It was all so... perfect." She closed her eyes.

Rico leaned in.

"Then there was... an accident. And it was all over in an instant. They were gone." She puffed. Here Tracy wiped her eyes with the side of her hand. "Sometimes I still see their smiles—in the faces of passing children on the street," she said with a nod toward the numerous young trick-or-treaters. "It eats me up inside."

"Tracy..."

"I can't go through that again, Rico." She finally looked him in the eyes. "I can't relive that experience knowing that it could all vanish without a moment's notice. Getting attached to kids—to *you*, even. Is it worth the pain—the *agony* of putting my heart—my *everything* into it just for it to be taken away?"

Castillo didn't have an answer. He clenched his fingers around the ring. "If you just need some more time...?" He trailed off, then slowly tucked the ring back into his pocket.

Tracy lowered her head, breathed in and out. She was about to speak when a loud barking sound echoed up the street. Both officers whipped toward it. It was faint, distant—originating from one of the houses closer to the island's entrance.

Tracy and Rico made brief eye-contact, nodded, then took off, jogging toward the sound.

There were fewer children in this section of the neighborhood, mostly a result of the darkened lights of a couple large houses whose owners didn't wish to participate in the giving of candy and treats. This made the officers' journey more swift, at least, and they slowed their pace to listen for the sound again.

This time, the barking had turned to more of a whimper—a pained, struggling sound.

Not good.

"It's coming from over there." Tracy pointed toward a hedge-lined property with a wrought-iron front gate. The gate was closed, chained with a padlock, but as they reached it the whimpers grew louder.

All of the property's lights were turned off, and there were no cars visible near the house. In the dim moonlight, however, both officers could sense some motion on the driveway. The pair pressed their bodies to the gate to get as close as possible, then Rico clicked on a flashlight.

Tracy gasped and Rico's hand went instinctively to his gun. There in the middle of the long, paved driveway was the source of the whimpering: it appeared to be some breed of terrier, but it was difficult to tell, for the creature was barely breathing. The dog's body was shriveled, like it had been sucked dry of its blood. The pavement beneath it was stained a dark reddish-maroon.

Rico shook his head as he took in the horrifying scene. "What the...?"

Tracy narrowed her eyes. "What do you think could have done this?"

He didn't answer immediately. Instead, Rico shifted the flashlight to the left, illuminating more of the driveway. "I don't think it's a *what*, Trace." There on the concrete were sets of bloody footprints, leading straight up to the gate, where they terminated abruptly. "I think it's a *who*." Rico knelt lower and shined the beam at the closest print: the shape of a bare, human foot.

Officer Jones didn't have time to make a response before she heard more barking—this time coming from back at the other end of the street from which they'd come.

Tracy angled herself to hear better. "Is that—?"

"Max!" Rico realized. "Something's wrong."

The street lamp nearest to them flickered above, almost like a power surge.

Officer Jones looked up at it, puzzled. "What the—?"

"We *have* to get back to Donna's place," Rico said, grabbing Tracy's hand. "*Now!*"

CHAPTER 14

"We're almost out of 3 Musketeers!" Sue called out to Donna from the front stoop, digging through the remaining goodies in the large bowl. A couple of kids dressed as ghosts swooped in and grabbed handfuls of candy then scampered off back down the long driveway. "Actually, scratch that; we're totally out," Sue shouted again.

"There's another bag on the kitchen counter," Donna hollered from her position at the gate near the road.

While Sue hurried inside, Donna turned and looked out across the road. As her enormous home sat at the tip of the island, she had an almost-straight sightline down both sides of the street loop. Donna felt a slight chill and wrapped her arms close.

Suddenly, Max let out a shrill *bark-bark!*

The sound startled Donna, who turned and hurried toward the golden retriever. "What is it, boy?" She crouched beside him and tried to follow the pet's gaze as he continued to yap, louder than before.

"What's got you all upset, Maxie?" Donna scratched the dog's neck with a gloved hand and looked out down one street, then flicked her eyes to the other. Her pulse quickened.

Way down at the farthest end of the palm-tree-lined avenue, Donna thought she saw a streetlamp burn out, followed by another—the next one. Then the next one. No. She wasn't imagining it. There was another. Then another.

Something was moving down the street—moving toward her.

No.

Not something.

Some*one*.

Marcus.

Lisa waded through the sea of costumed children. It seemed that almost every child in the neighborhood was Starla's exact height, and the majority of kids had masks covering their faces.

Of course. Lisa sighed, then decided to try a new method of locating the girl. "Starla? Are any of you Starla Gordon?"

No answer.

Lisa continued walking slowly as she looked down at the polaroid photo that Donna had given her. The ink at the bottom read: *Starla, Halloween 1981.*

In the photo, Starla was holding a paper bag and dressed in all-black, with skeleton bones painted in white down the front of her clothes. Her skull mask was lifted so that Lisa could see the girl's mischievous scowl, looking off to the side of the frame.

Where are you, kiddo?

Lisa raised her head as she took another step forward. Her eyelids fluttered quickly as a costumed adult brushed past her—closer than she had expected.

"Hey, watch it!" She turned and shouted after them. The figure never turned to glance back, so Lisa didn't get a good look at the person's face. Lisa shook her head and muttered under her breath: "Dummy. He oughta look where he's going—"

As she pivoted back in the direction she'd been walking, Lisa collided with another tall grown-up in a costume. *Oof!* This time, both Lisa and the other figure fell backwards, crash-landing on the rough pavement. Lisa released her grip on the photograph so she could soften her landing with both hands, and winced as she felt the gravelly ground digging into her palms. Her bone-shaped hair clip had dislodged itself, so a few strands of reddish hair hung haphazardly across Lisa's forehead.

The other person's fall had made quite a clatter, as the individual was dressed from head-to-toe in a suit of armor.

Lisa hurried over to help the stranger rise from the road. "So sorry, I wasn't looking..." As she approached, Lisa realized the armor was real metal. *Woah. That's commitment—especially in this heat!* "Here," she extended a hand. "Let me help you up."

The stranger's face was obscured by a helmet—the kind like a conquistador might've worn, with a faceplate covering the mouth and nose—but the two made eye-contact through a narrow slit. The stranger accepted Lisa's help. The woman pulled, lifting the other from the ground.

The armor-wearer stood up straight, around the same height as Lisa. "Thanks, niña," said the voice from within the helmet.

A woman's voice—she sounds old. "D-don't mention it," Lisa stammered. "Nice costume, by the way."

The armored woman nodded, then looked down toward her hand, where she held up a small squarish object: the polaroid of Starla. The old-voiced woman seemed to study it for a moment too long. Lisa started to fidget as the woman handed her the photo.

"Is that your daughter?"

Lisa shook her head. "Friend's daughter. I'm trying to locate her at the moment," she again began to scan the crowd. "She's out here somewhere."

"Good luck," said the stranger, then she abruptly continued on her original path, brushing past Lisa.

Huh. Lisa stared after her for a moment before shaking her head. *What a weird individual.*

Just then, Lisa heard barking—first from up the street near Donna's house, then in the other direction. A chorus of *yaps* at all pitches and frequencies.

"Starla?" Lisa muttered too softly to be heard. Then, when the barking continued to grow louder, she shouted:

"Starla, where are you, kid?" The woman started running, frantic, snapping her vision in each direction to try and spot the skeleton-garbed girl.

Then she froze. The farthest end of the street—near the entry to the island—had suddenly grown dark. Lisa took deep breaths as she watched the lampposts turn off one-by-one. No. They weren't turning off—their light was being taken. Drawn out by some invisible force. It was still a long way off, but now Lisa could begin to discern the shape of that force.

It was a man in the street. He made motions with his hands, as if pulling the light itself toward him—no—*into* him. Another figure walked at his side, keeping the pace. The pair moved quickly.

Lisa cursed under her breath then started running back toward the house. "Starla!" She hollered as she passed by children. "Starla, where are you?" She spotted a child in all-black and grabbed them by the shoulder. The child turned, frightened, revealing a boy with a half-eaten candy bar in his mouth. "Have you seen Starla?"

The boy shook his head, confused.

With another puff and a glance over her shoulder, Lisa again took off toward Donna's house. The darkness grew nearer. She made a final, fruitless sweep of the crowd before sprinting the rest of the way up to Donna's gate.

Donna's heart raced when she saw Lisa approaching without Starla.

"What happened? Where is she?"

Lisa shook her head, tears beginning to form at the edges

of her eyes. "I couldn't find her. I'm sorry, Donna, I—"

Sue returned with a bag of candy from inside the house, set it on the front step, then joined the other ladies at the edge of the driveway.

"We have to find her before *he* does."

Sue leaned in. "Before *who* does, Donna?"

Donna stood mesmerized, looking out toward the darkened lamps.

"Marcus. He's coming."

Calvin allowed the car to idle in an alleyway as he took nervous breaths. He rolled down the windows and twisted the key to turn off the vehicle, then exhaled slowly as he allowed himself to relax—only slightly—into the well-worn driver's seat.

Through the windshield, the recruit had a clear view of the Orange Street Mortuary & Funeral Home. There was a warm glow from the upstairs window—the spot that Dr. Blanche called her home—but the rest of the building remained darkened. With the car lights turned off, Calvin was confident he couldn't be seen by the doctor if she happened to peek outside, but he sunk down a little further just to be sure.

The long-range walkie crackled, startling the recruit. He turned the knob and clicked it into the *off* position, once again bringing quiet to the car. The young man set his hand on the door latch and took deep breaths. *Castillo's gonna kill me.* He wasn't entirely sure *what* he would find—if anything—but Calvin wasn't about to let go of a hunch—even if it meant disobeying orders for a few minutes.

With the windows half-lowered, the recruit listened to the distant sounds of late-night traffic. It was almost calming, peaceful. He checked his watch then flicked his eyes back up to the mortuary. *Running out of time. You can do this, Calvin. C'mon.*

He closed his eyes, inhaled deeply, then pushed open the door. Calvin closed it softly then started up toward the house.

Deep breaths.

I can't believe I'm doing this.

Calvin wasn't even sure what "*this*" meant yet—he was formulating the plan as he approached. *Break in and find some incriminating files? Interrogate Dr. Blanche myself and get her to confess to some involvement with the missing bodies?* None of these ideas had *actual* plans attached to them. But he kept walking, sticking as closely as possible to the shadows and walls of the adjacent high-rises.

As he reached the building closest to the mortuary and funeral home, Calvin paused. He looked all directions, checked that there was no one around, then darted across the pavement toward the side door through which Dr. Blanche had led them the prior night. The recruit slowly reached out his fingers and turned the door handle.

Locked. Of course. Drat.

Standing in the dark, Calvin considered his options. *Find a way to break in. Knock and ask nicely to speak with Eudora. Or leave.* He definitely wasn't about to leave, and the young man was sure the old doctor wouldn't be inclined to change her story just because he asked nicely.

Guess that means one thing: I'm breaking in.

The recruit felt his hands shaking as he reached into a pocket and withdrew his wallet. He pulled out a thick plastic credit card, looked around again, then carefully inserted a corner of the card into the gap between the door's lock and the frame.

They make this look so easy in the movies, he thought with a mindless bite of his lip. Calvin jiggled the card a little more. He was fairly confident he was doing it right. *Just have to get the card far enough in there to—*

A sound from the street startled him: a car engine. Calvin froze and whipped toward it. The vehicle rumbled around the corner at the end of the block, revealing a shiny black coat and heavily-tinted windows. The recruit was almost certain he'd be spotted, for the car came straight in the direction of the building, its front facing directly toward him. To his relief, however, the headlights were turned off.

That's a little shady...

Ideas flashed in Calvin's mind. He looked around then dove behind a set of prickly bushes that ran along the walls of the mortuary. The recruit tried not to breathe as he lay with his chest to the ground. Calvin was relieved to find that he had a partial visual on the car from this vantage point—a small patch between the leaves and bramble.

The engine continued to run while a door opened on the passenger side of the sleek black car. A figure in dark clothing stepped out onto the pavement. Calvin couldn't discern the stranger's face or identity, but the enigma looked like a man. He was tall and walked with purpose—right toward the mortuary's side door. Calvin tensed. *He'll see me!*

The man knocked on the door—a firm and specific series of seven quick raps—then took a step back to wait. *Some sort of code signal?*

Calvin gulped. The wait was agonizing. The recruit hadn't had much time to situate himself, but he realized now that he'd crouched in an uncomfortable position, with a root jabbing into his thigh.

Before he could think on it too much, though, Calvin shifted his focus again. The door clicked, unlocked from the inside, and inched open slowly.

"Trick or treat?" The man's voice was deep and dry, and his half-obscured face showed the slightest hint of a grin.

Eudora's head appeared in the doorway, her gray-white hair hanging in a tousled mess as she scanned the street. She whispered: "What are you doing here?"

"You said there were *developments*," the man answered.

"What if someone *sees* you, Rolf?"

The man waited before responding. "Then we'll tell them the truth—that I was just paying a visit to my old professor."

"Keep your voice down," Dr. Blanche hissed.

Rolf grinned again. "What are the developments, doctor?"

Calvin's mind turned again to the lumpy root under his leg. He winced and tried not to make a sound.

"The *police* were here last night," Eudora whispered.

"And?"

"They were asking questions."

"But you didn't give them any answers, did you?"

Eudora puffed. "No, but—"

"Relax, doctor. We *specifically* chose subjects with no living family or relations so that there would be no one to come along and mess this up—there's no one for these cops to interrogate."

"But they were asking *lots* of questions," Dr. Blanche continued. "And I know they suspect something." She paused. "Have you destroyed the tapes yet?"

"As I've told you many times, I have no intentions of destroying them. There's too much valuable research. And leverage."

"That's what I'm afraid of."

Rolf considered her words and glanced over his shoulder before speaking again. "They're in a safe place. You don't need to worry. You just focus on finishing your final task."

"And what about the Nightmare Array?"

"The Nightmare Array is complete—thanks to your work—and will ensure that all loose ends are... tidied up. You have nothing to worry about except making sure that you and the package are on that plane tomorrow night."

"You still haven't told me where we're going."

"Somewhere *they* won't find you." Rolf's voice was stern and decisive, and seemed to put an end to the conversation.

They heard a vehicle approaching down the street. The duo froze in the shadows as it passed by slowly, then continued driving.

"I should go." The man stuffed a hand in a jacket pocket and withdrew a small piece of paper, which he placed in Eudora's hand. "Here. See you on the tarmac. Don't be late."

Dr. Blanche looked at the paper. Calvin presumed that the mysterious flight's details were written on the note.

Without another word, Rolf proceeded down the pavement, got into the black car, and shut the door. The vehicle sped away as Eudora went back inside, locking the door behind her.

Calvin took quick breaths as he waited a few extra moments before climbing out of the bushes, then he sprinted across the lot and back toward the car. His adrenaline was pumping.

Castillo and Jones are never gonna believe this.

"I don't believe it," Tracy muttered under her breath as she ran beside Rico, the walkie in her hand. "He won't answer."

"Lemme try." Jones handed the walkie to Rico, who clicked the talk button. "Calvin! Come in, recruit! Do you copy? This is an emergency—we're headed for Donna's house—we need backup! Do you *copy?*"

Again, there was no response from the other end of the radio.

The officers had almost reached Donna's house when Rico glanced to his left. The lamps on the parallel street burned out one-by-one, just a few steps behind the officers. "C'mon, Trace. Almost there. Keep going."

The cool October breeze brushed past them as the officers reached the final stretch of the road toward Donna's home. Rico spotted Donna with Sue and Lisa at the edge of the driveway as they rounded the slight bend. The three women were huddled close, their gaze transfixed on the opposite stretch of road.

Rico and Tracy made it to the driveway, exchanging quick hugs with their friends to provide some sort of solace before returning their attention to the approaching darkness.

"It's Marcus," Donna whispered to the new arrivals. "And he's not alone."

Tracy looked around, saw Max, then asked. "Where's Starla?"

Donna's glassy eyes spoke clearly before any of the words came out of her mouth: "She's still out there."

Now, the group looked on. The last couple of the lampposts flickered, doing little to illuminate the approaching figures. Finally, they reached the top of the road's curve—just feet from the edge of Donna's driveway. Officer Castillo clicked on his flashlight, but the light immediately went dark. The moonlight gave just enough of a glow for the officer to make out the shape of the figure at the front of the pack: Marcus, his hand stretched out toward the darkened flashlight.

So it's true, thought Rico, his mouth agape. *Everything Donna said...*

Marcus stepped forward, out of a palm tree's moonshadow. He was accompanied by a handful of other figures, whose shapes and faces were still hard for the onlookers to discern as they lingered in the darkness.

Donna took a half-step forward. "Marcus, what are you doing here?" There was a tinge of hopefulness in her voice—hope that *her* Marcus was still in there, that this was all just a bad dream, a nightmare from which she would awaken any moment.

"He's here for the same reason we *all* are." The voice that responded to Donna did not belong to Marcus. It came from one of the figures behind him: a woman shrouded in a long, reddish overcoat.

Donna shot a look of concern to Rico. The voice sounded all too familiar, though it had been what felt like ages since she'd last heard it in person.

"We're here to clean up a mess," the obscured woman continued. "And to take what belongs to us."

Sue shouted at her: "What are you talking about? Who are you?"

Here the woman finally took a few steps forward, into the moonlight. Her red covering was accented by a matching-colored mask fashioned into the face of a dragon. Carefully, she raised her hands to the mask and removed it.

Donna's suspicions were confirmed. Before her stood a woman she hadn't seen up close—face-to-face—since the fateful day Marcus turned to gold: Angela Hyde.

Angela grinned, apparently gratified by Donna's baffled expression. "Good to see you again, Miss Locke. It's been awhile."

CHAPTER 15

Donna Locke clung tighter to Sue and Lisa as Angela appeared at Marcus' side. The rest of the figures near them still hung in shadows—Marcus had seemingly absorbed all of the lamp lights, leaving only the moon and a few carved pumpkins with votive candles to illuminate the street at the edge of Donna's driveway. The breeze fluttered the tiny flames in jack-o-lanterns placed along the curb and swept stray strands of blonde hair across Donna's face. As she looked out across the darkened streets, she saw that there were still a few children and families trick-or-treating in the dark, oblivious to the danger imminent at the end of the loop.

Starla's still out there. Where are you, kiddo?

Her shifting eyes settled back on the man before her. "Marcus, *please*," Donna asked earnestly. "Whatever she's told you, it's a lie."

The man's face was stoic. He didn't immediately respond,

and Donna wasn't sure he'd even heard her words until, finally, Marcus looked her straight in the eyes and answered: "I remember everything, Donna. *You* almost killed me. But Miss Hyde was there to save me."

Sue squeezed Donna a little tighter; she could sense the pain Marcus' words inflicted.

Donna's attention shifted back to Angela, who took another step forward, removed her hood and cocked her head. Her long, dark hair spilled out over her shoulders in tight, voluminous curls.

"Nice gloves," Angela sneered. "Did Roger make them for you?"

Donna didn't respond. She clenched her fingers.

"Too bad you didn't have them sooner," Angela continued. "Could've saved us all a *lot* of trouble—"

"Get to the point, *doctor*," Donna spat, her eyes finally starting to adjust to the darkness, where the shapes of the people in the shadows were becoming clearer. Donna counted three others, besides Marcus and Angela.

Angela sauntered toward Donna, her heels clacking as the red cloak dragged across the pavement. "I've already told you. We're here to clean up a mess." Here the dark-haired woman reached into the folds of her garment and withdrew a small, glimmering dagger.

Donna flinched and started to move one of her hands toward the glove on the other.

"Not so fast." Angela thrust the dagger toward Donna, stopping just shy of her neck, then eyed the still-gloved hand.

"You wouldn't dare."

Donna raised an eyebrow. "Don't try me." Between heavy, nervous breaths, she added softly, "Let him go."

Angela offered a disingenuous, wicked smile. "I assure you, Miss Locke: Marcus is here of his own accord. Now, be a good girl and don't make this any harder than it needs to be."

Donna glanced past Angela's shoulder to steal another look at Marcus. *I don't believe it—I can't believe that Marcus isn't under some sort of spell, some hypnosis, some weird science...*

Rico raised his handgun, pointed it at Angela—he couldn't bring himself to aim it toward Marcus, but the cop knew the moment might come. *He's my partner. Even if he doesn't remember it.* Officer Castillo waved the gun toward the figures behind them in the shadows, who had begun to look more familiar. "Who are they?" He shouted to no one in particular.

"Oh, how rude of me," Angela turned, lowering her dagger from Donna's throat. "I believe you've already met some of my... friends." Here she motioned toward the trio. Each stepped forward into the light—a horrifying lineup.

First, there was a man whose face seemed to be missing. Rico glanced at Tracy, recognizing the figure instantly. Castillo thought he felt his arm tingle, the phantom sting from the faceless man's shovel-swinging in the graveyard.

The next of the figures seemed only half human: he bore the body of a man, stocky and broad-shouldered, but his hands, feet, neck, and head were *far* from human. Instead, these body parts were those of a large, gray-green reptile—an alligator.

Sue whispered to Donna: "Those are *some* costumes. They really went all out for tonight."

"I, uh, don't think those are costumes, Sue."

The last of the three wore a tattered cloak that floated and fluttered slowly in the breeze. She had the face of a woman, half-obscured under a hood, and her skin was blotchy and rough. In her spindly, knobby fingers, she held a small animal—a limp and emaciated dalmatian puppy. Max whimpered and hid behind Donna's legs.

When she'd staved off the instinct to retch, Tracy's eyes moved lower, toward the shrively, cloaked woman's feet. *She's barefoot!* Upon closer inspection, the officer's suspicions were further confirmed: the subject's feet were covered in what appeared to be blood.

The sight of the strange ensemble only quickened Donna's pulse. She felt the edge of her glove on her right hand. With a deep breath, she tugged it with her left hand, baring her palm. Donna held it out, fingers spread and threatened, "Not a step closer or I'll *do* it!"

Angela twirled her dagger and smiled. "You're bluffing."

Donna kept her arm outstretched. *Am I?* She wondered. Turning another human to gold was as cruel a punishment as any, and almost as final as death—unless one had the ingredients and the expertise to develop a cure like Roger had. Still, Donna had serious reservations about it. Turning someone to gold was a last resort. Self-defense.

At that moment, the withered barefoot woman dropped

the remains of the dalmatian, where it fell to the pavement with a limp thump. She walked—no, *floated*—toward Donna and her friends.

"Get away from her!" Rico shouted, tightening his grip on his gun.

The barefoot woman kept moving.

"I said stop!"

Rico hesitated a second longer then pulled the trigger.

The blast was almost deafening—and the silence that followed it even more so. The woman in the cloak stopped in her tracks, angled her neck toward Castillo, then cocked her head to the side. She looked down at her torso, the place where a bullet hole *should* have been, but there was no hole.

"Uh, Rico?" Lisa spoke up and pointed toward the thick column that acted as one half of Donna's front gate. A large chunk of stucco had fallen off, blown away by the bullet, directly behind the floating lady.

What the—? Rico raised his eyebrows involuntarily.

"Who *are* you people?" Lisa wailed.

"They aren't *people* at all," Sue muttered a quiet reply, shaking her head.

"This is the Nightmare Array," Angela spoke again. "And if you and your friends are done playing games, Miss Locke, we have a job to finish." She pointed the knife at Donna once more.

"So you're just going to kill us all and be on your way?" Donna asked with a slight snicker, her hand still poised. "Not gonna happen."

"We aren't going to kill *all* of you," Angela replied. "Yet, anyway."

Before the group could process Angela's words, there was a shrill scream from down the street—it was a little girl's squeal.

Donna's eyes shot to the right, piercing through the thinning crowd of trick-or-treaters to the shape of a tall figure clutching a small girl. The girl wore an all-black get-up with a skeleton mask.

"Starla!" Donna screamed. "Get your hands off of her!"

The figure approached, wandering toward the group. When the kidnapper stepped into the moonlight, their identity became clearer: she wore the familiar, ancient armor of a conquistador, and a few strands of silvery hair peeked out from underneath the helmet.

Lisa recognized the armor from her collision with the woman earlier. The red-haired woman withdrew the polaroid photo of Starla and looked it over in the dim moonlight.

"Let her go!" Donna demanded. She wanted to run toward the girl, but Donna knew it would be foolish. She had no plan, and if she wasn't careful she could end up turning Starla into gold again. Donna took deep breaths and tried to hold back tears. "Why are you doing this, Angela?"

"We're here to finish what he started."

"He? Who is *he?*" Donna said the words out loud, but feared she already knew the answer.

Angela smirked. "Why, *Ducane* of course. You're one of his experiments that went awry, and you know far too much—you *all* do." Here she paused as if considering how much to say. "Ducane wants all of you—dead or alive." Hyde thrust the knife toward Donna once more. "He's already tried *alive*."

Donna's lip quivered as she watched the little skeleton girl wriggle and writhe, still clutching her candy bucket. "Marcus, you have to call them off—this is all a big misunderstanding—"

"No, Donna," Marcus answered calmly, his palms emitting a strange, flickering glow. "This is what *has* to be done. You're *dangerous*." He furrowed his brow; in his expression there was not even a hint of that kind, gracious man Donna once knew.

"W-whatever you do," Donna blurted out, "don't hurt her—don't hurt Starla!"

The girl kicked and squirmed. "Let me *go!*" The armored, frightening knight held her tightly, seemingly impervious to the masked child's actions. "I promise I only took one candy bar!"

Donna was furious and afraid. "If you lay *one* finger on her, I'll—"

Lisa elbowed Donna in the side and subtly nodded her head toward the polaroid of Starla.

"Not now, Leese," Donna dismissed.

"No," Lisa insisted in a whisper through clenched teeth. "Look. The candy bucket."

Candy bucket? Donna glanced quickly at the photo, then back to the writhing girl in the skeleton costume. *Starla didn't have a bucket; she had a bag!*

"Let me go!" The girl continued to shout, flailing the orange pumpkin-shaped bucket. "I wanna go home—"

The conquistador yanked the skeleton mask from the girl's head, allowing a tangle of blonde hair to spill out. Her eyes grew large as she examined the odd and terrifying gathering of adults. She locked eyes with Donna. "Miss Donna?"

"Tiffany!" Donna breathed a sigh of momentary relief that Starla had eluded capture, but this was immediately followed by another surge of fear and dread.

"That isn't her," Marcus said through gritted teeth.

Angela turned to Donna. "Where is she? Where's the girl?"

The nine-year-old girl in the homemade skeleton costume ran through the shadows. She could hear the sounds of delighted trick-or-treaters fading away behind her as she ran parallel to a thick wall that divided the neighbor's property from her home on the other side. The top of Donna's mansion was visible over the edge of the wall when Starla glanced to her right, but she didn't stop jogging until she came to a section of the stucco covered in vines.

Starla threw aside her skull mask and her bag full of candy and stuck her hands into the greenery. She felt around until her fingers gripped wood. The old trellis, fashioned in a crisscross pattern, made a perfect ladder. She'd climbed it many times when her aunt wasn't watching. The secret was taking each step slowly, to make sure her hands and feet slotted into the obscured grips.

The moonlight cast fluttering shadows over that segment of the wall as Starla pulled herself up the trellis. She climbed slowly, gradually. When she was near the top of the wall, Starla reached up and felt for the next grip. It was shrouded in thick, leafy vines, so the girl wasn't sure if she'd grabbed the right thing. She took a deep breath, wrapped her fingers around it, and released her weight to pull herself up.

Snap! The wood gave way, cracked in two. Starla reached out with her other hand and her fingers latched on to another grip, this time more secure. As she hung flat against the garden wall, she took deep breaths. When she'd composed herself, Starla started climbing once more, this time moving slow enough to test the hand-holds more thoroughly.

When she reached the top of the wall, Starla swung her body over it and dangled her feet off the other side, now facing the three-story mansion that she called home. As it was so deep into the lot, this part of the wall was shielded from views of the street, so Starla breathed easily knowing she would be invisible to her aunt or any curious passersby.

The girl eyed an upstairs window—darkened and dim. She examined the distance between the wall and the house. A narrow-trunked palm tree stood tall, close to the side of the house, and sprouted up past the window.

I can make it, Starla told herself.

If she jumped, she could land halfway up the tree trunk and shimmy the rest of the way up to the window.

Deep breaths.

She poised herself along the top of the wall, bent her legs, then launched, pushing away. Starla sailed through the air—several feet—and reached out her arms. Like a spider-monkey, she touched the tree and immediately wrapped her arms around it. Her face pressed against the trunk and she winced. It was covered in splintery spikes that poked at her cheek.

Ouch. Starla breathed a sigh of relief that she'd made it across the chasm—and that the rest of her body and hands were spared a splintery fate on account of her long-sleeved costume. She leaned her head around the tree and realized she was closer to the window than she'd intended. She stretched one foot toward a section of roof that protruded out between the first and second floors. It touched. Carefully, Starla swung her body around the tree and managed to transfer herself onto the roof.

She took another moment to breathe, then turned toward the window. She scrambled up the slight incline, gripped the window, and pulled upwards. With only a little resistance, the window screeched open and the girl climbed inside.

Starla closed the window behind her and felt around the dark space. She was in a room reserved for guests (not that they had many). She hurried toward the door into the hall. The girl ran quietly, her soft shoes barely making a sound on the carpet.

Finally, she reached a closed door. Starla clicked it open and walked inside. The faint hum of machinery and electronics could be heard immediately as the girl stepped across the bedroom floor. Slivers of moonlight danced through gaps in the blinds, casting parallel lines across the woman asleep on the bed in the center of the room.

Mom.

Starla moved closer and sat in the chair beside the bed. She reached out and felt Sondra's hand; it was cold but there was still a discernible pulse.

"Hey, mom," the girl whispered. "It's me." Starla waited, hoping for some sign that her mother was listening—or at least aware of the girl's presence. But there seemed to be no change in her pulse or brain activity. The displays monitoring Sondra's vitals remained unchanged.

"I need to know something," Starla started. "I need to *try* again. Aunt Donna says I might have powers—like hers, but different." The girl squeezed her mother's hand a little tighter. "So I'm going to try again, okay?"

Starla settled into a more relaxed position in the chair, still gripping her mother's hand. The girl closed her eyes and began to breathe in and out, slowing her heart rate. *Focus. Breathe. Reach out.*

She had no idea what she was doing, or if it would even work. But she was sure it had happened before—that she'd heard her mother's thoughts. Now, like a good scientist, she was doing everything she could to replicate the circumstances as closely as possible, to see if the proverbial lightning would strike twice and prove her hypothesis correct.

I'm listening. Searching. I don't see anything...

The girl let out a dejected breath and opened her eyes. Her

mother's expression had seemed calm when she walked in, but now Starla thought she discerned a hint of some other emotion. *Worry? Sadness?*

No.

Fear. Or regret.

Starla leaned in and closed her eyes once more. *I can do this. Listen. Focus. Breathe. What are you thinking?*

Another long moment passed and Starla began to grow discouraged. Then, with her eyes shut, Starla saw something: a faint glow in the darkness. It undulated, a blob of light until it scattered into smaller dots, which gradually spread out into an image.

Starla kept her eyes shut, trying to focus.

The scene became clearer. With her eyes closed, Starla envisioned her hand holding something small, flat, rectangular. A blurry photograph—no, her vision itself was blurry.

Only it wasn't *her* vision at all. The hand became clearer. It wasn't Starla's; it was from someone much older. *Mom? This is you. I'm seeing inside your mind... a memory?*

Starla shifted her mental gaze back to the photograph. There were three figures in the image, all standing in some sort of laboratory. One-by-one their faces gained detail—two men and one woman. Starla's pulse quickened. She knew these faces, and it frightened her. With her eyes still shut, Starla watched as the memory-scene continued to play out.

No, wait. I don't understand. What is that? Where are we?

The girl took short, furtive breaths as images played and flashed. In her periphery, Starla heard a sound growing—like a motor. An engine.

A car? Moving fast.

The girl's eyes snapped open as she realized the sound was not part of her mother's memory; it was happening just outside the house. Starla released Sondra's hand and ran to the window. Down past the long driveway, she could see a pair of headlights. The car accelerated at breakneck speed down the island's interior loop—headed right toward the house and a group of people near the edge of the driveway.

Aunt Donna's down there!

The car horn blared. Starla's eyes betrayed her shock as the car screeched into a sharp turn. It collided with one of the figures in the street then spun over, smashing into a column of the front gate. The girl held her breath as smoke began to drift from the disfigured, damaged vehicle.

CHAPTER 16

"Let me go!" Tiffany shouted and squirmed. "I don't know where Starla is!"

Angela rolled her eyes then nodded to the woman in the conquistador suit. "Go ahead—she's not the one we want."

The armored woman complied and set the girl down. As soon as the woman's grip was released, little Tiffany took off running down the loop toward the island's exit, tossing her candy bucket aside. When the child had vanished into the shadows, all eyes turned back to Angela.

"Kill them all," she scowled. "Then find the girl."

Her companions began to move forward slowly, closing in on Donna and her friends.

"Marcus," Donna pleaded once more. "You don't have to do this. Please understand that what happened to you was an accident—"

"Why should I listen to anything you say?"

"Because," Donna searched for something to say—anything that might sway him. "I spent an entire *year* looking for you—to find a way to *fix* the biggest mistake I ever made."

"Turning me to gold?" Marcus planted himself in a ready stance and held his arms out at his sides, their glow growing brighter.

"No, Marcus. My biggest mistake was letting you go."

Donna took deep breaths, waiting for him to reply, hoping she could get through to him and snap him back to reality. She noticed a flutter of his lip, a slight glint in his eyes. *I know you're in there. I know you know the truth—*

"That's really touching, Donna," Marcus replied softly, his head downturned. "But lying to me again—to my face?" He looked her in the eyes. "That's the last mistake you'll ever make."

Donna held back tears. *He's really gone, then.*

"I told you, Donna. You can't stop what's coming." Marcus raised his arms and moved his palms to face toward the group. He flinched as he listened to the faint sound of a revving car engine in the distance. It seemed to be growing louder, closer.

The man with the head of an alligator took a few more steps in, then let out a chilling, gurgling roar, scum and slime dripping from his dozens of sharp teeth. The creature moved faster, starting to run toward Donna with heavy leaps.

Rico fired his gun—two shots at the pavement that stopped the gator-man in his tracks.

"Get back, you revolting son-of-a—"

Beeeeeep! A shrill car horn sounded from behind the gathered array of monsters and enemies. Every head turned toward the noise at once. The gator-man was the last to turn. His beady eyes dilated as two bright white headlights drowned him in their beams. *Smash!* The vehicle braked, collided with the creature, throwing the car into the air in a spin. A moment later, the car smashed into one of the columns of Donna's front gate, while the gator-man was pinned—motionless—between the wall and the car. The vehicle was upside-down, totaled, and began to emit thick, blackish smoke.

Tracy had wrangled Sue, Lisa, and Donna just in time to clear the area, while Rico hurled himself out of the way of the car. When he rose to his feet, Officer Castillo had placed himself between his friends and the eclectic cadre that wanted them all dead.

From within the smoke and haze, someone started coughing. The sound came from the overturned car. The windows had been shattered and the driver was still in his seat, belt fastened in place. The onlookers watched as the man struggled and freed himself of his bonds then shimmied across shards of broken glass as he climbed out through the broken window. Finally, he stood, his back slightly hunched, and faced the small crowd.

"Declan!" Donna gasped. She started toward him from the driveway, but he held up a hand for her to stay back.

"I'm fine," Declan shouted, wincing. His arms were scratched and bleeding. He was *far* from fine, but he wasn't about to let Donna foil his attempt to save the day.

Angela fanned a wisp of smoke from her face as she reassessed the situation. "Well, there's a face I haven't seen in a long time."

"Miss Hyde," Declan said, gritting his teeth. "What an unpleasant surprise. Still trying to impress my dad by doing his dirty work?" The battered man couldn't see her expression in the smoke and darkness, but he was certain she wasn't smiling.

Donna squinted through the thick smoke. *What's he doing? He's going to get himself killed—along with all of us!*

"He and I have a deal," Angela answered.

"C'mon, Angela. I thought you were an independent woman?" Declan continued, glancing around near his feet. "But then again, you'll never be *truly* independent until you step out of the shadow of the great Rolf Ducane."

The overturned car had landed with its back end facing the onlookers. The trunk had popped open when it crashed, littering the street with its odd and assorted contents. From the corner of his eye, Declan inventoried a car jack, tangled jumper cables, and a crowbar. *Crowbar! That'll do.* He inched closer to it, keeping his body angled toward Angela.

"When we finish this job," Angela explained, "I'll cast my own shadow, and Rolf Ducane will barely be a footnote in the history books."

Declan moved closer. He could reach the crowbar if he crouched. "You won't finish the job, Angela."

"Why's that?" She seemed flustered.

"Simple," Declan grinned. "You're outnumbered. There's more of us than you." His smirk slowly sank into a frown as he locked eyes on the woman in the conquistador suit. "Oh, great. You again?"

As in their previous encounter, Declan watched as the woman's body contorted, morphed, and split into two identical entities, both clothed in the ancient armor and each holding a long, sharp blade.

"Terrific," Declan mumbled under his breath.

Angela leaned toward Marcus. "Kill him," she said loud enough for all to hear.

Donna shrieked. "Dec! Look out!"

Declan gulped as he watched Marcus raise his glowing palms toward him. They grew brighter then let out a blast of light. Declan leaped to the ground. He rolled, grabbing the crowbar and evading the deadly white-hot beams.

The blasts grazed the rear of the car, blowing through one of the tires.

Declan clutched the heavy metal implement as he refocused his attention on the foes ahead. He felt something wet on his hand and looked down: a pipe had been punctured in the wreck, causing fuel to leak on the street and into the gutter-swale that ran across the edge of Donna's driveway. In a few moments, the paved indentation would be full of gasoline.

Beside him, Declan sensed motion. His eyebrows raised involuntarily as he watched the half-gator-half-man struggle and work his way out from underneath the mangled car. He limped, clearly wounded, as he ripped free of his own tail, leaving it writhing under the massive weight.

"You've gotta be kidding me," Declan puffed. He whipped around in time to see one of the two conquistadors running at him with her sword drawn. Declan thrust the crowbar toward her, blocking the attack. She then tried again. This time, Declan ducked quickly, and the sword lodged itself in one of car tires. The woman seemed caught off-guard and frustrated, so Declan smirked and swung the crowbar, bashing her helmet off her head. "That's for last night."

Officer Jones joined Rico at his side, both aiming their guns at their attackers as they watched Declan continue his duel. "Don't come any closer," she yelled at the villains, who had once again begun moving toward the driveway.

Donna breathed heavily. *This can't be happening. They're going to kill us all, and then they'll come for Starla.* Sue and Lisa stood at her side, both keeping their distance from Donna's ungloved right hand. *My power's of no use if I can't get close.* She carefully placed the other glove back over her fingers and took another look at Marcus.

"He's gone, Donna," Sue muttered. "The Marcus you knew is gone."

Donna knew she was right. She had to accept it or she'd risk putting everyone *else* she loved in danger. His memories were too far gone, and his powers too great.

His powers. Donna noted the burnt-out electric streetlights. *He pulled the light from them.* Her eyes drifted to the jack-o-lanterns lining either side of the driveway. The votive candles inside flickered, only beginning to fade as they neared the end of their short wicks. *The light is still there. Every other light is gone except for the flames.*

Flames. Worth a shot.

Donna glanced to the carved pumpkins again, then whispered to Sue and Lisa: "When I say so, grab one of those pumpkins and toss it as hard as you can."

"Don, what?" Sue raised an eyebrow. "Are you crazy?"

"Just do it, girls." Donna took a deep breath. "Three." She clenched her fists and looked ahead. Declan was once-again crouched near the car, locked in a tussle with one of the armored women. He turned, made eye contact with Donna, nodded.

"Two," she whispered.

Deep breaths.

"One!"

All three women lunged toward the pumpkins. Sue tossed hers first. It sailed through the air and smashed into the man with no face. The candle's flame caught his arm on fire.

Lisa had grabbed a larger pumpkin and hurled it toward the barefoot woman. To Lisa's dismay, the squash splattered across the pavement, snuffing out its tiny flame in the process. None of the pumpkin guts even touched the woman, who seemed to have an ability to pass through matter.

Donna's was the last chance before the group moved in to finish them. Her target was much closer. Declan sensed what she was trying to do and dove from the paved road to the driveway. Donna held her breath as the jack-o-lantern flew over the pavers and splattered into the swale full of gasoline. The votive candle grew immediately into a wall of flames, sweeping across from one end to the other right as Declan tucked and rolled to safety.

Now a barrier of fire separated Donna's friends from their assailants. As she suspected, Marcus seemed unable to pull power or light from the fire. This didn't stop him from sending a few more beams of searing light toward them, which they dodged as they retreated back toward the house. Rico and Tracy fired a few shots through the flames, momentarily forcing their foes to back away.

Over the licking of the growing flames, which swept up and engulfed the crashed car, Donna heard a sound: police sirens. Angela and her companions heard it, too, then saw the flashing red-and-blue lights making their way down both sides of the island's loop, accompanied by a firetruck.

"This isn't over," Angela screamed. "We'll be back."

With that, the group of strange figures hurried off into the darkness, cutting through one of the hedge-lined yards, where they disappeared.

Donna's sudden rush of adrenaline had entirely sapped her strength, and she nearly collapsed into Sue and Lisa's arms. Tears streamed down her face.

Max began barking at something—or someone—near the house.

Tracy crouched to the dog's level and followed his gaze. "What is it, boy?"

The door to the house swung open and a little girl in a

skeleton costume ran down the front steps. Starla cried out, "Aunt Donna! Aunt Donna!"

Donna gasped and turned to embrace the little girl as she ran into her arms. "Oh my gosh, Starla! You're okay." She smothered the girl in her bosom as both continued to cry. "Thank God, you're okay."

As Donna clutched Starla in her arms, the police and fire department arrived and began to suppress the flames. Rico and Tracy filled in their counterparts on the details of the night's events, and their forces fanned out across the island in search of Angela, Marcus, and the other strangers that had disappeared with them.

A lone car pulled around the loop several minutes later, which caught the attention of Tracy and Rico. They recognized the vehicle as the one issued to Calvin. The car came to a stop and the young recruit stepped out. The other two officers were there to intercept him.

"Did they make it in time?" He asked frantically as Rico and Tracy approached. "I heard the distress call and sent for backup—"

Rico grabbed Calvin by the shoulders and threw him against the side of the car. "Where the hell were you?"

"Just gathering important intelligence—"

"You weren't at your post."

Tracy tried to interject, "Officer Castillo, I think he's a little—"

"Because you didn't show, there was a gap in the perimeter. And do you wanna know how those crazies got in here?" Rico's face was only inches from Calvin, whose eyes were wide. "Yep, you guessed it: the gap in the perimeter," he nearly shouted. "So tell me, kid: *why* weren't you at your post?"

"Rico, give the kid a break," Tracy said, yanking her partner away from the lanky recruit. "Give him some air."

Rico backed off, but continued to stare down the young man.

"I, uh, went back," Calvin started.

"Back *where?*"

"Back to the mortuary," he raised his hands defensively, "but before you get even more angry at me, you need to know that I found out something."

The two officers made brief eye-contact, then Rico exhaled. "What did you find out?"

"Glad you asked," Calvin started eagerly, brushing out a wrinkle in his shirt. "I found out that Dr. Blanche is guilty, just as I suspected, and that she's part of something much bigger."

Over the next several moments, Calvin recounted the conversation he'd overhead outside the mortuary, detailing talks of a package, the mysterious flight, incriminating tapes, and the man named Rolf.

"Rolf?" Tracy repeated. "Like Rolf Ducane?"

"Possibly," Calvin nodded. "He called her his 'old professor' and he was really tall and kind of scary. Judging by the shiny car he drove up in, I'd say he's also loaded."

"It's Ducane. I'd bet on it," Rico added. "Miss Hyde all but confirmed that she's working for him when she was here just a few minutes ago. She also name-dropped the Nightmare Array."

Calvin lit up. "Dr. Blanche and Rolf both mentioned that, too. It sounded like some sort of... weapon or something."

"See this mess?" Rico motioned to the carnage of the evening's battle at Donna's driveway. "The Nightmare Array is the name of the group of weirdos that caused all of this. Seems like Angela is their manager and Ducane's the big fish at the top."

Calvin nodded. "Whatever the case may be, Eudora Blanche is supposed to be on a flight tomorrow night with that mysterious 'package' that Rolf spoke about."

"Any idea what it is?" Tracy asked.

The recruit shook his head. "Not a clue. Maybe she's using the mortuary as a cover for a smuggling operation? Time's running out, though. We've gotta get over there now and bust her."

"We can't do that," explained Tracy.

"Why not?"

"First of all, we can't do that because we haven't got the slightest clue what 'the package' is. For all we know, it could be something as innocuous as suntan lotion or toothpaste. And second: you went back there without permission or a warrant. So if we show up there, we'll have to explain that your 'probable cause' came from a conversation you overheard illegally—and then we're all fired."

Calvin slumped and looked from one officer to the other. "So what do you suggest we do?"

"We need something more on Dr. Blanche or her, uh, business—even something small—then we can get a warrant and search the place." Tracy motioned to the car. "How about you get some rest and we'll pick this up in the morning, okay?"

Rico grabbed Calvin's shoulder, startling him. The younger man turned to face the officer.

"Hey," said Castillo. "Sorry I flipped. You did good work, kid."

"Th-thanks, officer."

Rico smiled. "You're well on your way to becoming one yourself."

With that, the young man got back in the car and drove away. Rico and Tracy watched as the car disappeared around the tree-lined curve.

When Starla and Donna both had some time to calm down as they watched the fires get extinguished, Donna asked, "Why did you run off like that, kiddo? I was scared out of my mind—I thought they'd taken you again."

"Sorry," Starla answered, slouching with her head low.

"Where'd you go?"

The girl nodded toward the house and pointed up at a second floor window.

Sondra's room. Donna nodded. "Another test, eh? Anything this time?"

Starla didn't answer, but seemed to avoid making eye-contact with her aunt and caretaker.

"Star, it's okay; you can tell me. Did it work this time?"

The girl gulped, then nodded quickly.

"That's great news," Donna smiled. "Then you have powers—just like we thought?"

As she said this, Donna realized the girl was still acting strange.

"I thought you were excited that you might have powers," Donna offered. "Did something... *happen?*"

Finally, Starla lifted her chin and looked her aunt in the eyes. "It worked. I saw something in mom's mind."

"What, like you saw her thoughts?"

"Sort of. I think I saw," Starla struggled to put words to the experience. "I think I saw her *memories*. It was like a movie playing out, only my eyes were closed."

Donna put her hands on the girl's shoulders. "Star, honey: what did you *see?*"

Starla closed her eyes slowly, as if trying to recall the scene. "It was a picture. Mom was holding it. There were some people... I think it was a picture from a long time ago. Three people. It looked like..." Here the girl hesitated, then said, "It looked like the pictures of grandma and grandpa—your mom and dad."

Donna wasn't sure why Starla seemed so upset by it. If she had seen a memory from Sondra, it could have been any number of photos from their childhood. "You're sure it was grandma and grandpa? You never met them."

"I'm sure it was them," she insisted. "Just like old photos you've showed me. It was them."

"You said there were three people," Donna focused. "Who else was in the photo? Me? Your mom?"

"They were in a laboratory," Starla closed her eyes again, ignoring her aunt's latest inquiry. "Grandma and grandpa were standing on one side, and *he* was on the other side. They were smiling. They were friends or coworkers, I think."

"*Who?*" Donna's grip on Starla tightened involuntarily. "Starla: *who* was on the other side? Who was in the picture with my parents?"

A single tear formed at the corner of one of the girl's eyes as she opened them. "It was the bad man," she said softly. "The bad man who took me and mom."

"Ducane?" Donna's vision was focused and her voice was almost silent.

Starla nodded slowly, affirmative. "I think your mom and dad *worked* with him."

Donna nearly fell backwards but caught herself.

No. There's no way. There's not even a chance *that our parents worked with that... monster.* Donna stood slowly and her eyes glazed over.

"Aunt Donna, what are you gonna do?"

The woman looked at the scene around her: the crashed car, the burn marks in the street, the guts of slaughtered pumpkins. Finally she locked eyes with Starla once more and spoke in a soft but determined voice: "I'm going to get some answers."

CHAPTER 17

"Tell him what you saw," Donna instructed Starla in a soft voice. The woman nodded to Declan, who stood nearby. The three sat in Donna's living room, a warm lamp illuminating one corner while the Halloween moonlight and the flashes of red-and-blue sirens seeped through the cracks in the blinds along the front-facing wall. "Take all the time you need," Donna added.

Starla nodded and closed her eyes. "I saw the picture of grandma and grandpa," she started, then hesitantly inched open her eyelids to look at Declan and added, "And the bad man was with them."

Declan's face betrayed his surprise. "The bad man? You mean..."

"The one who took us," Starla clarified.

Donna nodded and turned to the man. "Your father."

Declan didn't answer immediately, but inhaled deeply, his

thoughts drifting.

"Did you know about this, Dec?"

"No," he shook his head. "I mean, my father didn't talk much about his work, so I don't *think* I knew." Declan looked up. "Do you have a photo of your parents?"

Donna nodded and rose. She pulled a thick photo album from a shelf, returned to her seat on the sofa, and began to flip through the pages. "Here." Donna held up the page.

Declan shifted his position to peer through the glare of the glossy plastic page protector. The photo, pasted onto a dated, patterned scrapbook page, featured four faces.

"That's me and Sondra." Donna pointed at two young girls—one blonde, the other brunette. "And our parents: Richard and Betty."

The man studied the photo for a few moments before speaking. "I can't say I recognize them." Declan sighed, then turned to Starla. "But what else did you see in the photo in your... what did you call it?"

"Memory," Starla answered. "I think it was one of my mom's memories. It... *felt* like her hand holding the photograph. Grandma, grandpa, and, er, your dad were all smiling, in a lab. They were close. Friends, I think."

The two adults shared a concerned glance.

"I'm sorry, Donna," Declan said, placing a comforting hand on her arm.

She flinched, wanted to pull away but refrained. "Do you realize what that could mean... if it's true?"

"Donna, we don't know for sure—"

"It could mean that my parents are responsible for all of the experiments, all of the terrible technology Ducane's developed," she gulped. "All of the bad things that have happened in my life—this stupid curse, Marcus, all of it. Knowing my own *family* made all of this happen—how am I supposed to live with that?"

Declan was quiet for a moment, then muttered. "Believe me, it isn't easy."

Donna's eyes softened. "I'm sorry, Dec, I didn't mean to—"

"It's okay," he smiled. "I've had plenty of time to come to terms with who my father really is."

The woman lowered her chin. "I'm not ready to come to terms with this," Donna shook her head. "I can't accept it. I need to know the truth—the *whole* truth—about my family. There has to be more to the story."

The room was silent. The police lights had disappeared from the front drive, and the space seemed still, expectant.

"Aunt Donna," Starla spoke up. "There *is* more to the story."

Donna leaned in. "What do you mean, kiddo?"

The girl bit her lip. "There was more to mom's memory."

"What else do you remember?"

Basking in the warm glow of the lamp, Starla took a moment to regain her thoughts and composure, then shut her eyes once more. "Mom was in a big office when she was looking at the picture. They were really high up—she could see the city outside the window and it looked really small."

"Who's *they*?" Donna pressed. "Whose office?"

Starla exhaled sharply and opened her eyes. "Give you one guess."

Ducane.

"There were papers on his desk," Starla continued. "An open folder and a pen. I think he wanted her to sign the papers."

Donna held Starla's hands. "Why? What was she going to sign?"

Starla shook her head. "I don't know. I could see it all, but the details are too small—too hard for me to read."

"It's okay, kiddo," Donna comforted her. "Um, what happened after that? Did she sign the papers?"

The girl squeezed her eyes shut again. "It's hard to tell," Starla began. "I see it all like a movie, but it's skipping around like a record, jumping over parts... First she's looking at the photograph, then she sees Ducane behind the desk. It skips a little here, but then he hands her the pen. Then it jumps again. He's holding the folder, walking—there's a TV in the corner—then the memory skips again and the folder's gone. Mom leaves."

Starla let out a huge breath and her eyes opened.

"I'm sorry," she shook her head. "That's all I can see clearly."

Donna offered her a kind smile. "That's alright." She hugged the girl. "You're incredible, kiddo. I'm so proud to be your aunt. You're more special than anything I could've ever dreamed of."

Starla beamed. As Donna looked at the girl's freckled face and pearly grin, her own words echoed in her mind.

Anything I could've dreamed of.

Dreamed of.

Wait.

Donna's pulse quickened and she turned to Declan.

"I have an idea," she said to the man. "Maybe *they* can help."

"Donna, what are you talking about?"

"Memories are sort of like dreams, right?" Donna asked, still cryptic.

"Y-yes," Declan started. "Wait, Donna, you're not seriously suggesting—?"

She nodded. "Maybe *they* can help us find something in the memory—to get it out of Starla's head."

"Well, I mean, it's *possible*," Declan replied. "But they're done running jobs like the old days. You know that. They'll never to agree to this."

Starla raised an eyebrow. "Who—?"

"Dec, c'mon," Donna insisted, speaking over her niece. "If your father's really sent his so-called Nightmare Array after us to clean up his past mistakes, then it's only a matter of time before he comes for *them*, too. They aren't safe. None of us are."

Declan considered Donna's words. Her point was well taken, but he hesitated.

"We might not have much time," said Donna. "They'll be back."

The man breathed in deeply, then slowly exhaled, crossing his arms.

"Fine. I'll see if they can meet us at the warehouse tomorrow. Been a while since the tech's been in use, but we'll give it a shot."

Donna threw her arms around him and gave him a light embrace. "Thanks, Dec."

Starla raised an eyebrow. "Uh, Aunt Donna, Mr. Declan: who are you talking about? Who's going to help us?"

"Some of our old friends. You've met them." Donna smiled. "The Dream Team."

Late the next morning at the station, Officer Castillo poured himself a cup of coffee, just barely filling the styrofoam cup halfway before the pot was emptied. He sighed, took a sip, wrinkled his nose, then stirred in a generous helping of milk and sugar. *It hardly qualifies as café con leche, but it'll have to do.* Rico headed around the corner, where he joined Tracy and Calvin in a meeting room.

The recruit looked up from a notepad as Rico walked in. "Good morning, Officer Castillo." Matt Calvin's glasses magnified tired, bloodshot eyes.

Tracy offered a soft smile. "Morning, partner." The two made prolonged eye-contact until Rico noticed more of his surroundings.

A bulletin board on the far wall was pinned with newspaper clippings, xerox copies, and hand-scribbled notes. "This is everything I could find on Mr. Ducane and Dr. Blanche on such short notice," Calvin explained.

"And? Find anything?"

The young man sighed and adjusted his spectacles. "Not yet."

The trio stood shoulder-to-shoulder, examining the smattering of seemingly-disconnected information.

Tracy crossed her arms. "Last night you said Rolf referred to Dr. Blanche as his 'old professor.' That might be significant," she suggested.

"Do we know where she taught?" Rico asked.

Calvin shook his head.

Tracy tapped a finger as she leaned against a table. "What about Ducane?" She pushed off from the table's edge. "Do we know where he went to school?"

"Palmhurst College, just like all the other rich kids," Calvin said, moving to a stack of yearbooks on the table. "There's no one by the name of Eudora Blanche in any of 'em, but be my guest."

The two officers began flipping through the pages. Rico slowed as he reached a section featuring the black-and-white photographs of students. He ran his finger down the side until it rested on one name: *Rolf Ducane*. "His kid looks just like him," Rico said, holding up the book so the others could see.

Tracy nodded, noting the man's resemblance to Declan. "It's uncanny, really."

Castillo and Jones continued turning pages until each reached the faculty sections. Tracy flipped forward, then backward, then looked up with a puzzled expression. "Weird that Dr. Blanche isn't in here at all. You'd think they'd at least mention her name as 'not pictured' or something. Maybe she married and changed her name since then?"

Calvin sighed. "Already checked on that. No marriage records."

"Wait." Rico held his page up to the light to get a better look. "I think I found her."

The others crowded around. Calvin eyed the names on the side of the page. "I don't see her name."

"That's because it's not her name." Rico pointed to a portrait near the middle of the page. "But that's *definitely* her face."

His companions agreed. The woman in the picture was undeniably the same woman that had greeted them at the mortuary.

"But why's she listed as H—?" Calvin's jaw dropped. "Oh my gosh: *Hazel Vance*."

Tracy raised an eyebrow. "Why does that sound so familiar?"

"The *headstone*!" Calvin continued. "That's the name from the grave our faceless friend was digging up before we scared him off."

"So you think Eudora Blanche is just an alias or something?" Officer Castillo asked.

"Seems like it."

"But if Dr. Blanche was the real Hazel Vance," Castillo continued, "then who's buried in Vance's grave?"

Calvin speculated. "Probably another Jane Doe, just like all of the other bodies they snatched up. Rolf himself said that they picked people with no living relatives or connections so nobody would go snooping."

The officers and the recruit lingered, staring down at the picture for several moments as they processed their next move.

"Hazel Vance wasn't in any of our files," Calvin recalled. "So she isn't wanted for any crimes—"

"But this could still be the evidence we needed to get our search warrant." Rico grinned. "No matter how you slice it, either Blanche or Vance is a false identity, and I'd say that's fishy enough for us to move in."

The officers and Calvin grabbed their things and started for the door, when Rico stopped and turned back to the recruit.

"Good work, kid." He smiled softly and patted the young man on the shoulder.

Calvin beamed. "Thanks, Officer Castillo."

"Please," he answered. "You can call me Rico."

"As long as you don't call me *intern*."

"Deal." The pair shook hands.

Tracy stood in the threshold and flashed a grin. "Ready to go, boys?"

The two men nodded and followed Officer Jones out of the meeting room, leaving Rico's unfinished cup of lukewarm coffee on the table.

The squad car screeched into a parking space a block away

from the mortuary. Calvin leaned forward between the seats as Officers Castillo and Jones silently surveyed the scene ahead.

"Something feels off," muttered Jones. "Stay alert."

Rico threw the car into park and the trio piled out. The two officers drew their guns and approached the property with caution, Calvin trailing a few steps behind.

When they reached the sidewalk, the group froze in place, staring at something near the side of the building.

"Is that what I think it is?" The recruit adjusted his glasses.

"I think it is." Rico nodded and they moved closer, their guns still raised.

Soon, they were near enough to read a small sign that had been nailed to the wall:

For Sale.

Rico and Tracy loosened and lowered their guns.

"She split," Rico spat. "Dangit."

Officer Jones pressed her face to a window and looked in. Most of the curtains were drawn and blinds shut, but she managed to find a sliver through which she could see inside. The space was dark and dusty. "It's completely cleared out," she said. "Looks like Dr. Blanche—er, Vance—left in a pretty big hurry."

Rico craned toward Calvin. "Sorry, kid. I shoulda listened to you. We should've come right away last night—"

Calvin raised a hand. "It's alright. Don't mention it. Maybe there's something inside—another clue that can help us figure out what's going down tonight."

"He's right," Jones nodded. "Let's check the doors."

Tracy tried the front door—locked. Rico surveyed the back side of the building while Calvin went to check the handle of the side door.

"Nothing around back," said Castillo when he returned. "A little odd. How about your door, kid?"

"Locked," Calvin said through gritted teeth. "But I've almost got it."

The officers crowded around and watched as the recruit finagled a thick plastic credit card between the door and the jamb's hardware.

"Done this before?" Tracy asked, peering over his shoulder.

"Almost had it last night before Rolf showed up."

After a few more seconds of struggle, Calvin exclaimed, "A-ha!" The door swung open and the three peered into the dark, vacant hall. Calvin gestured toward the doorway. "After you, officers."

Tracy felt along the inside wall for a light switch. "Power's already been cut off," she said when it yielded no light. "Declan's really got MPL working quick." She produced a small flashlight from her belt, clicked it on, and stepped inside.

Rico and Calvin did the same, following the other officer into the shadowy space.

"Let's split up," Tracy suggested. "Every second counts."

The men agreed. Jones took the main floor of the front-facing building, Rico moved upstairs, and Calvin was left to investigate the back room. "The creepiest room where the bodies were kept," he muttered to himself. "Great."

His light cast a thick beam, catching dust particles as the recruit neared the door. Calvin opened it and stepped into the stark-white chamber. The large stainless steel table remained in the center of the room, but the filing cabinet and all other accoutrements had been removed, the signs of their former presence scrubbed clean.

Calvin neared the far wall, lined with a grid of small, squarish refrigerator doors behind which the doctor's subjects had been kept while they awaited the next phase of their afterlives. A chilling thought crossed his mind. *Surely she didn't leave any behind...?*

The recruit's hand trembled as he reached for one of the metal door handles. He gulped, gripped it, took a deep breath, pulled. Calvin peered inside through squinted eyes, holding his breath to keep from smelling any accidentally-left-behind decompositions as the flashlight beam swiped across the space. The compartment was deep, but empty.

The young man breathed a sigh of relief and carefully shut the door. He moved to the next one, repeating the process. Deep breath. Latch-click. Pull. Nothing.

He opened a few more of the airlocked chambers and was starting to grow discouraged, but knew Castillo and Jones would expect nothing less than a full sweep of the room. Calvin cycled through his process once more, yanking the door wide.

As the light filled the small container, Calvin saw nothing of note. He was about to shut the door when he paused, turned, and cast the light toward the back of the body-sized fridge.

There is no back. Calvin stuffed his head into the square doorway to get a better look. Sure enough, this particular refrigeration chamber had no back to it. Instead, it appeared to connect to some sort of larger space beyond it. *Another room?*

Calvin inhaled a shaky breath. *It's probably empty, right? Or maybe it's just for the machinery that powers the fridges.*

His gut told him those presumptions weren't the whole story. *There has to be some significance to this.*

"Guys!" He shouted over his shoulder. "I think I found something!"

Before awaiting the arrival of his counterparts, Calvin pulled himself up into the backless body chamber and began to squeeze into it. There was not much breathing room, and Calvin felt the tightness closing in around him. He paused halfway through his shimmying and aimed his light at a mark on the side wall.

A speck of blood. *From the paper cut?* It looked fresh enough. Dr. Blanche had been through the space recently.

As Calvin pulled himself through, toward the end of the chamber, he heard steps behind him. Rico and Tracy hurried over and peered into the faux fridge.

"Calvin, what are you doing?" Castillo shone his light at the younger man.

"There's something back here," Calvin answered as he reached the end. "Oh my gosh. It's like a whole 'nother room!"

"What do you mean—?"

"Hard to say," the recruit shifted his weight and tumbled out of the body-tube and into the dark room. "Ow!" He winced and stood up. Calvin waved back through the tight tunnel. "I'm fine."

Tracy attempted to get a good look from the main room beside Rico. "What do you see?"

The young man whipped around and surveyed the dark room. There were no windows, so the only illumination came from the beam emanating from his tiny flashlight. Like the rest of the building, it appeared to have been scraped clean of whatever use it formerly held, but a few stray pieces of barren furniture offered some clues: metal tables, a refrigerated storage cabinet, and a large centrifuge.

"I think it's some sort of lab," Calvin hypothesized as he examined the equipment more closely.

"A lab?" Rico repeated. *What was the doc experimenting on? Her clients?*

Calvin continued wandering the space. There appeared to be no traces of research left behind in the storage shelves, so he continued to sweep the room. As his light landed on something in front of him, low to the ground, Calvin's jaw dropped and he reached down to inspect it more closely.

"Uh, guys," he muttered. "I think you're gonna wanna get in here and see this."

CHAPTER 18

The warehouse garage door creaked open and Donna's yellow convertible revved into the darkness. The large bay door closed behind the vehicle and Donna shifted it into park. She helped Starla disembark from the back seat then joined Declan, who had already exited the car and started across the voluminous space toward a seating area several meters away.

A hulking, bald man rose from his seat when he saw Declan.

"You'd better have a good reason for dragging us back here, Dec," the man boomed as he approached.

"Cool it, Buster," quipped a short and sprightly young woman who appeared at his side. Her hair was dyed an unnatural, vivid aqua color. "He *said* it's important, so it *must* be important." She stopped a few feet shy of Declan and mock-whispered. "It *is* important, right?"

Declan smirked. "Yeah, it's important. We'll tell you all about it." He gestured toward the car, where Donna and Starla emerged from the shadows.

"Well, would ya look at that!" The teal-haired woman smiled and hurried over to the two. "Long time no see, Goldilocks." The diminutive woman gave a sly grin. In the blink of an eye, an exact duplicate of the smaller woman appeared beside her. The original wrapped Donna in a friendly hug, while her double embraced Starla, whose eyes grew big with amazement.

"Good to see you, Kiki—and... *Kiki*," Donna chuckled, then turned to the large man. "You too, Buster."

He waved and flashed a hearty smile. "Hey, Miss Locke. Hi, Starla."

Starla admired Kiki's sudden twin, who vanished just as quickly as she'd appeared.

The remaining, original Kiki put her hands on her hips and raised an eyebrow as she returned her attention to Declan. "Now, you gonna tell us what this is all about or not?"

"Of course," Declan replied. He glanced around. "Wait a sec. Where's Mira?"

"I'm here," a voice echoed from another dark corner of the room. A door slammed shut and the sound of short heels clacked toward the group. "Sorry I'm late," said Mira as she stepped into the light. The woman had dark hair, a fuller figure, and a kind smile. She pulled Donna and Starla into her bosom for a group hug. "Been a minute."

"It's good to see you, Mira." Donna said in earnest. "We're

sincerely grateful that you all came here to help."

Kiki sighed and crossed her arms. "And we're *sincerely* waiting on the edge of our seats to find out what was so darn important that you called us back together after we've been disbanded for months."

"Speaking of seats," Declan gestured toward the couches in the seating area nearby. "Shall we?"

The group made their way to the sofas. Large rugs formed a sort of room without walls. Dusty white sheets covered a few tall, lumpy towers of unseen objects to one side, with only their protruding corners to suggest the boxy shapes of what technology lay underneath. It was exactly as Donna remembered from the last time she had been there, several months prior.

Just a little bit more dusty, she noted.

Donna remained standing and turned to face the group. "We need your help. Declan called you here on my behalf—well, *our* behalf," she motioned toward Starla, who sat quietly on the couch. "Recently we realized that Starla *may* have inherited some sort of special abilities."

"Woah! What's your *thing*?" Kiki asked.

Starla raised her brow. "My... *thing*—?"

"Your *power*, kid. What's your special power?"

The girl stuttered. "U-um, I think I can sort of read people's minds—or their memories, I guess."

"No kidding?" Buster nodded, impressed.

Mira turned to the girl. "So you're one of us. Welcome, dear."

"Thank you." Starla settled into her seat. "It's only happened once or twice," she continued. "It's all very new."

As the team speculated, Donna interjected: "The reason we're here with all of you is that Starla... um, *saw* a memory. And we need you to help us get it out of her head—just like you used to do with the dreams."

Kiki crossed her arms and kicked her feet up on a crate. "Dreams and memories are *very* different phenomena," she puffed.

Donna's demeanor sank. "What do you mean?"

"I mean they're not the same thing."

"W-well, do you think it could still work? Do you think the Dreamcatcher could help us see the memory?" Donna waited with bated breath for an answer, but none came. "Please, the things Starla saw—they're very important to me. Would you please just *try* it for me—for an old friend?"

There was a long lull in the conversation. The sounds of distant cars and passing sirens were the only discernible sounds echoing through the vast warehouse.

Buster was the first to break the silence. "Worth a try."

Donna felt her whole body relax. "Thank you. It would mean the world to me."

All rose. The big man sauntered toward the large cloth sheets and gently tugged on one. Immediately, a cloud of dust formed and the fabric fell to the floor, revealing a set of large electronics and computing devices. Buster took a few more steps, pulled another sheet, and uncovered a leathery medical chair upon which were attached a variety of mechanical accessories and a set of thick straps.

Starla shuddered when she saw it.

"You don't have to do this if you don't want to," Donna whispered, placing one of her gloved hands on the girl's shoulder.

"Does it... hurt?" The girl asked to no one in particular.

"Don't worry, kid," Kiki said, flipping a few switches to fire up one of the big computers. "This little thing just sucks your brains out like a Slurpee through a straw. Won't hurt *that* much."

Starla shuddered and took a step back, her eyebrows raised with concern.

Mira crouched at her side. "Kiki's teasing you. It won't hurt," she assured the girl. "We'll be gentle. You're just going to have to be very focused for a few minutes, which might give you a little bit of a headache afterward. It should fade quickly, though."

The girl nodded her understanding.

Mira gestured toward the chair. "Ready?"

Starla hesitated. Mira took another look at the bleak, cold chair and closed her eyes. She raised her hands and crossed them back and forth out in front of her.

Starla gasped and Mira opened her eyes to look upon the illusion she'd created.

The drab chair was gone, now replaced by a fluffy, colorful seat with rainbow plush padding that sparkled in the fluorescent lights. A nursery mobile hung above the seat with four birds—starlings—attached to strings, rotating in a circular orbit.

"They look so real," Starla remarked as she drew closer. "How did you do that?"

"It's my... *thing*," Mira answered, wiggling her fingers.

"Can everyone see this?" The girl asked, looking to her aunt.

Donna nodded. "I can see it, alright. Impressive, Mira."

Starla climbed into the now more palatable chair and settled in. Mira placed a hat over the girl's head—it looked like a bicycle helmet. The headgear was pink and colorful, a continuation of Mira's illusions. She clicked the strap under the girl's chin. "Comfortable?"

The girl nodded.

Buster yanked on another set of sheets, now revealing a tower of television sets of all different sizes, stacked in a sort of haphazard manner. Kiki clicked a remote control and all of the screens flashed on at once, showing silent static.

Donna gestured to the TVs. "So we should be able to see the memory on these—just like the dreams, right?"

"Let's hope so," Buster answered. He turned to Mira. "All set?"

She finished connecting a hose-like cable to Starla's helmet and gave a thumbs-up as she backed away. "All set."

Donna moved around to the front of Starla's seat and held the girl's hands. "You ready to do this, kiddo?"

Starla nodded. Someone flipped a switch and a loud whirring noise began, startling the girl. She quickly regained her composure and settled back into the pink chair.

"We recording this?" Declan asked. Buster nodded.

Declan joined Donna and began to guide Starla. "Alright, now just relax and close your eyes," he said. She obeyed, slowing her breathing. Declan glanced over his shoulder at the television sets. The static now turned to black. "Good. Now: do you remember what you saw when you looked into your mother's memories?"

"Yeah, I think so." Starla kept her eyes squeezed shut.

"Great. Think of it just like it happened the first time."

The others waited in silence, watching the screens. Slowly, the darkness began to turn into blobs of light and color. Three figures slowly morphed and gained definition. They were standing in a laboratory. The whole scene was quickly surrounded by a white, rectangular frame—this was the photograph of Donna's parents with Rolf Ducane, just as Starla had described earlier.

"It's him, alright," Declan whispered to Donna when the face in the photo became clear. "Gotta be when he was around my age."

Kiki stood close to the largest of the television screens, her face cast in its glow. "Wait a sec. You said this memory was from Donna's sister." She turned to Donna. "You mean your family's been in cahoots with that monster?" Kiki flitted her eyes to Declan and muttered, "No offense."

"None taken," Declan replied.

"It was a shock to me, too," Donna explained, her eyes fixed to the screens. "I couldn't believe it when Starla told me, but there it is—it's undeniable: that's our parents smiling, friendly with the man responsible for ruining my life."

The scene on the screens seemed to move in slow motion, a scene playing out from Sondra's point of view. Her hand held the photograph near the bottom right of the frame while details continued to fill in around it: a large desk, natural light from a massive window, Sondra's outfit—a green dress.

Donna crouched low and spoke softly into Starla's ears as the girl's eyes remained shut. "What happened next? You said there was more—the folder, the papers, remember?"

"Trying to remember," Starla replied.

"Maybe we oughta give her the sleeping powder," Kiki snapped.

Buster rolled his eyes. "She saw the memory while she was conscious. If we put her under, her subconscious will take over and skew the things we're seeing—"

"Guys!" Mira pointed at the TVs.

The memory scene started to play in something close to real-time, unpausing from the near-static shot of Sondra's hand holding the photograph. She looked up, allowing the screen to fill with a new scene.

A man in an expensive suit stood behind a large desk. It was Ducane. He placed a folder on the surface and opened it, revealing a stack of papers. The man set a fountain pen beside it and looked up. His lips moved, but no words could be heard by Donna and her friends.

"Is there any sound on this?"

Kiki fiddled with the remote. The volume bar increased. The audio was unclear and warbled, like being heard underwater or from the next room over. "That's the best we got."

Drat. Donna fixed her eyes on the screens again and whispered to Starla. "You're doing great, Star."

Sondra's perspective shifted. She glanced to one side—out the large window, revealing the city skyline—then to the other, passing over a small television set in the corner. The office walls flickered—brown wood paneling for a split second, then a soft, smooth pastel color the next. The reflection of the woman directly ahead in a large mirror on the far wall finally confirmed it: this was unmistakably Sondra's memory.

Donna covered her mouth with her gloved hand as she noticed another detail in the mirror's image of her sister: Sondra was visibly pregnant. *So this memory was from a little over nine years ago,* Donna connected the dots. *But what was Sondra doing in Ducane's office. How did she know about him? Was she working for him, too—?*

"Wasn't her dress *green* in the other shot?" Mira pointed at the screens, where Sondra's reflection in the mirror showed her pregnant figure sporting a blue dress.

The blonde woman nodded. "Yeah. It was." Donna held tight to Starla's hand and studied the image on-screen.

"Maybe the kid's getting the details fuzzy," Kiki suggested.

Starla piped in. "This is how I saw it. I pinky promise."

"We believe you, kiddo," Donna said, though she wasn't entirely convinced. She had noticed the change in the wall texture, too.

"So I guess that means your sister's the one with the fuzzy

memory." Kiki returned her attention to the nearest TV.

Guess so. She was in a coma when Starla saw this, after all. And it was a long time ago. Donna watched as Sondra turned back to face Ducane. She stepped forward, toward the big desk, looked down at the documents before her. Underneath the open folder, there were two others.

C'mon. Closer.

Sondra took the pen in hand and sat down. Her gaze focused on the two closed folders. Only the tab labels were readable:

Locke, Richard.

And: *Locke, Betty.*

Donna's breaths were short. *Mom and dad. Sondra knew.*

The focus of the images on screen shifted again, now to the page atop the open file. Slowly the words at the top of the page became clear and Donna felt her heart drop:

Termination of Parental Rights.

No. There's no way. It can't be, Donna shook her head. *She didn't go through with it, right?* Without thinking, Donna's grip on Starla tightened. She felt like Ducane was trying to steal the girl from her all over again.

Sondra looked up to Ducane, his mouth uttering some indiscernible gibberish, then she raised the pen and brought it to the bottom of the page, resting it at the edge of a blank line. She began to write.

The screens changed abruptly, jumping to another moment in the office. The papers and folders were no longer on the table, but now in Ducane's hand.

"Wait, Starla, what happened?" Donna asked, frantic. "Can you go back?"

"It skipped like this. Like I told you. This is all I saw."

Of course. Donna took a deep breath, fixed her eyes on the screen. Ducane flashed one of his disingenuous smiles at Sondra and moved toward a large painting—it looked like a Picasso—on the back wall. He motioned for Sondra to look away. She turned slightly, angled opposite the window-wall. When she glanced back, it was clear that the painting was a sort of secret cabinet door on hinges, obscuring a locked safe behind it. Ducane stuffed the folders inside, closed the safe, then swung the painting back into place.

Then, the screens cut to static.

Donna's glistening eyes shot wide. "No. Wait, is that it?"

Starla opened her eyes and nodded timidly. "That's everything I saw in mom's memory."

Mira removed the headgear from the girl and Donna unstrapped the seatbelt, helping the girl out of the chair.

"You did great, my little Starling." Donna wiped a tear from her own eye with the back of her glove and pulled the girl close. "You did so well."

The others in the group watched in somber silence.

"Aunt Donna," Starla said. "What did that all mean?"

Donna sniffled. "Well, kiddo. I don't think we... know enough yet to say." *We know far too much,* her thoughts jabbed in. *This changes everything.*

"Was mom going to... give me up for adoption—" she paused. "To the bad man?"

Donna's expression became stern, resolute, as she looked the girl squarely in the eyes. "I don't know, Star. But I'm not letting him come *anywhere* near you ever again, you hear?"

The girl nodded as Donna stood and turned to the team. "I have to find those files."

"Isn't this a memory from almost a decade ago?" Kiki crossed her arms. "And how would we even know where to start looking?"

Donna pointed toward the static screens. "That office. I'm almost positive it's one of the penthouse suites in the Pelican building. Can you play it back?"

Kiki punched a button on the remote and the tape began to rewind, playing the memory backward.

"There!" Donna interjected.

The tape paused, jittering on the frame of the view outside the large window.

"That's the downtown skyline, and the bay at the bottom," Donna indicated with her finger on one of the glowing screens. "They're in a skyscraper at the south end of the island. It has to be Pelican headquarters—it would have been finished right around the time Starla was born."

None of the onlookers disagreed.

"Was I the only one who saw that Ducane put the files in a locked safe?" Kiki pointed at the screen. "Not to burst your bubble, but we don't exactly have the combo."

Donna sighed and slumped her shoulders.

Starla perked up: "Yes we do!"

"Huh?" Donna moved back toward her. "You know the

combination?"

The girl shook her head. "No. But mom saw it—in the mirror." She pointed back up at the TVs.

"Play it back," Donna instructed.

Kiki navigated through the tape to get back to the moment in which Sondra turned away from Ducane. It began to play again. In the reflection in the mirror at the corner of the screen, the watchers could see behind the painting. Ducane twisted the dial carefully one way, then the other, then back again before it clicked open.

Donna and the others instinctively craned their necks and squinted their eyes to see the tiny details on the grainy recording. "Can anyone make out the numbers?"

Buster strained to inspect the screen. "An average combination lock goes from zero to thirty-nine," he said, "marked in increments of five. It looks like he's starting from zero before he turns—" The large man studied the slight rotations of the dial on screen.

Declan picked up a pad of paper and a pen and scratched out a rudimentary circle with notches and numbers around it to illustrate the dial for reference. "Here," he held it up for Buster to see.

"Play it again." Buster watched closely, his eyes flitting back and forth between the drawing and the largest of the TVs. Kiki paused the tape as Ducane finished entering the combination.

"Did you catch it?" Donna leaned in.

Buster nodded. "Based on the length of each turn, I think

he entered: 19-29-39."

"But remember the image is flipped in the mirror," Mira pointed out, "so the real numbers should be their opposites on the dial."

"Right." The big man nodded and traced the notches on Declan's illustration. "Got it," he scribbled the numbers on the bottom of the sheet of paper and tore that portion off. He handed the scrap to Donna.

21-11-1.

She read the combination then looked up. "You're sure that's it?"

"If your sister and her girl were showing the truth, then yes. I'm sure. Of course," Buster added, "if this memory is from as long ago as it seems, there's always the possibility that the combination's been changed."

Donna nodded her understanding.

The room became quiet until Declan spoke up. "So do you really want to do this, Donna?"

The blonde woman took a deep breath. She glanced to Starla, who looked at her with expectant eyes.

"Yes," Donna answered. "I *have* to do this."

CHAPTER 19

Tracy held Rico's hand as he rolled out of the end of the narrow chamber and into the dark room behind the fridge door. It was a struggle with his still-healing arm wound, but Officer Castillo managed to make it through. His feet landed with a hollow thud—a portion of the floor appeared to be made of durable aluminum. When both of the officers were situated and had made it into the small room, they hurried over to where Calvin stood near a far corner.

In the dusty light, the three cops hovered over a small metallic trash bin.

"Our doctor tried to wipe this place of evidence," Calvin said. "She missed a spot." He removed a fragment of paper from the bin and held it up: it was clearly missing a large portion and its edges were burnt.

The officers leaned in close.

"What's it say?" Rico cocked his head to get a better look.

"From what I can make out," began Calvin, "I see the words: *clinical trial*, *subject file*, some numbers—looks like a serial or case number—then some more text that's a little hard to read, as it's quite charred."

"Let me give it a try." Tracy reached out for the scrap and Calvin handed it over in a careful, delicate manner. The officer held it up closer to her face and cast the flashlight over it, squinting. "*Subject J.S. responded positively to newest—*," she strained. "I think it says *transfusion. In spite of*—dangit, I can't read that part. Um, lemme see—*In spite of*—something something—*subject developed desired sensory traits. Trial deemed successful. Recommend to include in package.*" She looked up. "That's all there is."

Calvin's mouth hung agape. "*Package*? Do you think it could be—?"

Rico nodded. "And the initials?"

"*J.S.*," Tracy read them again. "Jason Sunder?"

Officer Castillo smirked. "Bingo."

"Wait, so let me get this straight," the recruit pressed his hands together in thought. "Dr. Blanche—or whatever her real name is—was conducting secret tests of some sort of compound on the body of Mr. Sunder, and it gave him—what did it say?—*desired sensory traits*?"

"Sounds a lot like what happened to Donna," Rico muttered. "This has Ducane written all over it."

Tracy raised an eyebrow. "But didn't Roger say that the formula only worked on Donna because her blood was *special*? Sunder and the other missing bodies had been dead long enough that there wouldn't exactly have been much blood left—special or otherwise."

Calvin gulped and extended a hand. "Can I see that again?"

Tracy passed the scrap of burnt paper back to the recruit. "What is it?"

"The tests," he said, his eyes straining to read the paper. "They weren't just of some compound or chemical. It says *transfusion*." Calvin looked up and gulped. "They were giving them *blood. Special* blood—like your friend Donna's."

Rico's expression became serious, concerned. "This is not good."

Officer Jones spoke in a quiet voice, almost a whisper. "You don't think—"

Rico nodded. "Ducane's found a way to give extraordinary powers to ordinary people. Think of the implications of that—if that sort of power got into the wrong hands."

Calvin adjusted his glasses. "Uh, newsflash: it's already in the wrong hands."

Just then, there was a sound like a door closing, latching.

"You hear that?" Rico whipped toward the sound—the fridge door through which they'd entered the small room. Then a realization set in: "Someone's here."

The three hurried over to the hatch. Calvin shimmed into the space and yanked on the door's handle. He shouted back through the tight space: "It's locked!"

"You sure?" Tracy hollered.

"Very sure." The young man wrestled the handle some

more before giving up. He began to bang with his fist on the back of the door. "Hey! Let us out!"

"Guys," Rico muttered, but he was overshadowed by Calvin's shouts.

"Open this up right now—!"

"Guys?"

"—or else you'll be sorry you ever stepped foot in—"

"Guys!" Castillo shouted. The others became silent. "Do you smell that?"

Tracy sniffed. "Smoke!"

"It's getting stronger," Rico observed.

"I think it's coming from out there," Calvin pointed at the door. "They're going to burn us alive!" Again he began to frantically beat on the door. "Hey! Open the door! Let us out!" There was no response. Finally, the recruit tried the handle again. "Ouch! It's hot!" Immediately, Calvin shimmied backwards out of the compartment and back into the secret room.

The three cops fanned out across the small room, running their hands along every wall and crevice in search of a way out. The tunnel through which they'd entered now began to glow red as flames ate through the door.

Calvin exhaled sharply. "We're trapped," he said, keeping his head lowered, turned away from the others. "I'm so sorry. It's been nice knowing you both." The recruit wiped his glasses, which were fogging rapidly as the room became warmer. "There's no one else I'd rather spend my last dying breaths with—"

Skreak!

The recruit winced and whipped around at the grating metallic sound to find Rico and Tracy pushing their weight against a large desk.

"A little help?" Rico snapped.

Calvin ran over to them. "Uh, yeah—"

"I think that hatch might be a way out," Officer Castillo explained, nodding to the large plate of textured metal on the floor as the recruit got into position between the officers. "On the count of three. One. Two. Three!"

In unison, the cops thrust their weight against the desk, sending its legs screeching across the metal and concrete. The desk toppled over, freeing the hatch from its mass. Tracy hurried around to the side of the metal panel and jammed one of her keys into a gap to use as leverage. When she'd raised it enough to grab hold of the grate, Officer Jones wrapped her fingers around the door and heaved upward. The hatch opened with another loud slam and the trio peered inside.

Calvin shone his flashlight into the dark space, exposing a rusty metal ladder that lined the inside of a concrete shaft that seemed to stretch at least twenty feet down. The young man looked up at the others and grinned. "After you."

Tracy puffed and swung herself around so that she could begin climbing down the ladder. The others followed suit. When the woman reached the final rungs, she stepped down to touch the ground. Instead of solid concrete, though, Tracy's feet met mushy, wet sludge. *Ugh,* she retched. Jones carefully allowed her feet to settle until she could feel the firm ground underneath; the sludge rested at about ankle-height.

While the others hurried down the ladder, Tracy waved her flashlight around the echoey chamber and sloshed toward a tunnel. "This way," she instructed the others as they hopped down into the grime one-by-one.

Calvin came last. His hand slipped near the end of the rungs. "Woah!" He sailed down to a soft, gushy landing, which splattered the disgusting goo across Rico and soiled the entire backside of the recruit's clothes. "Terrific." Rico helped him stand and the young man attempted to brush off some of the unidentifiable green-brown gloop.

"C'mon," Jones urged with a nod. The men followed her into the dark cement tunnel.

The network of underground tunnels was a maze that snaked back and forth until, finally, it came to a dead end. "Another ladder," Officer Jones noted, craning her neck up toward a closed metal cover at the top. Without another word, she began to climb.

When she reached the top, Tracy pushed against the round metal cover. It budged a little, but was heavier than she hoped. "A little help," she hollered down. Rico climbed up next and braced himself opposite Tracy at the top of the ladder. "Push!"

Together, the two were able to shove the cover open, sliding it with a grating sound across a glossy tile floor. The two peered out into the bright space, then slowly stepped up to the surface as Calvin followed at their heels.

Dozens of pampered, astonished faces stared at the three

muck-covered cops, surrounding them while seated at small tables. It took Rico a moment before he realized where the tunnel had spit them out: a ritzy cafe a couple blocks away from the mortuary. "Good afternoon," he said with a wave and a forced grin.

The room filled with gasps from the onlookers as they took in the sight of the dripping strangers.

"It's alright," Rico added as the trio began to saunter away from the grate. "We're Metro-Dade PD—everything is under control."

The guests began to rise from their seats and move away from the cops, disgusted and afraid.

Tracy whipped toward a server who stood on the fringes with a tray holding two glasses of water: "Call 9-1-1. There's a fire at Orange Street Mortuary around the corner." The young woman nodded and hastened away to make the call.

Rico, Tracy, and Calvin hurried across the dining room and out the front door into the street. The early afternoon light was almost blinding after spending the past several minutes in near-complete darkness, but when the trio's eyes had adjusted, they sprinted down the block.

As they rounded the corner, all three let out audible gasps. The mortuary was completely engulfed in flames that miraculously hadn't yet reached the tall buildings on either side of it. The sounds of sirens echoed off the skyscrapers and finally came into view at the end of the block as the firetrucks raced to the scene.

The officers and the recruit returned to the squad car,

still safely parked at the next block. Rico eyed a phonebooth nearby and hurried toward it. "Just a sec," he said to the others. "I have to make a couple calls."

Donna Locke flicked on a fluorescent light and closed the door to the small, spartan restroom, shutting out the rest of the shadowed warehouse. She leaned against the wall, closed her eyes, slid slowly down until she was in a crouched, huddled position in the corner. The woman let out a deep sigh as she clutched her handbag across her chest.

For the first time in a long time, Donna had a moment to breathe and think and feel the weight of the past days. The revelation that Donna's own parents and sister might have been in league with the man responsible for so many terrible things. The adoption paperwork. The close calls. The sudden reappearance of Marcus—a fundamentally *different* Marcus than the one she had grown to know and love.

Donna took another deep breath then felt the handbag with her gloved hands. She opened it and rifled through its myriad contents before pulling out a loose cassette tape. There was lettering scrawled across the label on the front—Marcus' handwriting.

The woman smiled to herself and shuffled through a few other tapes, found the one she was looking for, then withdrew her walkman and put its big headphones over her ears. Donna inserted the cassette and pressed the chunky *play* button.

Immediately, the tape's spools started spinning and a faint

crackle filled Donna's ears, mixed with the ambient conversations and clinking silverware of a restaurant on an average weeknight. The familiar, rich voice of Marcus spoke out—*the Marcus I used to know:*

"Dear diary—" His voice began before being cut off by a high-pitched chortle in the background. "What?"

"Dear *diary*?" It was Donna's voice, younger and smitten, with a playful chuckle. "That's how you're going to start this?" She sipped on a fizzing beverage through a straw.

"I guess," Marcus answered. "You got a better idea?"

"*Anything* but 'dear diary,'" she laughed again. The older Donna couldn't help but smile as she heard the happiness in her recorded voice. *Life was so much simpler.*

"Fine. Um, let me think. How about, uh..." He paused as someone shouted unintelligibly in the background. "To whoever is listening to this a thousand years in the future, let it be known that I, Marcus Myles, am madly in love with the one and only Donna Locke."

Donna's younger self let out a nervous, compulsive laugh.

"Hey, it's true." Marcus said with a discernible grin in his voice. "Nothing can change that."

The recording of Donna breathed deeply. "Well, people of the distant future, you should know that I, Donna Locke, feel the exact same way about Marcus Myles."

As she huddled in the bathroom corner, Donna listened to the subtle sound of sneaking smiles from the two young lovebirds, followed by the gentle, brief meeting of lips. Their first kiss. Donna breathed in. She could almost smell his cologne, his minty breath, intermingled with the savory scents of garlic and baking bread that filled the little pizzeria that night.

A knock on the bathroom door startled Donna. She stopped the tape and yanked off the headphones.

"Hey, Donna," Kiki's voice came from the other side of the locked door. "Some friends of yours are here."

Friends? "I'll be right out," she sniffled and wiped her nose with a wad of toilet paper. Donna stuffed the walkman and loose tapes back into her bag, stood up, and headed back into the large main room of the warehouse.

Donna's eyes adjusted again to the dim expanse, where she saw three newly-arrived figures conversing with Declan, Mira, and Buster near a police car. She recognized one of the figures instantly. "Rico!" Donna's shoes clacked a little faster across the concrete warehouse floor as she moved to greet her old friend. As she got closer, Donna confirmed that the man's companions were Tracy and the new recruit—Matt Calvin. "What are you guys doing here? How did you find this place?"

Officer Castillo started: "Roger gave us the address—"

Donna followed a gesture of Rico's hand toward the car, where the doctor emerged from the backseat with a grin. "Hello, Miss Locke."

"Hi, Roger." Donna turned back toward the cops, then retched and covered her nose. "Ugh! Is that you guys? You smell like crap."

Calvin took a step back. "What an astute and perceptive

sense of smell you have."

Tracy rolled her eyes. "We were just telling Declan and the rest of the team: there have been some developments."

"Developments?" Donna raised an eyebrow as Starla hurried over to her side.

Declan motioned toward the seating area. "Shall we?"

The group followed his lead and assembled on the sofas opposite the stacked television monitors. "I, uh," Calvin took another look down at his soiled clothes, "I guess I'll just stand right over here."

Kiki crossed her arms. "So you gonna tell us what's going on now, officer?"

"I was getting there," Rico answered. He took a deep breath. "As I think all of you know by now, there have been some strange occurrences around town as of late."

"You mean those monsters who tried to storm our house?" Starla piped in. "Who—or *what*—are they?"

"They're called the Nightmare Array," the officer replied. "And we've all but confirmed that they're part of a secret project that originated with Rolf Ducane."

Kiki raised her hand. "Uh, is someone going to tell those of us who weren't at Donna's mansion what the heck you're talking about?"

Rico breathed in and exhaled slowly. "Of course." He nodded to Donna, Declan, and the others: "Feel free to fill in any gaps." The officer moved over to a large bulletin board and wheeled it closer to the group. He carried a thin manila folder. "So as far as we know, the Nightmare Array is comprised of a group of individuals who each have some sort of ability—like most of you here." At this point, Rico reached into the folder and produced a flyer with a familiar sketch of a half-man, half-alligator hybrid, which he promptly pinned to the board.

"Now there's a face only a mother could love," Buster muttered.

"This was the first one that showed up on our radar," Officer Castillo continued. "Snatched up a kid and vanished into a canal—"

Roger interrupted: "Which leads me to believe he's more animal than man. He's the first of his kind that I've heard of, anyway."

"That's messed up." Mira shook her head.

"Then there's the man formerly known as Jason Sunder." Castillo added Sunder's case file to the corkboard, which featured the xerox copy of a tiny mugshot. "According to evidence left behind in a secret lab, we have reason to believe Sunder's developed heightened sensory traits."

"You said he was *formerly* known as Jason Sunder?" Mira raised an eyebrow.

"He died," Tracy said with an abrupt frankness.

Buster relaxed his crossed arms and cocked his head. "So that's one less nightmare to worry about..."

Tracy raised a finger. "Uh, sorry. I meant that he died years ago, but *somehow* he's alive again."

"It seems Mr. Ducane has cracked the science of resurrection at last," Roger explained. "Or reanimation, at least. No doubt he used stolen research to do it," he mumbled as an afterthought.

Castillo continued: "Sunder died in a fire. He suffered severe burns to his face, and it looks like Ducane or one of his associates stitched a skin graft over it."

Kiki moved closer to the bulletin board and gave a skeptical glance back to Rico. "So old Patchface here can't see but he—*what?*—uses echolocation to get around, like a bat?"

"Something like that."

Donna raised her hand. "What do we know about that old lady who can float through walls and stuff?"

Calvin took a half-step forward from his place on the outskirts of the group. "We don't know much," he began. "But her name was Marjory Beauregard, and she was also dead once."

"I can make it happen a second time if you want?" Buster smirked.

Roger ignored the man's joke. "From everything Officers Castillo and Jones shared with me on the way here, it would seem her ability functions something like a sort of ghoul."

Kiki puffed. "You mean like the kind that run around in a white sheet with two holes cut out for their eyes?"

"That's a ghost," Roger noted. "A *ghoul* gets its power from feeding on flesh and—more specifically—*blood*."

"That would explain what happened to my neighbor's poor puppy." Donna squirmed and pulled Starla closer on the sofa.

Declan had moved over to a table upon which was scattered an assortment of loose papers and pamphlets. He picked up a brochure and returned to the seating area to show it to the group. On the cover was the title *Age of the Conquistadors* with a colorful photo of an ancient suit of armor on display beneath the lettering. "What about her? At the museum the other night I came across a woman with silver hair—she could duplicate herself, just like Kiki—"

The aqua-haired woman crossed her arms quickly. "*No one* is just like Kiki." A duplicate copy of herself materialized at her side.

Declan smirked. "You're right. You're unique—just like everyone else." The man turned back to the others and pointed to the pamphlet as Kiki's double quickly vanished. "Anyway, the woman stole this *exact* suit of armor."

"That's odd," Mira placed a finger on her chin. "Does that booklet say anything about the significance of the armor? Maybe she's connected to it in some way."

Declan skimmed the folded piece as Mira looked over his shoulder. "It says the armor belonged to a Countess Francesca de la Fuente—a conquistador who explored Florida in the 1500s with Ponce de Leon."

Starla wondered aloud: "Do you think that lady was the Countess?"

"She looked *old*," Declan affirmed, "but not *four-hundred-years-old* old."

Donna reached in her bag and pulled out a polaroid photo. She looked at it longingly for a brief moment before holding it up for the others to see its face. "What about Marcus?" In the picture, he was smiling, dimpled and handsome. "What *happened* to him?" She handed the photo to Declan, who moved to add it to the board while Roger chimed in again:

"It seems that your golden touch may have *activated* something in him—abilities we couldn't predict."

"*Abilities* is an understatement." Rico shifted his weight. "He's shooting lasers out of hands, for crying out loud."

"Well, to be technical," Declan butted in, "I think he's shooting *light* out of his hands. He... absorbs it. Pulls it from streetlamps and flashlights and things like that."

Mira mused: "What I don't understand is how Marcus got those powers when he turned back from gold, but Starla hasn't shot a single laser—er, light—out of her hands."

Donna and Starla made brief eye contact. The girl had the beginnings of what appeared to be special abilities like the rest of her family, but that knowledge was still kept to a limited few. *At least until we know more,* thought Donna. There were enough people interested in her while they only knew of her *potential* for powers; Donna could only imagine what might happen if they knew the girl could possibly read minds.

"I suppose it might have something to do with the duration," Roger continued, shifting the focus off Starla. "The girl was only golden for a few hours; for Marcus, it was more than a year. As far as we know, some of these—I mean, *you*—er, *anomalies* have abilities inherent in the blood, which seem to be latent until activated—either chemically, as in the case of Donna and many of you, or by some sort of other adrenal stimulus, like the hormonal shifts of puberty, for example." He seemed to drift into a thought before continuing: "And now in Marcus' case, it seems, abilities can be activated through an event that alters the cellular makeup in some way. Either way, Mr. Myles is powerful. And dangerous. They all are. So I recommend you use caution and do your best to avoid running into them again."

As the doctor said this, Donna's gaze rested on the polaroid of Marcus that had now been pinned to the board. After all that she'd been through to undo her accident of turning him to gold, Donna felt a sense of resolve welling up inside her. *If he really is gone for good, then our only option is to stop him.*

Roger sighed, interrupting Donna's thoughts. "And then there's Angela."

Mira raised an eyebrow. "What's her power?"

"Ruining people's lives," Donna muttered and crossed her arms.

"She's the ringleader," Rico clarified. "Ducane's right-hand woman."

"Speaking of Ducane," Calvin interjected with a raised finger. "The reason we all rushed over here was to let you all know that Ducane is currently set to meet Dr. Blanche with a mysterious *package* today, and time's running out."

"Package?" Starla mused. "Like a present?"

"I'm afraid not," Calvin answered. "The package is the formula—the same one he used to build the Nightmare Array."

The group was silent as they let the recruit's words sink in.

"As I shared earlier," the doctor started, "most seem to be born with abilities—or the potential for them—but now Ducane has crafted a way to *give* abilities to whoever he chooses. To transfuse *special* blood into ordinary people to give them supernatural abilities—whatever abilities he can imagine or conjure up. This all has its limits, of course, but I know Ducane: he'll push every limit, no matter the cost."

Declan had kept quiet as the conversation drifted to talk of his father, but he now took a step back toward the group. "It makes sense. My father always envied those with powers. And it explains our encounter with him months ago—his abilities to shapeshift into a beast like me. That wasn't just a one-off experiment. He was the guinea pig for *this*. The implications are infinite; the doctor's right: my father's going to see this through to the end."

"We can't be sure," Tracy spoke up, "but we've got a strong hunch he intends to send this formula offshore so he can mass-produce it away from domestic oversight."

"Then what are we sitting around here for?" Kiki raised her brow. "Let's go stop him."

Donna lowered her gaze, and Kiki noticed. "Something wrong, Goldilocks?"

"I'm sorry," she shook her head and gestured toward the stack of TVs. "I just can't stop thinking about what we saw—my sister's memory, the photo of my parents. I *have* to know the truth about my family." Donna insisted. "If there's even a chance that those old files are up there in the Pelican tower, I have to go. And if Ducane is going to meet that doctor for this *exchange*, that will be the perfect time to make our move—when he's out of office."

"We already know of the existence of some incriminating tapes," Calvin added. "Mr. Ducane mentioned them in his conversation with Dr. Blanche. There's no way to know for sure, but I wouldn't rule out the possibility of Ducane keeping those tapes in a certain safe with all of his other important and sensitive files."

"You both have a point," Rico affirmed. "If we can get our hands on what's in that safe, there's a good chance we can bring down Ducane—and his whole operation."

"If and when you *do* find the tapes," said Roger, "there's a high-powered radio transmitter built onto the roof of the Pelican tower—it can override the local stations if calibrated correctly. It may require some tinkering, but you'll be able to broadcast any of your findings for the whole city to hear. It may seem a bit grandiose, but I believe that's the best way to ensure the message doesn't fall on deaf ears."

Rico nodded. "Perfect. Primetime. So you'll join, Doc?"

The doctor raised his hands defensively. "I've had enough action for awhile. I think it'd be better if I got back to my lab at the house—I've got a radio there. I'll keep an ear out and hit record when I hear your transmission come through. That way we'll have a backup recording in case you don't—" Here the doctor stopped mid-sentence and lowered his head.

"In case we don't make it out?" Kiki finished.

"Well, I wasn't going to say it," Roger mumbled.

"I'll handle the transmitter," Buster chimed in. "I know my

way around that kinda tech, if the doctor will be so kind as to fill me in on any important details of this particular model."

Roger nodded his agreement.

There was a lull in the conversation until Officer Jones raised her hand.

"I hate to be a downer, but what about the Nightmare Array?" Tracy nodded toward their clippings on the cork-board. "Your friend Angela said they'd be back—back for us, and back for another raid on Donna's house."

Donna pulled Starla close to her instinctively.

Rico sensed Donna's concern for the safety of her family "We'll reinforce your block, send in as many officers as we can spare. And we'll call in a favor to the Coast Guard and get them to add Star Island to their regular patrol of the bay." Officer Castillo moved closer and crouched so that he was at the level of Donna and Starla, who were seated on the sofa. "You'll be safe. I promise."

Tracy took a deep breath. "I'll go," she interjected, with a hint of wavering in her voice. "I'll go back to the house with the kid and Sondra and the doctor—that way Donna can go do what she needs to do."

"You sure?" Rico raised an eyebrow. It wasn't like Tracy to volunteer for a glorified babysitting shift, especially after everything she had shared in their Halloween heart-to-heart.

She nodded, offered him a soft smile. "I'm sure."

Though they could have spent several more hours discussing the nature of the Nightmare Array and the potential ramifications of Ducane's formula, the group commenced with dividing into three groups: Tracy and Roger were to take Starla back to Donna's house and keep watch over the girl and Sondra, with the help of Sue, Lisa, and the squads of officers on patrol; Declan offered to help Calvin intercept the package before it made it onto the flight.

"If my father's involved," Declan explained, "then I need to be the one to stop him and put an end to his madness."

Last of all was Donna's infiltration of the Pelican tower to find incriminating evidence of Ducane's foul play and secure the documents that held the truth about her family—or so she hoped. Rico was the first to volunteer, but Kiki, Buster, and Mira quickly followed suit.

Kiki quipped: "You're gonna need all the help you can get to break in there and get out in one piece. And," she added, "if there's even a chance of taking down that psycho, I am *definitely* in."

Donna accepted the help with gratitude then turned so that she and Starla sat face-to-face, angled toward one another on the sofa. The woman took the girl's hands in her own gloved pair and spoke softly. "Officer Jones and the others will keep you safe, little Starling. I won't be gone long."

The child's puppy-dog eyes began to glisten. "Will you be okay, Aunt Donna?"

She nodded. "I'll be fine."

"Be careful."

Donna smiled. "I love you, little Starling." She wrapped the girl in a warm embrace, squeezed her tight, then slowly rose and helped Starla to her feet.

The girl started to walk away but then hurried back. "Here—" Starla fished around in her pocket then held out a fist toward her aunt. She opened her fingers to reveal a shiny metallic object surrounded by crumbs of lint and a couple small paperclips.

Donna gasped when she realized what it was: "Your starling pin—?"

"You hold on to it," Starla insisted. "For good luck."

"But—" The woman started, then sighed. "You sure, kiddo?"

The girl nodded, tossing her wavy reddish hair up and down.

With another deep breath, Donna took the pin in her hand then hugged Starla once more. When they were finished, the girl flashed a freckled smile and turned away. Donna watched as Tracy and Roger ushered Starla to the police car in the shadows.

Rico called after Tracy. "Hey, wait up!"

She turned around as she opened the door for Starla.

Castillo moved close. His hand hovered over his pocket, sensing the weight of that tiny, precious metal ring. The man opened his mouth to speak, but decided against it.

"You okay?" Tracy cocked her head.

Rico breathed in deep, nodded. "Yeah. Just be careful, okay?"

The woman smiled. "You, too, partner."

Tracy entered the vehicle and slammed the door. The car revved on, blinding the onlookers with its headlights, then swiveled out through the rising garage door. When the bay door closed once more, Donna and Rico turned back to the remaining group.

Kiki took a deep breath and crossed her arms. “Guess it’s time to hammer out a plan. But first,” she scrunched her nose as Calvin stepped nearer. “I think a few of you could use a shower.”

CHAPTER 20

It was late afternoon and the sun began its descent behind a sea of burnt-orange and gray clouds as the off-duty squad car sped across the causeway. The heavy clouds rolled in off the coast, inching to swallow up the island up ahead.

"That doesn't look good," Roger remarked from the passenger seat, craning his head to inspect the ominous clouds.

Tracy felt her fingers tense, tightened her grip on the steering wheel, and she glanced in the rearview mirror. Starla was buckled into the back seat, watching the downtown skyline and shipping vessels move on parallax planes.

"How about we make a quick pit stop at Spec's and grab a movie?" The officer suggested, making eye contact with Starla's reflection in the mirror.

The girl became visibly excited and nodded.

Droplets began to appear on the windshield, quickly

displaced by a flick of the wipers. Jones added, "We'll have to make it quick, though. Before all hell breaks loose."

Roger switched on the radio and the car whizzed on toward the coming storm to the soundtrack of some unrecognizable synthesizer-heavy dance-pop track nearing its end.

Tracy took deep breaths as her mind zeroed in on Rico. Something didn't feel right to her about the plan he was walking into. It was haphazardly-formed, to be sure; but no matter how hard she tried, Jones couldn't shake the feeling that they were missing something. *What if it's a trap—a setup?* She speculated as the clouds grew closer, darker. *Or the combo—we're trusting in the reflection of a combination of numbers from a memory of a comatose woman filtered through the mind of a child, which was then visualized on an old, grainy television screen in a dark warehouse?* Tracy smiled. If the other happenings of the past days hadn't occurred—monsters, ghouls, flaming pumpkins—she might have thought the scenario much more far-fetched.

But now all she could do was breathe. In. Out. "Here we are," said Jones, wheeling into a parking lot. "You two keep the car running and I'll grab us something to watch." Before either Starla or Roger could protest, Tracy had pulled the car into park and disembarked, slamming the door shut behind her on her way into the video store.

"You're sure you wanna do this, Donna?" Declan leaned in as he watched the woman's eyes study the crackling television screen before her—the image of the penthouse office from Sondra and Starla's memory.

Donna nodded. "It wouldn't be the first time I've broken into Pelican HQ."

The two were joined by Buster, Kiki, and Mira while Rico took a call on a corded phone in a dark corner of the warehouse. The sound of running water emanated from the small bathroom, where Calvin attempted to scrub the smell of sewage out of his hair.

"No doubt they've made a few security upgrades since then," Kiki suggested.

"I *have* to do this," Donna finally shifted her eyes from the screen to look at the group. "I have to know what my parents—and Sondra—were doing with that *psycho*—" She glanced at Declan. "Sorry; no offense."

"None taken." Declan grinned. He didn't exactly see his father as a role model.

The woman pressed a gloved finger to the TV screen. "I need to know what my sister did with that paperwork—I need to know if she signed her rights away. For the past year, I thought everything that happened to me was just a coincidence, but now I know it's all connected. I just need to know *how*. I need to know that my parents and my sister weren't part of Ducane's evil."

For a moment, Donna even doubted herself. *What about the details in the memory—the changing color of Sondra's dress? The ways the walls shifted?* The screen flickered, a pixelated skyline and office. *No memory is perfect,* she reasoned. *We remember what we care about most.*

"We're with you," Mira offered with kind eyes. "We know how much this means to you, and we *will* get you to that safe."

Kiki and Buster nodded their agreement.

"Thanks, guys," the blonde woman half-nodded and clenched her gloved fingers.

Rico reappeared with a pep in his step. "Good news," he said. "I just hung up with my old buddy Jock—the pilot that helped us extract Marcus back in the Bahamas. With all of his transit out of MIA, he has access to the flight logs."

"And?" A voice echoed from the dark—Calvin, rubbing his hair dry with a towel as he walked toward the group. He was dressed in a set of Declan's musty hand-me-downs that had been found in an old box in the warehouse. "Did your buddy find out about our *package*?"

"It just so happens," Rico started, "that there's a routine flight tonight for a South Coastal Electronics, which just so happens to be a subsidiary company of Ducane Enterprises." The officer checked the expressions of the group, hoping they would find his sleuthing impressive. Instead, they seemed to be ripe with anticipation. "Fine. The flight's at 8 p.m. tonight."

Declan nodded. "That's definitely one of his companies. I'd bet that's the one we're looking for."

"Then you two had better be on your way to MIA," Buster suggested with a glance at his watch. "You've got less than an hour."

"Us, too." Kiki threw on a jacket. "Sun's almost gone. The Pelican building should be mostly cleared out by now."

The team scrambled to make last minute preparations and gather their necessary gear. Donna pulled her bag over her shoulder, the plastic cassette tapes clacking together inside. Declan approached and placed a gentle hand on her arm.

"I hope you find what you're looking for, Donna."

Donna returned a somber nod. "Thanks, Dec. Be careful out there. Your father's a dangerous man."

"I'll be fine." He lingered a moment, then met Donna in a brief embrace. When the duo had met just a few months prior, Declan couldn't have anticipated growing so close to Donna. But after everything they had experienced together since, Declan now viewed her as one of his dearest friends. Declan tried not to think about the possibility that this might be the last time he would see Donna. *Best not to dwell on thoughts like that.*

When all were ready, the members filed toward the vehicles. Buster yanked a dusty sheet to reveal a familiar, beat-up conversion van. It was the vehicle of choice for all of the Dream Team's former heists, and they had grown fond of the spacious, dated ride.

Donna grinned. "Just like old times, eh?"

Kiki smacked the hood twice as she rounded the vehicle to enter. "Let's just hope she runs as good as she did then."

"She's perfect," Buster chided and squeezed into the driver's seat. "Just get in."

Donna rode shotgun while Rico piled into the back with Kiki and Mira. The officer was about to slide the side door shut when he noticed Calvin standing, looking confused.

"Did Declan leave you behind?"

"He said he's, uh, going to get our ride," Calvin twitched nervously.

Suddenly, a loud revving echoed throughout the warehouse. The recruit jumped and turned toward the sound. From yet another dark corner of the warehouse, a pair of headlights awoke and caught Calvin in their blinding rays. He blocked the light with his hands as the car rolled closer. A bright red convertible emerged from the shadows, spotless and immaculate with pristine leather seats and its top in the upright, covered position. Declan rode in the driver's seat and pulled up beside Calvin and the large van.

"Get in, kid." Declan nodded toward the passenger seat and Calvin hurriedly complied.

Rico shouted over the engines. "Nice ride!"

"Thanks," the driver answered. "I was hoping for something more discreet, but I just couldn't say *no* to this beauty." Declan tapped the side of the car.

"Let's hope she doesn't end up like your last car," Rico grinned.

Declan rolled his eyes and pulled forward. The garage door lifted and the sportscar wheeled through into the dusky, humid air. The van followed closely behind, after which the bay door closed once more. The two vehicles split off in separate directions and headed off into the night as rain began to patter across the street.

The squad car skidded around the curvilinear loop of

Star Island as it moved toward the house. Through the rain and gathering dusk, Tracy could discern the silhouettes of a pair of boxy cop cars flanking Donna's driveway. She slowed as she approached the gate and rolled down her window halfway. The woman winced as the cold rain pecked at her face.

One of the windows rolled down on the cop car opposite Tracy's, revealing a mustachioed officer. "Jones! Didn't know they had you on patrol detail, too."

"I'm just here to keep an eye on the kid," Officer Jones elevated her volume over the gathering deluge, with a nod toward the backseat. Roger, in the front passenger seat, waved at the officer with an awkward wiggle of his fingers.

"We've got things covered out here," the officer snapped back. "They're paying us to babysit now?"

"Off the clock," she answered. "The woman who lives here is a friend. I'm just doing her a personal favor."

The officer leaned closer, his cap catching more of the rain. "Hey, you know why they've got so many of us out here? Seems a little excessive, right?"

Tracy sighed and considered explaining, but decided against it. "It's a long story, but just keep an eye out, okay? Can you buzz me in?"

The other officer nodded and rolled up his window. Tracy did the same as she watched the man reach for a walkie talkie. A moment later, the gate began to open. Tracy navigated the car up the long driveway and came to a stop as close to the front door as she could manage, just behind another car—

she recognized it as Sue's. When the car was off, she leaned around to look at Starla. "Okay, ready to make a run for it?"

Starla grinned and nodded eagerly.

At least someone's *going to enjoy this.* Tracy took a deep breath, grabbed the plastic bag with the videotapes in it, and began to count. "Ready? 3. 2. 1. Go!" In unison, the trio scrambled out of their respective doors, slammed them behind them, and rushed through the downpour toward the front door of the house. They huddled under the meager overhang as Roger fished around in his pockets for the key.

His face showed a sudden distress. "I think I've forgotten my key."

Tracy wiped a bead of trickling rain from her forehead and nodded toward the second car in the driveway. "Shouldn't be a problem, doctor."

The woman gave a rap on the sturdy door.

"Ah, yes," Roger breathed in. "I'd almost forgotten."

A vibrant shock of lightning cracked nearby, illuminating the entire front courtyard in a flash brighter than daylight. Starla jumped toward Tracy and wrapped her arms around the woman's waist. Jones cringed, tensed. A couple seconds later, a loud peal of thunder crashed, deafening.

"Yikes," Tracy mumbled, mostly to herself, trying to obscure her fear as she eyed the dark violet sky with suspicion. "Sounded pretty close."

"Actually," Roger began, "they say you can determine how close the storm is by measuring the amount of seconds that pass between—"

"Roger? Tracy!" A woman's voice behind them startled the sopping wet guests.

The trio turned toward the sound to find Sue and Lisa standing in the open doorway.

Lisa knelt and opened her arms toward Starla. "Get in here, kiddo. You're gonna catch a cold!"

All of the new arrivals followed the women through the doorway into Donna's expansive entry space and Sue closed the door behind them, with Max scampering over to lend his own slobbery greeting.

"What's going on?" Sue asked with obvious concern as she opened a nearby linen closet and produced a stack of towels for the guests. "Where's Donna—and Rico?"

"And what's with all the cops?" Lisa added, locking the deadbolt. "It's like Fort Knox all of a sudden."

Tracy bent to remove her wet shoes and gave Max a quick tousle. "Donna and Rico had to, uh, take care of something important. They'll be back later." She set one shoe on a mat by the door and started working on the other. "The patrol is to protect us from the..." Tracy paused, yanked on her remaining muddy shoe, then looked up at the inquisitive ladies, receiving a towel from Sue. "Thanks. The patrol's there to protect us from the Nightmare Array."

Both Sue and Lisa's faces betrayed their confusion and more than a hint of fear.

"You mean those goons that tried to burn the place down last night?" Lisa asked.

Tracy nodded and rose.

Sue leaned in. "You think they'd be stupid enough to come back here?"

"They threatened as much," Jones reminded them. "But that's what the patrols are for."

"So, are we safe?" Sue pulled Starla close and wrapped her in a towel.

Tracy glanced at Roger and the two made eye-contact.

Sue raised an eyebrow. "Should we take that as a '*no*'?"

"No—" Tracy shot back. "We're safe. No one's getting in here without our say-so."

A muted rumble of thunder reverberated throughout the house, rattling the glass windows and the chandelier above them. Max yapped. Tracy took this as her cue to change the subject. She held up the bag of video cassette tapes and started for the living room.

"How about we put on a movie while we wait for Donna and Rico to get back?"

"Whatcha got?" Lisa eyed the bag.

"*Flash Gordon*, *Alien*, and *The Shining*—just released on tape this week." Tracy fished a chunky tape out of the bag and grinned. "I was thinking *Alien*, at Sue's recommendation. I haven't seen it yet."

Lisa cocked her head and mock-whispered: "Don't you guys think that might be a little scary for a nine-year-old?"

Before any of the other adults could interject, Starla piped in. "I can handle scary."

"I'll sit next to you so I can cover your eyes at the gory parts," Sue offered.

"*Alien* it is!" Jones nodded, satisfied.

The red-headed Lisa puffed and rolled her eyes at Tracy and Sue. "Fine," she said, starting for the kitchen. "I'll throw some popcorn in the microwave. Donna's got a secret stash in the back of the fridge."

"Roger?" Tracy raised an eyebrow and rattled the video in its clamshell case. "Wanna join?"

The doctor had already started down the hallway toward his above-garage residence. "Actually, I've got to man my post so I can be ready with a tape when Donna and our friends transmit the recording, but send me a buzz if you need me." He pointed toward the intercom on the wall in the next room, then scurried off.

While Lisa started the microwave, the others hurried into the living room. Sue took the tape and put it in the VCR, then turned on the TV and flicked through to channel 3. A light through the back slider caught Tracy's attention and she moved toward the glass doors. The officer peered through the blinds and looked out across Donna's backyard. The light passed by again, this time clearly visible as the tell-tale green of a Coast Guard patrol vessel. Officer Jones exhaled slowly, relieved. *We're safe,* she reminded herself. The officer's mind drifted to her sidearm, which she promptly unbuckled and set on the kitchen counter, then returned to the living room.

"Miss Tracy," Starla beamed. "I saved you a seat next to me!" The girl patted the sofa cushion with her small hand as the previews for other upcoming movies began to play on the screen.

Officer Jones took a deep breath, forced a smile. "Uh, thanks," she said quickly. The woman sat and sunk into the soft couch beside the girl. Immediately, Starla nestled her head into Tracy's side. The cop tensed, unsure how to react. When she pushed past her discomfort, Tracy lowered her arm slowly and brought it to rest around the girl. Starla looked content, serene. *Safe.* Jones inhaled, then released the breath slowly.

Sue sat on the other side of Starla and leaned toward Tracy. "So, how are things between you and my brother?"

"Fine, I guess—"

"He, uh, *ask* you anything lately?"

"Ask me—?"

"Shh!" Starla interjected. "The movie's starting!"

A blaring trumpet fanfare accompanied the 20th Century Fox studio logo in all its glory, with the animated searchlights waving to and fro. As it ended and vanished, the screen went dark. A sea of stars appeared along with a planetary ring.

Beeeeep! The shrill alert from the microwave resounded through the entire house. Lisa removed the inflated paper bag, winced as she felt the heat. A few moments later, she appeared in the living room with a large bowl full of buttery, steaming popcorn and settled into a seat at the end of the couch as the opening title sequence of the film built to a crescendo of eerie strings. Max circled a place at the foot of the couch, lowered himself, and allowed his eyelids to droop.

A motion out the back slider caught Tracy's attention. She whipped her head toward it, eyes alert. A green, blinking light passed by. She relaxed. *Just the patrol boat.*

Starla must have felt the tension in Tracy's movements, for she craned her head up and asked, "Are those bad guys gonna come back here?"

Tracy took her time before answering, narrowly evading the actual question. "You don't need to worry. I'll protect you."

The officer said the words to comfort the child, but now it was becoming a mantra for her own peace of mind. *We'll be okay.*

Buster guided the van across the long, slick causeway and veered off through the rain toward the south end of Miami Beach. The Pelican Innovations headquarters served as the anchor of that tapered corner of the long island strip.

"If anyone from the station asks," Rico said, "I was never here."

The windshield wipers squeaked a struggling rhythm, fighting the downpour.

"You know, you don't have to do this," Donna assured him, leaning back to look over the front passenger seat.

He nodded. "I know. Might lose my job over it, but it's worth it to get the answers you're looking for—and hopefully bring down Ducane and Pelican while we're at it."

"Thanks, Rico." Donna offered a slight, somewhat-somber smile then took a long swig from a water bottle.

The van rounded a bend, splashing through a large puddle. The towering high-rise became clearly visible up ahead, even through the rain—a bastion of modern architecture that had set the trend for many of the other offices and hotels in the area when it was built in the early 1970s. Blue-green uplights intermingled with the thick sheets of rain and cast a tactile glow around the base of the building, illuminating the round emblem of a large-beaked bird—a pelican.

Buster parked a block away in a poorly-lit alley and turned around in his seat so he could view the entire group.

"Mira, you're sure you can cast an illusion that hides all of us?"

"Yeah, no problem," the woman nodded. "With this many of us, though, you'll need to take extra care that you neither touch anyone nor make a sound. We make the slightest mistake and the whole illusion falls apart. I've grown in my ability to convince senses beyond just sight, but even *I* am not quite powerful enough to do that perfectly for a group of us this size."

Rico leaned forward and pointed up toward the top of Pelican tower. "So we just make our way up there—past the guards—to the penthouse, crack the safe to find the incriminating tape, broadcast it off the roof for Roger and the whole city to hear, then get out, right?"

"That's right," Buster nodded.

"Great." Rico exhaled sharply and mumbled: "Simple. What could go wrong?"

"Sounds just like our old dream heists," Mira mused.

Kiki snapped back: "Except for one crucial difference: everyone will be *awake* this time."

"Here," said Buster as he began to distribute walkie talkies from a padded duffel bag. "Everyone take a walkie in case we have to split up."

"Split up?" Kiki raised an eyebrow as a duplicate copy of her head split off and appeared beside her real one for a brief moment.

"You know what I mean."

The beginnings of Kiki's double absorbed back into her natural body. "I'll take that extra one just in case." She tucked a second walkie onto her belt.

"Keep 'em switched off until we get inside," Buster added.

Each of the members put on a rain jacket or poncho, ensuring that they were pulled tight to keep them as dry as possible. The group piled out of the van into the pouring rain.

Mira—always the grounded and logical member of the party—asked, "So what happens if there's nothing up there? Or worse—what if Ducane's changed the combo to his safe?"

Donna flexed her fingers, scrunching the leathery gloves—a nervous habit—as she trudged toward the tower with her eyes focused ahead. She had heard Mira's questions, but remained silent. Those weren't scenarios she wanted to consider. *The tape. The documents—my family's story. They have to be there.*

The group clung to the shadows as they made their way up the street, dodging flooded potholes. Finally, they crouched behind a set of hedges that bordered the Pelican property. Rico peered around the corner, counted only a couple security guards patrolling the exterior.

"Alright," he turned back to the group. "Mira, time to do your thing."

CHAPTER 21

"Walk slowly," Mira whispered in her usual calming way. "Lift your feet directly upward and set them straight down, carefully." Any careless misstep on the wet, porous pavement could make a loud enough splash to alert the guards who stood perched on raised embankments to either side of the Pelican HQ entry road.

The driveway was essentially a large circle—a cul-de-sac loop that allowed for wealthy investors and other important guests to pull right up to the front entry, where they would receive a typical high-level of service from an attentive concierge. This circle of pavement was flanked by a pair of raised portions of land and shrubbery, artificially sloped and elevated to form a barrier that sent the clear message that common passersby—and curious members of the local media looking to unearth a scandal—were not welcome. The guards, wearing matching ponchos with embroidered pelicans on the shoulders, paced the length of the elevation, keeping watch over the grounds at night.

Without Mira's ability to make the guards see an illusion, the five individuals would have appeared to be walking straight down the center of the curved road toward the front doors. Mira's mirage was like an invisibility cloak over the entire team, which allowed those underneath it to see one another. Rico noticed Donna biting her lip in concentration, a raindrop snaking down her face.

Rico set a gentle hand on her arm, slowly, quietly. She turned to him and he offered a thumbs-up and his usual congenial grin—this time with only a hint of his own nerves shining through.

One of the guards stopped pacing. Mira threw her hands up wide at the front of the pack and looked back over her shoulder, eyes alert, mouthing: "Freeze!" Buster, Kiki, Rico, and Donna obeyed. The rain pattered, a droning white noise.

The security guard was angled directly toward the interlopers. In the wet and windy palm frond shadows, Mira couldn't tell if they had been spotted, but she waited. Each of the five held their breath.

When it came to using her powers, Mira was an experienced professional—an artist, really—but occasionally she missed a slight detail, like the rate at which a leaf fluttered in the breeze or an aberration of shadows cast on textured surfaces. One had to be especially observant and meticulous to pull off a convincing illusion. Her mind raced, thinking through the whole scene all at once.

The guard's gaze was intent now, but not on the group. Mira and the others locked on and followed his sightline to an area just beyond them. There was a slight release of tension as the guard's fixation became clear: a tall, elegant bird with pencil-thin tangerine legs, a white feathery torso, and a long angular beak. Water dripped from its waxy feather coat.

"Can it see us?" Rico whispered to Mira, overemphasizing his mouth movements.

Mira hesitated for a moment before shaking her head.

The great white heron took a step toward them, angled its dark-ringed eyes. Mira tensed.

"Ay, Gustavo!" One guard radioed to his partner across the wide entry loop. "Get a load of this thing!"

The second guard, perched on the opposite barrier, directed his attention toward the bird as well. "That's a big one," Gustavo noted. "Those feathers? We'd get a good price for those." The man started for a pistol at his side, when the first guard barked back.

"You crazy? Someone will see."

"Who?" Gustavo cocked his head. "It's just you and me out here—and I ain't gonna squeal."

"I dunno. What if someone hears it?"

"That's what a silencer is for. Plus, the rain doesn't hurt either."

Gustavo now took the gun in both hands, attached a silencer to the barrel, clicked the safety off, and aimed down toward the regal bird as it continued its slow saunter across the slick road.

The eyes of the five invisible people on the loop below grew wide in unison. If the heron continued walking on its current path, the bird would move straight through the middle of the frozen group, potentially placing all five members between the gun and its feathered prey. To get safely out of a bullet's path would require sudden—and potentially loud—motion.

Donna locked eyes with Rico, gulped, clenched her gloved hands. *This was supposed to be the easy part.* She took a deep breath then glanced up the muddy slope as she watched the bird pass behind Kiki, then Buster, then Rico. Next it would be behind her, placing her directly in the bullet's path.

The guard licked his lip and followed the heron's movements with his pistol, half-squinting in one eye. The creature slowed its lanky but graceful steps, nearing Donna, bending its beak to fish between a crack in the pavement. Donna held her breath and closed her eyes.

Phhlinkkk!

Even with the silencer, the pistol shot resounded off the barriers and the glass of the high-rise ahead. Donna opened her eyes and looked up toward the guard. His smoking gun was aimed several yards to the left of the group, but the heron had remained near Donna. When it heard the shot, though, the bird fluttered its feathery crest and massive wings and lifted off from the ground to seek shelter in the trees that bordered the Pelican property.

"Drat!" Gustavo lowered his gun, exhaled slowly, then removed the silencer and holstered the weapon. He wiped the gathering water from his face.

Before the group could take a collective sigh of relief, Mira waved them on toward the entrance to the building. Now that the guards' attention was directed elsewhere, they could hasten under less scrutiny.

Finally, they made it to the base of the tower and huddled into a shadow. A section of the building jutted out above them, shielding them slightly from the rain.

"What the heck just happened back there?" Rico asked.

"I coulda sworn he was aiming right at the bird—and me!" Donna's expression betrayed her concern.

"He was," Mira muttered, taking deep, labored breaths. "Or at least he *thought* he was." When the others offered confused looks, Mira continued. "I let him see the bird, but made him think it was in a different spot—safely out of range of us."

"Thanks," Donna nodded and noticed the weary look in Mira's eyes. "You okay?"

She winced but replied, "I'll be fine. Just took a lot out of me."

None of the other four seemed convinced of Mira's self-assessment of her wellness, but they knew time was of the essence. The mission couldn't wait for Mira to regain her full strength.

"So are we going in through the front door?" Kiki asked, leaning around the corner to get a better look. "Looked like there were a few more security guards inside."

Buster shook his head. "We were thinking something a little more discreet." He pointed toward the back of the building. "Service entrance."

The group shuffled along the building's shadow to the next corner, following Buster's lead. The back door was plain, accompanied by a keypad and watched by a set of security cameras. A single fluorescent light from a small overhang cast a wide glow.

"Alright," Buster began in a whisper, "Donna's going to turn that door into gold, soften it up a bit. And that should knock out the emergency alarm trigger. Then I'll do what I do best." He flashed a toothy grin and formed a fist. "Mira will make sure the cameras out here *and* in there keep seeing a boring, people-less scene."

Buster started toward the light and Mira grabbed his arm. "Just please try not to smash up the door *too* much. Once we're inside I'll have to release the illusion, and I need it to look as close to the real thing as possible."

"No promises." Buster smiled. "Ready?"

She rolled her eyes. Mira took a deep breath and raised her hands, palms out. "Ready."

Donna and Buster locked eyes then moved toward the door with haste, running through the rain for a brief moment toward the next overhang. Donna eyed the security cameras with suspicion, the little red light blinking every few seconds. *They can't see us.* She took deep breaths. When she was next to the door, Donna carefully removed one of her special, leathery gloves and placed her bare hand against the solid metal. Immediately, a wave of shimmering gold spread across the door, neatly terminating at the edges and corners of the door frame. Donna removed her hand, took a deep breath, and placed the glove over her hand once more.

Rico watched from the shadows. "It still amazes me every time she does that," he muttered.

Kiki nodded, mesmerized. "If I had that kind of power, I'd be richer than Pablo Escobar."

As Donna stepped aside, Buster now took his place in front of the small door. He had to crouch to avoid hitting his head on the overhanging light. "Open sesame." Carefully, he pulled at the door's handle. The entire edge of the door began to warp toward him like soft butter, effortlessly clicking free from the frame and its latch. When he held the door wide open, Buster turned to the others and flourished with one of his bulky hands. "After you."

The other four filed into the narrow hallway, wiping their wet shoes on a conveniently-placed doormat. Rico spotted a camera aimed directly at them. "You got that one, too, right?" He whispered to Mira as he removed his raincoat.

She nodded as they continued under it. "The illusion is like a blanket that covers us. Anyone under the blanket—those whom I allow—can see the reality. Anyone—or any camera—outside sees the illusion."

Buster pulled the golden door back into place, doing his best to straighten the bent edge so that it looked as close to normal as possible. "Best I can do," he shrugged to Mira as he finished and removed a poncho.

The door was a golden color and showed the clear signs of warping in-person, but the monitors and recordings from the cameras would be taped in crackled, low-resolution black-and-white.

Mira exhaled sharply. "Let's hope no one notices."

The group stuffed their rain gear into a small storage closet, did their best to dry off their shoes, and continued on down the hall.

Pelican Innovations headquarters was massive—a maze of offices, labs, and corridors fashioned of the finest (and most expensive) finishes available. Though Ducane had heightened security since Donna's last nighttime break-in there, the addition of Mira's powers made their trek up to the penthouse almost too easy. *Something feels off,* Donna thought as the group piled into an elevator, which lifted them swiftly upward. She quickly brushed the thought away as she felt her ears begin to pop from the pressure of their rapid ascent. The elevator slowed, rose to a stop, and offered a pleasant chime to indicate their arrival. The shiny doors slid open.

The five spread out onto the darkened penthouse floor. Rico immediately noticed the lack of cameras. *No doubt to allow Ducane to hide his shady dealings.* Mira relaxed as she noted the same, releasing her power of illusion.

Donna recalled the images of her sister's memories as she looked around and zeroed in on a set of wooden doors just beyond a secretary's desk. "Ducane's office is through there." She tried the handle. *Locked.*

"I can bust through this one, too?" Buster offered.

Donna shook her head. "We can't let him know we were up here. There's gotta be a key somewhere. Start looking."

The group split up across the large room. Kiki began searching a drawer of a decorative table near the large floor-to-ceiling glass windows. The view outside mesmerized the teal-haired woman and she looked out across the bay toward the downtown skyline. "Can't blame that old monster for picking this spot for his evil lair," she said, loud enough for the others to hear. "This view is incredible."

"We're not here for sightseeing," Donna chided, feeling around in one of the drawers of the secretary's desk.

"Alright, alright, give me a break!" Kiki started toward a section of a large bookshelf when something outside the window caught her eye. She doubled back, looked past the trickling raindrops clinging to the surface and angled toward the base of the tower, twenty-something stories down. Her mouth hung agape involuntarily and her eyes grew wide. "Uh, guys—"

"What is it now, Kiki?" Donna's voice betrayed the slightest hint of irritation.

"We've got company."

Mira and Rico were closest to the window and crowded at Kiki's side to get a look through the glass.

Mira gasped. "Is that—?"

Kiki nodded. "Sure looks like it."

"Of course. The Nightmare Array," Rico muttered under his breath. The figures on the street below appeared small, like bugs or a miniature model display. It was difficult to make out their features due to the rain and distance, but the onlookers' fears were verified as the lights from several streetlamps suddenly went out. *Marcus.*

Donna looked up from behind the desk. "They're *here?*"

"Yep." Rico exhaled quickly, his pulse quickening.

"Wait a sec." Kiki strained to see. "I only counted four of them."

Mira did the math in her head. "What about the other two? Where are they?"

Rico locked eyes with Mira and gulped.

"They're going exactly where they said they'd go."

Thunder rumbled, shaking Donna's entire house.

"Cover your eyes, kiddo. This next part'll give you nightmares."

Sue placed a hand in front of Starla's face. The girl tried to maneuver and sneak a peek at the TV screen, but finally gave up right as a small alien creature burst out of an on-screen character's chest. Lisa screamed.

Tracy felt tense, but her mind was somewhere other than on the film. She glanced past Sue to catch another look through the back sliding glass door. There was the same green light of the patrol boat, as before. *Everything's fine.* Jones repeated the words mentally, but her pulse remained heightened.

A bloody struggle played out on the TV. Out of instinct, Sue clutched Starla tighter and kept her hand over the girl's face. Starla caught glimpses and slivers of the scene through the gaps in the woman's fingers but obediently resisted the urge to break free of Sue's well-meaning grip.

Officer Jones turned to look out the back slider once more. It was dark, still raining hard. She waited for the light to appear again. *One. Two. Three.* There it was. The green blink of the patrol vessel, right on cue. It slowly lulled across Tracy's frame of view.

Suddenly, it disappeared.

The light reappeared a second later.

Blinked?

No. Something—or someone—had moved between the boat and the house, blocked the view for a split second. That would mean that *something* was in the backyard. Tracy's hand tightened to a fist. Her breathing became quick.

"Turn off the movie," she said to no one in particular, almost a whisper.

Lisa answered back, her eyes locked on the screen: "The scary part's almost over, Trace—"

"Turn it off!" Tracy nearly shouted as she leaped up from the couch.

The red-headed woman complied and clicked off the TV. As they'd turned off all of the lights to set the mood for the movie, the room now became almost completely dark and noiseless, except for the sound of pattering rain on the roof and outside. Max awoke and offered a curious whimper.

"Tracy, what—?"

"Shh!" Tracy placed her finger over her lips as she inched toward the back sliding door in the adjacent dining room.

"What is it?" Sue pulled Starla close.

Starla trembled. "The bad guys?"

Tracy didn't answer but continued toward the glass. The patrol boat had continued on its usual route and was now out of view, leaving the backyard completely unilluminated. Officer Jones moved closer, her face inches from the glass. She strained, squinted. Moved closer.

Lightning flashed.

For the briefest moment, Tracy saw two figures in the center of the lawn. She gasped.

"Hide!" Tracy stepped away from the glass and bolted toward the kitchen as the trio in the living room scrambled and crouched behind the furniture. Jones hurried toward the counter where she had left her gun earlier, but found that it was gone. She breathed quickly, scanned the entire kitchen. "Where's my gun? Lisa?"

"It freaked me out to have it just lying around there on the counter," the red-headed woman shouted from the living room. "I put it in the cabinet."

Tracy yanked open one of the cabinets. No gun. Just a set of bowls and plates. "*Which* cabinet?"

"The one by the fridge—"

As Officer Jones turned to try another cabinet, she stole a glance toward the back slider. *All clear.* Lightning flashed again. With quick steps, Tracy continued checking the cabinets, growing more infuriated with each failed attempt to locate her sidearm.

Dammit, Lisa—

The storm strobed again as the woman looked toward the glass door. Tracy jolted backward, catching herself against the counter as she let the cabinet slam shut. The two figures stood just outside the door now, their bodies outlined by the flash for only a fraction of a second. A man and a woman.

Tracy braced herself near the oven, whipped her head in another quick sweep of the kitchen. She caught sight of a knife block and reached for the largest butcher blade. As she removed it from its solid wood resting place, the officer ducked behind the kitchen island and crawled across the kitchen tile. She leaned to get a view beyond the doorway toward the sliding glass door. Her eyes drifted up toward the latch. *Locked.* It would have given her greater relief if the door itself wasn't fashioned out of thin, easily-breakable glass. But it would delay an intrusion at least, buying precious time for the others to hide.

A hand slapped against the glass, accompanied by a humid, foggy outline. The intruder's other hand moved to grip the sliding door's handle, applied pressure. The door didn't budge.

Tracy adjusted her stance, gripped the butcher knife tighter. In another burst of lightning, bright as day, the officer saw the first figure's face. Or rather, she would have seen it if the interloper *had* a proper face.

Patchface, Tracy almost grinned. *That's what Kiki called him.* But the officer had grown accustomed to referring to him by his given name—the one that belonged to him in another life: Jason Sunder.

He died once.

She braced herself.

If he so much as touches any of them, I'll make sure it happens again—for good this time.

Sunder tugged on the door again, confirmed that it was indeed locked, then stepped aside. Tracy now saw the man's partner: the woman once known as Marjory Beauregard, her decrepit skin and wet, wispy hair fluttering in the breeze. Her nickname terrified Tracy even more, for it conveyed the ghastly nature of the old woman's powers:

The Ghoul.

Just like her namesake from legend and lore, this Ghoul could float through solid objects as if they were no more dense than a cloud. But she needed one thing first.

Blood.

Max let out a bark and appeared at the threshold between the dining and living rooms.

"Max," Starla called out to him from her hiding place behind the sofa in the next room. "C'mere boy!"

The golden puppy ignored the girl's calls and snarled at the figures through the glass. The Ghoul crouched, lowering herself to the dog's level, and extended a crooked finger in a beckoning motion reminiscent of a cartoon witch. The small dog inched closer to the glass.

"Max, no!" Tracy muttered, nodding her head toward the living room in hopes that he would comply.

His growls intensified into loud yaps at the wet strangers on the other side of the transparent door. Marjory beckoned still, pressed herself close to the glass. She appeared to be hovering, her feet no longer touching the ground as she crouched.

Tracy tried again to call the dog toward her, but to no avail. The Ghoul bent her arm and reached toward the dog on the other side of the glass door. Officer Jones' eyes grew wide as she watched the decrepit woman's limb pass through the glass as if the door were mere tissue paper. Marjory reached for Max, lowered her hand to grab his collar.

"Maxie!" Starla cried out in another shrill whisper, barely heard over the rain that tapped relentlessly at the roof and windows.

The dog turned and backed away, just out of the Ghoul's reach. Max barked again, then scurried into the living room. Marjory seemed to be annoyed by the furry creature's maneuver, but she now rose back to her full height. Her arm remained halfway through the glass door as she now shifted to reach around to unlock the door from the inside.

Officer Jones took quick breaths. *Why didn't she just pass her whole body through? Last time she floated away with the whole Array.*

Max snarled in the other room.

It suddenly made sense. *She needs his blood. She's running low....*

After a few seconds of feeling her fingers up the side of the doorframe, Marjory alighted on the lock. It took a fair amount of strength, but Tracy heard the heavy *click* as it became unlatched. The old woman withdrew her arm from the glass so that her entire body was now fully on the outside of the now-unlocked door. She placed her bone-thin fingers around the handle and pulled.

CHAPTER 22

Declan sped up the car and skidded through the raised security gate across the wet tarmac at Miami International Airport. Calvin had used his Metro-Dade credentials to procure access to the landing strips, and the pair now followed the painted markings on the ground, which ran in solid and dashed lines toward the airport's main structure.

"Rico's buddy Jock said the South Coastal flight should be docked at Gate 7," Calvin pointed up ahead, the view slightly obscured by the rapid motion of the windshield wipers against the rain.

"How much time do we have?" Declan was determined not to miss the window to secure the package and stop his father.

The recruit checked the clock on the dashboard console. "Five minutes til they push off."

Declan bit his lip, heavied his step on the gas pedal. The

tarmac was deceptively more expansive than it appeared from up in the concourse, but the little convertible raced across the pavement as fast as Declan could get it to go.

Finally, they rounded the building and could view a row of planes of varying sizes docked along the gates, readying for international flights. The sportscar rushed past the first large airplane, where the pair could see glimpses through the airport windows of passengers filing down a jet bridge.

Calvin squinted out the side window and caught the gate number on the side of the building—the number 1. He turned and looked up ahead, following the progression of digits, pointed. "There it is. That small cargo jet should be the one we're looking for."

With a nod, Declan maneuvered around a slow-moving gas tanker vehicle and zipped on toward the jet at Gate 7.

Both Declan and Calvin breathed sighs of relief when they finally got a clear view of the plane and the blue lettering emblazoned across its side and wings: *South Coastal Electronics*. Exactly as they expected. Calvin couldn't help but slip a slight grin.

Suddenly, the plane began to move, a lugging jolt backward. Calvin's expression melted and his shoulders slumped as he watched men with glowing sticks and raincoats guide the jet as it slowly pulled away from the retracting bridge.

"What? They're taking off early! Do you think they knew we were coming?"

Declan shook his head. "Doesn't matter. We're going to stop them."

The convertible passed Gate 4. The driver yanked the wheel and the car lurched around a baggage car. Declan slammed his foot on the gas and the convertible skidded across the slick pavement. The compact car swerved. Calvin gripped the hold on the door and looked ahead as the car straightened out: they were now on a trajectory that—in a matter of seconds—would put them directly in the path of the plane.

"Are you crazy?" The recruit shot a look of concern to the driver.

"I'm not letting my father leave this tarmac." Declan's knuckles whitened and he took short breaths.

The distance between plane and car shortened. The engines of the two machines blared in competition with each other and the growing storm. One of the marshals finally caught sight of the revving car and leaped out of its path, tossing his orange glowrods aside as he hit the ground.

Declan winced. "Hang on, kid." Before the recruit could respond, Declan thrust his foot on the brake pedal. For a brief moment, the pair felt weightless as the vehicle around them shifted from rapid motion to full-stop.

The car hydroplaned, squealed as it spun—back wheels first—over the wet black tar. Declan attempted to regain control, but the wheel locked up. He and Calvin clung to the sides of the car and caught alternating, flashing glimpses of the plane through the windows.

Finally, the car screeched to a halt, now directly facing the reversing plane. The massive back tires rolled toward the convertible. The engine rumbled as the gap between the vehicles tightened.

"What are you waiting for?" Calvin shouted at Declan. "Move!"

Declan shook his head, braced himself, and locked his eyes ahead.

The airplane engine grew faster, louder.

Calvin reached for his door handle, heard the lock click, and whipped around. "Are you out of your mind?"

"They're going to stop."

The plane kept moving.

The recruit clenched his whole face and curled toward his corner of the car. "I'm not ready to die," Calvin muttered. "This is insane!"

Another roar of the engine startled Calvin so that he inched his eyelids open to steal a peek. The plane was now mere feet from the car.

With a sluggish lurch and a loud metallic grating sound, the plane came to a stop.

The engine decelerated. Calvin let out an enormous breath and sunk his head back to the headrest. Through his deep exhales, the recruit managed: "What the heck were you thinking?"

"Hey, it worked," Declan pointed out. His eyes drifted to the clock on the dashboard. "And would you look at that? Three minutes to spare." The man unlocked the car and opened the door, letting in a flutter of rain. "You coming? We've still got my psycho dad to stop."

Calvin regained his composure, nodded, and followed Declan out into the rain. Droplets formed on his large glasses, which he promptly wiped away before they were replaced by more.

One of the air traffic marshals hurried over to them. "Hey, you! What the hell do you think you're doing out here?"

Declan ignored the man and kept walking toward the front of the plane. Calvin noticed that the man was following them.

"Uh, I think he's talking to us—"

"—you coulda got yourself killed!" The disgruntled airport employee continued, trudging after them in his waxy raincoat.

Declan spotted one of the motorized metal staircases and pointed at it. "We need to get on that plane," he said, finally acknowledging the angry marshal.

The rain soaked the man's bushy, graying mustache as he stopped in his tracks. "You serious?"

Calvin panicked and fished around in his pocket. "We're, uh, with Metro-Dade," the recruit produced his temporary station access card and flashed it at the man quickly, hoping it might pass for a badge. "We have reason to believe there's a dangerous fugitive on that plane with a large quantity of contraband."

"Please," Declan urged as a rivulet of rainwater snaked down his face. "Time is of the essence."

The glowrods cast a red-orange glint over the grumpy marshal's weathered skin. He silently considered the plight of the two intruders before taking a deep breath. "It'll just take a minute to get the steps into place," he said finally, stomping through a puddle toward the motorized staircase.

Declan made eye-contact with Calvin as they followed the man. "Good story."

"It wasn't *technically* a lie," Calvin mumbled.

Within a few moments, the marshal had navigated the slow-moving staircase and docked it against the front of the plane. He clicked a brake into place and nodded to Declan. "She's all yours."

Declan gripped the slick rail and clambered up the metal steps with Calvin at his heels. The two worked together to release the lock on the aircraft door. It let out a puff of pressurized air as it shifted open and the men hurried inside.

The jet appeared to be a passenger vessel that had been retrofitted for use as a cargo plane, so the area that typically housed hundreds of seated flyers was now instead partitioned off as a separate, seatless compartment. Declan tried the door. It was locked. As the two men entered the plane, the pilot appeared behind them in the cockpit doorway.

"You wanna tell me what's going on here—?"

Declan didn't wait for the man to finish. He pointed at the door to the cargo area. "Open it."

"Metro-Dade," Calvin repeated his badge trick.

The pilot seemed unconvinced.

"We believe there may be dangerous individuals and contraband on board." Calvin nodded toward the cargo door and forced a pleading grin. "Please?"

"There's no contraband on here." The pilot puffed, fumbled for a set of keys around his neck, then made his way toward the cargo door. He unlocked it and swung the door open. "See for yourself."

As the pilot stepped out of the way, Declan and Calvin passed through the threshold into the cargo area.

The large space was packed tight with crates and metal cages containing an assortment of items. Calvin's eyes flicked from computer monitors to keyboards to calculators before he finally made eye-contact with Declan. *It was supposed to be here.*

The pilot chuckled. "That the contraband you were looking for? Everything's clear and accounted for on the inventory."

Calvin moved toward one of the containers and rifled through its contents. More of the same. "I don't understand," he muttered. "I heard them myself. This was their plan."

Declan sensed the younger man's growing frustration and motioned with his hands. "It's alright, take a deep breath."

The recruit shook his head and allowed his gaze to drift out the window. "I mean, they couldn't have known we were coming—"

"It seems unlikely, but—"

"Oh my gosh." Calvin's mouth hung agape and he stared through the layers of clear glass and plastic.

"What?" Declan forced his way through a heap of cargo to look through another window. His eyes grew wide.

There across the tarmac—just a couple gates up—was a

smaller cargo plane. A man in a dark raincoat stood at the top of a lowered ramp near the back of the craft, while another figure hobbled at the base of the ramp near a cart stacked with what looked like small, metallic suitcases.

"It's them," Calvin gasped and pressed a finger to the plexiglass. "That's her. Dr. Blanche." He turned to Declan.

"We got the wrong plane."

"I think I've got it!" Donna shouted from behind the secretary's desk. She rose to her feet and held up a small key between gloved fingers, glinting in a sliver of moonlight caught through the big windows. As the others crowded closer to see, the blonde woman hurried over to the double-doors that led into Ducane's office. She inserted the key into the lock, fiddled with it a little, then turned it.

Click.

"Bingo!" Kiki grinned.

Donna swung open the doors. The group was greeted by another set of panoramic windows that stretched the full height of the adjacent walls. A flash of lightning illuminated the vast penthouse office, briefly highlighting the display of trinkets and artwork scattered about—artifacts that Ducane had no doubt acquired through means of questionable legality, Donna presumed. These distractions faded as Donna locked eyes on a framed painting that hung just beyond a large mahogany desk.

The safe. Behind the painting. Just like in Starla's memory tape—it was a modern cubist piece made of thick lines and boxy shapes that appeared to depict a man's face. A second figure resembled a dog or wolf. Both the man and the beast each extended a hand toward the center of the frame, where they shared grasp of a single, wilting rose.

"Okay, let's make this quick," Rico urged. "Marcus and Angela and the others will be up here any minute."

Donna nodded. She made her way to the painting and carefully placed her gloved fingers around one edge. She pulled it away from the wall carefully, sensing the release of a weak magnetic pull. The painting swung on a hinge like a cabinet door, revealing the small locked safe behind it.

So far, so good. Donna took deep breaths as Rico and Mira crowded at her sides.

"You remember the combo?" Mira asked.

The blonde woman nodded. "Yeah. 21-11-1." Donna inhaled for several seconds, then breathed out slowly before finally placing her hand on the combination dial. *Clockwise three times to clear it first.* Donna twisted it, barely breathing, until it came to rest at the first number in the combination.

Now left, past the first number. She switched direction and slowly brought the wheel and arrow to meet at the second set of digits.

Donna made eye-contact with Mira, who muttered: "Moment of truth."

As she started to turn toward the last number, Donna's hand began to tremble slightly. She steadied her hand, inhaled, then held her breath as she inched the dial to the final number: *1*.

Click.

Donna, Rico, and Mira all released gasps of relief at once.

"Holy cow," Rico shook his head. "I don't believe it."

Donna swung open the small safe door and lowered her jaw involuntarily. Her fear that the safe would be empty was put to rest when she saw a stack of papers, folders, tapes, and other loose items sitting inside. "Believe it," she half-grinned to Rico.

"What's inside?" Kiki asked, too far away to see.

Donna reached into the safe and withdrew a few of the items, then held them up for the others to see. "There's a lot in here," she said.

"Time's ticking," Buster stole a glance into the penthouse lobby space to ensure the Nightmare Array had not yet caught up to them. "We need to find the tape that will bring Ducane down once and for all—fast!"

"I know," Donna flipped through a stack of papers. "And I'm not leaving here without finding out the truth about my family." She could feel her pulse rising with every second that passed.

"What's this?" Rico examined a cassette tape, encased in a generic plastic case with a handwritten label. "*Formula 31: Sunder, J.*," he read. "Sounds promising."

"There's a tape deck over there on the credenza." Kiki angled her chin toward the device.

Rico hurried over to the modern furniture piece, removed the cassette from its plastic case, and inserted the tape into the player. As it was already rewound, he pressed the clunky play button. The reels began to spin and a grainy room noise came through a set of auxiliary speakers hidden inside the webbed cabinet doors of the credenza.

On the tape, Ducane's voice spoke with a hint of weariness: "As before, my name is Rolf Ducane and this is trial number..." He seemed to be searching. "Uh, number sixty-seven. My colleague, Dr. Eudora Blanche, and I have composed a compound tailored to the genetic makeup of our subject J. Sunder. For the record, Sunder was pronounced dead approximately four years ago and has no known living relatives. Dr. Blanche and I are ready to administer Formula 31 to the subject, which should not only reanimate his body, but imbue him with heightened sensory abilities."

Donna made eye contact with Rico across the room. *Sounds familiar*, she thought.

The tape continued: "Dr. Blanche, would you like to do the honors?"

"Certainly," the old woman's voice crackled. The tape was quiet and muffled for a few moments as the doctor apparently administered the mysterious formula to the dead subject.

"Think there's enough on there for your buddies at Metro-Dade to lock 'em up?" Kiki whispered, trying not to overpower the recording.

"Him being dead with no relatives means they couldn't have gotten proper consent for this trial," Rico nodded. "But I need to hear a little more before I can say for certain."

"While you keep listening," Buster said, taking another nervous glance back into the penthouse lobby, "I'd better go and get the radio transmitter ready. It's going to take time to warm up and get it configured to the right frequency. The doctor said it has to be powered up from a generator room two floors below us. We've got to get that recording out in case..." He trailed off without finishing his sentence, but everyone knew what he intended to say.

In case we don't make it out.

"I'm coming with you, Busty," Kiki offered.

Mira and Donna looked up from the files.

"You guys be careful," Kiki added, already following Buster out of the office. "They'll be here any minute."

"We'll be right behind you," Rico assured them as the two ladies near the safe returned to their frantic flipping of folders and documents.

Kiki and Buster started out toward the elevators. Kiki hollered back: "If anything happens, you can get us on the walkies. See you on the roof!" The two piled into one of the luxe elevators and the doors closed quickly behind them.

"Any luck?" Mira muttered to Donna.

She shook her head and let out an exasperated sigh. "Nothing. Just old receipts and faxes. You?"

Mira shook her head. "What if—?"

"It's *got* to be here," Donna insisted. *The adoption papers. The truth about my parents. I have to know why they were working with Ducane.* "Keep looking." She finished skimming a file folder and moved on to a stack of loose papers.

A sudden loud noise came through the tape recording—an eerie, nasal gasp, as from someone who has held their breath underwater and has no mouth. "Hold him down!" Ducane's voice shouted. Rico, Donna, and Mira listened intently to the struggle. "Calm down, calm down," Dr. Blanche tried to sooth the newly-awakened body. "Jason? Jason Sunder? You're alright. Check his vitals," Blanche said, presumably to Ducane.

As he listened, Rico's gaze wandered toward the elevators and his eyebrows shot up as he looked above one of the sets of doors. On the wall space atop each elevator was an old-fashioned semi-circle of brass with a small hand like a clock. The thin hand pointed to one of a sequence of numbers that lined the rounded edge of the brass dial, indicating the floor at which the elevator car currently rested. Rico tensed as he saw that the dial above one elevator now started to move from some mid-building floor number down toward the ground floor. *That wasn't the elevator Buster and Kiki used.*

On the tape recording, Ducane answered back: "Vitals are stable. It worked, Dr.—"

Castillo turned to the women. "Uh, guys?" Rico pointed at the floor indicator, though the women could barely see it from their position near the safe. "I think our old friends are on their way up."

CHAPTER 23

Donna barely glanced toward Rico and the elevators before returning her attention to the remaining documents and evidence inside the safe. *It's got to be here!*

"It's moving again," Rico locked his eyes on the metal hand of the floor indicator dial. It had reached the ground floor and now started to ascend. "They're coming up. Fast."

"We need to go, Donna," Mira muttered in her usual gentle but firm manner.

Donna flipped a page then reached into the safe to inspect the next set of documents. "Not until we find what I came for."

Mira took a deep breath and exhaled sharply. She stole a glance toward Rico across the penthouse space.

"They're halfway up already," he gritted his teeth.

"Just give me a minute," Donna begged, her eyes flicking across a xeroxed page. She cursed under breath.

Mira hollered to Officer Castillo. "Go! Get the tape to the transmitter—Buster and Kiki will meet you up there."

"What about you guys?"

"I'll handle it," Mira assured him.

Castillo inhaled then clicked the *stop* and *eject* buttons. He grabbed the tape, shoved it into its plastic case, and took one more look across the expansive room. "You got maybe ten seconds."

"*Go!*" Mira urged, adjusting the walkie talkie strap slung across her body.

Rico hurried toward a door in the corner of the penthouse lobby and disappeared into the fire exit stairwell. *Clunch!* The door clicked back into place behind him.

"Donna, we have to wrap this up. *Now.*"

Donna shook her head, reached for the next stack of papers, then froze as she looked into the safe. A large, thick manila envelope sat in the small space, one of the last remaining items in Ducane's safe. The woman moved her gloved hand toward it and lifted the envelope with a sense of reverence. On the flap were two letters: S.G.

"This is it," Donna whispered as she read the initials. She started to pry open the soft metal clasp but stopped as she and Mira heard a frightening sound:

The ding of the elevator. The Nightmare Array had reached the penthouse.

Mira grabbed Donna's shoulder as both turned to get a view of the elevators.

Before Donna could make another move, the elevator

doors slid open. Each of the women froze, held their breath, and watched as four figures stepped out into the dark penthouse waiting area. Lightning flashed through the large windows, illuminating Angela and Marcus at the front of the pack. Behind them lurked the duo Donna's friends had affectionately labeled Frightknight and the Gatorman.

Angela looked straight through the open doors to Ducane's office and sauntered toward them. As she reached the doors, the woman stopped and stared directly in Donna's direction across the wide office. Thunder rumbled and the rain continued to patter, muffling the faintest of sounds.

Donna gripped the manila envelope. She was about to speak—to try and convince Angela to step aside and let them go on their way—when Mira touched her arm and leaned toward her.

"Whatever you do," Mira whispered. "Don't make a sound—and don't touch any of them."

For a moment, Donna was baffled. Angela was looking straight at them. They'd been found. There was no easy way out.

Finally, it clicked and Donna understood. Mira had cast one of her illusions over the two women, obscuring them from the new arrivals. Angela's attention wasn't on Donna, but the open safe beyond her.

"Move toward the window," Mira instructed. "Slowly."

Donna nodded and took a half step to the side of the desk.

Marcus now entered the office and looked around, bringing his focus to rest on the safe and its scattered contents on the large desk. "We're too late."

Angela narrowed her eyes and kept her focus locked on the safe.

Donna froze, took a quiet breath. *She can see me—sense me.* Angela had no "powers" to speak of, but she was a shrewd and unforgiving woman. That's what made her so dangerous.

As Donna Locke took another small step toward the enormous windows, her hip clipped the edge of a loose sheet of paper sitting on Ducane's desk. Her eyes widened as she watched the page ripple slightly, then settle and flatten once more. Donna couldn't move. She looked up at Angela. She had most certainly noticed the slight movement.

Angela held up a hand. "They're still here." She turned to her two other companions. "Guard the elevators and the exits. Don't let them escape."

Mira nodded toward the window and Donna carefully followed her guidance. The two lifted their feet gracefully, trying to avoid any sound of shuffling soles.

"I know you're here, Miss Locke." Angela taunted, shifting her eyes around the room as she approached the safe. "How about you and your friends quit playing games and just give up? It's no use trying to escape."

Marcus moved toward the windows, looked out across the skyline. He was mere feet from Donna—the closest the two had been to one another since Marcus had been freed from his gilded prison. The woman studied his face, searching for a glimpse of the man she had loved. Marcus Myles was stoic, nary a trace of his infectious dimpled smile. He flinched, twitched, and turned his head right toward the two hidden women.

He can't see us. Right? Donna's eyes met his. *Marcus.* The woman clutched the manila envelope in one hand while her other rested on the bag slung at her side. She felt the outline of the walkie talkie and the tape recordings buried in the bag, memories of their earliest days together. *Are you still in there?* The moment dragged on and Marcus breathed in deep, then turned and continued on toward Angela to join her behind Ducane's desk.

The storm rumbled and rattled the glass windows and Donna and Mira inched closer. Donna was about to take another step forward when Mira grabbed her arm. The women made eye contact and Mira shook her head. She pointed at the floor in front of the window. Donna raised an eyebrow, then nearly jumped as lightning flashed, casting a bright and blinding burst of electric light into the room.

"Our shadows," Mira mouthed.

Of course. Donna tried to remain calm. *Mira can't know the exact timing of the lightning strikes, which means she's going to have trouble masking our shadows.*

"Between flashes," Mira suggested, again mouthing the words without a sound.

Donna looked around the room. As long as no one was watching, there would be no problem. But a single out-of-place shadow could be their death sentence. *No pressure.* Donna nodded her agreement to her counterpart and followed Mira's lead.

"What are they looking for?" Marcus asked as he flipped through the loose pages strewn across the desk.

Angela rifled through the few remaining contents of the safe. "Whatever it is, I think they found it," she muttered, turning back to survey the room. Her eyes narrowed. In one corner of the room was a closet. "Check in there."

Marcus obeyed and moved with haste across the office. He yanked open the closet door and looked inside. "Empty. Except for some suits and old catalogs." The man closed the door and pivoted back to Angela, who seemed to be listening for clues to the presence of her invisible nemeses.

Donna and Mira shuffled quietly but quickly across the wide expanse—the glass stretched across a significant section of the office's outer edge. They were nearly past the windows when lightning flashed again, twice in succession. The two women paused.

Angela appeared bewildered. She had seen the peculiar shadows. "Did you see that?" She moved toward the windows quickly, with Marcus just behind her. "I know you're there, Donna," she taunted in the general direction from which the shadows had originated. "I'll give you one last chance to come quietly." She locked her gaze ahead, where she imagined Donna's eye level would be, and slowly sauntered forward.

A curtain at the side of the window fluttered, catching Angela's eye. She darted toward it with her arms outstretched, hoping to grab on to some part of the unseen woman. But her hands met only air and the gauzy cloth. She puffed, fumed, and eyed the office doors. "Watch the elevators—and the fire exit," Angela called out to her two cronies in the lobby area. She muttered under her breath: "You're not getting out of here alive, Donna Locke. And neither are your dear friends back at your island home."

Donna and Mira had made it safely out of the office and into the penthouse's lobby. *So they did send some of the party to the house, after all.* Donna knew Angela was just trying to get in her head. As she and Mira clung to the wall, they studied their escape options: the woman in conquistador armor had split herself into two identical figures, one guarding each elevator. The half-man, half-gator hybrid held his back to the fire exit—the only other way out of the penthouse.

Not good. Donna bit her lip and held tight to her belongings.

Before the two women could think further, they tensed up. The Gatorman began to sniff, the round nostrils at the end of his scaled snout expanding and contracting. He directed his head in the general direction of the unseen women and let out a low, guttural growl.

The sound made the hairs on Donna's neck stand up, and she clutched her handbag tighter. Then, she felt it: the walkie talkie in the bag. Donna turned to Mira and nodded down at her partner's own walkie. "I've got an idea," she articulated without a sound. Mira seemed to be putting the pieces together. She took a deep, silent breath and began to back away from Donna toward the opposite side of the lobby.

Angela and Marcus reached the large doorway between the office and lobby and stood at the wide threshold.

"Well?" Angela put her hands on her hips as she awaited

an explanation from the others.

"They're in this room," the woman called Frightknight said, interpreting her unspeaking reptilian counterpart's actions. "He can smell them."

Angela took a deep breath and looked around the expansive room. "Donna," she spoke into the space. "Spare the antics and show yourself so we can all go on with our lives."

There was no answer. In fact, the room had become eerily quiet, save for the pattering rain on the glass. The members of the Nightmare Array flicked their eyes across each part of the room, watching for the slightest movement or motion that might give away the location of their invisible enemies.

Angela spoke again, into the silence: "We both know how this is going to end—"

A sudden sound drew their attention to the far corner of the room: the crackle of a walkie talkie.

Like a predator locking on to the scent of its prey, Angela lurched toward the sound, nodding for the others to follow. One of the knights stayed near the elevators, but the gator-headed man moved in behind Angela and Marcus. "We've got you now, Miss Locke. Show yourself."

The walkie crackled again. Angela smiled, gritted her teeth, and stretched out her arms: "Show yourself!" She shouted.

Clunch!

Angela whipped around toward the new sound: the fire exit door had been flung wide open and now creaked slowly back into place. *Clunch!* It latched. "Get after her!" The group hurried toward the door but froze as something even more surprising happened.

The drab, inconspicuous door began to change. A wave of gold swept across its surfaces, spreading to the edges of the door frame, which also turned to gold within seconds.

Angela pushed on the door. It wouldn't budge. "It's been melded shut," she puffed and turned to the Gatorman. "Break it open." As the speechless henchman moved toward the door, Angela looked beyond him to the other two: "She's not the only one in the building. Take the elevators." The fuming woman pointed at the floor indicator above the elevator opposite the one they'd used. "They're two floors down. Find Donna *and* her friends. And when you do," she looked into Marcus' dark eyes. "Kill them all."

Boarding the South Coastal Electronics cargo jet was an honest mistake. It was Calvin and Declan's best guess at the time given the limited information. But there was no mistaking the identity of the aging doctor just two gates away. Matt Calvin was sure this time.

"We gotta go," Declan nodded as the two started for the cargo door. "Now!"

Calvin was only a couple steps behind as the two pushed past the confused pilot and exited the plane, back into the rain, which seemed to have intensified over the past few moments. When his view was unobstructed, Declan stole a glance up ahead at the other, smaller plane two gates away—the pair had driven right past it as they entered the tarmac.

The hunched woman—it was *definitely* Dr. Blanche—pushed the cart of armored metallic briefcases up the slick ramp, where she handed it off to the man in the dark raincoat. Though the figure wore a black fedora that shaded most of his face in the rain and waning twilight, Declan immediately recognized the man.

Dad.

Dr. Blanche descended the ramp once more and moved out of view—presumably to gather another cart full of cases. *The package*—the formula that would allow Ducane to bequeath uncanny abilities to whoever he wanted. Or, more accurately, whoever was willing to pay the most for it.

As Calvin and Declan bounded down from the metal staircase and onto solid ground, they strained to see past a large passenger plane that was pulling in between Gate 7 and Gate 5—where the plane of Ducane and Dr. Blanche was docked.

Just before the larger plane reached its final berth, Rolf Ducane looked up beyond it. His eyes met Declan's and betrayed a hint of surprise. The dark-garbed man ducked into the plane.

"Shoot!" Declan puffed as he darted back towards the sportscar at the edge of Gate 7. "He saw me."

Calvin struggled to keep up as he took labored breaths a few steps behind. "You sure?"

"Positive," he glanced between the landing hardware of the plane beside them and saw the flurry of propellers spinning into motion on Ducane's plane. "He's taking off."

The duo was almost to the car when Declan shouted, "You're driving," and tossed the keys to Calvin.

"Huh?" The recruit fumbled. The keys jangled onto the pavement, splashing into a shallow puddle. Calvin fished them out and continued on to the driver's side door. He settled into the leather seat and started the engine—a smooth roar.

On the passenger side, Declan pressed a button and the canvas top began to roll back.

"Uh, it's raining," Calvin noted, his eyebrows raised. He winced as the cold rain speckled his legs, arms, then face as the convertible top swung back into its retracted position, tucked into the frame of the car.

"Drive." Declan commanded. Ducane's small jet had begun to taxi away from the gate, the cargo ramp still lowered. "Follow that plane." Declan pointed as Calvin revved the cherry red convertible and swung the wheel so they were now facing their quarry.

"What about Blanche?" The old woman hadn't returned to the plane before it pushed off.

"We'll worry about her later. We *have* to stop that plane."

"Alrighty, hang on." The younger man slammed the gas pedal, jolting them forward. The tires skidded across the wet tarmac as the rubber barely gripped the road. Calvin maneuvered to avoid hitting a marshal, then rounded the butt of the large plane beside them.

The tiny cargo plane picked up speed, following the painted lines and signs on the ground toward the runway. As the convertible gained on the small aircraft, Declan shot a brief glance over his shoulder and back toward the shrinking gates. Dr. Blanche stood there dumbfounded, having just loaded another cart out of a large van parked at the edge of the airport building, only to find that Ducane had left her.

Left her behind, Declan thought, turning back to face the plane. *Guess he really hasn't changed all that much.*

"Uh, what's your plan exactly?" Calvin watched the speedometer hand rise, pushing dangerously close to the car's maximum velocity.

"Get as near as you can," the other man explained. "I'm going to cut those carts free." Declan pointed up toward the open cargo door, where three, wheeled carts were stacked high with metallic cases full of formula. Each cart was covered in a thick net made of two-inch-wide polyester strips criss-crossed and secured with metal clamps to the sides and floor of the cargo hold. "If we can't stop the plane, we've got to at least ensure those packages don't leave the tarmac."

As he was focused on maintaining a tight grip and a steady course, it took Calvin a moment before Declan's plan fully registered. "Wait—you're going to try and get *on* your dad's plane? *While* it's about to take off?"

Declan gave a quick nod and a half-smile. "Not *try*, kid. I'm gonna *do* it!" Immediately, Declan straightened out, gripped the side of the car, and began to shift and rise so that he was perched with his feet on the seat cushion.

"You're insane!" Calvin shouted, watching from the corner of his eyes.

"And you're doing great," Declan assured him. "Keep it up." The man now lifted himself so that he was nearly standing, gripping the edge of the windshield to keep his balance against the wind and rain.

"Just a little closer!"

Calvin eased his foot forward on the gas pedal.

"Get beside the ramp," Declan now instructed. Calvin complied. "There we go."

Declan eyed the metal cargo ramp, scraping and sparking against the wet pavement as it dragged along. He bit his lip, steadied one foot on the top edge of the slick car door. Carefully, Declan lifted his other foot up from the seat cushion, balanced for a split second, then leaped across the gap.

Declan's heart raced, thumping against his innards, which felt weightless for a brief moment as he floated through the air. His feet met the ramp, slamming the cargo door hard against the ground beneath it. Declan reached out and grabbed the interior edge of the plane's doorframe and steadied himself. He glanced back, gave a quick thumbs-up to Calvin, and proceeded into the cargo hold as the recruit kept the car close behind.

The cargo hold appeared to be devoid of all life except Declan, so he surmised that Ducane was the pilot.

Didn't know dad knew how to fly a plane.

The son didn't linger on this thought for long, but withdrew a pocketknife and flicked out a serrated blade. Immediately, Declan began to saw at the straps that held one of the carts of formula in place.

Within a few seconds, Declan sawed through one strap and moved on to the next. The woven straps were tough, built to withstand intense wear and tear. Finally, Declan felt the tight strap slacken, and the cart full of sealed metallic cases rolled toward the ramp.

Calvin swerved to dodge the oncoming threat. When the cart hit the tarmac, the cases scattered, tumbling in every direction. The recruit watched over his shoulder to verify that the cases of formula remained sealed—they appeared to be constructed out of some sort of bulletproof alloy—then veered back to tail the plane once more. The plane was nearing the end of the lane, where it would prepare to make a 180 degree turn to get into position for the final acceleration down the runway for its inevitable takeoff.

Declan repeated the process for the second cart, which broke free just as easily. The plane began its sharp turn and Declan was flung across the plane, narrowly dodging the now-free cart. As he watched the cases from that cart disperse across the tarmac, Declan grabbed a support beam and took a deep breath. The plane's trajectory straightened out once more and Calvin and the car revved back into view. Declan turned to face the third and final cart, stacked with dozens of sealed containers of his father's formula.

He could've built an army with this much of his serum. Declan decided not to speculate any longer on the devious machinations of his father, but began to hack at the straps that secured the remaining stack.

The first strap was the most belligerent, resisting Declan's sawing motion. With much effort, Declan finally managed to cut it loose. He started toward the final strap. The sound of the engines began to grow, ready for takeoff.

Beeeeeep! Beep-beep!

Calvin slammed the car horn. Declan turned to him, offering a quizzical expression as he tried to read the young recruit's lips.

"What? I can't hear you!" Over the droning sound of rain and the plane's accelerating engines, he couldn't figure out what the recruit was trying to say. Calvin's mouth was blocked by the top edge of the windshield frame, making it impossible for Declan to read his lips.

Declan returned his attention to the thick strap, beginning to saw at it again. With only a few loose strands holding it together, Declan sensed movement in his periphery. He looked up, back toward Calvin. The cargo door began to close, lifting upward. Declan's heart rate accelerated and he scrambled to cut the final threads of the net strap. He was too late.

The cargo door slammed shut, sealing with a loud latch. Declan held his breath, trembled, then exhaled sharply. The entire space was now dark, illuminated only by a few red bulbs spaced out every few feet along the length of the hold. Declan turned toward the front of the plane where he saw a door had opened, leading into the cockpit. A figure stood in the threshold, lit from behind.

"Looks like we've got ourselves a stowaway," the man spoke over the accelerating engines. He stepped forward so that his face was now bathed in reddish light.

Declan took quick breaths as he stared into his father's face.

"Hello, son."

CHAPTER 24

The glass door to Donna's dining room slid open, the salty grit of sand and sea causing only the slightest friction against the decrepit Ghoul's efforts. The sound of the storm now swept in through the back of the house, echoing off the walls and tile floors.

Tracy bit her lip. As she crouched behind the counter in the adjacent kitchen, she clutched the handle of the butcher knife and readied herself as the old Ghoul floated through the space. Her patch-faced counterpart followed into the dining room, tracking a set of muddy footprints across the pristine tile.

Marjory, the Ghoul, took deep breaths, then let out a rasping, sing-song taunt: "Come out, come out, wherever you are."

Sunder craned his head to listen for any movement while he sniffed through narrow nostril slits—his defining facial feature.

As she pressed her back against the kitchen island, Tracy turned her head slowly to get a clearer view of the intruders. Her gaze locked in as Sunder turned his head abruptly—right in Tracy's direction. For a moment, she was sure she'd been spotted. Gripping the butcher knife, though, she realized she was as good as invisible to him. *No eyes*. She took a slow, quiet breath.

Her relief was momentary, though, for now Patchface moved into the kitchen.

With great care, Officer Jones began to orbit the island. Even though she couldn't be seen by the faceless monster, crouching in his direct path made Tracy vulnerable to detection by his other senses. Jones remained low to the ground as she stepped backwards and made her way around to the next side of the island.

Patchface walked in a half-hunched manner, taking slow steps as if testing the firmness of the ground with each step. His hands hung like the claws of a predator as he walked.

As the faceless Sunder closed in on Tracy, his counterpart Marjory floated in the threshold between the dining and living rooms. She hovered lower to the ground now, likely a symptom of a waning supply of fresh blood. The woman peered into the darkness, allowing her eyes to begin to adjust.

"Here, boy," the Ghoul rasped, trying to lure Max out of hiding. "Dinnertime."

Starla covered her own mouth as she leaked an involuntary gasp. The girl crouched behind the arm of the big couch, just out of the frightening woman's line of sight. Sue and Lisa had made it out of the living room and scattered to some other part of the house, but now Starla was too scared to move. She turned her head slowly so she could see the television set.

The girl studied the reflections in the glossy black rectangle. The faint backlight of the moon through the dining room slider created an eerie silhouette of the Ghoul, floating at the edge of the room. The woman rested her feet on the ground and took a step into the large, black room.

"You can come out now," Marjory taunted. "I know you're in here, child."

In the kitchen, Tracy held her breath. Patchface was closing in, following her scent across the expansive kitchen. The officer braced herself to make a move with the blade she held in her hand, but feared that the faceless man's counterpart would quickly swoop in for blood. *No. Best to hang on to the element of surprise for as long as possible.*

Patchface sniffed around the corner of the island. Tracy locked up. The near-featureless head was only a few inches from her now, his forehead coming into view. She had seen the brute strength with which Sunder had wounded Rico back in the graveyard. Facing him now would be a huge risk, but it was one she had to take. She gripped the handle of the knife.

Bark! Bark!

Sunder whipped his head around—away from Tracy—and scuttled across the tile and back into the dining room. For a moment, Tracy breathed again. But she knew what the sound meant. *Max—he's going to give away Starla's hiding place!*

Rrrark!

Max growled in the living room, scurrying and leaping in the middle of an area rug. Marjory smiled, flashing a set of rotten yellow teeth as Sunder appeared at her side. The old woman watched as the puppy growled at something behind the sofa.

"Bingo."

She tapped Sunder on the shoulder, prompting him to begin sniffing his way across the room to follow the scents of the home's hidden occupants.

Max continued to snarl and yap at the space behind the sofa arm. The two intruders closed in.

"Come out," Marjory continued. "You can hide, but we're going to get you."

Patchface neared the end of the sofa, crouched to all fours.

"—and your little dog, too." The woman tensed, readying herself to watch Sunder snatch up their prey.

The puppy turned to look at the intruders for a brief moment before returning to his yaps. Marjory and Sunder rounded the corner of the couch arm, ready to capture the dog and his little human master.

The old woman froze as she looked into the dark corner. Max was alone, snarling playfully with the remote control for the TV. The batteries had fallen on the floor and the plastic was covered in tiny teeth marks.

Marjory whipped her head around the room. "Where is she? The girl's supposed to be here."

Patchface turned his head as if to await further orders from the Ghoul. Max started to scamper away. Sunder reached out his arm and grabbed the dog by the collar, nearly choking him. Max whimpered as the faceless creature held the dog out toward Marjory.

She grinned. "Snacktime."

Donna and Mira hurried up the stairwell toward the roof. They could hear the hammering of the Gatorman's weight against the golden door behind them. Mira, with a weariness starting to creep into her eyes, trailed a couple steps behind Donna, who stopped suddenly.

"What is it?" Mira asked.

Donna pointed up toward the next landing. "Shouldn't there be a door to the roof right there?"

There was no door. The landing appeared to exist solely to grant access to a thick fire sprinkler standpipe with its large wheel painted bright red.

Mira glanced downward. The loud wallops had stopped. "There's another stairwell on the opposite side of the building that must go up to the roof. But we'll have to get onto one of the lower floors to access it."

With a deep breath, Donna followed Mira as she began her descent in the same direction in which they had just come. They passed the door that Donna had turned to gold and continued downward past another level—too easy of a chance to run into their enemies. When they reached the level below that, Mira was about to pull on the door handle when Donna shouted.

"Wait!"

Mira turned. "What is it?"

"They know some of us were on this floor." Donna tried to catch her breath as she spoke. "The indicator. Above the elevator."

"What about Buster and Kiki and Rico?"

"We should warn them," Donna reached in her bag and pulled out the pair's remaining walkie talkie. For their getaway distraction moments earlier, she had turned the walkies to a new channel. Donna now switched it back to channel three and pressed the talk button. "This is Donna to Dream Team. Come in?"

A moment passed before a voice crackled back. "Talk to us, Goldilocks."

"Kiki!" Donna puffed. "Be careful. We think they're headed to the floor where you, Buster, and Rico are."

"Noted," the young woman replied. "But Rico isn't with us."

"He's *not*?" Donna furrowed her brow. Before she could click back more questions, Donna heard the elevator *ding* from the other side of the door. *The Nightmare Array.* Mira urged her to continue and the two scampered down the stairs once more as Donna tucked the walkie back into her bag.

When they reached the next floor, Mira pressed her ear to the door. After a few moments of silence, she nodded and opened the door slowly. The two women peered into a dim corridor then issued through the door. They followed a faint glow around the corner.

The floorplan was spacious and open. A walkway split down the middle of a sea of cubicles and desks peppered with boxy computer monitors. Their glowing screens faced outward toward the exterior frosted glass walls, which contained private offices and conference rooms.

Donna quickly scanned the room for any sign of movement. Apart from the faint blinking of MS DOS underscore cursors on a few of the illuminated computer screens, the vast office floor appeared to be devoid of motion. The blonde woman allowed a quick sigh to release before angling her head toward the far side of the room, where a red exit sign cast a harsh glow.

"You think the other stairwell is that way?"

Mira nodded.

Without another word, the two women continued walking with haste across the eerie, empty office. When they were nearly halfway across the space, they heard a sound and froze.

The *ding* of an elevator car arriving at the floor.

Mira tensed as she and Donna exchanged a concerned glance then looked back toward the elevators.

"Hide!" Mira gestured toward the grid of desks. The two women threw themselves on the floor and crouched behind the bulky desks.

Donna heard the elevator doors slide open. She craned her neck to peer above the desk, where she could sneak a glimpse of the new arrivals: Angela and Marcus. *The group split up!*

Donna sank back behind the desk and pressed her back against it, counting out deep, quiet breaths.

"I know you're here, Miss Locke." Angela's voice taunted from across the room, unseen. "Your friends can't keep you hidden forever."

The woman took a few slow steps across the room, her thick heels thumping softly on the carpet. "Give back what you stole from us," Angela continued, turning her head toward every direction in which she presumed Donna might be hiding. "And maybe we'll let you live."

'Maybe' doesn't sound too promising, Donna mused. She could sense Angela and Marcus moving closer. The glow of the computers flickered. *Marcus. The light.*

Donna looked back at Mira. "Do something," the blonde woman mouthed.

Mira shrugged. Donna hadn't noticed it until that moment, but she could now see clearly that Mira looked exhausted. Her eyes were drooping and bloodshot. *From using her powers so much,* Donna presumed. *Not much energy left.*

That left few options. The best two Donna could think of were simple: run or hide. *Or some combination of the two.*

As Donna quickly considered the options, she settled on the first. They had to run. If they could get to the far stairwell first, Donna *might* be able to seal off the door with gold like she did upstairs. She cocked her head so that she could get a clear view of the red exit sign. *I can make it.* She turned to Mira. *But what about Mira?*

"You ready to run?" Donna mouthed.

Mira nodded her head slowly.

That's not very reassuring.

"On the count of three," Donna whispered. "One." She peeked around the desk to gauge Angela and Marcus' proximity to them. "Two." Donna whipped back toward the exit sign. "Thr—"

Donna felt two firm hands grip her from behind: one on her arm and the other over her mouth, muffling her countdown. Her eyes showed her sudden concern, too afraid to turn to look at her captor. Then, slowly, she angled her body to get a better look, holding her breath in anticipation.

A few moments earlier, Buster and Kiki arrived at the floor above Donna—two floors below Ducane's penthouse. When they disembarked from the elevator, the pair was presented with a long hallway stretching and branching across the length of the level. Numerous doors sprouted off from the main, narrow hall, hiding their contents from view.

"Any idea which one of these doors has our generator behind it?" Kiki asked as the two started walking.

Buster didn't answer, but tried the first unmarked door that they came upon.

Drat, he tsked. *Janitor's closet.*

"Guess we'll know it when we see it," Kiki mumbled.

The two came to a fork in the hallway, where the hallway branched off in multiple directions, forming three possible routes.

Buster looked at Kiki and raised his eyebrows.

"Don't worry, we got this." She smiled then scrunched her face and strained.

Her large counterpart watched as an exact double of Kiki materialized beside the original. The two identical women exchanged brief eye-contact before turning to face Buster.

He shook his head. "That's never *not* weird."

Kiki handed her duplicate one of the two walkie talkies that she carried. As soon as her double took it and fiddled with the volume, the walkie began to crackle.

"—Donna to Dream Team. Come in?"

Buster flicked his eyes from one Kiki to the next. "I have a bad feeling about this."

Kiki's double clicked the talk button. "Talk to us, Goldilocks."

"Kiki!" Donna crackled back. "Be careful. We think they're headed to the floor where you, Buster, and Rico are."

"Noted," the woman answered, looking up at the others. "But... Rico isn't with us."

"He's *not?*"

Buster's eyes were wide. Before any of the group could speak back to Donna, they heard the *ding* of the elevator. "Go! Find the generator room," the big man instructed as the trio split off in separate directions.

The elevator doors slid open, spitting out the woman in the conquistador armor and her alligator-human hybrid partner.

"They're here," whispered the woman, wielding twin

swords. "Can you smell them?"

The reptilian face sniffed and angled toward her, nodded his head, then blinked his filmy eyelids.

Frightknight—the armored woman—moved forward down the hall, her ancient metal suit scraping and clanking with each step.

The pair reached the fork in the hall. The gator sniffed, first in one direction then another. This continued for a few moments as the woman listened for any sounds.

"Well?"

The Gatorman grunted three times, each with a nod down a different route.

"They split up?"

The hybrid grunted again, affirmative.

"Two can play that game," Frightknight smirked. She cocked her head, causing her face to warp and contort. As this happened, a mass formed to one side of the woman's body—the severed portion now growing a new body until there were two, full women standing in front of the humanoid alligator.

Both Frightknights now wielded a sword apiece. The first woman pointed her sword—held in her left hand—down the winding hallway. "I'll cover this one," she said. Her two partners nodded and split off in the other two directions. "Oh," the woman added, turning with a gleeful grin. "And remember: when you find them, kill them."

As the others vanished into the maze of corridors, the original Frightknight moved with haste down her own path. She bent around a corner and slowly approached the first door she saw. The woman was about to enter when she noticed another door—just a little further down the hall—hanging slightly ajar.

Sloppy. Frightknight shook her head, a few of her wispy silver hairs drifting at the edge of her morion helmet as she stepped toward the second door. The woman cautiously placed a pair of fingers on the handle and pushed. The door easily swung open, allowing her to see inside.

There was a faint pinkish glow, a haze filling the room. At first glance, the knight thought she was looking at a group of men and women, standing in formation with their backs to her, still and at attention. They stood in rows—there were about a dozen figures in total. As the Frightknight walked into the room, she realized these figures were not alive at all: they were mannequins, dressed in an assortment of labcoats of various materials.

Clever. The woman looked around the room. "I know one of you is in here," she taunted.

She sensed a motion near the back of the room. She caught a silhouette of someone—this time it was a *someone* who was actually alive and moving—behind a half-wall of translucent glass blocks. This was the source of the pink glow: some obscured, ultramodern lamp.

Got you. The knight moved swiftly past the shadowed mannequins until she reached the block wall. Slowly, she crept around the corner, where she found a stack of crates. Frightknight craned her neck to see beyond the boxes and tightened the left-handed grip on her sword. With her free hand, she pushed on the stack, toppling the crates and revealing a young girl with teal hair cowering in the corner.

The young woman put her hands up—empty with fingers wide. "Please don't hurt me!"

The Frightknight grinned. "Kiana, isn't it? Miss Hyde warned me about you."

"I prefer Kiki, actually," she mumbled.

"You and I are quite alike." The older, armored woman took a step toward Kiki. Frightknight placed the tip of her sword to Kiki's chest. "The power to create an exact replica of our own self with only a simple thought to will it."

Kiki kept quiet, though she obviously resented the woman's suggestion that they were anything alike.

"I wonder if your ability works in the same way as mine," the knight continued. Now she applied a slight pressure to the sword. Kiki flinched. "If you eliminate the original, then the duplicate will cease to exist as well."

Kiki tried to hide the pain of the sword's poking sting, but she winced. "If you're so sure about how alike we are, then be my guest. Try it and see what happens."

The older woman flashed a grin, exposing a set of rotting teeth. "With pleasure, niña," she said. The Frightknight wound back her arm and jabbed the sword with one swift motion, piercing Kiki directly in the heart.

Kiki's eyes shot open as she made a final gasp for air. The knight withdrew her blade, prompting her victim's body to topple over. As Kiki's body went limp, the other woman gave a light kick to verify that she was dead.

A pity, she shook her head. *Was just beginning to like her.*

A moment passed and the Frightknight turned to leave, but she paused as something caught her eye. Kiki's lifeless body slowly began to dematerialize, vanishing like a mist into the air.

"Curse you!" She spat. *The real thing's still out there!*

Buster threw open a door and crouched to pass through the threshold. He closed the door carefully behind him, pressing his ear to it. Nothing. *Yet.*

The hulking man flipped a light switch and surveyed the room as the fluorescent overheads flickered and twitched on. Along the far wall was a stack of large, boxy computer towers, which seemed to be working on overdrive. The devices emitted a droning, whirring sound.

In another part of the wide room was an array of television monitors, attached to the wall in a grid formation. Each screen conveyed a black-and-white crackling scene from somewhere in the Pelican building. *Backup security feeds*, Buster mused. The man moved closer to one, which depicted the service entrance—through which the group had entered the building. Buster set his walkie talkie on a desk in front of the screens and strained to look at the monitor. He smirked when he realized the display was too grainy to discern any of the dents he had left in the golden door downstairs. *Didn't beat it up* that *bad.*

Buster continued examining the space and let out a quick

sigh when he realized that the generator was not in this room.

Suddenly, there was a thump on the door, followed by a scratching sound. Buster tensed. *They found me.* He eyed the light switch across the room—it was too far to reach in time, and he'd be seen if the light was still on when they entered. Thinking quickly, Buster looked up at the single fluorescent beam in the center of the room's ceiling, clenched his hand into a fist, then swung. His uppercut landed squarely, smashing the light into thousands of tiny pieces. The room went dark as the shards scattered across the concrete floor.

Buster took a couple steps back and pressed himself against the wall just as the door burst open. The silhouette of an alligator with human limbs stood in the doorway, hissing. Buster held his breath as the reptilian man slowly entered the darkened room. Buster inched toward the door, still in shadows, ready to make a run for it.

A crackle across the room startled both of them.

"Buster?" It was Kiki's voice, shouting through the walkie. "Come in!"

The Gatorman angled his snout toward the walkie—the device was perched on the desk beneath the dim glow of the security monitors. The creature took slow steps toward it.

Dangit, Kiki. Buster eyed the door once more.

"I think I found it," Kiki continued. "The generator room—come in, Buster."

The gator hybrid reached for the device then froze. The Gatorman's nostrils flared, sniffed. Suddenly, the creature whipped toward the door.

Buster observed a sliver of the light from the door casting a yellowish glow in the alligator's eyes. With a quick motion, Buster leaped toward the door and slammed it shut, trapping both he and the hybrid in the dark room. *I can't let that thing get to Kiki.*

"Buster?" Kiki's voice resounded again, this time more of a frightened whisper. "You okay? Listen, if you're there, I'm gonna need you to pick up. Talk me through this."

The gator growled, a guttural, palpable utterance full of phlegm and teeth.

Buster leaped out of the way of the door, for the slight screen-glow reflecting off the edge of the Gatorman's slimy body allowed the big man to see that the creature was now running toward him.

Without a second to catch his breath, Buster clung to the edge of the room and shimmied until he was nearly at the monitors. He reached out a hand and grabbed the walkie talkie, clicked the talk button: "Kiki! Tell me what you're looking at."

The reptile clearly heard the man's words. He turned toward Buster, licked his teeth with a long, slimy tongue, and began to amble toward him.

"Uh," Kiki scrambled. "It's a huge breaker box that says *Danger: High Voltage* in big red letters on the front. Should I be concerned?"

"Open it," were the only words Buster was able to manage before the creature pounced, leaping through the air. Buster tried to evade the reptile, but it landed on him, latching its claws into the man's flesh. "Gah!" He winced, losing his grip on the walkie. It clattered across the room.

Kiki's voice snapped back: "Okay, now what?"

"Get off me, creep," Buster struggled, but quickly tossed the creature aside with a sharp kick. His brute strength propelled the Gatorman into one of the humming computer stacks, resulting in a burst of sparks.

Buster scrambled for the walkie. "There should be some colored buttons next to a large switch."

"Yeah, I see all that."

"Pump the switch four times to prime it, then—" Buster felt a sudden pain in his leg and dropped the walkie. "Gah!" Alligator teeth dug into his calf, wrenching sharply. Buster let out a low scream as he tried to get a good look at the monster in the darkness. The security monitor glow reflected in the gator's eyes, and Buster planted a firm kick with his free leg.

Buster clenched his jaw as he felt the reptile's teeth rip through ligaments as the maw finally dislodged, the creature pushed away.

Kiki's voice crackled through the walkie as she counted off: "One. Two. Three," she strained. "Four. Okay, we're primed! Now what, Busty?"

Through gritted teeth, Buster clawed across the room to pick up the walkie. "Remember the colored buttons? Tell me what you see."

"There's a yellow button, and green and red ones. Which one do I press?"

Kiki's voice lingered in the dark room as Buster once

again brought the walkie toward his lips to speak. Before he could press the button, a flurry of scaly motion appeared, chomping down on the walkie—and Buster's hand. The man wailed and loosened his hold on the walkie. With his other hand, he gripped the upper jaw of the gator and yanked as hard as he could. The slobbering maw opened only slightly, just enough for Buster to pull his bleeding hand free of the vice grip. Buster socked the creature in the snout, sending it recoiling into the corner.

Buster crawled away and frantically looked around the room. There had to be a way to contain the violent creature. The man's eyes fell on one of the massive computers—the one shattered open by the Gatorman's collision with it. With only a single uninjured leg and arm, Buster struggled toward the computer. Its innards were exposed, a dangling mess of cords and wires.

The Gatorman locked his eyes on Buster, again caught in the eerie, reflective glow of the security screens. Buster huffed and reached his good hand up into the computer. He felt around before yanking his hand back out in a fist.

At that moment, the reptile hybrid scampered across the floor on all fours, jaws open, and lunged at Buster. Buster leaned out of the way, causing the creature to miss its target. While it was disoriented, the big man pressed his full weight over the creature and withdrew his quarry from the computer: a tangle of thick, multi-colored cables. A couple of the cords were several feet long—these Buster wrapped quickly around the snout of the Gatorman. When he was satisfied that the bindings were sufficiently secure, Buster took another few strands and crafted a pair of makeshift cuffs, pulling the beast's arms behind its back while the Gatorman's soft underbelly pressed against the cold floor.

Finally, Buster managed to stand up. He took a deep breath and opened the door, allowing in a stream of light from the hall.

"Alright, Gatorade. You stay put, alright?"

Buster hurried into the hall, slamming the door shut behind him.

CHAPTER 25

Kiki stood in front of the large breaker box, walkie talkie in hand as she awaited a response from Buster. She'd been the only one lucky enough to locate the generator room—the machinery that would allow Pelican's rooftop radio tower to function so they could easily broadcast the incriminating recording and bring down Ducane once and for all.

But I haven't got a clue how this thing works.

The red lettering that read *Danger: High Voltage* did little to comfort her.

"Open it," came Buster's words, rushed and breathless through the walkie speaker.

With a deep breath, Kiki obeyed, reaching for the small handle. The gray metal door creaked as it confronted her with a more complicated array of levers, switches, buttons, and lights.

Kiki snapped back through the walkie talkie: "Okay,

now what?"

A few seconds passed with no response. Kiki was about to press the talk button again when Buster's voice crackled through: "There should some colored buttons next to a large switch."

"Yeah, I see all that." Kiki nodded instinctively, even though the man couldn't see her.

"Pump the switch four times to prime it, then—" Buster's voice dropped out.

Then what? Kiki inhaled slowly then let out the air quickly. *Okay. I can do this. Focus on the first part. Four pumps.*

Kiki located the priming switch, gripped it, then counted off as she lifted and lowered it in succession: "One. Two. Three," she strained, yanking on the lever as hard as she could. "Four." Kiki exhaled slowly. "Okay, we're primed! Now what, Busty?"

Buster's voice came through the walkie, labored and quick: "Remember the colored buttons? Tell me what you see."

The young woman stood back to get a good look at the panel. "There's a yellow button, and green and red ones. Which one do I press?"

No response.

"Hello? Buster?" She waited. "Buster, which button?"

A full ten seconds passed. *C'mon, Busty! What's wrong?*

Kiki moved to click the walkie button again when she felt a sharp pang in her chest. She dropped the walkie and threw one of her hands over her heart. It wasn't the first time she had experienced that kind of pain; she knew what it meant, but it didn't hurt any less.

She's gone.

Whenever one of Kiki's doubles was wounded or killed, all of the other iterations felt it deeply, like a voodoo doll pricked with an unseen, sharpened needle.

No sooner had the pain begun to dissipate than a figure appeared in the doorway: the Frightknight, a sword in her right hand. *Or maybe it's her copy.*

"Don't make any sudden moves," the woman demanded as she waved her sword toward Kiki.

The teal-haired young woman glanced at the walkie on the floor, then back up at the armored lady. "What do you want?"

"We want you gone," the conquistador answered, nodding over her shoulder.

A second, identical woman in armor stepped in from the corridor. This knight held a bloody sword in her left hand. "You must be the original." The Frightknight cocked her head.

Kiki's eyes flicked between the duplicate women and the ancient weapons in their hands. They were closing in, and it was clear they intended to show Kiki the same untimely fate as her own duplicate in the other room.

The original Frightknight raised her left hand, gripping the sword. "I'm afraid the world isn't big enough for two of us with the exact same power." She gritted her teeth. "Goodbye, Kiana."

Kiki braced herself. She watched, helpless, as the knight thrust the blade, still dripping with her copy's blood, downward toward Kiki's heart. She gasped. The sword pierced her chest and Kiki stumbled backward.

The knight removed the sword and scoffed as Kiki's body went limp. She looked down on the bleeding woman then turned to her counterpart. Without a word, she nodded, and the two started for the door. They froze when they saw another figure in the threshold: it was Kiki, wearing a labcoat snatched off one of the mannequins from the other room.

A third version? But we killed the original—

The original Frightknight looked back over her shoulder. The slain Kiki's body slowly began to disappear. "What? How?"

"I'm the original. And I'm afraid our powers are not the *exact* same," said the Kiki in the doorway, gripping a walkie talkie. "What? You mean you can't make more than *one* copy of yourself?" Kiki smirked at the dumbfounded looks on the faces of the two armored women before her. "Guess that means my powers are just a *little* bit better."

The identical Frightknights glared at her and started to run toward the door.

"And I told you," Kiki added. "*Don't* call me Kiana."

Kiki scrunched her face, straining with all of her might. As she did so, a duplicate materialized in front of her. Then another, and a third beside that one. Immediately, these Kiki copies ran to intercept the knights, dodging the swipes of their swords. The original Kiki in the doorway, already showing signs of weariness, repeated this process a few more times, creating even more copies of the teal-haired woman to assist the small army that was now filling the room.

The knights managed to wound a few of Kiki's replicas, but they were no match for the sheer number of the young women who now immobilized the conquistadors by grabbing their arms and legs. The women's swords were tossed aside, and a pair of the Kiki duplicates found a coil of rope with which they bound the two knights.

Kiki now leaned against the doorframe, barely clutching the walkie talkie as her copies finished the job. One-by-one the duplicate women vanished at Kiki's command until only the prototype remained.

The young woman started to slip, her weary body drifting downward. But she was caught by a large, strong hand. Buster eked a smile. "Hey there, you okay?"

Kiki nodded, her eyes drooping.

Buster helped her stand and inspected the two women in the center of the small control room. "Not bad," he said, wincing slightly as he took a step forward. His arm and leg were bleeding and his clothing torn with bite marks.

Kiki gasped when she noticed. "What the heck happened?"

"It's only a flesh wound," Buster tried to grin. He pointed at the control panel. "Green," he said. "You press the green button next."

With a nod, Kiki hobbled over to the panel. She took a deep breath then placed her finger squarely on the green button and pressed. Immediately, a red indicator light began to glow near the top of the panel beside a label that read: *Generator system active.*

"Alrighty." Kiki glanced at Buster then inspected the tied-up Frightknights. "Now, what do you say we lock these two in a closet and get up to the roof so we can end this madness?"

Tracy peered around the edge of the dining room wall into the large, dark living room. Marjory—the Ghoul—clutched the small golden retriever puppy in her pasty hands while her faceless bodyguard stood beside her. Both had their backs to Tracy, but the officer could still hear the squeals from Max, desperate to free himself of the intruder's grasp.

Where's Starla? Tracy's eyes flicked around the dark room. *They'll find her next...*

Before she could decide on her next course of action, Tracy felt something touch her arm. She whipped around, gripping the butcher knife, but let out a huge, silent breath when she realized it was Starla.

"Thank God you're okay," Tracy gasped as she crouched to the girl's level and wrapped her in a brief embrace. "Thought they almost had you." The officer looked Starla in the eyes. "I need you to get upstairs—I saw Sue and Lisa go up there, and we can't let those monsters get to your mom before we do."

Starla hesitated. "What about Max?"

As if on cue, Max yelped as the Ghoul's incisors pierced his golden fur. The dog whimpered and squirmed, helpless. It would only take a few more minutes for the Ghoul to suck out all of the puppy's blood. If Tracy or Starla ran to try and free the dog, Patchface would most certainly apprehend them.

Tracy eyed the knife in her hand and an idea crossed her mind. "Get ready to run, kiddo."

The girl seemed convinced that Tracy had a well-thought plan and started to back away toward the far kitchen doorway that led toward the front entryway and staircase. Tracy peered around the living room wall briefly before looking back to Starla. The girl stopped near the fridge and opened the door.

"What are you doing?" Tracy mouthed, trying to keep her volume lower than Max's whimpers or the rain on the glass of the windows and the open slider.

Starla didn't immediately answer, but withdrew a translucent plastic pitcher half-filled with a bright reddish liquid. Tracy raised an eyebrow as Starla began to scan the countertops until her eyes alighted on a glass container of salt. "Just in case," Starla whispered back to Tracy and stood at the threshold, ready to run at the officer's signal.

In case of what? Tracy didn't have time to think on it much longer. Max growled and yelped again, clearly in pain. Tracy took a deep breath, shifted her hold on the knife's wooden grip, and stood up in the large arched threshold between the dining and living rooms.

"Ready?" She mouthed to Starla across the kitchen.

The girl nodded.

Alright, Dracula. Tracy narrowed her vision and muttered under her breath: "Suck on this, creep!" With a quick wind-up, Tracy hurled the butcher knife across the dark room.

Sphlinch!

The blade lodged itself squarely in Marjory's back. She shrieked and jolted at the sudden pain, dropping Max out of instinct. The little dog hit the floor with a thud, but quickly rose and padded out of the room toward the home's entryway, carrying a slight limp as he did so.

Starla took this as her cue and hurried after Max. The two made it to the stairs, only looking back briefly as the two terrifying intruders turned to face Tracy. The dog left a trail of dark red drips along the steps as he ascended with Starla.

The Ghoul reached around to her back and began to pull on the knife, but each attempt to move it caused her greater pain. She screamed in agony, then squeezed her eyes shut. The woman removed her hands from the knife and held them out, fingers spread.

Tracy's eyes grew wide as she watched the knife slowly begin to move, then suddenly it fell straight down—through her body—and clattered on the hard ground. *Her powers. She's regained some from Max's blood. Not good.*

Before she could calculate her next move, Tracy realized that the patch-faced man was running toward her. Officer Jones ducked back into the kitchen as Patchface trailed her, with the Ghoul remaining in the living room out of view.

Officer Jones ducked back behind the kitchen island and found herself in the same predicament as before, only this time the faceless intruder was even more angry and determined to find his prey. *Roger*, she remembered. *The intercom.*

There was another intercom in the hallway just outside the kitchen. Tracy just needed to lure the monster away to buy herself a few extra seconds.

Tracy's shoulder jostled a stack of metal saucepans tucked on a shelf of the island. She froze. Patchface sniffed and moved toward the sound with haste. Tracy's eyes shifted around the dark kitchen, finally resting on a pair of large ceramic jars that contained sugar and flour.

As the faceless man closed in, Tracy stood and took a few short steps. She grabbed the smaller of the two containers, on which were painted schools of tropical fish, and turned to see Patchface only a few steps away. The woman swung the heavy jar low like a bowling ball in a pendulum motion a couple of times to gain momentum, then allowed the container to slip free of her fingers as she brought it upwards once more.

The ceramic piece flew across the kitchen toward the dining area at the far side of the space. Tracy held her breath. Finally, the jar collided with the solid wall, sending a burst of shimmering white granules over the tile.

Immediately, Sunder whipped his head toward the sound and scurried toward it. Tracy used this time to move with quick, silent steps out of the kitchen in the opposite direction.

When she passed through the threshold, Tracy pressed herself against the wall outside the kitchen, took a few deep breaths, then eyed the intercom. She dove at it and pressed the button.

"Roger!" She spoke in a shrill whisper. "Roger, it's Tracy.

We need help! Two of those creeps are in here—the Ghoul and the one with no face. Get help—fast!"

Tracy's breaths were short as she released the button, waiting for an answer. She heard the rustling and jostling of dining room furniture in the other room. Patchface was quickly realizing that the thrown jar was a diversion, and the sounds stopped. Now his lumbering steps grew louder, moving back across the kitchen.

"Roger?" No answer. "Hurry!"

Tracy pressed her body against the wall again. Sunder approached the threshold of the kitchen, only a few feet away.

C'mon, Roger!

"Roger!"

Officer Jones?

The doctor whipped his head toward the intercom on the far wall as he remained on his droopy sofa clutching a boombox. There was clear distress in the woman's whisper.

"Roger, it's Tracy," her voice continued, hasty but quiet. "We need help! Two of those creeps are in here—the Ghoul and the one with no face. Get help—fast!"

Roger gulped. He wanted to get up, but even taking the few steps across the room could cause him to miss the incoming transmission from Donna and their friends. *Then their mission would be in vain.* Doctor Lansing eyed the intercom again, then looked back down at his fingers, hovering over the *record* button. He took a glance at his telephone, mounted to another wall in his compact studio apartment, which doubled as a makeshift lab.

"Roger?"

I'm sorry, Officer Jones. He took short breaths. *I can't miss this.*

"Hurry!" Tracy's voice gave one final harsh whisper before the intercom clicked off again.

The radio static filled Roger's ears as his mind raced through possible scenarios. *The transmission: we need it if we're to bring down Ducane once and for all. But Tracy. And Starla...*

The man bit his lip and his eyes drifted to the clock.

It read *8:18* in big, red, digital letters.

Suddenly, he had an idea. *Hang on just a little longer, Donna.*

Roger stood up and hurried toward the intercom. As he did so, he twisted the metallic tuner knob on the side of the boombox. A flurry of split-second bursts from dozens of stations blasted through until he landed on the intended frequency. He lifted the boombox and smashed the intercom's *talk* button.

Tracy pressed her back to the wall.

C'mon, Roger! Do something!

The man with no face crept closer, just around the corner in the kitchen. Tracy could hear his heavy breathing, warm bursts through his nostrils. The creature lowered his head and sniffed, then angled his head to hear for the slightest movements as he stepped into the hall. Tracy's foot slipped. She froze up. The patch-faced man whipped toward her.

Suddenly, the intercom clicked on at a deafening volume, a crackling static followed by the sound of an immense and furious drum solo. Tracy cracked a momentary smile of relief as the bassline came in, followed by the dark, sultry vocals of Phil Collins on *In the Air Tonight*.

Sunder was disoriented, scrambling his head from side to side until he eventually threw his hands over his ears. Tracy cranked the volume knob on the intercom, further confusing the creature that hunted her. Thinking quickly, Jones reached for a ceramic vase and brought it down as hard as she could over the monster's head. It shattered. Patchface went limp and fell to the floor.

CHAPTER 26

Donna held her breath as she felt the hand gripping her arm. It was warm, firm but gentle. She turned, relaxed slightly when she saw the face.

"Rico!" Donna mouthed, almost forgetting to stay silent, lest she attract the attention of Marcus and Angela, who were now closing in on them.

"I got a little sidetracked, but c'mon," he whispered and nodded back toward one of the offices. Donna crawled after him, keeping low behind the computer desks as Mira followed suit. Donna glanced back over her shoulder, verifying that they were out of the view of Angela and Marcus. As Donna continued toward the office door, she froze. She felt her handbag, slung across her shoulder, lighter than usual.

The documents! They were gone. Donna flicked her eyes back toward the spot where she had been hiding. She tensed as she set her gaze on the thick yellowish-brown packet lying flat on the carpet beside the desk—*it must have fallen out of my bag.*

Donna was about to crawl back to grab it when she felt Rico's grip again. He pointed past her. Angela and Marcus were walking right toward the manila file packet. If Donna darted back for it, she would be seen, without a doubt.

Rico angled his head toward the office once more and Donna followed. They entered the office, pushing through the frosted glass door in silence. Rico softly closed it behind them.

Inside, the three took deep, quiet breaths.

"I have to get that packet back," Donna whispered.

Officer Castillo shook his head. "No time. They'll see you. We have to find a way to get out of here alive and get to the roof. We've still got our *ammunition.*" He held up the cassette tape from Ducane's vault and rattled it.

Donna eyed the tape, but her thoughts remained on the manila envelope. *Those documents have the answers I've been looking for. The truth about my family.* Donna kept the words to herself. There was no use protesting. She knew Rico was right. *Doubling back for the files would only jeopardize the rest of the mission—and put us all in even greater danger.* But there had to be a way to get the documents back. Donna's mind raced through scenarios.

Mira leaned her back against a large desk on the far wall, her weariness now showing even more in her eyes.

"You okay?" Donna whispered and placed a gloved hand on the other woman's shoulder.

Mira inhaled slowly then nodded. Donna was not convinced.

Rico tried to make out the shapes and shadows of Marcus and Angela just outside. "We've gotta call in backup," he said. "And let Tracy know that some of those guys are headed to the house."

"With our luck, they're already there," Donna muttered and lowered her head. She reached into her pocket and withdrew the tiny, colorful pin that Starla had given her for safekeeping: the starling.

Castillo placed a hand over Donna's. "Tracy will take care of her," he assured her, though Donna could sense his lack of certainty. "She'll keep Starla safe."

Donna's eyes were misty as she nodded. "And what about us? Even if we make it to the roof and get that recording out for everyone to hear, we'll still have to get past *them*." Here she nodded toward their hunters behind the translucent glass wall.

The officer surveyed the small room. It looked as if the office had been vacated and mostly cleared of its usual trappings, but what remained were a bulky faux-wood desk, a swivel chair, a fax machine sitting on a corner table, and a tall floor lamp. "Like I said, we'll call in backup."

"How?" Mira asked. "We're trapped in here with no phone."

"There should be one on the fax machine," Rico pointed toward it, then cocked his head. "Huh? That's weird." He moved closer to it, realizing that there was no phone receiver attached—just a numeric keypad with some extra buttons. "Looks like some new-fangled prototype." He lifted the flatbed cover. "It scans things like a photocopier." Rico scratched his chin as he continued inspecting the device.

"It'll have to do," Donna moved closer to the man and machine. She dug through her bag and produced a black Sharpie marker, which she promptly handed to Rico. "Here, use this. We can send a message to the machine in my home office back at the house and, er, hope Tracy hears it coming through. Then she can call in backup for us *and* the girls at the house."

Rico took the marker and thought for a moment. The whole idea was absurd. Sending a fax would be both loud and time-consuming, but it seemed like the only somewhat-viable option at that moment.

A crash outside the office made all three friends freeze.

"We're not going to get *any* calls or messages out if they catch us first," Mira whispered.

Donna and Rico shared a quick moment of concerned eye-contact before the officer finally turned to Mira. "Do you think you could—?"

"Yes," Mira nodded.

"Mira," Donna leaned toward her. "You've barely got enough strength to walk, let alone conjure up some elaborate illusion."

"I can buy us time," she answered. "Precious time."

"Mira—"

"It's my choice to make."

Donna knew from her determined expression that Mira would not be dissuaded.

"Okay," Donna said softly. "Then it's now or never."

Rico began to look through the drawers of the desk while Mira closed her eyes and leaned back. She held out her hands, waved them, her fingers dancing through the air as if weaving thread on an invisible loom.

Donna turned to Rico as he looked up from the desk. "What's wrong?"

"There's no paper," Rico answered quietly. He checked the tray under the fax machine and found it empty. "What kind of office doesn't have any paper?"

"Uh, I dunno, use your hand or something?"

Rico nodded. "That'll do." He uncapped the marker and began to quickly scribble letters on his open palm.

As he finished the message, Donna punched in the number for her home fax machine and Rico slid his hand under the flat top so it rested on the glass scanner.

"I think you've gotta hold it there while it scans," Donna noted, pressed the *send* button, then moved back to crouch beside Mira, whose hands were outstretched. Donna whispered: "What are they seeing out there?"

"A forest," Mira answered, her eyes still shut. "A maze of trees. It'll keep them occupied until..." She trailed off, winced, and took a deep breath.

"You okay?"

Mira nodded quickly. "Just hurry up."

Donna rose and joined Rico at the fax machine. The light

beams of the scanner spilled out from the glass underneath the flatbed. Donna scrunched her eyes a little as it inched its way across Rico's hand.

Donna's mind began to drift as she clutched her handbag. "This is all my fault, Rico."

"What, that we're trapped in here sending fax messages via my sweaty palm?"

"No," she rolled her eyes. "All of this. I turned Marcus to gold. I'm the reason he's like *that*—" She nodded toward the door. "I should have never agreed to Ducane's experiments in the first place. If I had just been grateful for what was right in front of me—Marcus, Starla, my sister, you." Here the woman looked up at Castillo. "Now I might lose everything, and hurt all of you in the process."

"Donna—"

She continued, "I've already lost Marcus. I can't lose anymore."

"Marcus isn't lost," Rico insisted. "He's still in there. I have to believe that."

"Then why does he think I'm the enemy?" Donna wiped a tear with the back of her glove.

"I don't know," Castillo admitted, glancing to check on the progress of the scan. *Almost there.* "Maybe all that time he was, er, golden, he forgot—forgot who he was, forgot about what you two had."

What did we have? Donna lowered her head. She felt her satchel, the cassette tapes. Memories recorded in thin magnetic plastic strips. Her mind drifted for a moment before she looked back at Rico.

"What about you and Tracy?"

"What about us?"

"Sue told me you were thinking about popping the question," Donna clarified. "Did you do it yet?"

Rico shook his head, his face turned away. The scanner completed its cycle and the machine began to buzz and beep, dialing the number to send the message.

"Are you going to?"

The man removed his hand from the machine and looked Donna in the eyes. "I don't think she's ready. There's too much..." Rico searched for the words. "Too much baggage she's still got to sort through."

"So you haven't even *asked* her yet?"

"Not exactly. But she wouldn't say *yes* if I did." Castillo raised his eyebrows.

"You're making the decision for her before she even has a chance to respond," Donna smiled. "If you love her as much as you say you do—and I *know* you do—then let her make her own decision. In her own time. But she can't give you an answer if you don't ask."

The officer remained quiet, considered Donna's words. He felt the weight in his pocket. That tiny, consequential object which he had carried around for what felt like ages.

The fax machine blurted out some string of electronic tones from somewhere inside its hard plastic body.

Donna read the digital display: "It sent."

"Now let's just hope they get it in time." Rico breathed in

deep.

"Mira," Donna said, moving back across the room. "How you doin?"

"They're getting *very* frustrated," she answered, her voice shaky and thin. Marcus and Angela's muffled outbursts could be heard through the frosted glass. "But I can only hold them for a few more minutes."

"Enough time for one more fax?" Rico asked, his hand stuffed in his pocket.

Mira nodded. "Should be. Make it quick."

Donna turned to him. "Rico, we've gotta go—"

"It's important," he said. "And it might be the last chance I get."

Tracy took one more look at the unconscious patch-faced man sprawled across the tile floor, his body framed by shards of ceramic pottery. The officer barely had time to catch her breath before she caught sight of the Ghoul entering the kitchen from the living room.

Now's your chance. Go!

The woman sprinted across the hall toward the stairs as the Phil Collins track continued to blare, muffling Jones' footsteps as she made her ascent. Her hand glided along the railing and she took quick steps.

When she reached the second floor landing, Tracy looked both ways down the carpeted hallway. "Starla?" She called out in a loud, harsh whisper—wanting to be heard by the child but not the ghastly intruder downstairs. "Starla, where'd you go?"

Officer Jones gasped when the music downstairs suddenly stopped. *Well, guess it was good while it lasted.* She started down the hall toward the nearest door—Sondra's room. The door hung slightly ajar, and Tracy nudged it open. Through the widening crack, her eyes took in the lumpy form of Sondra, nestled under the covers—the way she spent most of her days. Jones stepped forward and noted the metal IV pole beside the bed, a hook holding a small plastic bag full of crimson blood. As she finally rounded the corner, Tracy nearly jumped. A small hand grabbed her own.

"Miss Tracy, we have to go!" It was Starla. Her freckled face betrayed a look of fear and urgency.

Tracy gestured toward Sondra's bed. "What about your mom—?" The girl tugged on the officer's hand, pulling her back toward the hallway.

"She'll be okay, but we have to go." The child pulled on Tracy's hand again, this time successfully compelling the woman to follow back into the hall.

As the girl led her down the hall, Tracy caught a glimpse downstairs through the railing.

The Ghoul was headed for the stairs.

"Starla, I promised your Aunt Donna I'd keep *all* of you safe." Tracy started back toward Sondra's room.

"And you will," Starla grabbed her hand and wouldn't let go. "Just *trust* me. We have to hide."

Tracy bit her lip. She wanted to believe the girl had a plan, but she wasn't about to sacrifice her mother in the process.

Time was running out, though. The Ghoul reached the foot of the stairs and began to hobble up.

Starla nodded toward another door at the end of the corridor. With a deep breath, Tracy followed as the girl led her into the shadows. Once inside the room, they closed the door most of the way. Tracy pressed herself up to it, peering through the remaining sliver.

The officer took a moment to survey the space they had entered. It was a bedroom, all the lights switched off. *A guest room, by the looks of it.* There was a queen-size bed in the middle of the room, covered in a trendy floral duvet, an intercom on the nearest wall, and a set of built-in cabinets and a desk on the far wall. She didn't look close enough, but Tracy noted what looked like a computer and some other bulky tech on the desk. Her eyes continued around the room.

An en suite bathroom, too? Tracy raised an eyebrow at the open door into the tiled restroom. *Fancy, Donna.*

"Where are Sue and Lisa?" Tracy wondered quietly.

"In there," Starla whispered and nodded to the bathroom.

Only slightly relieved, Tracy's attention turned back to the narrow field of view, the sliver through the door. The Ghoul's shadow danced ominously on the walls near the stairs as the old woman worked her way up to the second floor.

Starla crouched beside Tracy and whispered. "As soon as she's in the room, you've got to close the door. Put this around the handle," Starla said as she handed Tracy a length of thin but sturdy rope tied into a loop on one end. "And tie the other to the banister. Tight! That should keep her from opening the door from the inside."

The kid's really thought this through. Tracy nodded. "What about your mom?"

"I told you," Starla leaned in. "She'll be okay. Quick. Here she comes!" Starla ran across the room and climbed onto a short stool near the wall, leaving Tracy at the door.

Tracy watched as the frightening, haggard woman reached the top of the steps. Her wispy hair and tattered clothes moved with less flow than usual as she took a brief inventory of her surroundings. *She still hasn't had enough blood to use her powers.* Marjory's weary, furious eyes lingered on the half-open door into Sondra's room. Tracy held her breath, waiting for the Ghoul to proceed. The old woman started toward it, then paused.

Slowly, with a stilted movement, Marjory turned her head to look down the hall, into the shadows—right at the door to the guest room.

Tracy tensed and she softly closed the door. She was sure Marjory had seen her.

The Ghoul course-corrected and began to limp in that direction down the dark hallway. Her steps betrayed her injury, the knife wound that remained open on her back and torso. When she was mere steps from the door, the woman stopped, turned her head to listen.

A voice crackled from the other room—back near the stairs. "Hey," said the young voice. "What are you doing here?" It was Starla.

The Ghoul grinned and turned to follow the child's voice.

"I'm here to finish a job," she muttered. She licked her lips and continued walking with heavy steps across the carpeted landing.

"You aren't going to hurt us," Starla's voice said—it was coming from Sondra's room. "Are you?"

Tracy raised an eyebrow and turned to see what Starla was doing. Jones had heard a slight echo when Starla spoke. She was still in the guest room just a few feet away from Tracy. The girl's little finger was pressed against the intercom button, projecting her voice through another identical speaker in Sondra's room.

"Great idea, kiddo," Tracy smiled when she realized what the girl had done. She once more cracked open the door a sliver and peered through just to be sure it had worked. Sure enough, the Ghoul continued walking into Sondra's room, following the crackling voice.

Marjory crept into the dark room. Lightning flashed through the gauzy curtains, illuminating the near lifeless shape of Sondra's lumpy form on the bed. "Where are you, girl?" She wondered, searching for the source of the voice that had summoned her into the room.

"Come out, wherever you are," the Ghoul taunted as she passed by a dresser, upon which rested a stack of children's books. *Where the Wild Things Are* topped the stack. "I'll eat you up, I love you so," the woman muttered. She turned back toward the immobile Sondra, covered in thick sheets. Her eyes drifted, following a tube of red liquid from Sondra to its attached bag that hung from the metallic IV drip stand.

Marjory licked her lips. *Blood.* "I'll eat you up, indeed."

The old woman reached out her hand and removed the bag of crimson fluid from the hook. With a smile of delight, she brought it to her mouth. Her teeth punctured the plastic and she immediately began to suck the liquid. It was only a matter of moments before the bag was half-drained.

In the guest room, Starla signaled Tracy. "Now—go!"

Tracy took a deep breath, swung open the door, and sprinted down the hall with footsteps as quiet as she could manage, holding the length of looped rope in hand. She reached Sondra's room, tossed the loop around the lever handle, and quietly pulled the door shut. Finally, Tracy turned and stretched the rope toward the nearby banister. She tightened it and tied a sturdy knot, fulfilling Starla's instructions so that the door was now nearly impossible to open from the inside. Jones backed away from the door and took a moment to catch her breath.

Inside, the Ghoul sensed that the door had been shut. She finished slurping up the last of the liquid from the blood bag and tossed it aside, then slowly moved toward the door. She jiggled the handle, pulled, and found that the door would not budge.

Marjory grinned and spoke loudly so she could be heard through the door. "You're a fool if you think a door can stop me." She closed her eyes and raised her hands, her usual ritual for focusing her special through-passing abilities. The old woman opened her eyes and stretched out her hand toward the door. Her fingers met the wood—and stopped.

What? Marjory pressed her hands against the back of the door, attempting to will herself through it. *It's not working! But the blood—how—? No matter.* She eyed the lumpy form of Sondra on the bed. *I'll just have to drink a little more.*

The woman stormed over to the bedside. She pressed her hand against the duvet, right where the woman's head should be. Instead of a face, though, Marjory felt a strange solid shape. A high-pitched, childlike voice spoke out from the bed:

"I love you very much."

Marjory's eyes widened with rage and she ripped off the covers. Underneath was a mass of pillows, stuffed animals, and a doll. "I'm getting hungry," the doll's voicebox spoke. "Will you feed me?"

The Ghoul ripped the head off the doll, stomped back to the door, and tried to pass through again. Instead, she met the solid wood with a thud. "Let me out right this minute, or I'll break down the door!" Marjory rammed against the door.

Tracy, still in the hall, turned to make eye-contact with Starla, who stood in the guest room doorway. "There was a ton of blood in there. How is she not passing through the door right now?" Tracy was baffled and hurried over to the girl. "And where's your mom?"

"Mom's in there with Sue and Lisa," the girl motioned toward the guest room's connected bathroom, which had a second door off the hall. "And that wasn't blood," Starla grinned. "It was Kool-Aid mixed with salt."

"Salt?"

"Yeah," the girl answered matter-of-factly. "One time I got a cut on my lip and some of the blood got in my mouth and it tasted salty. I thought it might make it more convincing."

Tracy was dumbfounded—and impressed. "Good thinking, kiddo." She gave the girl a quick squeeze then turned back to hall. "It worked—"

The Ghoul continued to rail against the door.

"—but that won't hold her for long."

Before the pair could exchange any more words, a telephone started ringing. It was coming from the guest room.

Tracy looked around for the phone. "Should we answer that?"

Starla pointed toward the built-in desk on the far wall of the room. "It's not a call—it's Aunt Donna's fax machine. There's something coming through."

While the Ghoul continued hammering and clawing against the other room's door, Starla and Tracy hurried over to the fax machine. It made a few strange noises, then began to print out a black-and-white image on a sheet of paper that slowly inched its way into the tray. The officer angled her head to read the half-printed message—words scribbled in Sharpie on the palm of a hand, with some spilling onto the fingers. The shadows on the scan made it difficult to read, but Tracy was sure of one thing:

"That's Rico's handwriting. And—" she craned her head, "I think that's his hand."

Her heart was racing faster. The message finished printing and Tracy held it up:

SEND HELP. ½ ARRAY HERE. ½ DONNA'S.

"A little late, but I appreciate the warning," Officer Jones mumbled. "Rico and Donna and the others need backup. It sounds like the rest of the Nightmare Array ambushed them at Pelican. I need to let the station know so they can send a squad to help." She turned back to the fax machine. "Can this thing make outgoing calls?"

"Uh, I don't think it's configured for that," Starla shook her head. "You'll have to use the phone downstairs."

Of course. Tracy cursed under her breath. Just then, she heard a splintering sound from the hallway. "She's breaking down the door!"

A voice shouted from the en suite bathroom. "You mean it didn't work?" It was Lisa.

Tracy hurried over and peered into the restroom. Sondra had been placed carefully in the bathtub, padded with pillows and blankets. Sue crouched on top of the toilet seat while Lisa paced the small space.

Officer Jones took in the scene from the doorway then shook her head. "No. She's breaking through. But I'm going to protect you. Stay here—"

Lisa shook her head. "We can't just *stay* here—she'll get through!"

Tracy's mind raced. She had sworn to protect Starla and all of the women in Donna's house, but they were running out of options.

"Miss Tracy—" Starla's voice rang out behind her. "There's another fax coming!" She pointed at a blinking light as the attached phone started ringing again. Tracy darted toward it.

The machine started to beep and whir as it began to receive the incoming message. It began to translate the data into a printed output, the process continuing just as slowly as the prior message.

A loud cracking sound echoed down the hallway. Tracy glanced in that direction, watching as one of the Ghoul's hands emerged through a large fracture in the door. She was almost through.

The fax machine queued up a sheet of paper, seemingly taking its time.

The Ghoul took another swing at the door, this time hurling a piece of furniture at it. Another large cleft formed in the door.

C'mon, c'mon! Tracy urged and willed the fax to print faster.

Suddenly, there was another noise from the hall. Tracy and Starla watched as the en suite bathroom door swung open. Lisa ran out, slamming the door back behind her.

"Lisa, no!" Tracy shouted, starting toward the hall as well.

Lisa sprinted toward the stairs and began her descent. Tracy hurried out of the guest room to follow her. Before Tracy could catch up, though, Sondra's bedroom door burst open, shattering pieces of wood across the hall. Tracy flattened herself against a wall, clinging to the shadows.

The Ghoul emerged through the jagged hole, catching

a fleeting glimpse of Lisa's red hair at the foot of the stairs. Marjory followed quickly, with lumbering movements down the steps.

No! Lisa! Tracy followed, grabbing a piece of splintered wood as she reached the stairs. She ran downstairs, skipping every other step to move faster. Tracy reached the foyer.

The Ghoul followed Lisa into the kitchen, just out of view, where the monster would easily corner her. There was no escape.

No, no no! Jones pulled all of the adrenaline she could muster, gripping the wood so tightly that its splintery grains dug into her flesh. She leaped over the still-limp body of Patchface, nearing the doorway to the kitchen.

Cracckk!

A gunshot rang out. Tracy froze. *No.* She took a few more steps and peered around the doorway into the kitchen, expecting the worst.

Lisa stood at the far end of the room. She held a pistol with both of her hands, aimed directly at the Ghoul. A wisp of smoke surrounded it. The Ghoul grabbed her chest and tumbled backwards onto the hard tile with a *thud.*

The red-haired woman's expression betrayed utter horror at what she had just experienced. When Lisa made eye-contact with Tracy, she pointed at an open cabinet near the fridge. "*That* cabinet," she said. "I put your gun in *that* cabinet."

Lisa tossed the weapon on the kitchen island as Tracy hurried to comfort the weary woman. A moment later, Sue and Starla appeared in the doorway, inspecting the fallen, lifeless Ghoul and her faceless counterpart.

Starla ran to Tracy, who crouched low to catch the girl in a tight embrace.

"It's okay, kiddo," said Jones. "You're safe. I've got you." Tears began to well up in Tracy's eyes as she held Starla close.

After a few moments, Tracy finally remembered Rico's urgent plea. She stood and hurried to the telephone. "Gimme a minute," Tracy said as she punched in the number, fiddled with the long cord, then stepped around the corner to make the call just out of earshot of Starla, Sue, and Lisa.

Starla heard a whimper and turned to see Max limping toward her from the living room. "Maxie!" She crouched and threw her arms around his golden fur, careful to keep clear of the fresh wounds from the Ghoul's vampiric incisors.

Tracy finished the call, returned to the kitchen, and hung up the phone. "There's a squad on the way to Pelican now," she explained. "Let's hope they're not too late."

Starla allowed Max to lie down, then the girl stepped toward Tracy, holding something in her hands. It was a piece of paper, folded a few times. "The other fax came through," she said. The girl carefully unfolded it and handed it to Officer Jones. "I think it's for you."

Tracy took the crinkled sheet in her hand. As she read it, she instinctively placed her other hand over her mouth, a mixture of shock and deep emotion washing over her. Slowly, she folded the page and lowered herself down to the tile floor, resting her back against the lower cabinets. She began to sob as the others huddled around her while the rain continued to patter through the open sliding-glass door.

CHAPTER 27

Rico hovered over the large fax machine in the small office, tapping his finger on the table beneath it. The beeping and rotor noises stopped. "Is it sent?"

"Yeah," Donna confirmed. "Now let's get out of here and up to the roof."

Rico grabbed a small object from under the flatbed scanner and stuffed it into his pocket. "How exactly do you plan on doing that? Mira won't even be able to stand up."

Donna knew he was right. Mira had expended all of her energy forming and sustaining the illusion to keep Angela and Marcus occupied just outside the office. There was no way she'd be able to keep up if they had to make a run for it.

"Go," Mira muttered, her eyes still closed as she waved her hands to form some new variation in her illusion.

Donna crouched to her level. "Mira, we're not leaving you—"

"You have to. Now! I-I can't hold it for much longer."

Rico and Donna exchanged a worried look.

"You heard her," Rico nodded.

Donna placed one of her gloved hands on Mira's shoulder. "We'll come back for you. Wait here."

The woman nodded, then rasped, "It's slipping. You have to go—*now!*"

The pair started for the door, Donna adjusting the strap of her bag over her shoulder.

"Keep away from them," Mira added. "Hurry."

Rico opened the door and spotted Marcus and Angela in the center of the office, clearly frustrated at whatever confusing circumstance Mira had conjured up for them—it wasn't visible to the officer. Donna noticed that Angela carried something in her hand—the manila envelope. She was about to speak when Rico held a finger to his lips. The two shuffled out of the office and clung to the wall.

Marcus must have sensed the motion, for he now aimed a blast of searing hot light at the office door. The frosted glass shattered, startling Mira so that she lost focus. She tried to regain control of the vision, but the forest maze began to flicker and dissolve from Marcus and Angela's view. The dark-haired woman was the first to spot Donna and Rico. "There! They're getting away."

She pointed and Marcus fired off another blast in their direction.

Donna screamed as the light and heat scorched the drywall near her head. Rico grabbed her by the hand and urged her on until they rounded a corner. Finally, they reached the fire exit and pushed through the door into the stairwell.

"Four flights," Rico nodded as he started up the stairs. "We can do this."

Donna followed suit, her gloved hand gliding along the railing. "Let's just hope Buster and Kiki got the generator up and running."

As the duo cleared the second level of stairs, they heard their pursuers enter the stairwell below them.

"Stop them!" Angela shouted.

Marcus held out his hands as he ascended, pulling the light from a wall-mounted fluorescent emergency illuminator. He then stretched his arm out and upward—toward Donna and Rico—sending a beam at them. A chunk of the concrete steps crumbled, almost tripping Donna. Rico caught her by the hand and pulled her up. The two continued their ascent.

At last, Rico and Donna reached the roof. The roof access door creaked open and they rushed out.

The rain had slowed, but it still fell in thin, cold sheets, pecking at Donna's face. She winced as she surveyed the rooftop.

"Donna!" Kiki's voice rang out. "Over here!"

The pair turned toward the voice. Kiki stood near a large steel tower, upon which rested a large satellite dish. Buster was huddled at the base of the broadcast tower, fiddling with the controls. He turned to the new arrivals.

"Is it ready?" Donna asked, hurrying across the slick roof.

"Ready," Buster nodded. "You have the tape?"

Rico reached into his pocket and pulled out the cassette from Ducane's safe. "Right here." He handed it to Buster, who promptly inserted it into a slot in the control panel.

"Don't even think about it," rang a voice from behind. Angela sauntered across the flat, wet roof, Marcus at her side. She stood precariously near to the edge of the roof and removed her hand from behind her back. She held the thick manila folder, dangling it over the precipice.

"If you broadcast that recording," Angela taunted. "I'll drop it. And you'll never know the truth about your family."

Donna's eyes flicked from Marcus to the radio tower, then back to Angela. *I have to know. I'll never be able to have peace—to have closure—if I can't know what really happened.*

But we have a chance to bring down Ducane—to put an end to his whole operation. This nightmare.

Angela extended her arm a little more. "What's more important to you, Miss Locke: knowing the truth about your family's involvement with Ducane, or trying to stop him from getting away with it?"

Donna carefully removed her bag from over her shoulder, handed it to Rico with an earnest nod, then stepped toward Angela with her hands raised—a gesture of peace. Marcus took a fighting stance, bracing himself with his hands ready to weaponize at a moment's notice.

"Marcus," Donna pleaded. "I know you're still in there—she's using you." She stepped forward, wiping away a streak of rain from her face. "Don't let her do this."

The man's brown eyes remained fixed on Donna,

unflinching and unmoved by her words.

"He's mine now, Miss Locke." Angela steadied herself. "Now, what'll it be? Destroy the tape and I'll give you your family's file."

Donna's blonde hair was drenched now, and she glanced over her shoulder at Rico, Buster, and Kiki. "You have to promise to let my friends go free, too."

Angela cocked her head. "If you destroy the tape?" She seemed to consider the woman's proposition. "Deal."

With a deep breath, Donna turned back to her counterparts and nodded. Buster placed a reluctant finger on the eject button, prompting the interface to spit out the tape. He handed it to Kiki, who brought it over to Donna and placed it in her gloved hands.

"Good," Angela nodded, still dangling the manila packet over the edge of the skyscraper. "Now, destroy it."

Donna looked down at the tape in her hands. Her breaths were short. She knew it was the only way to save her friends, but she couldn't shake the feeling that she was making the wrong choice. There was no going back now.

She crouched and placed the plastic cassette on the wet ground. Then Donna raised one foot, took a deep breath, and slammed her heel down on the tape. It shattered instantly, cracked right down the middle. Donna reached down and picked up the fragments of the tape, holding them out for Angela to verify that the tape was no longer usable.

"I'm impressed, Miss Locke." Angela smirked. "Choosing your friends over the greater good." She scowled, then released her grip on the thick brown envelope. It fell.

"No!" Donna started forward as she watched the sealed packet plummet rapidly—sailing down the side of the tallest building in Miami Beach—gone forever.

"Oops." Angela wiggled her fingers and took a step away from the edge. "Guess you should be careful who you trust, Donna."

There were a hundred nasty things Donna wanted to call Angela at that moment, but she was too furious to speak. Donna stood with her jaw agape, taking deep breaths.

"I'm afraid you're just one in a long line of obstacles, Miss Locke—obstacles that have kept me from what's rightfully mine." Angela stepped toward Donna. "And do you know what I do with obstacles?" Here she leaned close so that she was nearly whispering. "I break them, step on them, and continue my rise to the top."

Buster, Kiki, Rico, and Marcus stood by, unsure how or if they should intervene.

Donna was mere inches from Angela now. She gritted her teeth. "I'll give you what's rightfully yours." Donna swung at Angela. Her gloved fist knocked the woman across the jaw.

Angela recoiled, wiped a spot of blood from her lip, then smiled at Donna. "If that's how you want to do this..." The dark-haired woman swiped a kick at Donna's legs, knocking Donna flat on her face, where she splashed in a puddle. Angela straightened out the collar of her long overcoat and planted a second kick at Donna, this time directly to her face.

Thwack! Donna cringed and squirmed, rising to her feet.

She returned the favor with a kick of her own, then threw her body weight at Angela. The two struggled, their arms locked in a tussle as the others continued to look on.

Marcus intervened, grabbing Donna by the arm. He swung her away from Angela. Donna slid across the slick roof toward the edge of the building, grabbing onto a protruding conduit to bring her motion to a halt. She glanced over her shoulder, looking down at the ground hundreds of feet below. A squad of police cars approached the building, sirens blaring.

"Marcus," Donna winced, starting to rise. "Help me! You have to remember who you were—who you are. I'm not the enemy."

He moved toward her, unfazed.

"What happened to you was an accident—I didn't mean to do it, I promise." Donna's eyes welled with tears and rainwater. "It was Angela." As Marcus and Angela closed in, Donna glanced to her gloved hands, then over to Rico. She nodded to him.

Rico lifted one of the cassette tapes from Donna's bag and pushed it into the radio transmitter slot. He pushed play. A red light turned on and a faint crackling began to emanate from a set of compact speakers on the interface. Castillo cranked the volume and turned back to Donna.

"Marcus," Donna insisted. "You *have* to believe me. You have to *remember*. Listen!" She pointed at the tower as a voice came over the recording:

"Dear diary—" It was Marcus' voice, on the tape. He chuckled. "What?"

"Dear *diary?*" The reply was in Donna's voice, younger and playful. "That's how you're going to start this?"

"I guess," Marcus answered. "You got a better idea?"

"Anything but 'dear diary,'" Donna's younger self laughed again.

On the rooftop, Donna watched as something shifted in Marcus' eyes—his expression changed. He was listening. *Truly* listening. Donna put her hands behind her back and tugged on one of her gloves as the voices on the tape continued to crackle through the rain:

"Fine," Marcus' voice continued. "Um, let me think. How about, uh... To whoever is listening to this a thousand years in the future, let it be known that I, Marcus Myles, am madly in love with the one and only Donna Locke."

"Hey, it's true," young Marcus said. The corporeal Marcus stood motionless on the roof, his hands still clenched, ready to fight.

In front of him, Donna mouthed Marcus' next recorded words, having listened to them so many times she had committed them to memory: "Nothing can change that."

It was true back then, Donna was certain. *I know you're still in there.* She gazed at Marcus intently, searching for some glimmer of the man she loved in his eyes.

The recording of Donna breathed deeply. "Well, people of the distant future—"

Angela shouted at Rico. "Enough! Turn it off!"

"—you should know that I, Donna Locke, feel the exact same way about—"

Click.

Rico complied.

"Enough of your games, Donna Locke." Angela snarled. "Let's finish this."

Angela ran across the slick roof and landed another punch at Donna, causing the blonde woman to lose her balance. Donna's pulse quickened as she felt her body falling backward. She flailed, trying to find a grip on something—one hand gloved and the other bare. There was nothing to grab.

Except the hem of Angela's coat. Donna reached out, gripped the thick edge of the long coat with her bare band. The momentum pulled the coat—and its wearer—over the edge of the building as well. In mid-air, Donna watched as a wave of gold swept out from the place where her hand had touched the coat, quickly working its way up the garment until it met its wearer.

Angela's eyes grew wide and she tried to pull herself back and remove the coat.

But it was too late. The two women were falling.

Donna felt a strong grip on her other arm, meeting her gloved hand.

Marcus! He pulled as Donna released her grip on Angela.

Angela's entire body had completed its transmutation into pure, solid gold. It nicked a protruding edge of the Pelican building, bounced off the wall, and tumbled quickly down, gaining speed. Donna looked down as Marcus pulled her to safety: the golden woman hit the concrete driveway and shattered into shimmering pieces.

Donna collapsed into Marcus' arms as she caught her breath, keeping her ungloved hand away. She looked up into the man's deep brown eyes, clear and bright for the first time since before he had been turned to gold.

"Marcus—" Donna panted. "You remembered."

He nodded. "I-I'm sorry, Donna," were the only words he could muster before he was overcome with tears. Marcus buried his face in Donna's wet hair and wept as the others approached.

Marcus turned and met eyes with Rico. Castillo smiled. "Hey, partner."

The two men hugged while Donna covered her bare hand with a glove.

Marcus returned to Donna's side, and the woman introduced him to their other friends. "Buster, Kiki; meet Marcus Myles."

When the greetings were through, Rico handed Donna her bag. "I hate to cut us short, but I need to get back to the house—Tracy's in danger—"

Marcus raised an eyebrow. "Who's *Tracy*?"

"We've got a lot to catch up on," Rico assured him, starting for the door to the stairwell with the others in tow.

"What about Ducane?" Kiki stopped. "Are we just going to let all of that work go to waste? How are we supposed to stop him now?"

Donna shook her head and stepped forward. "That's how." The woman pointed up in the night sky, past Kiki, toward the city skyline. A small aircraft was headed over the bay, swerving and dipping in unusually dangerous maneuvers for a typical cargo or passenger plane.

"It's Declan," Donna muttered. She wasn't sure how she knew exactly, but her intuition had her convinced it was him.

Donna watched in silence as the plane headed toward the ocean, its winglights blinking in time.

Declan. It's up to you now.

Just minutes earlier, the plane rumbled across the tarmac. Declan gripped the pocketknife as he stared down his father across the small plane's cargo bay. Ducane intentionally blocked the controls to the cargo door, which would require Declan to remove his father if he wanted to escape from the moving aircraft.

"You can put an end to all this, father," Declan urged. "Stop the plane and turn yourself in. That formula is dangerous." He gestured toward the remaining case, still clinging to the plane's interior wall by its one remaining strap.

"It's only dangerous in the hands of those who don't know how to use it," Ducane smirked, clenching and unclenching his fists. "That formula has given me a power I'd only dreamed of. Imagine how it could change the world for the better."

"Not every dream is meant to be realized," Declan said.

"Well," his father raised his eyebrows and gripped the metal doorframe, "it's too late to turn back now." A voice from the front of the plane crackled through a small speaker near the door.

"Cleared for takeoff." It was the pilot. "Strap in."

A few seconds later, the plane jolted. Declan tumbled backward, his knife clattering across the floor of the cargo hold.

The plane was taking off. It accelerated rapidly and lifted away from the tarmac, soaring into the rainy night sky.

"Like I said," the older man smiled. "It's too late to turn back now."

Declan regained his balance and hung on to the side of the hold until the plane began to level out once more. His plan of escaping out the back door and onto the tarmac was now moot, which left few options. Only one, actually:

Get the pilot to fly us back to the ground.

It seemed easy enough, barring the only obvious obstacle: *Father.*

Rolf Ducane began to move toward his son, a scowl across his face. "I'm afraid if you can't see things from my point of view, you're only going to drag me down."

Declan eyed his pocketknife a few feet away, just out of reach.

The father took another step forward, running a hand across the top of the thick case of formula before turning back to Declan. "It brings me no pleasure to do this," he started. "But you've become a liability, son. You're going to have to die now." Ducane reached beneath his coat and removed a shiny, compact handgun. He cocked it and pointed the weapon at his son.

The younger man bit his lip, his pulse pounding. Another glance at the knife. He could reach it if he dove at just the right moment.

"Goodbye, Declan."

Declan leaped across the cargo hold, diving at the knife.

Ducane fired the gun.

Splink! The bullet grazed the metallic wall and ricocheted off into a pile of cargo crates on the other side of the vessel.

While his father was disoriented, Declan held the pocketknife by the blade, wound back his arm, then threw the weapon at his target. The serrated knife lodged itself in the soft flesh of Ducane's shoulder. He gasped as he felt the sharp pain fill his body.

The father dropped his gun atop the formula case to free his hand and reach for the knife's handle, and the man took several steps backward as the plane shifted slightly. Ducane pulled slowly, winced as the serrated edges tugged at tender flesh and muscle. Finally, the blade was removed. He inspected it, dripping with his own blood, then glared at his son. "I thought I taught you to respect your elders, boy."

"Hard to teach when you're not around," Declan quipped, still catching his breath.

Ducane gritted his teeth. His eyes flicked to the interface on the wall just behind him. He hit the cargo door's control button and immediately felt a grating sound rock the entire plane. A moment later, the back hatch began to lower, ushering in a loud wind.

Declan once again reached for one of the wall supports as the rushing gust swept through the hold. Ducane's handgun rattled briefly before being swept away, clattering out the open back door and into the night void.

From the other side of the plane, Ducane aimed the bloody knife and threw it with as much force as he could muster. The rush of air accelerated the weapon's trajectory—moving like a projectile toward Declan.

The younger man's eyes shot wide. He felt a tingling sensation in his chest, then his arms and neck. With an animal-like instinct, Declan dodged the knife, which sailed past him and joined the handgun in the wet blackness of the night sky.

A quick glance after it revealed that the plane was now flying over the city, headed across the bay toward the ocean. Declan caught a brief glimpse of the iconic Pelican building, towering above the rest of the skyline. When he turned back, Declan witnessed a strange and horrifying sight: his father's body contorted and rippled, transfiguring into an enormous creature. Veins protruded and popped from his tightly-stretched skin, visible between the patches of fur and hair that covered most of his body.

Yikes. It's even more hideous than I remember.

Declan maintained his grip on the plane's wall support beam. He could feel the tension rising inside his body, a swirl of emotions kept at bay. *It's the only way I'll stand a chance against him.*

"I don't want to hurt you," Declan gritted his teeth as he shouted across the hold which now felt more like a wind-tunnel. "But I *will* if that's what it takes to stop you."

"Try your best," Ducane smiled, saliva dripping from his incisors. "Pain is fuel."

Alright, then. Declan took a deep breath and closed his eyes. He winced, cracked his neck. He felt a chill come over his entire body, then his muscles shifted, grew, expanded. Last came the fur—growing out of his skin until it covered his whole body in a chestnut coat that matched the hair atop his head.

"So glad the beast could come to play," Ducane growled when the son's transformation was complete. The two grotesque, hairy figures now stood poised at either end of the cargo hold, each waiting for the other to make the first move.

Suddenly, a red light began to blink through the doorway behind Ducane. Declan watched past his father's hairy shoulder as the pilot came into view, a pack strapped to his back. With frightened eyes, he looked into the cargo hold, shook his head frantically, then disappeared. The pair of beasts heard the sound of a side hatch opening, and more rushing wind filled the space.

Declan whipped around to glance out the open back cargo ramp: the pilot had jumped, sailing downward. His parachute expanded, inflated, slowing his descent toward South Beach as the plane continued its course out over the Atlantic Ocean—without a pilot.

"Guess it's just you and me now, boy," Ducane flashed a set of slobbering teeth.

Declan felt the pressure shift. Without its pilot, the plane was losing altitude—fast. The younger man turned his attention to the final case of formula. He pounced toward it, digging his talon-like claws into its strap. This had little effect, so Declan sunk his teeth into it, biting at the thick strap.

A blur of silver and brown appeared out of the corner of his eyes, and Declan felt the sudden force of his father collide with him. The son's teeth were yanked from the strap, and the two beasts tumbled toward the cargo door. It was slick with rain. Both of the humanoid creatures grasped at the plane's structural frame, narrowly avoiding being sucked out into the sky and sea.

Declan looked ahead, past the blinking red light and toward the cockpit. Even if he could fly a plane, he was certain there was no way he could stop the inevitable fall. *We're descending too rapidly.* He turned. His father clawed at the inside of the plane, slowly gaining a better grip as he moved further in.

This ends tonight. It ends now.

Ducane eyed the case of serum, then looked out the back door.

Declan could sense his father's plan being formulated. *He's going to try and jump—and take the formula with him.*

The son took deep breaths, his claws clinging, scratching the metal wall frame.

No. I won't let that happen. There's only one way to stop him.

Declan gulped.

His father crawled across the cargo hold and clutched the remaining case of formula. With his teeth, he gnawed at the threadbare strap.

Declan's attention shifted to a dangling strap—one of

the others he'd sliced apart while the plane was still taxiing across the tarmac. It whipped and snapped in the wind, one end still fastened to the wall. He reached out for it, grabbed it, and crawled closer to his father and the formula case. The son tied the end in a loop and stretched it toward his father's leg. *Almost there.*

The plane would hit the ocean in a matter of moments. Declan was confident in his plan: tie his father to the plane so he would go down with it. Declan would make a jump at the last minute.

Ducane was determined, chewing and sawing at the thick strap. Finally, it snapped. He smiled, clutched the case in his large, sinewy arms and jumped toward the open back hatch.

Declan held his breath as he watched the strap tighten around his father's foot and grow taut as he neared the back door. Declan scrambled toward the open door to make his own escape, but his jaw sank as he watched the strap break. His father was free of the makeshift binding.

No! Declan gripped the edge of the plane once more. He took a glance out the back. The moonlight on the waves was bright and nearer than ever. *Do it. It's the only way.*

As Ducane wound up to leap out the back door, Declan threw himself across the space, grappling with his father's beastly form. He grabbed him, pushed the father toward the opposite wall, and gripped the support beams. Declan had pinned his father to the wall—the older man-beast still clutching the case of formula.

The father struggled to break free, but it was no use.

Declan whispered his last words. “Goodbye, dad.”

The plane collided with the ocean with a furious splash, bursting into flames at impact. The scorched fuselage quickly filled with water, submerged, and sank beneath the surface, drowned, down into the depths.

CHAPTER 28

No one spoke as the elevator descended from atop Pelican tower. Buster held Mira's weak, limp body, the occasional flicker of her eyes assuring the others that she was still alive—still hanging on. Donna stood between Marcus and Rico, a gloved handhold connecting her to both of the men, while Kiki tapped a nervous finger on the elevator's metallic wall.

When the group piled out of the elevator car and into the lobby, they were greeted by flashing red and blue lights and a squad of Metro-Dade police with their handguns aimed at the new arrivals. The cops relaxed their stance and lowered their weapons when they saw Rico, the first to step forward and flash his badge.

"Oh, Officer Castillo," the captain nodded. "Didn't realize you were part of this operation."

"Just trying to get these civilians out of here," said Rico.

He gestured toward Mira. "She needs medical attention."

"Of course, sir. There's an ambulance right outside."

Castillo thanked the captain and the group continued on toward the doors. The captain caught sight of Marcus, head lowered, and pulled Rico aside.

"Is that—?"

Rico nodded.

"Didn't he, uh—?"

"It's a long story." Rico guided Donna as they continued out the glass doors, but the officer turned back once more to the captain, who trailed just behind them as they stepped outside. "There were a couple of suspects—a woman in armor and, uh..." He trailed off, unsure of how to explain the hybrid creature.

"You mean that ugly reptile thing?" The captain smirked. "We got 'em both." He motioned to an armored vehicle. "Luckily we got a heads up to bring animal control along—someone called it in."

Tracy. Castillo eked a half-grin. *She got the message.*

A cadre of paramedics approached, wheeling a gurney. Buster eased Mira onto the stretcher and followed as the medics hurried her toward the ambulance. Kiki started after them, then doubled back to Donna and the men. "I'm gonna stick with Buster and Mira until we know if she's gonna pull through." Kiki handed Donna the keys to the van and started to turn back. Donna held on to her hand a moment longer.

"Hey," she looked Kiki in the eyes. "She's going to pull through." Donna believed it. She gave Kiki a squeeze then watched as she followed the others.

The ambulance pulled away, leaving Donna with Rico and Marcus. "C'mon," the blonde woman started down the street and jangled the van keys. "Let's go home."

Donna's mansion swarmed with cops. When she saw the flashing siren lights as they approached around the island bend, Donna's pulse quickened. Since the driveway was teeming with police cars, they parked the van on the street and Donna ran toward the house with Rico and Marcus at her heels. A quick flash of Rico's badge gave them swift access to pass through the security checkpoint at the front door.

When they were inside the expansive foyer, Donna immediately noticed the shards of broken pottery. She covered her mouth when she saw a stain near it on the tile: blood.

Before she could catastrophize too much, Donna heard a shrill voice ring out from the living room.

"Aunt Donna!" Starla ran and leaped into Donna's arms.

"Little Starling." The woman wrapped the girl in a tearful embrace. "Are you okay? Are you hurt?"

"I'm fine—they didn't hurt us," she assured her aunt. "Miss Tracy kept us safe." The girl turned to look over her shoulder as Officer Jones approached from around the corner.

Rico hurried toward her and wrapped his arms around her. The two immediately started crying, unable to speak.

Finally, Rico managed: "When we knew they were coming for you, I was so worried. I wasn't sure if I'd ever see you again."

Jones nodded. "I'm seeing you now," she placed a gentle hand on his cheek. "We're safe."

A pair of paramedics pushed past them, carrying a stretcher from the kitchen. A sealed black body bag rested on it, strapped to the stretcher.

The Ghoul.

Tracy spoke up as they passed: "Is she—?"

The paramedic shook her head. "She's gone."

Officer Jones exhaled slowly as the duo carried the corpse away. She turned back to Rico. "They already got Sunder—he's locked up."

Rico assured her that the Gatorman and Frightknight shared the same fate. "And Angela—she's gone. For good."

At this point, Tracy noticed Marcus, who had lingered near the front door. She tensed when she saw him, starting for the gun at her side.

"It's okay," Rico placed his hand on hers. "He's okay."

Officer Castillo locked eyes with Marcus and motioned for him to join them. The man approached, timid and reserved.

"Tracy, meet Marcus," Rico gestured to him. "Marcus, this is Tracy. My, uh—my partner."

The pair shook hands, Marcus offering a weary, hesitant smile. Before they could speak much further, Donna took Marcus by the arm and leaned toward the pair of officers: "Hey, have either of you heard from Declan yet?"

"Calvin called right before you got here," Tracy explained. "He said they managed to round up a couple cases of the formula, and they got the doctor locked up with the others. Calvin's on his way here now."

Donna spoke softly. "With Declan?"

Tracy shot a concerned glance to Rico before turning back to Donna. "I'm so sorry, Donna," she started. "Declan, uh—" She shook her head. "He didn't make it. He went down with the plane—Ducane was on board, too."

No. Tears began to well up in Donna's eyes as Marcus pulled her close.

"I'm sorry," Marcus whispered as Donna buried her face in his warm chest.

Donna had grown fond of Declan. *He was a good man. A good friend.* As she mourned, she thought of his final, noble sacrifice.

"Ducane is gone," Rico muttered to her with a gentle pat on the back. "He can't hurt you anymore."

Sue, Lisa, and Roger were in the living room, just around the corner, with Sondra sprawled across the sofa while they finished giving statements to the police. When that was complete, the trio joined the others and exchanged greetings and hugs with the newcomers.

As the conversation died down, Tracy nodded for Rico to join her on the back patio. They crunched through sugar and terra cotta on their way out the slider. The rain had stopped, leaving only the trickle of water dripping off roof tiles and planters. At the edge of Donna's property in the distance, the bay waters lapped up against the concrete barrier wall, a calming, familiar sound.

Tracy stood angled toward Rico, her face downcast. "I, uh, got your fax." She withdrew the folded crinkly paper from her back pocket.

Rico gulped. "Oh. And?"

"And I'm sorry—"

Sorry? Rico's pulse quickened.

"—sorry that it took me so long to tell you about, er, what happened in the past." She took a deep breath. "After what happened, I thought I could never get attached—never make a commitment like that again. Losing him and the girls was too much—too painful. I couldn't even be around kids without imagining something terrible happening. I never want to feel that again."

Castillo wasn't sure what to say. He kept quiet as Tracy continued.

"When that *thing* was coming for Starla in there? I thought it was going to happen all over again."

"You kept her safe."

"I won't always be able to keep *her* safe. Or *you*." She placed a gentle hand on his cheek and whispered: "I don't want to lose you, Rico."

"Listen, if you're still not ready, you don't have to answer—"

"No, I mean, I *can't* lose you. I want to be with you."

Rico's jaw lowered involuntarily. "You do—?"

Tracy took a half-step closer. "Love isn't worth a thing if you aren't willing to risk losing it." She reached down and unfolded the piece of paper, holding out the black-and-white faxed document. It was the message Rico had hastily faxed, scribbled in marker on one of his sweaty palms. The sloppy letters read:

When you're ready.

Just beneath the words was the scan of a small, metal ring.

Tracy placed the paper in Rico's hands and leaned close.

"I'm ready," she whispered. Tracy planted a soft kiss on Rico's cheek. He grinned ear to ear and the two shared another kiss—this time on the lips—as the moon shone bright on the bay.

The next morning, Donna awoke to the dappled sun dancing over her eyes. She squinted and rolled out of bed, hobbling down the hall. She paused, peered through a cracked-open door into the guest room. There was Marcus, asleep. *Peaceful*, Donna smiled. *There's so much we have to talk about. And we will. Soon.* She closed the door and headed downstairs.

As she prepared breakfast, a skillet of scrambled eggs sizzling on the stove, Donna swept up some of the prior night's remaining debris into a dustpan. She dumped the dust and sugar into the trashcan, then heard a knock on the front door. Donna switched the burner to its lowest heat setting and went to answer the door.

Donna let out a sigh of relief when she discovered that the visitor was Rico.

"Morning," he said. "Didn't mean to scare you. It's just me."

"You're fine," Donna waved him in. "Come in, I was just making breakfast."

Castillo followed Donna into the house, his hands behind his back as they entered the kitchen.

"Is everything okay?" Donna grabbed the spatula and stirred the eggs.

"Yeah," Rico nodded. "I just, uh, wanted to give you something." He moved his hands in front of him, revealing a large, damp brownish envelope. "They found it at the scene shortly after we left."

Donna's hands trembled as she reached to receive it. The initials S.G. were smeared but unmistakable. *The documents—my family's story.* "Did you open it yet?"

The man shook his head. "Figured you should be the one to do the honors. Hope the rain didn't do too much damage."

Donna turned off the stove then placed the envelope on the kitchen island. She carefully unfastened the metal clasp and opened the flap. The envelope and its contents were still damp, sticking to each other as Donna gently tugged them free. She removed a stack of pages and file folders, some clipped together, others stapled, while a few hung loosely in place.

At the top of the stack was a file folder. The tab on the side read: *Locke, Richard. Just like in the vision,* Donna recalled. She carefully opened it, its contents stuck to the inside. She peeled two fragments of a thicker paper away and turned them over. *Not paper, exactly.* Photographs. Or rather, two pieces of a single photograph. The same one from Sondra's memory vision—a group in lab coats that included Donna's parents next to Rolf Ducane. The photo had been ripped in two, its jagged edge separating Ducane from the Lockes. Donna ran her fingers over the small, young faces.

"Sondra saw this, but it wasn't ripped yet."

The woman set the photo fragments aside and inspected the next piece: a brief letter, handwritten to Mr. Ducane. "It's signed by my parents," Donna whispered, glancing up at Rico. Most of the ink had bled, turning the cursive letters into blobs, indistinguishable from one another. Donna ran her eyes down the page, making out only short phrases:

... clear we have fundamental differences...

... what constitutes an ethical research organization...

... have no choice but to bring this to the proper authorities...

She carefully peeled the letter away. Beneath it was a formal, typewritten page of letterhead that bore an early iteration of the Pelican Innovations logo in the corner. This document was more legible than the last, but Donna zeroed in the words in the middle of it: *... serves as your immediate termination of employment from Pelican Innovations...*

There was a signature at the bottom: *Rolf Ducane.*

Donna let out a deep breath and closed her eyes. "My parents," she said softly. "They weren't trying to help Ducane. I think they were trying to *stop* him."

Rico shared a warm smile and nodded. "That's a relief. So your family's alright after all?"

Donna didn't respond. She flipped the page. Beneath

it was a newspaper article—the moisture made the article from the back bleed through, making the words on the front harder to read. But Donna could read enough. There were two small headshots—her parents—next to a small headline and blurb: *Local scientists found dead in canal... Autopsy renders suicide likely... Survived by two daughters: Sondra and Donna.*

Donna began to shake. She had grieved her parents' death many years ago, but this felt like a wound being reopened. Her eyes moved to the dateline at the top of the page. She raised an eyebrow and flipped back to the termination letter. "This article is dated the same week that Ducane terminated them from Pelican." She looked at Rico.

"Do you think he—?" Rico gulped.

She nodded slowly. "Yeah," Donna mumbled. "They got in his way. And... I bet they had powers, too... and he got jealous. Ducane had them killed. It's what he does, er, what he *did*." The woman went quiet, a moment to reflect in reverence on her parents. She lamented that she had so little time with them. *So many secrets. I hardly knew who they really were.*

Donna knew she could linger on their memory for some time, but there was still one more folder she had to find. She quickly but carefully separated the stack until she found it under the other items. The tab read: *Gordon, Sondra.*

Donna lifted the cover of this dossier. Inside was a stapled document—some sort of report, typed and organized. This, too, had significant smudging, making much of it illegible. The heading was clear: *Comprehensive analysis for subject* S.G. A date of birth listed beneath it confirmed that it was a report on Sondra.

The legible portion of the narrative was brief: *Subject exhibits paranormal abilities, verified through multiple rounds of testing. When others are nearby, control participants report hearing what they describe as voices in their heads. In one instance, all participants experienced and heard the same exact message when placed in proximity to the subject. Audio recordings of these sessions revealed no audible communication.*

Donna's brow furrowed as she continued reading:

Upon additional testing, lab technicians observed that subject's psychologically-transmitted messaging persisted even when subject was sedated.

At this, Donna's jaw hung agape.

Starla's powers—the messages, the supposed reading of her mother's mind, the vision. It made sense now why she was never able to do it with anyone else. *They weren't Starla's powers at all.*

They were Sondra's.

"In the vision," Rico said, "why was your sister talking with Ducane in the first place?"

Donna shook her head. "I don't know. I think maybe he was trying to get her to keep quiet—she knew too much about what he did."

"Do you think he—Ducane, I mean—do you think he's the reason she's—"

"In a coma?" Donna had considered it, but thought it seemed too far-fetched—even for Rolf Ducane. Not now, though. "I don't think there was any limit to the lengths he'd go to tie up loose ends. Maybe she knew—knew what he did to my mom and dad. I think she was trying to stop him, too." Donna stared back at the report.

"Is that what you were looking for?" Rico asked.

Donna inhaled and shook her head. "No. There's something else." The woman set aside the stapled report and moved to the next item in the folder.

Donna held her breath as she read the top of the next document: *Termination of Parental Rights.* The bottom portion had crumpled, folding over on itself and obscuring the place where the signatures were supposed to go. Donna reached toward the fold then paused.

"In the vision, my sister was signing her rights away," Donna muttered, her fingers searching for the moist edges of the folded paper. "If she did it, that means she was giving up Starla to that monster—for them to do all sorts of cruel experiments on her. It means that when he tried to take her from us—twice—he was just acting on his rights." Finally, she found an edge and started to lift.

Rico put a hand on her wrist. "Are you sure you want to know?"

"I *have* to know."

"Ducane's gone," he looked her in the eyes. "He can't take her now. Would knowing the truth really change anything?"

Donna maintained eye-contact with him. "It would change whether my sister is a decent human being—or a monster like him."

Rico breathed, relaxed his grip on Donna's wrist. "People

can change, Donna."

She didn't respond, but turned her eyes back to the page. Rico slowly pulled away his hand. Donna gripped the edge of the damp page and began to unfold it. Her breaths were quick and short. Finally, the page was unveiled, flattened.

The woman inspected the line where Sondra's signature was supposed to go.

It was blank.

"She didn't do it." Donna gasped. "I could've sworn she signed it in the vision—" *But she didn't.* Tears formed at the edges of Donna's eyes as she looked up at Rico. He wrapped an arm around her shoulders and stood by her side in silence as she cried.

A few moments later, Starla's small feet pattered across the tile as she entered the kitchen. Her reddish hair was tangled in a mass of bedhead, and her bright eyes sparkled. "Morning, Aunt Donna. Morning, Rico."

"Hey, Starlita," Rico smiled and swooped the girl up in his arms. He gave her a friendly squeeze then set her feet back on the kitchen floor.

Starla rubbed her eyes as she noticed the papers strewn across the island. "Is that—" She pointed. "From mom's memory?"

Donna inhaled deeply. "Yeah. Some of Rico's colleagues recovered it for us."

"Does any of it, um," the girl searched for the words. "Does it say anything about my powers?"

Rico shot Donna a glance. *You have to tell her the truth.*

Donna considered it for a moment, then answered. "Kiddo," she crouched to the girl's level. "It said some things about the, uh, powers. Your powers—reading minds, hearing things. Except... it said they aren't exactly *your* powers. They're your mom's. *She* was talking to *you*. She showed you her visions."

The child was silent, considering her aunt's words. Though it devastated her, Starla knew deep down that Donna was telling the truth. "I guess it makes sense," she mumbled. "If it was my power, I wasn't very good at controlling it."

"Hey, Star," Donna consoled her. "I love you just the same—powers or no powers." Here Donna eyed an object on the counter, glinting in the morning light. She reached for it and held it out for the girl to see: the starling pin. "You'll always be my little Starling." Donna pinned the ornament to Starla's shirt. "And who knows: maybe your powers are just waiting..." She trailed off.

"Waiting for *what?*"

"Waiting for you to grow up," Donna smiled. "But let's hope that doesn't happen too fast." Donna rose and grabbed a plate. "How about some breakfast?"

Starla nodded and took a seat on a stool at the island, as the table and chairs had been irreparably damaged in the prior night's skirmish.

"Rico?"

"It would be rude to turn down a meal," he smiled. "Thanks, Donna."

The trio settled around the island and enjoyed breakfast

as a salty breeze off the bay blew in through the open kitchen window.

CHAPTER 29

Late in the afternoon, a golden sky cast its warm rays across Donna's home. Upstairs, Donna moved toward Sondra's room, inspecting its newly-installed door as she entered the cozy space. The blonde woman looked over her shoulder, making furtive eye-contact with Marcus, who flashed her a dimpled grin as he ushered the repairmen down the stairs. Donna slowly half-closed the door, muffling the conversations of the men outside, and approached her sister's bedside.

A local news program droned on a television set in the corner of the room: "... after a freak accident just off the coast of South Beach. No bodies have been recovered from the scene of the plane crash, but tests revealed unknown, possibly-toxic chemicals in the water near the site of the crash. Officials are cautioning citizens to stay out of the water until the area is deemed clean—"

Donna clicked a button on the remote to turn off the TV,

then settled into a chair and placed a gentle, gloved hand on her sister's arm. "So it seems like there's a lot you didn't tell me."

Donna exhaled slowly, trying to imagine how she would even begin to have a conversation about everything she'd learned.

I tried, Donna thought she heard her sister say.

Wait. "Did you just...?" She let the words trail off as she inspected Sondra's soft face, framed by her chestnut brown hair. Her lips had not moved, yet her expression changed. Sondra appeared almost pained.

"Sondra?" Donna leaned closer.

Suddenly, Sondra's nostrils began to flare, inhaling.

Donna nearly leaped from her seat. "Sondra!"

Sondra began to breathe more deeply. Then her eyes fluttered open—*blue-green eyes,* Donna noted, now recalling how their mother used to compare the shade to Sondra's favorite childhood dress.

"Oh my goodness," Donna gasped. "Sondra? Can you hear me?"

Her sister slowly turned her head to face Donna. As the two sisters locked eyes, both began to cry, salty tears welling up in unison.

"Sondra, it's me—your little sister, Donna."

The older sister seemed to be examining every inch of Donna's face, every detail. Finally, she opened her lips and whispered: "You don't look so little to me."

Both sisters cracked a smile, Donna wiping her tears with

the back of her gloved hand.

"Do you know where you are?" Donna asked. "Do you know what happened to you?"

Sondra shook her head. "Don't remember much." Sondra diverted her gaze for a moment, then focused on Donna again. "My baby girl," said Sondra, her pulse beginning to rise. "Is she safe?"

Donna reassured her, "She's fine. Starla is fine. She's downstairs."

This seemed to confuse Sondra at first, but her expression gradually changed back to a smile. "I'm so glad you're here, Donna. I missed you."

Donna smiled softly. "I missed you, too, sis."

As Sondra's energy seemed to be incredibly low, Donna kept the rest of her questions to herself. *They can wait.* She took another good look at Sondra and gave her hand a light squeeze before hurrying out of the room to call a doctor. Donna was elated, hollering to Starla as she moved down the stairs.

"She's awake," Donna nearly shouted. "Your mother's awake!"

Standing at the foot of the steps, Starla froze briefly then sprinted up the staircase to see her mother.

A wave of emotions crashed over Donna, but the prevailing two were hope and gratitude.

Thank God—Sondra is finally awake.

It was a cool, humid evening when the sun began to set,

bathing the tops of fluttering South Beach palm trees in warm gold. Soon the sky turned salmon pink and gave way to purple dusk as neon lights flickered on to welcome the nightly visitors to the strip.

Donna Locke and Marcus Myles kept along the sidewalk that ran adjacent to the beach, buffered only by grass and dunes. The two walked slowly, Donna's arms crossed to keep warm. The cold front was brisk by South Florida standards, even for the early days of winter, but neither of the pair had worn jackets.

"You cold?" Marcus asked.

Donna shook her head. "I'm fine."

"If I had a jacket, I'd let you wear it."

"I said I'm fine." Donna looked at him, rubbed her arms with her hands.

Marcus cracked a smile. "I may have been absent for the last year, but I can still tell when you're bluffing, Donna Locke. C'mere."

The woman exhaled slowly, then nestled close to Marcus. He wrapped one of his sturdy arms around her and the two continued walking.

"That's some place you got," Marcus said after a lull in the conversation.

"Yeah, it's..." She trailed off. "It's a lot, isn't it?"

He chuckled.

"I've been thinking about moving, selling it. It's too big. Too much." She kept her eyes on the sidewalk ahead. "When you were... gone, I did a lot of searching. For you, for anything that would make that terrible feeling go away."

"What feeling?"

"The feeling that it was all my fault." Donna's breaths were short. "What happened to you, I mean. So when you, uh, came back, and you blamed me for it, I actually believed that it was true."

"I'm sorry, Donna." Marcus stopped walking and removed his arm so that Donna could face him. "I was confused—that whole gold thing did something to me. I needed answers, and Angela fed me lies that I believed all too easily. I wasn't myself."

Donna stared into his deep, dark eyes, searching for the soul of the man she'd known and loved so well—just to be sure it was really, truly him. "I know, Marcus." She held out one of her gloved hands. He placed his hand in hers, then clasped the other around it. "I'm just glad you're back."

The two continued walking. Donna gestured toward a crosswalk and the two crossed as the signal changed.

"Where exactly are you taking me?"

Donna grinned. "You'll see."

The two walked past a sizzling hot dog stand and a jewelry store, then ducked into an alley. It was a shortcut, Donna explained. Finally, the alley spat out the couple, back onto another crowded sidestreet. Donna pointed and they continued walking, hands interlocked.

He looked around. "How much further?"

"Almost there." Donna took both of his hands and pulled him along the sidewalk. "Close your eyes."

"Huh?"

"Close 'em," she chuckled. "I'll tell you when to open."

The man smirked, revealing his dimples, then shrugged and complied. "Fine. You better not let me trip."

"I won't. Follow my voice." Donna led him down the sidewalk, narrowly evading a group of boisterous, staggering passersby.

"I never stopped looking for you, ya know," Donna said quietly, glancing up at him.

Marcus nodded, his eyes still closed. "I know. Rico told me."

"Do you remember... *us*?" Donna kept her eyes ahead, navigating through another small crowd of tourists.

"What do you mean?"

"I mean, do you remember what we *had*—together?"

"To be honest, I can only recall bits and pieces," he replied.

Donna's shoulders sank.

"I do remember one thing—vividly."

The pair stopped walking. Donna turned to Marcus. "What's that?"

He took a deep breath, kept his eyes closed. "I remember how it felt whenever I was around you."

Donna's eyes grew moist and she took slow, calculated breaths. Her gloved fingers gripped Marcus' hands as she looked up at him. "Open up," she sniffled.

"I'm trying to—"

"No," Donna chuckled. "Open up your *eyes*. We're here."

Marcus squinted one eye, then opened them both wide.

He looked around, glanced at Donna, then focused on the sign painted on the window.

"What's this?"

"You don't remember?"

He started to shake his head. "Should I?"

Donna exhaled sharply. "It's okay. One thing at a time. It'll come back to you." She maintained a gentle hold on his hand. "I brought you here because I thought it might help you remember more. They say smells and sounds are deeply connected to memory."

"And why *here* specifically? This place looks like a dump."

"Shh!" Donna smiled, throwing a hand over his mouth as a satisfied customer exited onto the sidewalk, a bell jingling as the door closed behind. "It's a family-owned establishment; they've been here for years. It's legit. Trust me: it's not as bad as it looks." Marcus raised his eyebrows and Donna continued: "I brought you here *specifically* because this is where you took me on our first date. And several after that."

Marcus cocked his head and flashed another dimpled smile. "You're a real wonder, Donna Locke."

"And *you*, Marcus Myles, look incredibly hungry." Donna nodded toward the door. "What do you say we continue this discussion over the best pizza in town?"

"After you," Marcus motioned toward the door. He held it open as Donna entered, and he followed closely behind.

A hostess welcomed them, gripping a stack of menus in one arm. "Welcome to Jaci's Pizza. Table or booth?"

Donna pointed toward a booth. "That one taken?"

"All yours, lovebirds." She handed them menus and the two settled into the sticky red faux-leather seats.

Marcus eyed the colorful stained-glass lamp that hung above the table and clenched his fist. The light flickered for a moment until Marcus looked away. He surveyed the room, listening, inhaling, taking in the smells, sights, and sounds of the small pizzeria. "I remember the tape recorder," he said finally, rubbing his forehead as if he had the beginnings of a headache.

"Good." Donna took his hand. "The rest will come. It might take time, but I'm not going anywhere. Afraid you're stuck with me, Marcus Myles."

Marcus flashed another soft smile. "I can't think of anyone else I'd rather be stuck with than *the* Donna Locke."

She felt her cheeks grow warm and red.

"No, I mean *truly*: I don't remember anyone but you. And Rico."

"How romantic," Donna rolled her eyes.

Marcus gestured at the menu. "So, what's good here?"

"Most of the pizzas are excellent," Donna explained. "But you haven't *lived* until you've tried the garlic rolls."

The two burst into laughter once more, and the night seemed to go on for hours and hours. It was a blur. But Donna was sure of one thing: Marcus was really, truly back.

Donna's story is over,
but another is about to begin.

Song of the Starling:
A Magic City Wonders Novel
(Coming Soon!)

If you enjoyed *Nightmare Array*,
would you be so kind as to leave
a review for it on Amazon or your
preferred book vendor's website?
Every review helps my books
get found by new readers!

Thank you for reading,
- Taylor

ABOUT THE AUTHOR

Taylor Thomas Smythe is a native of West Palm Beach, Florida, which has been a source of inspiration for a variety of his creative works. Smythe is the author of the acclaimed seven-book *Kingdom of Florida* middle-grade fantasy series, which was a silver medal winner in the Florida Authors and Publishers Association President's Book Awards and a finalist in the National Indie Excellence Awards. *Goldie*, the first installment in his *Magic City Wonders* series, was a gold medal winner in the Independent Publisher Book Awards and silver medal winner in the Florida Book Awards. Taylor enjoys creative writing of all kinds and topics, but he especially likes to write stories about imaginative places and secret, magical worlds.

Visit lamplightuniverse.com *for more.*

www.ingramcontent.com/pod-product-compliance
Lightning Source LLC
Chambersburg PA
CBHW020532310726
48979CB00014B/2296/J
* 9 7 8 1 9 5 9 3 4 5 1 5 2 *